The Gabriel Club

The Gabriel Club

Joydeep Roy-Bhattacharya

Granta Books
London

Granta Publications, 2/3 Hanover Yard, London N1 8BE

First published in Great Britain by Granta Books 1998

The translations of the poems of Miklós Radnóti are reproduced by the kind permission of Jascha Kessler, from *Under Gemini: A Prose of Memoir and Selected Poetry*, 1985, Ohio University Press, Athens © Jascha Kessler.

A CIP catalogue record for this book is available from the British Library.

1 3 5 7 9 10 8 6 4 2

ISBN 1 86207 165 9

Typeset in Janson by M Rules
Printed and bound in Great Britain by
Mackays of Chatham plc

Acknowledgements

My gratitude to Becky Hardie, whose editorial acumen has been a revelation.

Thanks to Frances Coady at Granta Books, Simon Trewin at Sheil Land, Karl Heinz Bittel at Albrecht Knaus Verlag and Plien van Albada at Prometheus/Bert Bakker.

I owe a great debt to those who inspired me to persevere: Giovanna Andrian-Sforza, Déa del Asturides, Gyula Bakacsi, Thomas Bartscherer, Susan Behr, Torgil Lenning, Claudio Magris, Lisa Puccinelli, Nicholette Roemer, Laura Susijn, Vladimir Tismaneanu, Emily Thompson, Michel Tournier.

Above all, I am grateful to Alexandra Ludwig, lambent companion, reader.

Contents

Book One

Whatever is sacred, whatever is to remain sacred, must be clothed in mystery.

Stéphane Mallarmé

The essence of mystery is to remain perpetually ambiguous, to have two or three aspects or possible aspects.

Odilon Redon

Book One

Budapest, 1976

Prologue

Entries in a Diary Found on the Banks of the Danube

L ast night I was writing my journal when I heard footsteps running rapidly away from the house. As the sound receded into the distance, there was a gunshot, followed by a scream. Walking over to the window, I opened it, scanning the street. It was too murky to discern anything, the uneven patchwork of dark and shade wrapping around my eyes. Convinced that I had made a mistake, I was just about to turn around when a car parked about two blocks away exploded, a sudden bright flame lunging into the night. A man was hanging by his neck from a tree in front of the car, his face battered to a pulp. His naked feet danced circles in the air, swinging round and round, slowly catching fire and turning black. Trembling, I backed carefully into my room, latching the window firmly behind me.

Deep in the folds of the night, as I lay in bed, half-asleep, half-awake, I heard water lapping at the steps to the house. I opened my eyes, wondering what could be going on. Drawing aside the sheets, I put on my nightgown and lit the candle by my bed. In the dead of winter, I walked out to the terrace and looked down. The Danube had overrun the garden below, the street beyond, the city beyond the street. The water was glacial, inexorable. It was rising slowly, the currents surging in the grey half-light. Most of it had frozen over with the cold. Budapest lay under a sheet of ice, a crystal city. Only the ramparts of the

Citadella and the twin spires of the Mátyás Church broke through that shining opalescent swirl.

Back in my room, I sat down on the bed, lit a cigarette, and waited. The smoke curled up in jittery spirals and scaled the walls, only to be trapped by the beams of the ceiling. Some of it settled around my face, clouding my eyes and making them smart. I swallowed hard, my lungs constricting. Across from me, the clock on the wall continued its temporal progression, phosphorescent fingers restlessly probing, waiting . . .

Father walked into the room, a cold draught from the corridor following him inside. As he closed the door, I looked down instinctively at the floor and clenched my teeth, my knees drawing up so tightly it hurt to breathe. The thin cotton coverlet clamped into an impregnable shield around me. I folded my frame into a fortress. My fingers clenched, the nails gouging into my palm. Sparks from the dying stub scorched my lips. He made a face and cleared his throat, saying that the room was unbearably stuffy: I knew he hated my smoking. Walking over to the windows, he flung them open, the water gushing in as he did. The candle blew out, a wisp of pale smoke where the flame had been. But I just lay there, watching him get drenched as the water rushed in, the sweat trickling slackly between my legs.

America stirred beside me at that moment; she reached over sleepily to link her hand with mine. When she sensed me moving away, she woke with a start and hitched herself up. Then she moved closer, gently wiping the wet off my face and holding me, while at the same time clutching the knife she always slept with. The clock on the wall shifted to the left, interrupting that fleeting moment of comfort. Suddenly, there was a roar of water, the sound reverberating into the room from the outside. Father staggered back from the window, fighting against the swirling tide. He knocked over a partly submerged chair and lost his balance, plunging backwards. The rising waters churned as he went under, his hand breaking the surface as he grasped for support. He must have given up the struggle shortly after because he was sucked out of the room as we looked on in horror.

Turning me away from the sight, America shielded my eyes, running her fingers lightly over them. Using her knife, she cut

4

up the pieces of ice hardening around the bed and prised the blocks loose with her hands. We skated free, on our giant sledge, right out into the open. I could see Father suspended below, frozen in mid-stroke, his arms outstretched like wings. Death had come . . . so easily. Below him, I could see the garden as if through a thick slab of clear glass. I stared down through that prism, the ice distorting and twisting him out of all recognition, but he was already lifeless, inanimate, his face contorted in agony.

We slid away from the house, watching it sink under the ice sheets. For a moment it teetered, as if at the edge of some mysterious abyss, and then it disappeared from view without a sound.

I looked up: it had turned from night to day in a matter of seconds, here, on the surface of a new world. A flock of seagulls flew swiftly past, heading towards the silence in the east. All around us callea lilies were opening up like crimson gashes in the ice, their black roots shooting fissures through the white glaze. In the distance, I glimpsed an immense ivory gate arching into the sky and, beyond it, the shimmering plains of Pannonia, harvested fields of sunflowers stretching away towards the horizon. But even those sunflowers were white, as if made of stone, with slate-coloured fish frozen on to them. I sensed America reach out to me then, rocking back and forth, her voice softly crooning a lullaby.

It was very, very cold.

September 23

A long time ago, Mother whispered to me that I would always be different. She drew me to a corner, covering my ear moistly with her mouth, out of the hearing of anyone. I pressed closer to her, engulfed by the warmth of her skirt. We didn't speak, our sounds merging with the silence. She was young then, her face imprinted on mine, bone copying bone in profile. Later, when her hair had turned grey, I would trace that profile with a finger-tip and whisper that she was beautiful still, and she would bite her lips, holding back the words until there was nothing left to say.

5

Instead of words, she would bring me flowers and fragrant twigs, cuttings from the garden, river water in a cup. We would arrange all of these in careful symmetry, hiding them in secret places, guarding them against impatient footsteps, faces. Sometimes, huddling in the stairwell, out of sight of the rooms that brought her madness back, I would hold her hands and try to wish the present away. Sometimes I would even fall asleep, trying to decipher her silences.

As I grew older, I tried to reach out and make her speak. At other times, I wanted to run away. Sensing my confusion, Mother would cross herself over and over again, the lines on her face growing deeper still as I held on to her and wiped away her tears.

We used to go to the Mátyás Church together. Standing side by side in the nave of that cavernous cathedral, we'd watch the sunlight streaming into its dark interior. Lighting a single white candle, she would lead me by the hand down the dim central aisle, past the stained glass windows, past the gloomy recessed tombs, past the velvet-curtained confessional, past the glittering golden chapels, past the fenestrals, past the modest rows of pews, past the pulpit made of plaster, past the ornate bronze baptismal, past the choir, past the chancel, past the baluster . . . until we were standing before the gleaming marble altar, face to face with the tabernacle.

Outside, the river stretched away as far as the eye could see.

In a while, that river would begin to bleed.

In a while, that river would begin to flower.

September 30

It is going to rain today. I can sense the turn in the weather. The city has gone behind a cloud, and I can no longer see the sun. I gaze down from my terrace, the Danube a shape in the distance, dark water cresting horizon.

Turning my back to the river I contemplate my house. I was born in this house, I grew up within its walls. I've lived here all my life. All my dreams, all my nightmares, all are held within these confines. I suppose that's why, when I think about it, I can never quite decide whether it has been sanctuary or prison.

I cross the terrace and enter the light-filled room that overlooks the river. A mirror greets my entrance, and I move within its captive walls. All my childhood images crystallize around this room: four-poster bed in the centre, white sheets like snowfields regardless of season, the smell of polish on wood-panelled walls, vases filled with flowers and marbles made of crystal, toys in sunlit processions along the floor, pitchers of fresh milk on the table, the scent of crinoline and perfume.

There are other rooms, of course, and long, endless corridors. Lace curtains. Trophies on the walls. Forests of crowded antlers. Shrouds.

When I was young I loved to fill the house up with people. Every room had its own imaginary inhabitants and I dedicated entire days to playing with them. But as I grew older, I replaced the imaginary people with real ones. Together, we formed the Gabriel Club. It was my dream, my inspiration. My one lasting creation.

Or so I imagined.

October 2

There are stories told of dissidence that are filled with drama and with danger. Of nights spent in dark streets dodging pursuers. Of months spent in prison. Border crossings. Underground conspiracies. Public protests. Exile.

The Gabriel Club was nothing like that. Our resistance was compelled by exhaustion, not confrontation. We were exhausted with compromise. Tired of our generation's lack of ambition, we turned away and turned inwards. There was no flamboyance in what we did, no resonant clarion calls to rebellion. Bastards of our times, we repudiated the unspoken contract that enabled our contemporaries to survive: the agreement that the regime would leave its citizens alone if the citizens did not interfere with the regime. We were committed to an open society and to the dissemination of ideas independent of the regime. To bring this about, our means were almost absurdly simple. We held seminars and meetings where we freely debated ideas, we made copies of banned books and journals, we circulated news from the outside world by word-of-mouth and, above all, we wrote and wrote to keep our spirits alive.

In the beginning, our enterprise was relatively open, but it gradually transformed into a far less public undertaking due to the surveillance and other pressures exerted on us. We became virtual recluses, dedicated to opposing the system with the force of our creativity. This transformation, from a relatively well-known collective that produced material and held discussions on a serious and regular basis, to a shadowy group of young artists waging our own, very introverted war against the repressive regime, caused a certain amount of confusion among dissident circles. Some people thought we were going too far; others accused us of self-centredness and arrogance. Out of step with the underground *avant-garde*, we began to be left alone to our own devices.

A visitor from the West with vaguely humanitarian tendencies once expressed her bewilderment at the things we saw fit to publish. Where were the revelatory indictments of the system? Where was the sense of apocalyptic condemnation? Where the calls for a new millenarian creed? As a case in point, she singled out one of our recent publications, the text of which was entirely made up of abbreviations, acronyms and the sort of mind-numbing bureaucratese familiar to all who had to live and work in close proximity to the regime. What was the point, she asked, of this? Or of the output of the disenchanted true believer who'd volunteered to write about a single day of her working life within the Party's higher echelons? When she'd handed in her effort, it had come to one hundred and fifty-eight pages of closely type-written script, and we'd printed it in its entirety as an unparalleled depiction of the near-farcical requirements of her daily routine. I refrained from pointing out the obvious to our well-intentioned Western friend: that she'd grown up in a milieu less obviously exposed to absurdity. That's why, when it came to foreign writers, we translated Kafka instead of Joyce, skipped Orwell for Beckett, preferred Platonov to our own home-grown

Koestler. The distinctions, while hardly subtle, made much more sense under the conditions we lived in.

The work exhausted us physically. Much of it was drudgery, most of it was thankless. We derived our excitement from the most tedious enterprises. We slept little, ate even less, and our exhausted bodies struggled to cope with the goals we set ourselves. There were frequent disagreements among us, many leading to open altercations and fights. We were not a stable organization, there were no fixed regulations or rules of conduct. We were a group of like-minded individualists committed to the freedom of the mind, and we pushed ourselves mercilessly and to the limits of our endurance. It was a deliberate and principled rejection of the stasis that surrounded us. We were compelled by a simple moral imperative that sustained our hopes, an imperative that grew out of the determination, modest enough, to live and not merely to survive.

Our tools were patience and persistence. We resisted conspiratorial activities because we recognized this would play into the hands of the regime. The idea of terrorism was anathema to us, and we went out of our way to avoid provoking the police. Instead, we promoted the values of compromise and engagement. We refused to demonize those who opposed our aims, even when they made their contempt clear. We were determined to subvert the system from within by a peaceful and incremental disassembling. We were young, but we were not reckless; we recognized the long haul ahead of us, and we armed ourselves with patience. We were the Gabriel Club, determined to bear witness.

There were four of us in the beginning, and four at the very end.

I suppose I should be able to write it all down.

I suppose I should be able to put it all down.

October 3

There were four of us who led the Gabriel Club, a strange and driven quartet.

9

I am thinking, as I write, of András.

To this day I find it difficult to be coherent about him. Only one image recurs. On the morning of my twenty-sixth birthday, a message scrawled across the mirror in my room: *'There's so much left that needed to be said. So much that was left unspoken between us. I pray that you will find the strength to cope. I pray to God you don't lose hope.'*

I try.

In my last letter to him, I replied: *'In the depths of my guts your seed has burned out alive.'* A mangled citation.

He didn't reply.

October 5

When I met Stefán he was a beaten poet, a man nearly broken by his resistance to the regime. He claimed that he healed under my care. He was convinced that meeting me had turned his life around. And yet, I could never quite understand him. And I was never quite as comfortable with him as I would have liked. I told him that he made me nervous, that something about him disturbed my peace of mind. His response to me was terse and hurt: 'My heart is a tiger stalking my head through winding corridors filled with your blood. Let me be.'

Strange and foolish and tortured Stefán.

In another life, perhaps.

But in this one, enough.

October 8

And, finally, János . . .

János was a stranger when he first came to us. I was sitting with Stefán and András in Gellért Park when a solemn little boy approached us with flowers. On the point of placing the bouquet on our table, he drew back and proceeded to tear the flowers up. 'On the instructions of that gentleman in the black hat . . .' He pointed, and then he gave us an elaborate bow. By that time, the gentleman himself had sauntered up. He doffed his hat. 'I've just quit my former mode of existence as an insurance clerk. I'd like you to join me in celebrating my re-entry into the free world.'

János wrote to me once from a trip he made to Auschwitz. He said he was spending his time mending broken eyeglasses for the museum. He said it took him twice as long as everyone else. Twice as long because he kept breaking down.

János.

The night János blew himself up was the end of the Gabriel Club.

After that, I abandoned everyone and shut myself away. And once again, I began replacing the real people with imaginary ones. All around me, the rooms in the house began filling up. All the rooms save one. I decided to save that one.

Save that one for my one true love.

October 10

I am looking at a black and white photograph of András and János. I took it the day after András was released. He was detained for a week for 'disseminating illegal materials'. They told him he'd been under scrutiny for months and the next time around the sentence would be far more severe. They wanted to warn him beforehand, they said, because he was a first offender and obviously a rank novice.

In the photograph, János stands behind András, his head shaven clean, dark glasses concealing his eyes, a cigarette in his hand. András is the one closer to the camera; he is pale and unshaven, and there are dark circles under his eyes. He wears the guarded look I will soon learn to recognize. Behind the two of them the wall is a dark space filled with shadows.

I remember András telling me about the marble flagstones in the room they'd held him in; he was reluctant to say anything about the interrogation itself. They asked me questions, he said, that was all, the welts on his hands giving lie to his words. When I asked, What questions? he replied they'd taken him to a church.

11

A beautiful old church, rococo, with flagstones on the floor and a grey light pouring in from the courtyard. Square white flagstones, he said very precisely, about twelve inches across, with a hundred and forty of them along the width of the room and about three hundred down its length. There were flowers on the altar at the far end, he smiled; you have to hand it to them, sometimes they have a sharp sense of humour.

A woman had interrogated him in the beginning, which had caught him off-guard. She was very brisk, very professional, and she'd gesticulated with her hands a lot. She wore a necklace made of coral and he had focused on that and ignored her questions. Now I know more about coral than I ever wanted to, he smiled. Very useful information.

The woman had given way to a man, apparently her superior, and one endowed with less patience and a rather different technique. He'd asked András just once if he would collaborate, and then he'd told him to sit back and relax.

Don't tell János this, András confided to me, but the interrogator was his brother, Andor; he had specifically asked for the assignment. It made for a very interesting interaction, he added grimly, one loaded with innuendo, rancour and a peculiar kind of hatred.

Looking at the photograph now, I wonder if János had known about his brother's role, despite our precautions. It would explain the look on his face, that stony mask of anger. Not long afterwards, he'd turned to me and said he'd been contemplating killing his brother.

October 12

Less than a week later we began to see the same grey car parked across the street from the house. There was usually one man at the wheel and another slumped beside him reading a newspaper. Sometimes, though, only the driver turned up. He lounged behind the wheel and littered the kerb with cigarettes. There wasn't even the slightest attempt to keep up pretences.

One extremely hot and muggy afternoon I took him a bottle

12

of water but he left before I could cross the street and realize my good intentions. Another time I positioned myself in front of their car and treated them to Bach's suites for unaccompanied cello. A sophomoric gesture, perhaps, but one eminently filled with satisfaction. They lasted through the first three suites and then they gave up and drove away. I wondered what they'd found more objectionable: Bach, or my evident composure.

They came back, of course. I was on the terrace waiting for András when I saw him bicycling down the street, the grey car following closely behind. When he alighted at the gate, they pulled up beside him and there was an instant confrontation. By the time I reached the scene, I could hear András protesting, his voice brittle with anger. I burst out of the gate to find them searching through the contents of his bag. As they turned towards me, a gust of wind snatched away some of the papers. They spiralled down the street, one of the men in hot pursuit. His partner pushed András against the car and held him there. They had a quick conference and then they let András go. The car pulled away as I stared at András in confusion. He returned my look with a mysterious grin. We walked down the street towards the scattered pieces of paper. I picked up the first sheet and stared at it in surprise. Then I began to laugh. András had been carrying the score of Beethoven's Opus 130. I'd asked him to bring it and had forgotten all about it in the excitement.

So that's how it was: Bach and Beethoven on the same afternoon.

Quite the day for internal security policemen and musical interludes.

October 15

When András suggested to me one morning that we go down to an abandoned church he knew of, thirty-seven miles from Pest, I wasn't in the least bit surprised. He appeared to have developed a fascination with churches ever since his interrogation. He kept talking about the different churches in the city, but almost always in terms of their architectural features. This is not a turn towards religion, he assured me slyly, simply a new-found interest in a certain kind of aesthetic.

We took the train there, the three of us: András, János and I. On the way to the church they walked on ahead across the broad undulating fields and left me far behind. I watched their briskly striding forms and wondered if I should be jealous. I sat down on a rock and reminded myself of what I loved most about András – his freedom from emotional artifice of any kind – and I wondered if I even had the right to feel dismay. Now that I think about it, I can't quite recall what my conclusion was. Nor can I remember much about the church except that it was low-roofed, with a wide-open courtyard and a steeple that was the sole indication that it had once been a place of worship and not a barracks house. But I do remember the fields, the endless fields floating towards the horizon, not even a blanket of cloud thrown across their shoulders.

October 18

A night in András's room. It is winter, it is cold. This night occurred four years ago but I have trained myself to think back like this; I have trained myself to remember the past and to write it down. This is not because I am living in the past, or that I can't let go of it, but because I am trying to understand what went wrong, so terribly wrong with us.

András lives in a room that has two levels. A flight of steps separates the upper level, where he has his bed, from the lower one, where I am sitting on the floor. I have my hands around my knees, my body hunched forward to ward off the cold. András says he doesn't mind the cold; sometimes, to prove his point, he leaves his windows open at night.

Now he paces the room, reciting from *Hamlet*. He reads from Pasternak's translation, which he says he prefers to the original. His thin face is in profile to me, and his right hand rises and falls with his declamation. I cannot take my eyes off him.

Later that night I watch him as he lowers himself naked into the metal trunk that serves as his bath. He has coated it with

14

bitumen to make it watertight. He perches on the rim, his feet immersed in the water, a candle lighting up his face and ribs. He cups his hands and washes his face. The water drips from his hands, it trickles down his face and his chest. The room around him is dark, only that single candle lighting up the haiku of the bath.

That was the night András gave me the orchid. It was a white giant, its flame replacing the candle as we put it out. A white gift to make love with, our breaths quickening and slowing, our flesh clothed in petals.

In the deserted street outside, snow. In that room from a long time ago, instead of a bed, a sarcophagus.

October 20

András was my lover for three years. He was my lover and the man I respected most of all. We tried to keep our relationship secret, each reluctant to compromise the integrity of our work with our private passion. He was a writer who wrote with a poet's grace and a child's clarity of vision; I was a musician who resorted to writing when my music became impossible. I looked to him for inspiration, and he . . .

He.

October 21

He is laughing inside my head tonight; I can see his white teeth glinting in the dark, the veins standing out on his forehead as he throws his head back and laughs.

I wonder if he is laughing at my visitors from this morning. There were three of them, all men in plain clothes, completely at ease as they arranged themselves around my front door, one on either side of the path, one in the centre. I recognized only one of them, János's brother, his eyes riveted to the ground, shoulders tense, left hand clenching and unclenching.

The man on the right lights a cigarette, his hands cupping the

15

flame. He is bearded, the only one without a jacket, he looks like a young poet, not a thug. Next to him, hands in pockets, legs wide apart, the stereotypical state security agent looking for trouble.

I wait for them to speak but as usual they are silent. This is a game to them, a game without rules, a game they have played with me for over four years now.

The man with the cigarette throws his match into the shrubbery. He steps forward and offers me a cigarette and I indicate my refusal. He looks confused, then disgusted. He steps back and looks at János's brother for guidance. On cue, Andor raises his eyes to me and says, 'It is time for you to go.' His voice is low, so low I can hardly hear him. I stare at his tightly set jaw, sense his barely contained anger. This is a man waiting for a pretext to explode.

I deny him the pleasure. I say nothing at all.

They glare at me; then they turn to look at each other. The man in the middle takes his hands out of his pockets and folds them into fists. I notice – and he makes sure that I do – his large hands. Finally, after an acceptable period of intimidation, they turn around and walk away and I am left alone until their next visit.

October 23

There is nothing of János in his brother. János was a gentle giant; his brother is a stranger looking for violence. There is something vicious about him, a fire threatening to spill and spin out of control. Had I the choice, I would have gone to great lengths to avoid him. As matters stand, he has made my house his main theatre of operations following his brother's death. It is a subtle and inverted form of revenge. There is little that I do that is not under his surveillance. Once he accosted me on the street and thrust a diagram of my house in my face, a blueprint of great finesse. You are that red mark in the diagram, he said grimly, the fly caught in the web. His thumb encircled the mark and pressed down on it. From now on there will be little in your life that will be private.

To counter this, I developed new habits. I stopped bringing friends home, stopped going out as often, gave up the telephone, kept more and more to myself. It was a battle of attrition, and I was willing to invest all the time I had to play it out to the end.

It was as János had taught me, his advice one evening as he'd lain bare-chested on the terrace, staring at the sky. The only weapons we have are time, ingenuity and patience, he'd said; they have everything else. We live inside their cage, the bars are invisible, they hold the keys to all the gates. But time is a powerful antidote to oppression, and our ingenuity more than matches theirs. We know how to play their game, we know when to take advantage of them and when to draw back, and we can keep them constantly guessing. The joker in the pack is patience, that is the rogue that will determine who wins out in the end.

That's what he'd called it, the joker in the pack, laughing softly as he'd pronounced the word, then increasingly with less control. Patience! he'd cried out: Patience! The world will be won with a little bit of patience! – his laughter rising to a shout, his head rising from the ground only to fall back again. All we need is a little bit of patience!

I walk out on to the terrace and lie down where he had lain that evening. Last night's rain has left the terrace drenched and dark. I turn on my stomach and press my face to the ground. The flagstones smell of rain, dust, pollen. There is a shadowy trellis of trees on the window panes. I listen to their rustle the way I had listened to his laughter, his lesson about patience. I enter his memory and the burn is instant. Instant the pain.

He'd ended his life the same way he'd lived it, impulsively and with the minimum of fuss. An object lesson in ingenuity, decisiveness, self-discipline and courage. But emphatically not in patience.

And now I write everything down.

Everything is written down in an attempt to overcome, to salvage, to assuage.

I can see János standing in my room on the evening before his death. He stands before the window, his eyes gazing out at the marbled sky, his forehead pressed against the glass. Although it is still light outside, in the room it is already dark. He gestures at the grey sedan on the street and speaks in an undertone about his brother. 'He is afraid,' he says. 'He is afraid of anyone who is different from him, and his fear has made him sick. His fear is a contagion, a fiction, and I feel a great pity for him. Which is a pity in and of itself, if you think about it . . .'

He walks over and stretches out on my bed. 'Everything dances with its shadows . . .' he muses, 'and all freedom falls before the dark line of fate.'

He rises from the bed and crosses out on to the terrace. I watch him walk over to the parapet and point his finger like a pistol at the car on the street. He lingers there for a moment and then he turns around and walks away. Entering my room again, he says briskly, 'Perhaps I'm going to have to kill him to prove to myself that I'm still alive. Or kill myself to bring him to his senses.'

'What is that?' I ask tentatively. 'A rhetorical statement?'

He turns his head to consider my question, his face in shadow.

'I feel in pieces, you know . . .' he says slowly, 'the pieces of a person waiting.'

'Waiting for what, János?'

'For an end to this sense of helplessness. Hopelessness.'

'And this, from the great proponent of patience?'

He doesn't respond directly. Instead, he says, 'I've always believed that when things are as dark as they are now, we must recreate them in our own image.'

I try to understand his words, but unknown to me it is already too late.

The next day he walks straight up to the police car and easily disarms its startled occupants. Trussing them up securely, he places them at a safe distance on the pavement. 'Tell my brother this is for him,' he says. 'Fingers of fire, like birds, embracing kin. A gift for his conscience.' Ever the ironist, he inserts a photograph of himself and Andor, taken when they were children, in each of the bound men's pockets. Then he returns to the car and douses himself with the petrol he has brought with him. The match lit, the deed done, the explosion can be heard for miles around.

October 26

The day after János's death there were only three of us inside the frosted church: András, the black-clad priest, and I. The coffin was white. It could be no other colour. In the diffused darkness, I lit thirty candles, one for each year of his life. Later, I filled a cup with water from the river and watched the setting sun colour it over, only to drain away death-like soon after.

When I came back home that evening I sat down at the piano that had meant so much to him. After a while, I realized that I just couldn't bring myself to play. I shut the lid, turned off the lights and walked away.

The days that followed were like dead and dark weights pressing relentlessly down on me. I tried exorcizing them with water from the river – cool, damp splashes on my face. Sometimes it worked, reviving me. Most other times the memory of János resting in a cold coffin overwhelmed everything and I would wish for night again, pray for sleep again. I would lie motionless in bed, listening hour after hour to the whispering growth of mould on the walls, my mind weighed down by a sense of the most terrible solitude. Beyond me, beyond the boundaries of my room, I could see the vibrant summer shadows of trees, a blend of street sounds drifting through them. Within me, fatigue . . . fear and fatigue . . . tongue pressed against the sharp edges of teeth. Courage, I counselled myself. If I could find the strength, despite everything . . .

And so I existed, hesitating to enter into conversations with anyone but myself. In the sleeping hours I covered my eyes and tried to forget the past. In the waking hours, I covered my mouth, mute like Mother, voiceless, speechless. The comfort of company passed me by as I withdrew from the world and attempted to reconstruct my life. I wandered in and out of books, streets, rooms with people, pages in my diaries, memories, events, my intuition always several moments too late to make a difference, especially to myself.

These stumps of memories, their deadening glitter.

October 29

For almost three months following János's death, I managed to maintain his cyclostyling machines and turn out copies of forbidden materials just as he would have wanted. But the task soon proved too much without his expert guidance. The machines started breaking down, and there were more and more errors. Then András suggested disposing of the machines altogether, their presence in the house a continuing reminder of János. After initially resisting the suggestion, I agreed to let go of the larger machines; they were simply too cumbersome to be of any use and we gave them to friends who were eager to make use of them. The smaller ones I moved down to my cellar. People I knew advised me against this: the house was under constant surveillance; any kind of illegal activity on my part was bound to be instantly reported. I listened to their advice in good faith, but my natural stubbornness intervened. I continued to hold seminars and circulate banned materials, albeit to a steadily diminishing audience. Over the next few months I exhausted all of my strength and most of my resources with little to show save a litany of mishaps that reflected my intransigence. Soon even I had to acknowledge there was no point in carrying on. And still I kept postponing a decision, unwilling to come to terms with the inevitable. There was more to this paralysis than I was willing to admit. Printer's ink washed over my conscious moments; it coloured my sleep every night when I closed my eyes and fell into exhausted oblivion. Every day I agonized over the decision to terminate the last vestiges of the Gabriel Club. I took long walks by myself, going over the alternatives. And I maintained my journal, faithfully recording the tedious procession of days, each one exactly like the next in all but the smallest details.

I was wiping printing ink off my hands one evening when the waiting finally caught up with me. As I was drying my hands on an apron I suddenly felt an immense sadness flood through me. I threw away the apron and switched off the machines. (Despite that apron, I invariably ended up getting ink all over myself, the brackish taste of it lingering in the skin long after I had stopped working.) I knew I had finally reached the decision to close down the press. For an instant I held the moment in my hands, mentally crafting alternatives. Outside, the city seemed to pause as well in quiet consideration. Then it resumed its motion with a shrug, brusque bustle, while I locked the door to the print room one last time and threw away the key.

I woke up today thinking about that. For a while, I simply lay in bed, looking around the room. It was difficult not to notice the paint peeling on the walls, the curtains fraying. Everything looked so utterly worn and threadbare.

As I lingered between the sheets, a single shaft of sunlight crept across the room. There was a peculiarly enticing quality to it. Clambering out of bed, I chased that fleeting bar of light to the ground. Cornered, it gave up, turning around and slipping in through my skin, golden. Sensing the warmth within, I clapped my hands, the sound breaking through the surrounding silence. I could still hear the cadence echoing through the empty rooms as I walked over to the mirror and brushed back strands of hair from my face. I looked at my eyes and they looked back. When I turned away, they were still watching me.

Leaving the room, I walked out on to the terrace. I drew a deep breath, the crisp, dry air rushing into me. It was a beautiful day: gorgeous white-hot sun cresting the sky. The radiance wrapped around me like a sunflower.

It reminded me of America.

21

November 2

I returned home one evening and ran into America – Ami – walking out of the house. Since I never locked the door, a practice I refused to abandon despite the surveillance, I stopped, wondering whether the stranger had come to the wrong address. She stopped as well, looking at me uncertainly before extending her hand in greeting. Taken aback, I replied that I was sorry and that I didn't intend to appear rude, but I didn't think we'd met . . . when she smiled quickly and introduced herself. She'd heard a lot about me, she said, and she'd been looking forward to this meeting for a long time. Before I could respond, she stepped forward and kissed me on the mouth, and I remember moving back a few steps and almost losing my balance. I felt breathless and overwhelmed, and she must have noticed my discomfort, because she hastened to apologize for any assumptions she might have made. It was just that she'd heard so much about me, she repeated, reaching forward to hold my hand, but I turned away and sat down on the steps. With a look of concern she sat down as well, her hands clasped before her, her face suddenly tense. I think she expected some kind of rebuke from me. She waited for me to speak, her expression defensive and tremulous, but also defiant. It took me a moment to collect myself. More composed now, I reached out to touch her in lieu of words. I could also see that our meeting had been witnessed: my friends in the car parked across the street were staring fixedly at us. In the meantime, she had already begun telling me she would come back another time when I persuaded her to stay, letting her know that her visit had attracted attention, that it would be unwise to leave just then.

We went into the house, and she stayed for almost two hours, an encounter alternating between mordant curiosity and understandable reticence.

November 5

The night following Ami's visit I went down to the river. I had taken to going there in the evenings because my watchers were less vigilant once darkness fell. There was a stretch of river outside the city I had discovered a few years ago and I went there to swim at least once a week.

There was a bridge across the river, and a spiral stairway that led straight down to the water's edge. I walked down the steps and undressed behind a bank of rocks, the river less than a silhouette over my shoulder. I hung up my clothes on the branches of a willow tree, only the sound of my breathing disturbing the silence. I did not come here for comfort, I came here to renew myself.

The water was warm and it surrounded me with a wash of silence. I swam out to where the river was deepest, in the shadows under the bridge, where the bedrock buckled and dipped and there was nothing under my feet save a sudden, sharp void. I closed my eyes and immersed my head and when I rose again there was a sliver of silver outlining my ascent. I was halfway across the world now, all my anxieties and cares forgotten. I had shed my customary skin and I looked for a different kind of truth under the cover of water. The river was my armour, and there was nothing anyone could do to me there. My subterranean skin had made me impregnable.

I lay down on the river bank and gazed up at the night sky, my mind so concentrated that the stars appeared invisible. It was my visitor from the morning who occupied my thoughts, she who had suddenly made my world unstable. There was something about her child-like assurance, her familiar, easy confidence that undermined my sense of self. I tried to pinpoint what it could be that was upsetting me. I questioned my own suspicions; perhaps the life I lived had made me paranoid, unable to trust the way a normal person should. There was a difference between faces in the light and faces in the darkness. And yet, despite all these careful considerations, the more I thought about the matter, the more I was led to question her *intent*.

Who was she and what were her motives? Why had she chosen to seek me out precisely when my past history and my present circumstances had combined to leave me at my most vulnerable?

She was the most self-absorbed person I had ever met. She loved to talk about herself, blissfully oblivious to everything else. It was integral to her charm, reminding me of a film or a book wrapped up in the circle of its own narrative. I told her that in one of our fleeting early conversations and she came back the following day, asking me to explain what I had meant. I purposely decided to be a bit perverse. I said that she was much less profound than she imagined herself. Shocked by my forthrightness, she stared at me in silence, slowly drinking her coffee. Then she told me, in a small voice, that she didn't want to have anything more to do with me.

We met again the next day, of course.

She mentioned later that she had been attracted precisely by my willingness to criticize her. I provoked her to think, unlike the people at the artists' cooperative where she lived. They were intimidated by her, she said, and, for her part, she felt nothing but contempt for them. The important thing, though, was that they left her alone, it was a cheap place to stay, and she had all the studio space she needed to pursue her painting. Would I like to visit? She invited me there one bitterly cold evening.

The building turned out to be a warehouse that had once been used to refrigerate meat. In its present incarnation, it was so littered with the paraphernalia of an art studio it was almost a cliché. Wherever one looked there were endless rolls of drawing paper, dozens of frames used to stretch canvases, discarded paintbrushes, balls of cotton wool, wood shavings and, of course, stacks of canvases. The predominant features, though, were the banks of easels leaning against the walls, some carrying finished paintings on their backs, others standing bare, like scaffolding.

Ami's room was tucked away in the basement, accessible only by a narrow flight of steps. It was tiny and freezing; it had been used to store blocks of ice. The only source of light was a rusty iron grate sloping down from the ceiling. Transparent plastic sheets covered it in an attempt to keep out the draughts. A lamp with an orange shade stood in one corner, next to a bookcase and a dresser camouflaged with a kilim.

Intrigued by the austerity of her surroundings, I asked for a little more light and she switched on the lamp so that I could better examine her motley collection of things. Like the room, they were spartan and eccentric, a comment on their owner. There was a cluster of meat-hooks suspended from the ceiling, a plastic bag filled with fish scales in one corner, a hamper to hold her paint-brushes, a battered leather suitcase with clothes spilling out of it, a bookcase made from wooden packing cases, a couch in the shape of a panther with a cushioned seat astride it and, of course, the ubiquitous canvases. I later discovered that Ami slept on the floor, squeezed into the tiny space between the panther and the door.

Walking over to the bookcase, I took out a cyclostyled edition of Endre Fejes' *Generation of Rust*. It proved impossible to read, however, with a red neon street sign alternately flashing '*kávé*', '*tea*' and '*kakaó*', into the room and effectively drowning out the feeble lamp inside. I turned to examine her canvases and met with the same result. She watched my efforts with amusement, suggesting that we have coffee instead while she explained the paintings to me. She poured ceremoniously; we drank from tin cups. She said she modelled herself after Cézanne; I confessed to admiring Delacroix and David. We discussed surrealism, symbolism, the meaning of life, the bag of fish scales in the corner, the pursuit of art, free will. And we agreed to disagree on most of these topics, laughing. We were of one mind, though, when it came to artists who sold themselves to the regime. With droll understatement she referred to these individuals as revolutionaries, while at the same time delicately rolling her eyes as she parodied the usual justifications offered to explain compliance: '*Everything* has to be sacrificed to the steamship of the regime. And *everyone* must learn to content themselves with borrowed beliefs and borrowed lines.' I burst out laughing. I knew too many people who used exactly those words in exactly that tone of voice. Then she suddenly turned serious. 'I have burned many bridges to reach this place,' she said. 'It didn't always use to be this way; in the past I was quite the materialist. Now I have no regrets about living like this. From that single grate in the wall I get what light I need to paint. And every night, as I lie on the floor, I can see the moon track down the centre of the room and surround me with its radiance. That is all I need to sustain me.'

Occasionally, as she spoke, I could hear the steel-shod tramp of boots from the street, marching past the warehouse in unison. Flurries of snow would slide into the room through the grate when that happened. Ami explained that there was a police station directly across the street. It makes it very safe here, she joked, but she didn't smile.

I noticed that she had a completely idiosyncratic habit of emphasizing certain words, especially when she was excited. The words were preceded by a quick intake of breath, her speech becoming correspondingly breathless. It was a verbal tic, a charming oddity. She punctuated these moments with vigorous gestures, her face becoming increasingly animated. Very different from my own pronounced stillness.

'But I'm forgetting my obligations as a host –' she exclaimed. Was I hungry? A plywood board balanced on books transformed the room into a dining space. We each had a boiled potato garnished with herbs and cream. She ate hers with ferocious abandon. I was more sedate, sitting across from her and gravely contemplating her ebullience.

There was much about her that reminded me of quicksilver. The constant changes in expression, the swift shifts in conversation, the inability to focus on any one thing beyond a certain point. Also, her habit, whenever she moved around the tiny room, of moving over objects rather than around them. Combined with her sinuous and almost boneless beauty, the effect was startlingly fluid. To my eyes, that strange and quick litheness went with the rest of her. She was smaller than I was, slighter than I was, and much more active and restless. She held herself with a dancer's impatient grace, the mercurial quickness of her movements communicating a sense of fleeting impermanence. Next to her, I felt large and awkward, ponderous even.

November 10

I went back to her place again – how could I resist? She showed me her latest painting, which was incomplete: she had a problem finishing her work, she said. I brought my notebooks over, I was working on my first novel. We smoked like maniacs, keeping warm. From time to time, I showed her what I had written and she would point to a particular phrase and give me her verdict. For instance, once, having picked up a piece of paper that I had summarily discarded, she said: 'This is good work. Let it be.' She made it sound like a command. Surprised, I stared at her but she only broke into an effervescent smile, making her words seem more like advice and less like a decree. I did as she suggested, feeling inexplicably reassured, while she turned away from me and went back to her painting.

One evening she put her canvas aside. She couldn't seem to focus, she said, gazing at me with a fierce intensity. Disconcerted, I tried to return to my writing but found myself increasingly unnerved by her scrutiny. When I looked up again she asked me if I realized that things between us were not as simple as they seemed. Mistaking my silence for assent, she walked over and touched my lips. Then she asked if I would agree to model for the incomplete painting. She needed inspiration, she said, and she believed that she would find what she was looking for in me. What exactly would that involve? I asked. She didn't reply. Instead, she continued to regard me with an enigmatic gaze. I lit a cigarette, stalling for time, my hands beginning to tremble. She noticed my nerves, I think. I lay down, the room suddenly very warm and oppressive. I realized I had to get out of there. I rose to my feet and made for the door.

She let me leave without saying anything.

November 12

Fathomless.

Fathomless to describe how, on my next visit, I walked in on her unintentionally. She didn't notice me. She was crouched on the floor, her back to the door. She was wearing men's clothes: brown canvas shirt, brown jacket, padded overcoat. She was naked below the waist. Her legs were damp and she was shivering violently. I saw her face in the mirror that she was holding. She'd painted a beard on her chin. I heard her speak. Her voice sounded deeper somehow. 'I am your sun,' she was saying. 'The mind is a parody. You are my sun.' She flicked the mirror with her tongue, her lips arrowing into a kiss.

I backed out of the room. Fingershocked, catatonic, she was crying silently.

November 15

Despite my better instincts, I went back two days later. She met me at the door. Her hair was damp, she'd just stepped out of the bath. She seemed preoccupied and subdued, and I sensed her hesitate before she let me in. Halfway down the steps to her room, she turned, her face troubled. In a low voice, she said that I should leave, that this was not a good time to be visiting. I was mortified. We walked back to the door and she opened it for me, stepping aside to allow me to leave. It had begun to rain outside, and as I walked down the steps the wind buffeted me from all sides and a flash of lightning pierced the street. I came to a standstill, my face mirroring my panic: I was terrified of lightning. My hands clenched by my sides, I waited for a moment, willing myself to keep on walking. On the verge of breaking into a mad run, I felt a tap on my shoulder, and then Ami rushed into the driving rain and yanked me back in. Caught off guard, I slid back to the steps, resisting her attempts to pull me in. She grabbed me by the arm and slammed the door shut behind us, and then she literally dragged me back to her room. She handed me a towel, looking on as I attempted, quite unsuccessfully, to dry myself, my numb fingers getting the better of me. Finally, to my great relief, she took the towel from me and pressed it to my face and covered my eyes with it. She rubbed the towel against my face, at first slowly, and then with a savagely circular motion so that my cheeks came up in bright red welts. Then she let go of me and sat down abruptly on the floor, her shoulders beginning to shake uncontrollably. I knelt before her, about to ask her what the matter was, when she reached out and took hold of my wrists, grasping them tightly, like a child. I closed my eyes, her head resting on my shoulder. We crouched there in the silence for a very long time. It was as if we shared a secret, but neither one of us was willing to acknowledge it.

It was still raining when I left that night.

November 17

The next time I saw Ami was by sheer accident. I was hurrying down a street on my way to the river. Turning a corner, I was brought to a standstill by an immense rose bush bursting out of a snow-covered mound. In the dead of winter, it was flowering with a wild and gay abandon. As spectacular as that was, it was Ami who caught my attention. She was sitting cross-legged in front of the bush, a canvas on her lap, her face serene. She glanced at me with a smile, accepting my presence there as a matter of course. 'Look!' she said affectionately, 'look at this mad rose! How it has lost its head! And what an exhibition it is making of itself! It has no secrets, no cryptograms hidden in its flame! It's so completely narcissistic and shameless!' Standing up, she took my hand and pointed feelingly to the grey winter sky: 'What guts it must take to bloom in a climate like *this*!'

November 18

I called her from a pay-phone the following morning. My timing was perfect, she said. The painting wasn't going too well, she was immensely frustrated, and she could certainly use my company. Why didn't I come over? Very well, I replied with alacrity. I took a bus to the warehouse. I walked into her room, expecting the usual breathless greetings and progress reports; instead, I found a surprise. She had emptied the room. All the eccentric trappings were gone; a single canvas on a large wooden easel was all that remained. Even the walls had been stripped. She said the dislocation was strictly temporary. She needed the empty space to create the atmosphere necessary for her latest painting. She'd reached a dead-end with it, she'd needed to do something different to achieve a breakthrough. Bemused, I stood in a corner and watched her as she walked around the room, talking energetically. She paused under the open grate; she'd taken off the plastic sheet. She surveyed the room with a speculative eye before positioning the easel directly below the grate, the light washing across it. That done, she studied me over the rim of the canvas, paint-brushes held at the ready. I asked to see the painting, which she'd covered with a burlap sheet. 'All in good time,' she smiled at me. 'Meanwhile, I have a request. I'd like to look at you for a full five minutes without any conversation or movement. Could you do that for me?' Intrigued, I agreed. Pleased, she lit a cigarette, adjusting the folds of her painter's smock as she brought a chair into the room and sat down facing me. I gazed back at her, trying my best not to look self-conscious. She seemed quite unruffled, her gaze remarkably composed and placid. It made me want to reach out and touch her, but I remembered our agreement and resisted the impulse, knowing that it would displease her if I did. So we both sat there, the smoke from her cigarette intermittently screening her off from me. Gradually, her expression began to alter, her face becoming cold and impersonal. She turned very pale, her lips narrowing into a thin line. And the look in her eyes! For once I was truly baffled. I read fear there, and hate. Taken aback, I tried to find a semblance of love, or even friendship. But she only leaned forward on her chair, her entire being focused on me with that strangely intent antipathy. Her hostility seemed to weigh down on me with a centrifugal force and I had to look away, aware that she was examining me almost as if I were an inanimate object, or, even worse, a freakish curiosity.

Five minutes seemed like a very long time. When they were finally over, I wrenched myself away from her prying gaze, asking her what the matter was. It's nothing, she said. You're lying! I accused her, losing patience for once. Yes, of course I am, she replied. That much must have been obvious . . .

30

I turned my back on her after that and left almost immediately, running most of the way home.

November 20

I returned the next morning. I had to. It must have been earlier than I realized because she was still asleep. She was curled up on the floor within a crumple of plastic sheets. She woke up as I walked in. I must have shown my surprise at her rather unusual sleeping arrangements because she smiled disarmingly. 'It makes me feel protected,' she explained, 'as if I were a chrysalis.' Pulling me down beside her, she threw a bare leg over me and pressed her mouth affectionately to my cheek. She was in a much better mood today, she said, and apologized for yesterday's incident. She was planning to go into the city, she wanted to buy paints and a canvas. Would I like to accompany her? Of course I would, I said, relieved that the misunderstanding had resolved itself so easily. I made some tea while she left the room to wash. Our strange interaction from the day before seemed entirely forgotten.

We walked through the city on the way back from the art supplier. The day was very clear, the light bright and sunny. There wasn't a single cloud in the sky, everything stood out in sharp, focused detail. Ami complemented the weather with her exuberance. She seemed elated, exalted, and I wanted to share in her excitement. We sat down by the river and I told her about myself. I spoke about my early determination to become a musician and the difficulties that I had faced. I talked about my subsequent turn to writing. I told her about the Gabriel Club and why it had meant so much to me. Some of it must have sounded naive but she hung on to my every word, asking me the most specific questions. I don't know how long I talked, but I remember it being such a relief. I found it easier to confide in her than I had almost anyone in the past. But I didn't tell her about my personal life. And I didn't tell her about András.

She didn't ask.

Instead, she requested my manuscript. She said she'd been wanting to read it for a while but she'd been too shy to ask. She

31

suggested going back to my place and getting it. Caught up in her mood, we hailed a cab, an unprecedented luxury. Once we reached my house, however, she insisted on waiting outside. 'It's better this way,' she insisted, stubbornly resisting my attempts to coax her in. Resigning myself to these sudden shifts in mood, I moved away, not knowing what to make of this new reticence. I unlatched the gate and walked down the driveway, looking back on the off-chance that she might have changed her mind. But she was standing erect and still, her back firmly to the house.

When I returned with the manuscript, she swivelled around and thrust her face at me. 'Do you believe the past can ever die?' she demanded aggressively. She waited for a second to gauge the impact of her question. Then she spun on her heels and marched off even as I searched for a reply.

November 23

An entire week went by before I could see Ami again. She had asked me not to visit; yet another of her capricious decisions. Overruling my protests, she'd explained that it was a test. A test of what? I'd asked resentfully. Of our friendship, of course, what else?

We met at her place, as usual. I was still very sullen and made certain that she understood that I was reaching the end of my tether. Our conversation, already desultory, began to falter hopelessly until she took the matter in hand and asked me to leave. She said it was obvious I didn't understand her, and she saw no point in our wasting each other's time like this.

For the first time, I refused to agree with her. I held my ground and insisted that she explain what she wanted from me. She eyed me hesitantly, obviously uncertain about how to deal with my intransigence. Then she asked if I was certain I could face up to the consequences of my question. I told her to stop being so patronizing. In reply, she walked over to a shoebox and took out a photograph from it. She paused for a moment before handing it to me. This is for you, she said. I stared at it, my hand closing over it in surprise. It was a postcard-sized photograph of

Ami lying naked. A clear, startling detail: the amber tuft between her thighs exactly matched the amber of her eyes.

I handed back the photograph without a word. My throat felt parched and dry, and I found myself unable to speak. She stepped forward with a strange smile, her face set and white. 'Now you know what I want from you,' she said calmly. 'Come here. Come to me.'

I didn't move. I couldn't move. She walked up to me. I watched her, my eyes smarting as if they'd been staring at the sun. She stopped before me and reached out to touch my lips. Her hand was cold, her touch like frost. 'Tell me what I have to do . . .' she said, 'to escape memory.'

I opened my mouth, barely managing a 'Why?'

Her lips were trembling. Her hands clenched into fists. Her voice broke as she replied, 'Because I am tortured by this moment.'

My eyes fell. 'I am very tired.'

'We are all very tired,' she replied. 'Look at me.'

I kept my eyes fixed to the ground. I couldn't fight her, I didn't want to. She was in my blood, already in my blood. I wanted to surrender.

She leaned her head against me. Her face slid down to my shoulder, then lower. She straightened up and slipped off my jacket. Her hand moved to my face and she touched my lips, her fingers brushing my cheeks. I raised my face. I let her kiss me. Our lips were dry. She kissed me again, her mouth searching. I held on to her hands; they were surprisingly strong and wise, the fingers rough-grained and blunt.

I let her undress me. She did it calmly. I felt my clothes drop away, aware that everything was moving slower than usual. I wanted to laugh. I wanted to break down. Instead, she made me lie down. I stretched out on the cold stone. She turned me on my side, my arm stretching out towards her. Her hair fell across my face, across the white-eyed staring of my face. She covered my head with a velvet sleeve. Inside my mask, a shiver of possibilities, dark. Outside, the rasp of her brushstrokes on the canvas as she painted recklessly, furiously.

Later that night, she showed me the results of our joint undertaking. I gazed at the canvas in fascination, taking it in with half

33

my mind while the other half sensed her slipping out of her clothes behind me. I was still staring at the canvas when she touched my back, her fingers running down my hips, shivering, quick. I closed my eyes and clenched my teeth to keep from crying out, my hands gripping the canvas as I leaned into the painting of me leaning into a painting of me . . .

November 26

To be turned into a painting.

Or a photograph. To be turned into a print. To be laid out bare. To be displayed. To be transformed. To have skin turned into black and white, flesh into tint. To have clothes stripped away; to watch clothes drop away, winged. To be made to stare at oneself. In a photograph. As an object. From a distance. Or up close, on a canvas, splayed. Right side up, as on a wooden block; or flattened against a metal press. To be framed on a wall, naked frame within space of naked frame. To be bent forwards, backwards; to be made into a collage, dismembered, separated. To be forced to assume a hundred different forms and shapes. To be moulded; to be folded. To be transformed, willingly in the beginning, and at the very end, without will.

There was no point in my denying it. I was obsessed. I was obsessed with Ami. But obsession should be like that – like a convulsion. I was intoxicated. But passion should be like that. A transcending of space and time. Things spinning out of control. Day after day after night.

December 2

One day Ami turned to me and confessed that she was painting better than ever before since we had become lovers. It was strange, she said, this intensity of feeling, but she found my company immensely reassuring. She said she sensed my intuitive faith in her abilities. She said she knew that I believed in her. In the final analysis, wasn't that what was most important in a

34

relationship? And now it was almost as if she needed my appreciation in order to be able to create. 'It's almost as if I *need* to believe that you care for me . . .'

Did I feel the same way? Did I sense a feeling of release, a liberation?

Yes, I did, I replied hesitantly.

Then this was good – no? There must be a certain reciprocity.

I walked home thinking about what she had said. Although it wasn't that simple for me, even I could feel my natural reserve begin to ebb away. It was her sense of vitality that was most affecting me. The way she lived, so carelessly, so independently. The way she drew me out – entering the space around me and instantly suffusing it with energy, electricity. I envied her confidence and her ease. Against that, my own attempts to get to know her better must have seemed like stilted geometry. I told her that in one of our meetings. That's right, she laughed, teasing me. It was her invisible aura: she was proton-woman, electron, neutron, turn-on, everything!

December 6

That was the way it was between us in the beginning. Her constant laughter bubbled and welled over my own melancholic temperament, washing through it like a stream, bringing the light back in. She was just like a wilful child in the many ways in which she lured me out of my self-imposed cage, her incurable optimism a constant source of amazement to me. We began writing to each other almost every day, her letters to me as long and involved as mine were becoming. There seemed no end to the things we could learn from each other. There were differences between us, of course. Very early on, I realized that there was an air of calculation in everything she did or said that was entirely alien to me. But it didn't matter; nothing mattered in the light of what she was giving me. I felt as if I constantly needed to contain the relationship in order not to let it exceed its proper boundaries. There was always the danger it would swallow my entire world. It was unnerving to have to treat something so good with so much caution.

35

It was only a matter of time before I asked her to move in with me. She hesitated in the beginning; there was a curious ambivalence on her part about the prospect of living in my house. She even suggested that we take an apartment in the city and share the rent, an idea that had to be rapidly discarded given our financial straits. I kept at her, however, with a doggedness that surprised both of us, and eventually she gave in. Less than three months after our first meeting, Ami agreed to live with me.

It was a revelation, the speed with which she imprinted her personality on mine. Together we wandered around the house naked, writing, painting, making music. I wrote fugues dedicated to her; she made tiny wooden sculptures for me. White horses were especially important to her. White horses that 'ran faster than the wind'. I called them the white horses of Lilith.

She had all these aspirations to art, the rooms littered with incomplete canvases. Pride of place, however, was reserved for a work she entitled 'Gemini'. It hung over the mantelpiece in my room, the only one of her paintings she deemed complete enough to put on display. A blank white canvas with a straight black line running diagonally across it. Nothing else was allowed to mar its perfect symmetry. It seemed the ideal metaphor for our relationship. I told her so, but she only smiled.

In the afternoons, she tended to curl up with a book, her lips pursed in concentration, feet swinging in the air, small white soles flashing like minnows. I would often find her like that, sighing in rapt little rushes of sleep, the book discarded in a spiral of open pages. I could stare at her sleeping face for hours, losing myself in her smallest sounds. I savoured those moments of being with her, watching the gentle ebb and flow of her chest, my fingers running over her, never actually touching. She had the softest skin. When I brushed my fingertips along her arms, I felt instantly reassured, my own flesh prickling in sympathy. Sometimes I even wondered if I preferred these times when she was asleep to her waking moments when everything seemed so much at sea.

When I look back, I recognize how taken I was with her. Or maybe we just had very different ideas of love and sharing. Very different ideas of giving. At the time, though, the mere idea of having her all to myself was enough to banish all my doubts and self-questioning. Every night I found myself lying wide-awake beside her after she had fallen asleep, my eyes staring at the ceiling, my mind wondering about the future. I think I was realistic enough to know that things couldn't go on like this indefinitely. Nothing in my life had, and there was no reason to believe that this would turn out any differently. Sometimes, almost as if she'd sensed my unease, Ami would wake up whispering.

Once, for instance, almost inaudibly, 'Do you . . . do you think it's raining in the woods, in Central Park, in New York?'

'In New York?'

'Yes, yes, can't you hear the thunder, the deluge . . . the traffic rushing down the rain-drenched streets?'

I smiled. 'No,' I said, 'all I can hear is the tremor in your voice.'

We would sit together on the terrace every evening. I loved to watch the light retreating along the Danube; I never tired of it. Ami jokingly referred to it as my evening tonic. It brought me an uncanny sense of peace, a sense of the day's natural ending. We would lean against each other, our shadows mingling and spilling to the floor, the flagstones around us dyed golden.

'Is it raining in New York, London . . . the Amazon?'

'Yes, my love, close your eyes, can't you hear the thunder, see the shadow of bells in the sky . . . lightning?'

She would laugh and open her eyes wide, her hands stretching out and merging into me in an endless embrace, an endless kiss.

December 10

When the time of troubles began, it was Judas-like: swift and without warning. One day Ami told me she had found a job at a local theatre. She was going to be working there from the early evening until late at night. Surprised at the hours, I asked her where the theatre was, but she wouldn't tell me. I asked her if it was safe to be working those hours and offered to escort her there every evening. She turned me down, as I suspected she would, telling me there wasn't any cause for concern. I tried

37

reasoning with her, but that only made matters worse. Soon she took to staying out all night, sullenly wandering home the next morning and sleeping through the day until it was time to get up once more and leave. I confronted her, telling her how worried I was by her secrecy. She reacted with a breathless belligerence, almost shivering in her fury. What was the matter with me, she demanded. Did I envy her freedom? Did I want to completely stifle her creativity? Taken aback and hurt, I asked her what she was implying. 'Can't you see?' she burst out. 'You're so dreadfully earnest! You're draining the life out of me! I need colour, life, danger, uncertainty! I need the sharp edges of things! You can't give me that! You're draining all that out of me!'

Then she accused me of following her; she said that I knew exactly how things were degenerating between us and, as far as she was concerned, she had had enough of me. Of course, I had to deny it all, my voice rising in anger. I realized that she had turned the tables on me, that she had suddenly become the victim and I the persecutor. There were a million things I could have thrown back at her in response. Instead, I controlled myself and said that she was reacting with a ferocity quite out of pro-portion to my original question, and that there was something unnerving about this overnight transformation of love to an almost pathological distrust and hostility. She replied that she was fed up with my morbid seriousness; she said it reminded her of decay and of dying; that it was just like my writing. I looked at her in disbelief. I told her she couldn't possibly have meant what she'd said. She countered by handing me back my manuscript. 'I couldn't finish it,' she said, cold and brisk, 'I didn't have the energy. It was far too tedious and debilitating.'

After that, I studiously ignored her presence, believing that there had to be a limit to how bad things could get between us, and that she would eventually come to her senses and apologize. I cared about her and she was being completely unreasonable and selfish. I was not a confrontational person by nature, and I was willing to wait for her to realize how despicably she was behaving.

We had our next altercation a few days later. It began with her telling me I could never be a man. Before I could react, she had already changed the topic and accused me, once again, of following her: 'I *know* you're following me. Don't try to hide it. I know you're spying on me!' She said she wanted me to know she carried a gun, and when I looked at her, bewildered, she rushed out of the house. I watched her as she ran down the street. I made no attempt to stop her. I knew she didn't have a gun. But after that, I could no longer concentrate on anything. I kept thinking about our exchanges, disturbing in so many ways, but also good; sobering for my passions. My thoughts wandered back to the feelings of affirmation that had used to run between us, my mind searching for a return to that communion. I told myself I had always been aware this was a dangerous game, but wasn't all love like that? Was that why she had become so tense? Why were we even in this battle? We were both losing out, couldn't she see?

Then, one day, she failed to come home at all. Instead, I was woken up the next morning by someone banging on the front door. Thinking that it was Ami, I hurried down, wondering what could have happened to her keys. Perhaps she had lost them. It didn't matter, I was prepared to be nonchalant. What did I care that she was becoming so callous and erratic?

I opened the door. There was a man standing there, a blond stranger, very muscular and athletic. He said he had come to take away her things.

'And who are you?' I asked.

'I'm a friend of hers,' he replied, handing me a crumpled envelope.

I ripped open the envelope in my haste.

She had written two words on a torn piece of paper.

Two words. That's all.

'*Useless explaining.*'

Two words.

The blond man left with her belongings.

December 15

A week later there was a letter from her. It was postmarked in Venice. I opened it with trembling hands, not knowing what to expect. There was nothing inside. No letter, no photographs, no odds and ends, nothing. Instead, in one corner, I found a minute splinter of stained glass. I placed it on my hand, closing my eyes.

Tell me, tell me please, is it raining in New York?

What?

New York . . . is it raining there?

Yes, my love, it is, and the storm has swept away everything. It is a deluge, after all, and the water just keeps on rising. And I can see your shadow in the sky – fly, America, fly. You spread your arms, but you have no wings.

America, my love, my flesh was far truer than the entire kingdom of words exchanged between us. And now, even in my deepest sleep, you are the sore festering below my breast, the open wound I lick from lip to lip, worn, threadbare, with no idea of what happened to you, to me, to us . . .

December 19

Enough! Enough of this yearning backwards, this bitterness, this futile reminiscing! Enough of this living like a shroud!

Long ago, Ödön Diósy wrote that memory is a receptacle, full of nothing, a dangerous maze to lose oneself in. Escaping from the bondage of my past, I fled today to the banks of the Danube, the voices and the memories cluttering up my mind. I took a tram to hasten my flight, but it broke down half-way to the river. We trooped out of the stalled car in single file. An old man in front of me turned around and leaned into my hearing, speaking bitterly: 'Nothing functions in this damned country any more! Nothing, man or machine!' His voice broke: 'They are slow-poisoning us, mark my words! – they are poisoning the little that's left with kerosene.' I didn't quite understand his allusion but I knew exactly what he meant. I took his arm, helping him across the street. He gallantly raised his hat to me, but, by that time, I was already on my way to the river.

In school they used to teach us that the Danube was the embodiment of history and memory. Today I could almost believe that as I felt myself slowing down, calming down, thinking of the comfort that Mother had used to draw from its waters.

The riverfront was unusually deserted. There were no tourists, no Russian officers strutting officiously down Széchenyi Rakpart and forcing everyone to step aside. Relieved, I took off my shoes and walked down to the river's edge, the water rolling slowly past in an opaque brown haze. I lay down on the ground and stared at the sun, its brightness painting pointillist dabs of colour on my eyes. Dazzled, I turned away and glanced up at the Chain Bridge, at the red flags fluttering violently along its length, their garish chiaroscuro stripping me, once again, of any real sense of peace.

A while later, I sat up, shivering. I caught my reflection in the water, noticing how thin I had become over the past few months. I remembered how I had run into Elemér, a friend, a few days ago, and he, obviously embarrassed at my condition, had offered to help me out with money. He said he had friends in high places who could be persuaded to find work for me. He said it didn't look good for an Emperházy to fall to pieces like this. Anyone else, perhaps, but not an *Emperházy*. The way he said that made me smile. My family, the Emperházys, the 'once and eternal princes of the realm', had owned Slovakia a long time ago. Before that there'd been a prolonged and bloody history of river piracy, of brigandage and the swift disposal of travellers foolish enough to believe the Danube waterways safe and free. But that was how the fortune was first amassed. It was only after that initial plunder that the family had civilized itself, becoming respectable in the usual progression of things: robbers and murderers the first few generations, patrons of the arts through the following centuries.

I related some of that history to Elemér, while at the same time reassuring him that little of that bloodthirstiness remained in me. There was too much inertia in me, I said, and probably too little ambition. Unconvinced, he agreed to accompany me home, stealing glances at me from time to time to make sure I hadn't been pulling his leg with my family stories. It almost made me regret having so cavalierly disabused such an obviously hallowed mythology. Once home, I made amends by serving him some appropriately exotic Turkish tea, accompanying that

41

sweet-tasting brew with passages read from my manuscript. The book was nearly complete, which was a relief; only a few finishing touches remained.

Elemér taught photography at a local college; he was steeped in the lore of dark-rooms and chemicals and film-developing techniques. He went through the motions of listening to me read, his hands restlessly shuffling through the pages of the manuscript. He didn't quite know how to respond to my book, but he tried to disguise it manfully. 'You need a ledger to hold these pages,' he suggested. 'One of those big box-files, with adjustible clips and inserts. I could get you one from my department. It would also be sensible to number the pages, organize them.' He paused, looking at me with a noticeable awkwardness. 'You need someone to look after you, to remind you what it's like to live in the real world.' Aloud, he wondered about the point of spending so much time writing a book we both knew could never see the light of day under the present regime. He muttered something about the need to come to terms with the powers that be. I leaned over in response and kissed him on the cheek. Poor, dear Elemér, he could never quite get himself to say what he wanted. He left shortly thereafter, flustered, as always, by our meeting.

I must have fallen asleep beside the river. When I woke up, it was late in the afternoon. A cool, steady breeze ruffled the water. Groups of schoolchildren in blue and white uniforms played along the embankment. A solitary cloud shaped like a sword brandished its tip alternately at each of the four points of the compass. A flock of ravens crossed silently over the river, heading towards the round grey towers of the Fishermen's Bastion.

Gradually the sky clouded over, leaving only the remnants of a pale golden sheen over the city. I rose to my feet and brushed the dust from my clothes while absent-mindedly glancing up at the bridge. A woman was standing there, too far off for me to make out her features. She was leaning against the railings, a palette in her hand, the sky opening up above her like the vast vault of a cathedral. She reminded me of Ami – the way she moved, so carelessly, so independently – the way she held her brush at an angle and swept it across the canvas. I wanted to walk over and watch her paint.

42

Instead, I turned around and took the long way home, my memories like metonymous warders muttering at me through the bars of my prison.

December 20

I woke up this morning to find a brown leather glove lying on the pillow next to me. It was a man's glove; the leather worn and creased and smelling of cigarettes. I sat up in bed and a shadow fell across the room. I glanced at the terrace: there were two men standing there, their faces pressed to the window. They must have walked right through the house.

I recognized one of them, I had seen him before, he often came with János's brother. He was the man I had once mistaken for a poet. When he saw me looking, he thrust his hands into his coat pockets and took out a pair of wine glasses. Holding them high in the air, he brought them together with a sudden crash, the glass shattering to pieces. With a sudden lunge forward, he bent over and picked up a shard of glass, slicing it across the flat of his hand, a gleaming red line marking the incision.

They began to back down the terrace after that, their eyes on me until they reached the balustrade. They exchanged a quick glance, and then they turned around and vaulted, of one accord, right over the balustrade and down to the garden.

I scrambled out of bed and rushed out on to the terrace. There were pieces of broken glass scattered all over the flagstones. The men were already crossing the street when I leaned over the balustrade. They glanced at me as they entered their car, the man in front wrapping a handkerchief around his self-inflicted wound.

I swivelled around and ran back to my room. The leather glove had fallen to the floor. I picked it up and took it downstairs to the kitchen. I placed it in a brown paper bag and put a match to it. The flames enveloped the bag with a dull blue glow, the room filling with smoke.

I opened the windows and fanned the flame, tufts of fibres rising in the air. They drifted like motes, grey shapes rising to the ceiling. There was a crackling sound. Then the fire died down and I swept up what remained of the glove and put it out with the rubbish.

December 21

A visit from János's brother is always worthy of record. He is by himself today and he stands stiffly on the steps and gives me the once-over. We both know why he is here. 'Today is the day my brother killed himself,' he says. He is nothing if not direct. 'I come here every year to remind myself. This is where it happened –' he points to the street. 'Just there. On the street. You can still see the melted tar.' He pauses to give me a malevolent look. 'János was a fool to have fallen under your influence. You have his blood on your hands. You will have his blood on your grave.'

I move to close the door but he puts his foot in the way.

'There've been all kinds of reports, all kinds of incidents.'

'Like what happened yesterday, for instance? Your men have taken to making house calls. They walk right in and leave their litter behind as evidence.'

His face blanches as he looks away. 'We're keeping an eye on you,' he says. Then he adds, 'We're looking after you.'

'Those are two entirely different things,' I point out.

He leans forward until his face is inches from mine.

'I know,' he replies. Then he turns around and walks away.

Night

I was reading Akhmatova when I heard footsteps racing into the house from the street. I hurried downstairs, turning on the lights as I ran down the steps. There was no one in the hall, no one on the steps. I opened the front door to make sure, looking out into the garden. It was too dark to discern anything. The first signs of fog were descending on the city; nothing else disturbed the silence. Convinced that I'd been mistaken, I was about to turn away when a car parked further down the street exploded, a

44

ball of fire shooting into the night. A man was walking slowly in front of the car; he was pushing a cart, his body hunched over. I stared at him, my vision obscured by the flames. Something was huddled inside the cart – it was a dead child, an infant – its head covered with a dirty white cloth, feet sticking out. The man was crying soundlessly as he pushed the cart, tears pouring down his face. I edged back inside, closing and locking the door carefully behind me.

December 26

I woke up in the middle of the night in a cold sweat. I dreamt that Father was in my room again. I had to hold on to myself to keep from shaking. I sat up in bed, and then I walked across the room and opened the big bay windows that looked out over the city. Moonlight glinted on my black Danube, white water ghosts coasting its surface. A passing steamer left a milky streak in its wake. It was headed upstream for Vindobona, Parnassus, Avalon, and then . . . who knows? Its lights kept going on and off, as if signalling to me. It perched precariously on the horizon for an instant, then it took off into the clear dark sky, water streaming from its underside.

I turned away from the snow-covered windowsill and walked into what used to be my grandfather's study. When I was a child, the high ceiling had always seemed to defy gravity. Round brass chandeliers hung from it like planets in a strange static cosmology. Delicate spider nets encased some of the globes. I could easily have dusted them clean a long time ago, but it seemed such a waste then, as it did now, to obliterate such painstaking craftsmanship.

The walls of the study were covered with rows of plushly bound classics, volume after volume sandwiched into shelves made of teak and mahogany. Close up, a faint yellow mould could be seen impartially chewing through the books, the paper already quite brittle, the pages crumbling at the slightest touch.

At the far end of the study there was a wooden screen painted black and inlaid with ivory. Behind it nestled my favourite

45

armchair, with a silk-covered ottoman placed before it. The armchair faced a gigantic fireplace with an elaborately carved mantelpiece. Above the fireplace, on a giant canvas dominating the wall, Grandfather glowered down in the full splendour of his uniform. Colonel-General Emperházy of the army of the dual empire, Ambassador-Plenipotentiary of the 'k. & k.', the Imperial and Royal Austro-Hungarian Monarchy. The painting, executed on commission in Vienna, showed him standing next to a trophy – a dead man, probably a Serb – on a Montenegran battlefield. Grandfather had been known to discipline his soldiers by shattering their kneecaps with the weighted end of his riding stick. When news broke of the assassination of the Archduke Franz Ferdinand in Sarajevo, Grandfather was in Florence, elegantly promenading down the Via del Proconsolo with his wife and child. They had rushed home post-haste on the first train to Budapest, the Colonel-General departing almost immediately for the Eastern front. Poor man, he had had his horse and legs blown away from under him on his very first day on the battlefield. Events subsequently overtook his command and in the resulting pandemonium he fell prisoner to the Russians. Reportedly, he served out the remainder of the war in a hospital somewhere in Bessarabia. The family spent the rest of the war waiting for him. He never did return, but eventually the Franz Joseph Medal did, followed in 1918 by the *Umbruch*, the collapse of the Empire. After that we drifted into penury, my father able to do very little to salvage the situation.

My father . . .

His was a very different story from the Colonel-General's.

In his youth, my father had been a man of exceptional beauty, tall and dark, with a fairy-tale profile. They said that women had lined up in provincial capitals to watch him ride past. A man of strong passions, his way with women was the stuff of legend, an example held up without envy by his peers. Unknown to them, though, he was given to sudden and uncontrollable bursts of temper that marred the otherwise idealized perfection of his features. He was also addicted to the gambling table and always on the run from his creditors. As a way out of his financial straits, he wooed Mother with single-minded intent, winning her hand despite her family's strenuous objections. The couple settled in Vienna with the greatest of fanfares, commencing a lifestyle incongruously out of keeping with his earnings. Soon the debts began to accumulate and scores of irate creditors turned up, abruptly bringing the young bride face to face with her husband's sorry past. It was then that she realized that his motives for marriage had had much more to do with her money than any real affection. It must have been very sobering. When she confronted him, he turned on her violently and confirmed her worst fears. What had followed was the usual tedious litany of sins: gambling debts, poolhouse brawls, drunken fits, a slew of cheap mistresses. In the early years of the marriage Mother stoically bore the worst of these shocks, accepting them silently and without protest as the natural outcome of her being both Jewish and a woman. Father's frequent and cutting comments to that very effect only served to cement the imbalance in their relationship. He was the scion of one of Hungary's oldest families. She was the daughter of a Lithuanian grain merchant who'd made his fortune in retailing. To win him over, she had severed all ties from her family, but it wasn't enough. Nothing she ever did was enough. In time, he tired of her submissiveness and by the end of their lives she would cease to exist for him altogether, not only as a companion, but also as a person.

And that is where I came in.

For, within the four walls of his house, he'd found the perfect replacement to bear the brunt of his grievances: his own captive child.

I was born late in my parents' lives. It was probably an accident. In the beginning there had been two of us – myself and Gabriel, my stillborn twin. Father never forgave me that transgression. He said I'd killed Gabriel in his sleep. 'Murderer!' he'd scream out in the middle of meals, his face crimson. At other times he'd smash things, giving vent to his endless rage. He'd pick up my plate of food and hurl it at the wall, then order me to go and clean up the mess. Relations between us were practically non-existent by the end. I was an embarrassment to him, the unkindest blow in a battle he knew he had lost, the battle to save the only world he'd ever identified with, a world that was brittle and narrow-minded and brutish but, for its privileged members, filled with its own irrefutable benefits.

Father's conservatism was the natural outcome of his life-long inability to adjust to modernity's rapid and incomprehensible flux. In his youth he had tried to compensate by embracing the reactionaries when they'd driven out Béla Kun's short-lived communist regime in 1919. It was a not unusual phenomenon among people of his station and sympathies. The victors, in their turn, had been quick to utilize the indubitable value of the Emperházy name and connections, and Father had been more than willing to cooperate. To him they'd had one vital and extremely reassuring trait in common: a virulent and unadulterated anti-Semitism. The eventual outcome of this sordid alliance was a ministerial rank with corresponding privileges and benefits. But even here, as in most other things in life, Father turned out to be a failure. Just two years after his appointment he'd been 'transferred' and given a minor diplomatic post in Madrid. Ironically enough, that was the sole reason for his escape from the ignominy of the years of collaboration with the Nazis. In his absence, and to his lasting bitterness, his wife's background as daughter of one of the most illustrious Middle European Jewish houses would ensure the loss of most of his own remaining familial heirlooms and property. And whatever wasn't confiscated by the Germans during the war would then be snapped up by their successors, the Comrades.

A sudden gust of breeze from the river interrupted my thoughts. The room was getting draughty, the heavy damask curtains billowing in the wind. I decided to leave the windows open and walked back to my room, passing a photograph I'd once taken of Ami. She looked back at me, icily indifferent. I remembered the studies I had done of her in the nude, the light playing across her face. She'd liked being photographed on the terrace, especially in winter. I would bundle up against the chill while she sprawled naked on the snow-covered balustrade, directing me on her best angles, her body entirely sculpted of sunlight. She would always check herself in a hand-held mirror before I was allowed to craft her in film. At first I remonstrated with her – it destroyed the pure sensuality of the creative experience if everything had to be so contrived and deliberate. Art should be spontaneous, I protested, a sudden and instant communion between subject and artist. She was a painter, surely she should be able to appreciate that. She begged to demur – there was absolutely nothing sensuous about cold blue flesh against snow, and would I please stop being so typically abstract and metaphysical! Artifice was the key to the modern condition. We live in a world where everything is improved by its image, where the carefully doctored photograph is *always* superior to the original. It was as simple as that, she insisted, looking me straight in the eye. For instance, she said, consider these painted eyes, or these painted lips. Or consider this flower – this flower that is so red and dramatic but at the same time so predictable and boring. Tear out a petal or two, on the other hand, scatter them with carefully calculated narcissism on the floor . . . like this . . . while lowering the eyelashes just so, making the eyes dark and remote and mysterious, and what do we have? We have a moment of undiluted poetry, of passionate abandon, which I, especially I, should be able to most appreciate – case closed – her voice gurgling with laughter.

At other times she would use a knife as a prop. 'Look at this,' she'd drawl, 'ordinarily commonplace, at best mildly menacing in a *petit bourgeois* sort of way . . . and yet . . . placed . . . right here . . . extraordinarily sinister . . . and suggestive . . . especially . . . if . . . the merest drop . . .' her voice descending to a husky slur, '*Le Sang d'un Poète* . . . things must be *arranged*, yes?'

There, dear heart, hadn't she just proved that artifice and sensuality were both sublimations of creative energy, but that the one *obviously* took precedence over the other? After all, reason preceded inclination, and not the other way around. What did I think? Did I not believe that there was always a moment *after* sensuality, but that art had to be one of a kind, transcending all those purely spontaneous and intuitive moments of ordinary living? Otherwise there would be no room left for the intellect, unless that was precisely what I intended, a world that rested on necromancy and superstition, on spells and black magic. I was a musician, surely *I* should be able to appreciate the dangers of my beliefs?

49

I smiled in disagreement but went ahead and took the photograph anyway, her accomplice in artifice. She stood up, bending down to brush the snow off her legs. That's when I took her photograph again, surprising her in that one unguarded moment. In the dark-room, she looked on intently as the chemicals brought that second photograph to life, her outlines dissolving into the snow, only her head rising clear out of the white haze, eyes glowing in twin pools of lava flow, hair cascading down like rain.

She looked at that photograph for a very long time. 'This is so . . . elemental,' she whispered, overwhelmed. 'So . . . irrational, so . . . instinctive.'

'Yes, Ami, and isn't that true of life itself?'

She looked away.

There are all kinds of magic.

All of that was before she smashed my camera in one of her fits.

I crawled painfully back into bed, my stomach knotting over with cramps. The memories were back. If it weren't for the memories.

December 31

I was lying in bed when a barking dog broke into my sleep. I stayed there for a long time, listening. Then I walked out on to the terrace. The barking came from the street. I couldn't locate it. After a while I returned to my room, shutting the door behind me and trying to go back to sleep.

There must have been a New Year's celebration at Moszkva Square. Through the night, stragglers trickled by in front of the house in twos and threes, their voices drunkenly weaving in and out of my hearing. Someone flung a bottle high into the air. Sleepless, I watched its huge shadow play across the ceiling. Glass shattered against glass. I heard the sounds of raucous laughter, songs about history and *auld lang syne*. Meanwhile, the barking went on inside my head, uninterrupted.

I begin the new year with a different kind of visitor. She is a little girl named Clio. Clio and I first met about a year ago when I spotted her wandering around the garden one winter morning. I went out to talk to her and found her going barefoot in the snow, her shoes slung over her shoulders. I made her put on her shoes and she rewarded me by slipping her hand through my fingers. I took her into the house and gave her something to eat. She sat down at the table and pulled down her hood, surprising me with a wide bright smile.

We've become good friends. She is an only child, rather lonely, and her parents seldom seem to be at home. I've let her have free run of the house and she turns up every afternoon and spends hours playing on her own. She speaks infrequently or not at all. In her silence I sense some of my own childhood confusion. In her silence I find myself thrusting back to the edge of my world, passing once more into the land of memories – that counterpoint of life.

Her visits sometimes coincide with the times I play my cello. She sits on the floor near my feet, out of the way, and listens very carefully to the monotonously repeated notes. She never seems to tire of the fact that I am practising rather than performing a piece. I've been trying to teach her a children's piece by Prokofiev, but she seems intimidated by the instrument. Perhaps we'll have better results with the piano.

I've wondered if I should try to reach out to her in other ways. I asked her once if she would like me to walk her home and she protested so vehemently that I never brought it up again. There is a recognition from her side, I think, of my consuming preoccupations, and she appears to have decided to ask only so much from me and no more. This is quite in keeping with her overall seriousness; there is a quality of solemnity to her that I've seldom seen in one so young. I can't say that I remember the last time I heard her laugh, though she seems quite content. She walks around the house, eyes wide open, her lips pursed to a point as if she were memorizing its many nooks and crannies. I recognize that look, I used to have it myself as a child. It is the discovery of happiness within the confines of these walls. The bright vision of an imagined world. One best left to bloom on its own.

January 7

I went back to the Promenade today to sit by the river. There were quite a few people around me, enjoying the unseasonal sun. Opening the book I had brought with me to read, I looked up and saw Ami on the bridge. She was setting up a large white canvas on an easel, her back to me. Taking no chances, I careered right up the stairs to the bridge. As I reached the uppermost steps, a passing bus blocked my line of vision and obscured her from me. When it had passed, Ami was nowhere to be seen.

I walked breathlessly back to the riverside, my face red and flushed, my frustration showing. Heads turned to stare at me curiously. Oblivious, I sat down, drained by my emotions.

I dallied until sundown. A bright red glow dipped over the palace on the mount of Buda, the old city. More than two hundred years ago, Eugene of Savoy had quartered there, resting from his many campaigns. I felt the spirit of his age suffusing me as the last rays of the dying sun reached over the bastions. A horse-drawn carriage dashed across the bridge, coming to a halt near me. One of Eugene's courtiers slid out of it, mincing across to where I was sitting and going down on bended knee. In his hand he held an invitation from the prince. I succumbed to the feeling: timeless, formless . . .

Blue, blue darkness of the river, sustaining the night from the dissipations of daylight.

Blue, blue darkness, burnished by the waters of the Danube.

January 15

It rained all day today. Great squalls of wind whipped up the Danube, sending waves smashing into the city. Massive black clouds glowered over the surrounding hills. They gathered for the final decisive attack, waiting for the command to swoop down and devastate everything. This must have been the mood of the city when the Turks overran it centuries ago. I imagined Kara Mustapha, the Turkish commander, riding through the streets, abducting screaming women and children and decimating families. White streaks of lightning shot through the sky and gouged the earth wide open. Hail and baleful fists of sleet hammered against the windows separating my room from the terrace. I walked over to the phonograph and put on Liszt's *Mephisto Waltz* at full volume. In the distance, obscured by the storm, the Danube churned into whirlpools. Venturing out barefoot on to the rainswept terrace, I danced with myself. The howling winds blasted the waltz over the city and into the surrounding plains. Icy droplets combed my hair and skin, clothing me with a colourless robe of rain. The rain washed over me in waves. I tore off my shirt, bacchic first-born child of the union of light and darkness. I slipped twice in my frenzy, feet cutting open on glass fragments. Lying on the floor, vanquished by the dance, I sucked on my wounds. Feast. The rain swept into my open room, triumphant.

January 18

I dreamt that America touched me tonight. And that I told her that I still loved her. I heard her asking me, repeatedly and insistently: 'But will you love me and cherish me even if I only exist in your dreams?'

Night

I was lying in bed when I heard footsteps running away from the house and into the street. As the sound receded into the distance, I heard the startled tinkle of bells, followed by the dense flutter of wings. I walked over to the windows and scanned the street. It was too dark to discern anything. As I was about to turn away, a car parked about two blocks away exploded, the bright flames lighting up the night. A man was standing in the middle of the street. He was tall and slender, with jet-black hair and blood-red eyes, his form shrouded in a bulky overcoat. I recognized him: he was a writer, an intellectual, an engineer of human souls. A bevy of shadows flew out of the burning car behind him, materializing into ravens. Undaunted by the flames, they bustled around him, their wings flapping frantically. One of them flew over and alighted near me, its beak busily playing with a morsel that was red and wet and gleaming. I looked closer: it was a piece of human flesh, a piece of tongue. I glanced at the man again. He was singing to himself as he fed the birds, a gush of warm crimson flooding down his chin every time he opened his mouth, the mystery of bread and wine reaching its highest perfection in that metamorphosis of flesh and nourishing blood. I stumbled back into my room, leaning against the panes and pressing my hands to my mouth, my legs giving way under me.

January 24

When I was a child I loved playing outside in the garden. It stretched in a soft green swathe around the house, separated from the street by a tall wrought-iron fence. The fence had been manufactured on Grandfather's specifications in a foundry in Rapallo. He'd wanted a complex symmetry of double-headed Habsburg eagles and Emperházy sunflowers. The eagles used to feed on those sunflowers, Father once told me, it was how they survived day after day, holding up the fence. On windy days, I could hear them calling out to each other as they surveyed the torn Danubian valleys and fields of war – Ulm, Blindheim, Regensburg, Esztergom.

One evening, Father was busy with his printing press, the machines rearing and pounding as he tamed work out of them. I was playing in the long grass next to the fence. Suddenly there was a commotion above my head. A flock of black and white swallows was milling around the pointed iron spokes. One little bird had managed to impale itself. I called out to Father, my voice urgent and strained. He came rushing out, and I pointed in great agitation to the fence. He took in the situation at a glance, clambering up the railing and carefully prising the swallow off. It fluttered for a moment in his hands, and then it lay still. The rest of the flock gathered around in neighbouring bushes, watching us in silence. Father climbed down, his hands stained with thin, red streaks. He kept looking at the bird with narrowed eyes, his teeth a glimpse of white in the darkness. After a while, the tiny creature lay cold and lifeless, a still grey stone in his palm. It was just like one of those story books where wild things die, the feelings drained out of them. But I was still alive, Dadda, what should I do? He drew me close, his breath misting up the evening air. I held on to him, my face burrowing into the side of his neck. He buried that little bird while I looked on, his eyes shiny and red.

My father could be like that when I was a child, a kind and gentle friend.

He was the Envoy Plenipotentiary in Madrid when the communists usurped power in 1948. He lost his position immediately. Outraged, he hurried back home, convinced there had been some kind of mistake. In 1955, they finally let him open a printer's shop at home after denying him the right to work for seven years. They said it was the just retribution for a class enemy. To atone for his sins, he was made to print communist propaganda pamphlets. In 1956, when Imre Nagy declared his short-lived revolution, father rushed to embrace it. Nagy died, executed in 1958. Father lived on but his fledgling business never recovered. That same year the Party cut off his pension and stripped him of his benefits from his years of diplomatic service. I think it was that deprivation that finally broke his sense of manhood, permanently distorting it.

And so they hounded him, methodically twisting him, a stranger to his own family with every passing day.

January 29

I walked home from the river this evening, my daily round. It looked like rain overhead, the sky grey and crumpled with

55

clouds. The streets were jammed with traffic, everyone trying to get home in a rush. A Soviet convoy was passing through the centre of the city, tail-lights casting an orange glow as the vehicles headed towards the dusk. It began drizzling while I waited under an awning, the onset of rain hastening the darkness. When the drizzle turned into a downpour, I ventured out, my hair instantly plastered to my skull. By the time I turned into my street, the alchemy from day to night was complete. I was still some distance from my house when I noticed someone coming out of the front door. It looked like Ami. I called to her in surprise, but the rain drowned out my voice. Oblivious to my presence, she crossed the street, her cape flapping wildly as she picked up pace. I hurried after her, but she was walking too rapidly for me to catch up.

Darkness wrapped around the neon-lights and a gossamer fog quivered and spun through the deserted city. The houses sucked in the dim light given out by the infrequent street-lamps, their rain-soaked façades massive and grim. But my quarry seemed unmindful of their presence. She walked quickly in and out of the shadows, the fog around us now thick enough for me to finally lose sight of her.

I have no idea how long it took me to find my way out of that fog. It was as if I had fallen off the edge of the world, I could see absolutely nothing. Several times I thought I made out the shapes of houses, but as soon as I approached them they receded into that dank yellow sea. I was about to give up the struggle and wait it out when I glimpsed a mysterious line of lights in the distance ahead of me. As I blundered towards it, I slipped on the edge of a kerb and fell to my knees.

When I looked up again, I was in a forest of stone pillars – a construction site lit up by lamps. A flock of loudly honking geese flapped past, terrified and lost in the fog, hurtling from pillar to pillar. As I followed in their wake, the fog began to clear and I found myself near a fountain, the ground around me covered with mottled shapes. The shapes were flowers, crushed under the day-long tread of incontinent feet. The fountain lay next to a cemetery, the flowers intended for the dead. In the darkness surrounding the graves there were shadows passing like lovers on clandestine trysts. There was a faint smell of amaranth in the air. And yearning. Desire. In one corner, a wreath of red roses surrounded the gravestone of a young man who had gone mad and died (of unrequited love in 1829, the inscription read). In another, the wind kept up a muted beat as it conducted the play of rain on stone statuary: *introitus, kyrie, sequentia, offertorium, sanctus, benedictus . . . lux aeterna.* I listened to that requiem with my eyes closed, but after a while even that paled: the dead cannot indefinitely sustain, and the living cannot rest indefinitely on dead lips.

I returned to the fountain, sitting down and leaning my head back. A single street-lamp illuminated the fountain. Cigarette stubs floated in the water like charred fireflies. I gazed into the pool and saw myself stumbling through the dark streets again, my eyes searching. In that valley of dead flowers, between the cold stones and the chorus of cold bones, I tried to deal with . . . disappointment. Alone. Alone again in the hour of darkness.

February 11

Today I have been summoned by János's brother to his office. Usually I am the recipient of his visits but today it is the other way around. I wonder what could have occasioned the change.

There is a long line of people waiting in the corridor outside the office, and they watch me in silence as I walk past them, their anxiety and resignation manifest.

My interlocutor is not alone; there is a young woman standing behind him. They watch my entrance with indifference; I am not offered a chair. Instead, the woman thrusts a file in my direction while her superior gazes at me with thin-lipped distaste. 'You are hoarding illegal printing equipment in your house,' he says, his voice emphasizing his contempt. 'You must take us for complete idiots. How much longer did you think we'd look away?'

When I remain silent, he leans forward and places his elbows on the desk. 'For the record, please permit me to briefly catalogue your sins.' On the fingers of his right hand he ticks off the points one by one. 'Publication and distribution, despite repeated warnings, of pornographic literature by foreigners, *agents provocateurs*, and so-called dissidents. Clandestine exhibitions and photographic and film shows on gulag prisoners within the premises of your residence. Destruction and defacement of public property by putting up posters and flyers without permits. Illegal possession of unregistered typewriters, cyclostyling machines, and printers of various foreign and domestic makes. Conspiratorial meetings and other illegitimate activities with an aim to overthrow the government.' He pauses and looks at me drily. 'The list goes on and on . . .' he says.

He points to the file lying in front of me. 'If you would care to examine that, you will find a copy of the deed to your house. The original is with us in case we should need to initiate legal proceedings to confiscate the property. As you will see, the document was drafted in 1905 and expired five years ago, which means that you've been occupying the property illegally. Having made certain you understand where the matter stands, I am prepared to be reasonable.' He gives me a meaningful look. 'I am prepared to give you exactly one month to surrender all subversive materials. All the equipment, all the documents, all the books and letters and particulars of your associates. The lecture notes that you use for your so-called seminars you can either destroy or use as toilet paper, but the rest must be itemized, catalogued, and tagged for our inspection, and this in exactly one month's time from today. Do I make myself clear?'

I pick up the file and glance over the documents, trying to appear detached. I read through the copy of the deed and then I put the file down on the desk. He reaches over and sweeps the file into a drawer. A thin haze of papery dust blows into the air.

No more words are exchanged. There is a sense of finality to it all. A feeling of closure. They watch my departure in silence.

I return home and the first thing I do is to lock my doors and retrieve all my address books from their hiding places and set fire to them. I burn my lists of collaborators, the names of contacts in neighbouring countries, the lists of middlemen, the secret donors to the cause of resistance, the details of underground publications and their contributors. I burn drafts of articles, both published and unpublished, copies of letters written by me as well as letters received in support of our cause, thick piles of catalogues, inventories, documents. I work slowly, steadily, to achieve the complete eradication of evidence. It is hard work, hot work, and before long I have stripped down to my underwear, my hands and face sooty and smoke-stained. I consider the growing accumulation of ashes and tell myself angrily that this should have been done a long time ago. Although I've been very careful in the past – I've had to be – there is now an unmistakable exigency in making certain that I don't compromise anyone who's ever had the occasion to be associated with the Club.

My concerns prove eminently justified when I go to the terrace later that afternoon and spot not one but two cars parked across the street. There is a group of schoolchildren walking past, their presence adding an innocuous normality to the scene. For an instant I indulge myself with the idea of running over and confronting the occupants of the cars, but reason reasserts itself and I resume my arson with a renewed sense of urgency.

February 17

I've taken to spending my evenings on the terrace. I wear my most formal dress, put on my most elaborate masks, and hold solitary and brilliantly original conversations in my salon by the setting sun. It's a show I put on for the edification of my watchers across the street. I know it's a bit like wearing my defiance on my sleeve, but I would rather be this way than react submissively to their intimidation.

As always, I am witty and entertaining and an absolute delight to be with as I waft among my imaginary guests, telling the most absorbing stories. I imagine Mother hurrying over and asking me to put on something warmer. I reach out to hug her, but she has already found someone else to distract herself with.

It begins to rain, the force of the wind driving everyone inside. The crowd divides into two groups, some departing, while others, less hopelessly cynical about the past and more willing to be captivated by my presence, stay a while longer and are suitably entertained. Meanwhile, it continues to rain, the river rising steadily in the distance. The rainwater drips through cracks in the ceiling and gathers in restless pools.

The conversation turns to love and death. What is love? someone asks. And what about death? The conversation becomes a clever craft. I reason with myself: even true love is eventually nothing but a temporary contract, determined by context, terminated by death. It's all very cut and dried, a self-conscious ruse, deliberate, like a plot. I point to America on the wall – love is like that dead photograph. She had told me that once. She had told me, half-mockingly, that I didn't seem to be able to make up my mind whether our relationship was dilemma or artifice. Someone in the shadows, a kindred soul, walks up to the photograph and gazes at it. Dilemma or artifice? she muses. She turns around and pronounces love a deception instead. Someone else, obviously a hopeless romantic, asserts that we are bringing our personal biases into this – love is much more than that, it is a denial of desire, a rejection. We all laugh, though I want to break down and cry. The conversation continues: What about the love of life? A life of love? Living for love? Dying for love? The room fills up with thick smoke from my cigarette, each whorl a question-mark. In the dying light of evening, I walk into my room and stretch out on the bed.

In the distance, as I play my elaborate waiting game, the river begins to overflow on to the Promenade. Already the waters are lapping around the lowermost houses. Concrete foundations slowly turn into swamps, parts of the city cracking open and beginning to sag. The clock on the wall strikes the hour. As the chimes die down, the door to my room swings open and Father steps in. He coughs, his hands chopping through the smoke as he tries to locate me. Then he closes in.

He stands before me, his head swaying from side to side, his slate eyes opaque and strangely distant. His silhouette, squat and muscular, blocks the light. He slips off his shirt and folds it carefully over the back of a chair. I watch him from out of the corner of my eye, my hands resting on my knees, the smoke from my cigarette a shield around me. He flicks off the lamp, a stranger, a giant. I hear the rustling of his trousers, then a pause as he folds them in the dark. He leans forward and plucks the cigarette from my hand, stabbing it out on the face of the table. Then he rips aside the thin cotton sheet and exposes me, his hands gripping my shoulders with all his might.

The white sheet sails across the room into a distant corner and hangs there motionlessly, its folds suspended in mid-air like a dying light. The conversation in my mind becomes a complex ruse, a mechanism to distract. I cover my head, my companions drawn in a tight circle around me, mute, like Mother, watching helplessly. I draw up my knees, my stomach knotting in pain. I retch on the sheets, my fists crumpling to fragments. Millions of mouths cluster on my face, kisses raining wetly down. They press close to me, glistening, listening. They spread their slime over my eyes, inside my mouth, on and below the surface of my tongue. The slime trickles down my throat, choking me. I try to wrest away but my arms are pinned behind me. There is nothing to do but wait helplessly for the spear, the sword, the final thrust. I watch the silhouette lunge. The room turns upside down.

A second too late, the river bursts the levee with a rush, its waters pounding the concrete to dust, swirling through the city streets and racing towards us. Asphalt roads turn to slush, liquid boulevards streaming out of the black river. Spread-eagled on the bed, my body crushed on the sheets, I hear the sound of the water – the Danube smashes into the room with a deafening roar. The windows splinter, the room exploding into spray and light, the heavy wooden doors collapsing like reeds as the river thunders towards us. Father turns in alarm.

Matchstick, matchstick, matchstick man, sliding hopelessly into the deep. I watch him sink to the bottom without a sound, flotsam, jetsam, broken into bits, crushed. The swirling waters swing him around, bubbles clouding over him, his eyes shocked with disbelief as I push him right off, knowing full well he can't swim.

It is Budapest, October 1956, all over again.

I remember that night clearly – I am eight years old and confined to bed with a fever. Mother has the radio switched on, the metallic scrape of the announcer's voice filling the room with words. Imre Nagy is speaking from the balcony of Parliament House. There is a brief interruption before his confident baritone comes on the air. 'Comrades . . .' he begins, 'dear Friends . . .' The crowd roars its approval at this suddenly informal form of address. Then the announcer's drone again, reporting troop movements near the border, a new grain pact with Poland, the latest on events in the Suez. Twenty minutes later, a new announcer, a woman, her voice sounding strained. She reports that people have begun demolishing the Stalin monument on Dózsa György Avenue. She says that someone has slung a placard around the statue with the words, 'Russians, when you run away, don't leave me behind!' In the background, as she speaks, I recognize strains of Petőfi's 'Song of the Native Land'. I remember Mother listening to the report with growing alarm, her hands nervously playing with her apron. There is an urgency to her movements as she moves swiftly from room to room and fastens all the doors and windows. Father is late, out drinking again. In his absence, the house hunkers down like a shadow, becoming watchful and still. In the silence inside the room, Mother grips my hand like a vice, her knuckles standing out. We wait in the dark, quiet, like the rest of the city.

Suddenly, in the street outside, there are shouts, then the clatter of boots running helter-skelter and the sound of an explosion. Bright searchlights go on all around, drowning out the dark with a cancerous glow. They pierce surgically into our room through the shuttered slats, slicing it up into a rib-cage of black and dazzling light. I hear commands shouted in shrill voices, staccato bursts of gunfire, screams, then the low rumble of tanks from the east. Bullets zing around in the open air outside, Mother silently whispering prayers. Someone shouts: 'Open the door!' I hear the door to the house crash open, then bang shut again, whip-like. My toes feel hot and clammy. Strange eyes peer into the room through the shutters, past the corners of curtains drawn tightly shut. I recognize one pair, over there by the bay windows! There is another, I am certain, crouched under my bed. Soon, Mother and I are completely surrounded by those eyes. The fear grows. I watch us run from one corner of the room to the other, trapped. Then the eyes blink and Mother is whisked out of sight.

The radio fills with the fanfare of drums, confused announcements about the end of the world. More drums. A new VOICE comes on, suave, controlled, venomous. There is an enormous animal power in that VOICE. It slithers all over the room, supple, terrifying, exultant. It washes over me like fire, singeing me as I cringe down under the sheets, fascinated: it sounds like the Voice of God, Lord of the Idea, Substance of the New Man, Father, Perpetrator, Criminal. And even as It speaks, a small girl with my face and shiny cheeks and happy flowers in her hair climbs up to the edge of the bed and waves at me with a tiny clenched fist. I wave back, uncertainly, recognizing that she is tunelessly singing a familiar nursery rhyme. I start singing along with her, but as soon as I do, she alters the words into a chant, which others on the radio take up as well, their voices mechanically repeating over and over again: 'Pure self-recognition in absolute otherness. Pure self-recognition in absolute otherness. Pure . . .' I stretch out a hand to the little girl, scared. She is still trilling, the chanting in the radio rising in a crescendo, welling up to the ceiling and threatening to sweep even the VOICE aside as It clings to the airwaves, buffeted by the ecstasy It has generated. Then It reasserts control with a shout, words streaming out, frenzied exclamations acknowledging the rapture as It ejaculates in a final gush of rhetoric on the millions of faces pressed against radio-sets all over the nation, setting Its seal on the renewed journey of Scientific Man from mere sense-awareness to Absolute Knowledge. And as It dies down to a whisper, no longer the VOICE but only a murmur, It reaches out and with a hot slurp, swallows me up. Still hanging on by a slender thread of hope, hurting, aching, drowned by that sound, I cry out to the little girl, but it is of no use. Her head bowed down, wet from Its wet, skirt drenched in sweat, her stubby legs spread far apart and bleeding, she doesn't even look at me as she tosses the burning torch in my direction.

February 25

Solitude.
I went for a long walk today. I needed time and space to think. I started out at dawn. It was very dry, the cold air rasping in my

chest. The streets were deserted in the baleful morning light, block after block of grim concrete shells plodding into the horizon.

Some of the houses were beginning to stir, snatches of radio wafting out of them as I walked past. They stretched and shifted on their haunches to the sounds of the new day. Then, one after the other, they spasmodically vomited out the workers of the worker's state, each scurrying to his daily round with sweeping generalizations.

I wandered down to the waterfront and found that I was joining a party of seagulls. I watched them dive and turn and glide, their fleet forms chasing each other. They were as festive and witty as always, and they darted in and out of the water and under the piers on the dockside. The river exploded into bursts of light every time they crested its surface, the water turning silver, then black, then silver again.

I crossed over the Chain Bridge, half expecting to see Ami setting up her easel. Of course, she wasn't there. After waiting for a while I walked up the steep cobbled streets to the old quarter. I could hear a piano playing Mussorgsky inside one of the houses, someone really pounding down on the keys. I started running, my feet springing from one stone to another in a highly exaggerated parody of the beat, my grandfather's coat-tails fanning out behind me like wings. I swivelled round and round in the middle of the road, the dark clouds swirling overhead and serenading my dance. There was a church straight ahead of me, its massive brown door papered over with a poster of Lenin. Someone had blackened over his bald pate with paint. The Comrade looked young, almost dashing, his hands outstretched and urgent. I ran up the church steps and collided with the door. Staggering from the impact, I clutched at the loose ends of the poster to regain my balance. It tore off in my hands, and I fell to the ground. As I bounded back to my feet, in the distance a man in a brown jacket clapped mockingly. I looked down at myself: I had dark bruises on my right arm and knee. But then, I bruise easily.

I resumed walking, following the contours of the street as it wound up the hill. I cast a glance behind me and saw the man in the brown jacket. He stopped and entered a grocery shop when he saw me staring, but at the next street corner I glimpsed him again, lurking in the shade of a balcony. I decided to ignore him and continue walking.

Below me, the Danube curled past the city of man, its trajectory slow and meandering. I looked down, the land stretching away on all sides of me. In the West, I sensed a terrible silence. In the East, far beyond the Danube, glimpses of an alien normality.

At the top of the hill, I turned around and retraced my steps. I entered the grocery shop and waited behind the door with my eyes on the street. The man in the brown jacket hurried past, his eyes fixed before him. I watched him turn the corner and then I walked out of the shop and headed in the opposite direction. A fragment of coloured paper followed in my wake, borne upwards by the breeze. It was the poster I had torn off the church door, Lenin's eyes staring ahead sightlessly.

It was evening by the time I decided to return home. I stopped at the Fishermen's Bastion and watched the setting sun. A squadron of fighter planes roared overhead, pterodactyls burning across the twilight. Their afterburners left a swirling orange trail; people gathered around and pointed at the sight. The dying rays of the sun intensified the orange glow and deflected it to the river. For one breathtaking moment the Danube became a shaft of fire. Then the fire died down and the onlookers dispersed, their eyes still shining with excitement.

It was dark by the time I crossed the river.

She wasn't there on the way back over the bridge either.

Night

I was lying in bed last night when I heard footsteps running down the street. I heard a car gun its engine, I heard its squealing tyres, and then . . . silence.

In the dead of night I got up from my bed and walked out to the terrace. It was very dark and I waited for a moment, my hands resting on the balustrade. A shadow winged past in the dark, a night bird on the prowl. I could hear sounds of laughter in the distance, and then a piano, drifting.

65

I was about to turn around and walk back to my room when I heard someone call out my name from the street. It was a man's voice, and as I waited, I heard him call again. 'Who is it?' I called back. 'What do you want?' My cries were met with silence. Then a projectile hurtled out of the darkness and landed near my feet. I hurried over and picked it up; it was a rolled-up cardboard cylinder with a piece of paper taped inside. The note was unambiguous. It said: '*You are losing touch with reality.*'

March 8

I've been almost a week now without food.

They switched off the electricity yesterday, claiming four months of unpaid bills. Elemér dropped by yesterday as well and, appalled at the state of affairs, recommended giving up and giving in to them. I showed him the pages of my completed novel. He said that I was crazy, that I should accept the inevitable and fall in. At least it was far better than holing up in here and rotting away like this! He said that pride will have its fall. I handed him a briefcase filled with lecture notes on free will. 'Use them as firewood,' I said airily, 'or toilet paper, whichever you prefer. But don't ask me to give in. To do that now would be to make a mockery of everything.' He bowed his head in distress as he paced the length of my room, and then he marched into the study and gestured violently at the rows of books. 'My God!' he said, 'don't you realize that you've got to survive? If you won't be practical, then at least I will! All these useless books – there's good money in them if nothing else!' He yanked at the nearest volume, a first edition of *The World as Will and Representation*. The spine came off in his hand, a small, damp cloud of mould descending around his shoes. He looked down in confusion, and then he backed away from the book and stumbled out of the study. I asked him if he was feeling all right, but he didn't reply. I filled his cup with tea but he waved it away. Instead, he took his leave with a muttered promise not to return until he'd found a resolution to my situation.

March 12

The mould continues to grow under my skin. It is black in colour, I think, though I cannot, for obvious reasons, be certain.

I slit my wrist once and peeled the skin back but all I could find was fire.

I look at my eyes in the mirror. There's mould behind them as well. The mould's entered my eyes as well. It's just like passion. It's just like when a man looks at a woman – a mere glance, no more than that – and realizes that his flesh is on fire . . .

It's just like when a man looks at a woman.

You will never be a man, she said.

March 16

Elemér came by tonight, dejected. He said that he had asked around exhaustively on my behalf. The usual reply was that my 'case' wasn't the kind that lent itself to a simple resolution. Perhaps in a month's time things would begin to look different. It was all a question of my shaping up and being a little less obdurate.

In any event, he'd brought along a bottle of my favourite red wine, the legendary Bulls' Blood from Eger. I brought out glasses and we toasted each other in all solemnity. He got drunk rapidly and we reminisced about old times. Finally he clasped my hands and began to weep, becoming very loud and melodramatic. It was a side to him I had never seen. He kept saying something about 'life's fatal conceit', and about having failed me completely. I tried to convince him otherwise, telling him that things would work out, but he was inconsolable and insisted that he could no longer look me in the eye. I told him that he was behaving like Themistocles just before he killed himself with a draught of bull's blood. He took one last defiant swig from the bottle, then swirled to his feet, girding for battle. I looked at him with great affection as he ferociously strode around the room, sniffling all the while, his eyes running. Finally, he tripped on his shoelaces and sprawled out on the floor.

Before he left I gave him a box file containing my poetry and my novel. He clutched it to his chest, wrapping his braces around them, promising to read them as soon as he reached home. I corrected him immediately. 'No,' I said, very clearly, 'I don't want anyone to read them. I've given them to you as a friend, but only for safe-keeping.' His downcast expression told me that I had just made him very unhappy, but I stood my ground and he agreed to respect my wishes. At the door, he turned and, standing on tiptoe, kissed me gently on the cheeks. I watched him stumble down the street, growing smaller as he staggered into the distance.

March 20

More rain.

Walking along the river, cold rain burning into my skin, cold ice spreading over my face. Creeping along the ground that slopes down to the river's edge, I look into the water. From deep within its dark green sludge, a single blue eye comes climbing out, followed, in a moment, by another one. A head emerges next, swimming into view, disembodied, shapeless. Fascinated, I stare down. The rain fences me in. I am now a captive of a dark green mirror. Heat emanates from it. There must be a fire below it. The waves of heat soak into my face and I break out in a sweat. I sense the sweat. My eyes water with the heat. Ice-cold drops of sweat collect on my chin and drip down to the mirror. I watch them strike. I hear them strike. They sizzle and burn and instantly transform into the waves of heat that strike me on my face. I am drenched with sweat. The drops trickle to my chin and drip down to the mirror again. Bleary-eyed, I hover above the mirror, my reflection surrounded by that frozen fence of rain. My eyes grow dim. The first blue eye dissolves in the water, followed, in an instant, by the other. I peer down in surprise. Where is my chin? What has happened to my chin? I raise a hand, there is a crackling sound: my poor blue blood must be frozen stiff. That's when I realize I am turning into ice. My chin has melted away. My face is melting away. Eventually, there will be nothing left of my disembodied head.

(Behind me, a tug on my shoulder: 'Are you all right?'

'You're standing too close to the edge . . .'

68

'Look, are you all right? airtight? all right?')

Cold rain soaking into my skin; cold ice creeping over my face, my frozen head.

Burning.

March 25

I imagine I am listening to Shostakovich's Fifth tonight. My anthem. It spins round and round inside my head in a madding rush.

Outside, the Danube rustles sleeplessly in the darkness, true mirror of my nature. Dawn will bring the sun back, the brink of another day bleeding into the river.

Increasingly, I feel I am a driven creature, beating heart within beating rib-cage within the soaring space of a cathedral.

Twenty-nine years of leaning against myself. From this point onwards, it can only be a matter of time.

But then again . . .

Is it raining in New York? Do you know?

I think so.

You don't know any more?

There's no denying, my love, that every day I know less and less.

Yes, but is it raining in Central Park? Tell me again. Try.

I'm so tired, my love.

March 28

A knock on the front door. I open it to find János's brother standing on the steps, his collar turned up. It is very bright outside and I have to shield my eyes against the glare. I place myself directly in front of the door so that it is clear I have no intention of letting him in. He has some keys in his hand and he jangles them to fill the silence. I begin to tell him I am busy when he holds up his hand. To my surprise he attempts a smile. He clears his throat and asks me if I realize the full import of the position

I am in. When I continue to remain silent, he says slowly, 'I could institute a search of these premises right now and confiscate anything even remotely incriminating. I am not obliged to give you any more time, do you understand? I have waited longer than a month. I could produce a search warrant this very instant.' He hesitates to let the full import of his words sink in. Then he gives me a look filled with meaning. 'Has it occurred to you to wonder why I've allowed you so long to salvage your position?'

He has a point there, but I don't know the answer to his question, so I don't reply. He gives a nod, as if satisfied. Then he turns away and scans the garden and the street. He lights a cigarette. 'You're completely powerless,' he says flatly, 'and that must rankle someone with your instincts.'

'You're completely powerless,' he repeats, 'but you are not stupid.'

He makes a chopping motion with his hand and then he glances at me, his face flushed. 'I made an unusual gesture in giving you the time that I did. I expected you to respond to that gesture in some small way to show you'd understood.'

My continued lack of response makes him increasingly agitated. 'I have taken risks to buy you time. I have placed myself in a compromising position. There have been questions . . .' His voice trails away.

Then he starts speaking again, almost violently. 'There's no getting through to you! You're all the same! What did my brother have that made him different? What did he *do*? Why must I face this treatment? Tell me – *why*?'

I step back into the house and close the door in his face. There is a reassuring click as the latch falls into place. In the darkness I lean my head against the wall. There is a moment of silence and then I hear his voice again, low and rushed: 'We could have come to a civilized agreement. We could have reached a compromise. Everyone does! Would that have been asking for too much?'

In the silence I imagine I hear his breathing. There is a scraping sound. Then a sudden thudding kick against the door as he yells: 'To hell with you! You are your own worst enemy!'

He kicks the door again and I hear his footsteps receding.

70

In my room upstairs I lie down on the bed and stare at the ceiling.

I shut my eyes.

It is dark inside and for once I bless that darkness.

March 30

Cold. Cold now, the usual place by the river as I watch the snow falling. In the beginning, though I can no longer recall it that clearly, the snow was hard and firm and I could stand on it. Then the snow melted and the rock-like consistency turned to slush. I say slush because that is what it looks like even though it is olive-coloured and shot through with ice. And it yields to my weight far more than ice would, caving in to form gaping craters near the water. (The water that is as black as darkness.) Olive-coloured slush against jet-black water; black waters lapping against the soft olive slush until it rips off to reveal the strata immediately below it, composed not of shale or schist or granite or anything like that, but of quicksand, a sticky brown-green mass that moves with or against the current. Every step that I take sinks my feet deeper into that sand; I am sucked in to my hips but I struggle free every time, my ankles and feet coated with slime. And every time I retreat a bit further, seeking higher ground. (The urge to let go, give up, sink. But I contain myself, shivering.)

The river is motionless under the late evening sun although the current has already begun to shift as the light angles down from the western horizon. Behind me looms the steep grey slope of the embankment, the high-water mark half-way up its concrete face.

Giving up the urge to go down to the water, I return to the embankment, climbing up the steps to the deserted promenade. I greet its firm surface thankfully, sitting down and gazing at the black water.

I remember the day Father died, boating on this river.

I was with him.

He was leaning over the railings of the boat and looking down

71

at the water, his back to me as I moved closer. Reaching forward . . . my head instinctively looking down . . . sweat trickling slackly between my legs . . . I gave him a gentle push . . .

An accident.

It was effortless . . . he was as light as a feather . . . old, shrunken, giant no longer. I watched his shadow stain the water, slowly sinking down, lost in the depths of the river. I can still see him suspended below the surface, frozen in mid-stroke, hands stretching out towards me as I turned away, nine-inch long razor blades burying themselves under my fingernails.

He flailed around desperately for a while, drowning by degrees – he couldn't swim. He turned around in the water once, pale-blue eyes wide with shock and disbelief. Then a black-backed gull swooped down and scooped him up. The water wrinkled momentarily, and then it was still.

I remember his telling me once as he smiled out of the corner of his mouth: 'Immanuele, my dear daughter, don't you think we should be closer?'

Mother had watched it all, silently, hand trembling over her crucifix. She died four years after him, in 1969. Brain fever. All she had known was everything.

In the distance, a man with a ponytail begins playing folk-songs on his zither. He wears a crimson tunic, with gold braiding on the sleeves and the collar. He leans into the instrument as he plucks the strings, his fingers tapping out the rhythms on the polished fretwork. The zither's leather case lies open before him, snowflakes collecting inside. I walk over and drop a coin into the case. Then I return to my place by the river, the folds of my skirt spreading out around me. I sit there for a long time with my eyes closed, listening.

Nightfall by the Danube. The zither-player puts away his things and prepares to leave. Behind him, specks of light glisten along the bridges across the river. I watch his retreating figure, and then I draw my arms around myself and rest my head on my chest. A cold wind blusters against my face. I drink it in, long, deep draughts, savouring the chill. I lean into the wind and cover my face with my hands. Intent on oblivion.

Something brushes against my hair. It's a golden-yellow moth.

It alights on my shoulder and moves down to my wrist. As I reach for it, it rustles and takes off, its wings fluttering across the river.

It is late by the time I leave for home. A pale fog hides the houses, the streets are alabaster strips. Hunger does the strangest things to a person: over the last week or so, time has entirely lost its meaning for me, the days replicating each other endlessly. Tonight it only seems appropriate.

I reach home and walk around the house, opening all the windows to let the cold air in. When the windows are undone, I cover the furniture with white sheets. They flutter in the high breeze like candles.

Back in my room, I walk over to my bed and lie down, my knees drawn up against the chill. The white sheets surround me; I am lying on an ice-cold glacier, a moraine. The moon shines down on the deserted terrace. The moon glistens on my skin. Everything seems slower, the hours without integrity. Trapped in that space in-between, I sense my eyes closing and surrender myself to sleep.

When I wake, I am spread-eagled on the bed. My head is pounding and my throat is dry and parched. I feel exhausted, depleted. I feel deathly cold and ill. I turn on my side to find a man lying beside me.

It is András.

As if in a dream, I reach out to him.

He moves away. There is a woman on the far side of the bed next to him. I recognize Ami and stretch out my hand towards her, but she moves away as well. Beyond her I glimpse another shape, darker, indistinct.

I sit up with a start and open my eyes. I am soaked in sweat, shivering uncontrollably. I crouch there for a moment, my heart fit to burst. Suddenly, I hear footsteps running away from the house and into the street. As the sound recedes into the distance, I climb out unsteadily and walk over to the snowbound terrace.

It is pitch-black outside but, for once, not too dark to discern the car parked down the street. Too late I screw my eyes shut, realizing I am about to play out János's death in my mind again. I didn't see him die. All I heard was the explosion, followed by

73

the most terrible silence. I sag against the balustrade just as the car bursts into flames, one thought running over and over through my head:

To be able to end life like that: clear-eyed, without illusions, without regrets.

Far better than to die like this: bit by bit by bit.

Book Two

Budapest, 1994

Chapter One

The Restoration

The day began, as days sometimes will, with murder. It would end with murder as well, but that was different. In the beginning was the act, fierce and final. Just as he was about to enter the sun-drenched college courtyard, András heard a thudding sound ahead of him. Looking up, he was just in time to see a bird smash into a window at the far end of the stairway that led up from the courtyard. The bird was a black-backed gull, its underside dragging violently against the fractured pane. As András stared at it, horrified, the bird stabbed the pane with its beak and shredded it to pieces, a splinter piercing its heart. Then it slid down the glass, wing tips shuddering as it slipped out of sight.

Racing up the steps, András flung the window open, shattering the already fragmented pane. The injured bird was lying on a horizontal ledge below him, its lungs gasping for air. Blood was flowing from its open beak in a viscous dribble. It convulsed once, a tiny black maggot crawling out of its mouth. Then its beak clamped shut, its eyes glazing over.

Reaching down to the ledge, András picked up the maggot and placed it on his palm. Nestling against his skin, it turned out to be not black, but translucent, its flesh-coloured insides gleety and gorged. It spread out and began crawling towards the edge of his wrist. He blew gently on it, and it curled up into a ball. He

77

flicked it out of the window, watching as it landed on the roof of a van parked below him. It was a mover's van, with a golden butterfly painted on one side. A stocky man was standing beside it and wiping his face with a beret. He moved to the back and opened the doors, reaching in to take out life-sized marionettes from the van's crowded interior. He stacked them against each other, a gentle yellow light bathing the cobblestones around him as he worked. Noticing András looking down, he waved his hand in greeting. András waved back. The man pointed to the dead bird.

'Did you see that?' he called out.

'Yes, I did,' András replied.

'Strange, wasn't it? What do you think it was – suicide or murder?'

András scanned the corpse carefully.

'It's riddled with maggots,' he said, 'so I suppose I'd call it murder.'

The man considered that, blowing on his hands. 'I wonder,' he said, 'but I have to go now. I'm putting on a show for the kids at four.' He nodded towards the massive front doors of the college, and then he retrieved a pair of gloves from the roof of the van and entered the building.

Stepping away from the shattered window, András examined his hands. They were pin-pricked with blood from the dead bird. Wiping them clean, he walked slowly back the way he had come, his mind returning to the decrepit old man who'd accosted him as he'd stepped out of the taxi on his way into the building. It was as if the man had been waiting for him. 'You're the writer, András Tfirst, aren't you?' he'd demanded. He'd held his head low, nursing every word like a grudge. 'Yes, it's you all right,' he'd carried on without hesitation. 'I've seen your picture in the papers.' Thrusting his face forward, he'd forced a crumpled piece of paper on András. There was a message scribbled on it: *'The books you write are godless filth! They ought to be burnt! You will rot in hell for the state of your mind!'*

András had handed the note back, but the old man had refused to accept it, his mouth opening to reveal a thicket of ruined teeth. 'That's for you,' he insisted. 'Thank you,' András replied, 'but I don't want it.' The other crossed himself. 'Liar!' he spat venomously, the veins on his neck standing out. 'Liar for the things you put down on paper!' He carried a knobbed stick in his hand, the head shaped like a beak. Raising it threateningly above his head, he grated: 'Your blood's on fire, my fine-feathered friend! No good can come of that in the end!' The stick wobbled perilously in the air. András hastily stepped back, but the old man turned on his heels and stalked away, his back held straight, his head shaking from side to side.

Now, as András recalled the incident, the attractions of the courtyard's abundant green foliage were lost on him. He walked across the open space and entered a long corridor lit by a multitude of lamps. A sign on the wall directed him to a lecture theatre at the far end, where he could hear the murmur of many voices. At the head of the corridor, András hesitated and looked around, willing himself to go forward. He'd been here before, a long time ago, and now he tried to orientate himself. Remembering that there was a gallery overlooking the lecture theatre, he ducked in through a small side door. It led to the darkened gallery, its narrow space partially screened off by a plywood partition. A double row of chairs ran along its length. Choosing one in the back row, András sank into the quiet of the shadows, his eyes squinting as he examined the steadily filling room below.

The lecture theatre was large, with pale yellow walls and a rectangular blackboard flanked on either side by windows. They let in a sharp, clear light, the radiance streaming in and turning the walls to gold.

His eyes scanning the room, András contemplated the faces. The space was packed to capacity, with people sitting all along the aisles. Most of them were strangers, which he found oddly reassuring. He was already beginning to feel ambivalent about this engagement. An intensely private creature, over the past few years he had cultivated his reclusive instincts into a finely honed art. Besides, he abhorred speaking in public: it inevitably brought up reminders about the past and about himself. Now it irritated him to think about how easily he had given in to the invitation. With sudden impatience, he glanced across the lecture theatre

79

and into the courtyard where a window flashed open, its panes catching the sun. At least the impending ordeal, he consoled himself, had the saving grace of being finite.

In the room below, someone turned on a bank of lights over the blackboard. In the sudden glare, András noticed his hosts, Elemér Klein and Júlia Ambrus. Elemér was a member of the faculty here; it was because of him that András had agreed to appear. Netting the notoriously reclusive András had been a coup, and Elemér was already bringing that home in numerous small but significant ways to his fellow faculty members. He was a small man, and as he moved rapidly from person to person, shaking hands and exchanging quips, his eyes never left the door. He went busily to the stage and began arranging a semi-circle of chairs in front of the blackboard. He placed a lectern to one side and adjusted its height, angling it so that it faced the audience. He surveyed the room with narrowed eyes and then he dimmed the lights above the blackboard and walked away.

András realized that the time had come for him to go down: the air of expectancy in the room was tangible. He stood up and left the gallery, his footsteps leading him slowly down the corridor. His face was impassive as he entered, but inside his pockets his hands were clenched.

A hush of anticipation greeted him. Elemér rushed over and they shook hands. Taking him by the arm, Elemér led him to the front. Someone clapped as they passed, and there was an outbreak of coughing from one side of the room. When they reached the stage, András turned and bowed slightly, his movements controlled and deliberate. He nodded to Júlia Ambrus, and sat down.

Elemér's introduction was brief and to the point. When he'd finished, he smiled reassuringly at András and motioned him forward. András stood up, the rain of questions beginning even as he moved towards the lectern.

The first query was cutting and, as he had anticipated, directed at his past. 'Mr Tfirst –' the questioner began, 'I'm Max Südfeld from *The Literary Week*. Mr Tfirst, ever since you left Budapest some ten years ago and went into seclusion at your Abrahámhegy retreat, you've built up quite a reputation as a recluse. At the time you justified your decision as a way to concentrate more fully on your writing. But we've seen very little of that since. In fact, nothing at all. If one were to compare this to your rather prodigious output earlier on, your resolve to isolate yourself seems to have had rather questionable results. When are your readers going to see something new?'

András smiled. 'I don't know. I can only tell you that throughout this period I've been working on a single book – a book that, if I may say so myself, will far surpass anything I have written so far.'

His questioner sat down, and from three rows behind him someone else stood up. 'Mr. Tfirst –' he began, 'I'm Gusztáv Móra from *New Light*. Mr Tfirst, you're probably aware that there's been some comment about the fact that, unlike the work of most of your peers, your own books deliberately chose to ignore political realities and concentrate on the mundane personal. In the past, some critics saw in this both an abdication of your responsibility as a writer, as well as an inexplicable retreat from your activist heyday as a founding member of the Gabriel Club. Would you care to comment on this?'

'No, I would not,' András glanced away. 'Besides, I'm afraid I don't see the personal as mundane.'

There was a ripple of laughter around the room. The speaker crossed his arms with a dissatisfied air. When the noise had died down, he carried on with deliberate pointedness: 'To write about personal issues at a time of societal crisis was a bit of a luxury, wasn't it? Almost a glorification of the prevailing conditions, wouldn't you say?'

András smiled again, the man's obvious hostility paradoxically helping him gain in confidence. 'Mr Móra,' he said gently, 'you have yourself criticized me in the past for – and here I quote – "the bleak pessimism of my novels".'

'What is your point?'

'That it would take an idiot to contend that my books are non-political, and, therefore, some kind of glorification of prevailing conditions.'

The man who had asked the question looked completely taken aback. 'What do you mean?' he managed.

András placed his hands flat on the lectern. 'That I do realize that my books made no grand proclamations of dissidence,' he replied. 'My characters were ordinary people trying to lead ordinary lives and unable to do that under the prevailing circumstances. Reduced to living without a net, they bore witness to the system's failure. Tell me, what kind of glorification is that?'

'I don't know,' came the nettled retort. 'Why don't you tell me?'

András considered for a moment. Then he replied softly: 'What you have in my work is a narration of memory. A narration of memory stretched to breaking point. You may ask why this interests me. My reply is straightforward and, in that, perhaps simplistic, but it may be condensed into a single word: expiation. The expiation of guilt.'

'Guilt?'

'Yes, guilt.'

'I presume you mean our nation's collective guilt?'

'Oh no, not that at all. To attribute everything to a nebulous collective is an easy absolution, isn't it? In fact, I don't believe there is such a thing as collective guilt. There is my guilt and your guilt and everyone else's guilt about what was done to us for forty years, about what we allowed to be done to us. And then there is the guilt of our own very private associations. But all of that falls under the category of individual experience and can, therefore, hardly be considered the same thing as collective guilt. If one is to mention the collective at all, then I would rather speak of a collective responsibility, a responsibility to remember the past and to make sure it's never forgotten. That is why, for me, genuine awareness in the political sense occurs precisely when the present is bombarded with profane fragments from one's own history. It's the only way to write, I think: from the most personal of memories. Because conscience depends on memory. Anything else is propaganda, and that doesn't interest me.'

'And you don't believe that that has made you vulnerable to the criticism that your writings are apolitical?'

'Perhaps my writings are apolitical from a certain point of view,' András replied patiently, 'but I've learned not to let that bother me.'

'But literature that is serious must be overtly political, mustn't it? Especially in our part of the world.'

'Look, that's nonsense.'

'Nonsense? That's a strong word. May I be rude enough to ask, then, why you write at all?'

András hesitated and studied the piece of chalk in his hand. 'You've obviously missed my point,' he said slowly, 'which makes me wonder if you've been listening to me at all. But you want to know why I write? I write because I must. Anything else would reduce me to a state of absolute fear. You see, like everyone else, I suffer when I write. But unlike most others, I write because I fear what lies on the other side. I fear it absolutely. And what lies on the other side is silence.'

'But I don't understand, Mr Tfirst. How can you say that when you've only just emerged from ten years of silence? A silence, which, I might add, was self-imposed and without any explanation offered to your reading public.'

'Ten years is not a lifetime.'

'But ten years of silence, nevertheless? A period that encompassed the end of the communist nightmare?'

A thick-set man suddenly stood up and shouted from the back of the room: 'I think it's crazy to shut yourself up for so long! Writers have a responsibility! What were you thinking?' He sat down again, as abruptly as he'd risen.

The room was getting warm. András wished someone would open the windows. He wished he hadn't agreed to come. To his right, he heard Júlia clear her throat and use her mike for the first time, her voice gentle but firm. 'Ladies and gentlemen,' she began, 'we'd like to maintain some order here. We've been very fortunate in having Mr Tfirst address us. As you must be aware, this is his first public appearance since returning to Budapest and we're privileged to have him here. With that in mind, could we please refrain from personal comments and stick to the substantive?'

The thick-set man shot up again. He was shaking his head. He raised a fist as he headed for the exit. 'They're censoring us, I tell you, they're censoring us!' he yelled out. 'It's just like in the old days! Nothing's changed, nothing's changed, just younger faces, that's all!' He left the room, the door banging shut behind him.

There was a moment of nonplussed silence, broken only by a muttered expletive from Elemér. Then Júlia, sensing that the situation was getting out of hand, leaned forward. Tapping her mike very deliberately for emphasis, she said, 'My apologies, Mr Tfirst. I'm certain you appreciate that no one else in this room shares the sentiments that you've just heard. Once again, my apologies.' She turned to the audience. 'Any more questions?'

A clean-shaven man in the second row raised his hand.

'Mr Tfirst –' he began nervously, standing up, 'my name is Demeter Fülep, and I'm a student here. My question pertains to the structure of your novels. I'm fascinated by the motifs and patterns that recur across your books, such as the mysterious appearances of the woman in red. Is this some kind of hidden dialectic that should be telling the reader more about your work, or is it merely a personal conceit in terms of an instantly identifiable authorial signature?'

András contemplated the speaker. 'In general,' he replied, 'I cannot bear objective interpretations of literature, and I've always resisted that kind of analysis when it is applied to my own books. I suppose I've always believed it serves no purpose other than that of diluting the emotional and spiritual content of what is written down. That is why I am extremely reticent about analysing my own work, especially in a forum as public as this one.' He stepped away from the lectern, his face relaxing into a smile. 'That said, however, and in deference to my hosts, I will attempt to be a little more accommodating. The occasion demands it, I think.'

He cleared his throat before carrying on. 'To begin with, there are two answers to your question, Mr Fülep. The first, and the more specific response, has to do with my view of writing as being closely related to musical composition. Just as in a symphony, themes and motifs repeat and overlap and add to the fabric of the whole, so in my novels the repetitions serve a like purpose. That much is conscious and deliberate on my part, and I have no hesitation in acknowledging it.'

He turned to the student. 'Does that answer your question?'

The other shifted in his seat and was about to respond when someone else called out from behind: 'You said there were two answers.'

'Ah, yes . . .' András gestured in the direction of his unseen interrogator. He paused as he searched for the right words. 'I can probably explain it best by stating that my second answer has to do with a particular view of the human condition that sees it as undergoing a process of continuous enfolding. This owes a lot less to dialectics, as I understand it, and more to a kind of psychological expressionism. In my own work, the endeavour becomes one of exploring, with a child's sense of wonder almost, the peculiar chronologies of the individuals that I present to the reader as representative, without being caricatures, of universal archetypes. At the same time, I seek to trace universal experience through identifiable patterns. This explains my repetitive use of certain symbols. Through their visual resonance, they enable me to explore more fully the origins of what we claim to know and experience, our felt perception of the world, a perception that is emphatically not rational and is often completely enigmatic and mysterious.'

A woman in the front row interjected, her thick round glasses catching the light as she leaned forward. 'On a less abstruse level, what about your use of particular motifs like the woman in red? What is one to make of her sudden and inexplicable intrusions into the text?'

Before András could answer, he heard another voice, lazy and indolent: 'Yes, what about the woman in red? Is she someone you wanted to fuck?'

Elemér struggled to his feet, his face flushed with embarrassment. 'Dear God, André, you don't have to answer that! What is wrong with you people, why can't we be civil here?'

Someone at the back tittered.

András stepped away from the blackboard. 'It's all right,' he said, glancing curiously at the girl who had asked the question. She was pale and slight and dressed entirely in black, with black jeans and a diaphanous shawl wrapped around her shoulders. She held her head delicately balanced and at a slight angle, her appropriately jet-black hair drawn severely back and tied in a knot.

András gestured at her. 'May I know your name?'

'Clio,' she replied.

Someone tittered again.

'Just Clio?' András asked.

'That's what I said.' She spoke with a slight accent.

András waited for a moment before replying. 'No, Clio,' he said, 'she isn't someone I want to fuck. She simply happens to walk in and out of my books at will. One day, perhaps, she's going to make some sense. There was a time I used to believe she was simply a character awaiting resolution, one of many. But I don't know any more. In a lot of ways, I suspect I've given up on her. I have a funny feeling she's just going to disappear one day without any explanation, which would be fitting, don't you think?'

She appeared unconvinced, her faded grey eyes staring steadily into his.

He shrugged. 'It's the best I can do, I'm afraid, short of telling you once more that I simply don't know the answer to your question.'

Sensing his discomfort, the quick-witted Júlia stood up and tapped her watch to indicate that they had reached the end of their allotted time. She thanked the members of the audience, thanked András for his 'kind words', and, finally, reminded everyone that refreshments were being served in the room next door.

Twenty minutes later, András found himself reaching for his second cup of tea in an attempt to fend off 'Anna Márton, I do the celebrity interviews for *Public Eye*. You must have read our last issue on literary entrepreneurs and the marketplace, the one that's been the talk of the town? No? Oh . . .' She seemed momentarily at a loss, and then she perked up. 'Well, it doesn't matter, I suppose you've been more than a little out of touch. But I did find that question about the woman in red fascinating. Tell me – if you wouldn't mind my imposing on you a bit, there's such an air of mystery surrounding your personal life – isn't it time you dispelled some of that for your readers? You know, reach into the dark trough of memory, that kind of thing? It would be a scorcher, I can tell you that much. The famous, and might I add, famously reticent, Mr T first, in an intimate conversation with no holds barred . . .'

András smiled politely. 'I'm afraid not. I'm not very comfortable with that kind of divulgence.'

She wasn't going to be put off that easily. 'What about the Gabriel Club, then? After all, you were one of the founders, weren't you? What about the glamorous and reclusive Immanuele Emperházy, the legendarily difficult János Szegedy, the poet Stefán Vajda, and all of the others who stood up to the regime? There must be enough material there for an entire issue of my magazine! I mean, think about the packed turn-out at your reading today, and how young most of the faces were in the audience! Most of them weren't even born when the Gabriel Club fought its battles for freedom and democracy. Don't you think the younger generation deserve to know what you did for them? Don't you think they need the inspiration? Tell me how you began, about your early student days, your successes, your failures –'

András stopped her with a withering look. 'There's nothing I could tell you about that either,' he said. 'There's little to reveal, and what there is wouldn't be of interest to anyone, least of all to your readers. But you're going to have to excuse me. I'm out of the habit of closed spaces and crowded rooms.' He nodded curtly, turning around and retreating in the direction of the windows overlooking the courtyard. Behind him, he could hear his interlocutor busily scratching away on her notepad.

Elemér caught up with him and detained him for a moment. 'You're not making too many friends, I see,' he grinned. 'Not that I would have expected anything different. That Márton woman, for instance, the one you just disposed of so cavalierly, she's got a bit of clout. Not that that matters to you, I know, but you might think of working on those social graces a bit.' He paused, lowering his voice, 'But I'll leave you alone now, I can see that girl staring in your direction. What did she say her name was? Clio?'

András had to turn a full circle before he could locate the object of Elemér's attention. She was leaning with her back to the wall, her eyes staring listlessly at the crowd. She'd tied her hair back with a black bandanna, a few stray tendrils curling down. She looked up suddenly and noticed András.

He gave her a smile.

She smiled back, looking lost. That prompted him to walk across, and he manoeuvred his way through the crowd.

'Hello again . . .' he ventured, as he reached her.

She straightened up. At last she replied, a bit diffidently, 'I'm sorry, I wasn't paying attention. What did you say?'

'I said, hello again.'

She stared at him, her eyes widening slightly and accentuating the startling grey of her irises.

'I'm still a bit confused about your question,' he began, 'It caught me off guard –'

She cut him off, her voice low and rushed: 'I don't believe it could have. I think you were prepared for it.'

It was his turn to stare. Meanwhile, she had pressed defensively against the wall, her shoulders tautening.

He cleared his throat. 'Why do you say that? How could I possibly have been prepared?'

His words seemed to strike a chord because she slanted her head forward, her eyes lighting up. 'Well . . . I just thought it would be something you'd expect in the course of things. The way you deal with her seems to beg the question I asked.'

He studied her uncertainly, not quite sure what she meant, but she was already looking away from him, her chin resting on her shoulder. Then she glanced back at him, her expression changing and becoming strangely severe.

'Why must you keep bringing her back?' she asked. 'Someone like that should be sacred. If you have no use for her, let her be, leave her in peace.' Her eyes narrowed. Then she turned on her heels and crossed to the other side of the room. Taken aback, András followed. 'Look,' he began when he had caught up with her, 'it's difficult for me to respond if you walk away like that.'

'What if I'm not really interested in your reply?'

'Why wouldn't you be?'

'Maybe I like maintaining illusions.'

'Then it's a question of manners.'

'Manners don't interest me. Integrity is much more important.'

'You're just being difficult.'

She ignored his comment, stretching away from him and pressing back against the wall, the thin material of her black top accentuating the tapering slope of her figure: she had the wide, wing-like shoulders and narrow hips of a swimmer. One of the straps of the top was badly frayed and coming undone. It distracted him. For a moment, he imagined her breasts under the thin skin of the fabric. Embarrassed, he looked up, about to point out that the strap was loose, when he saw that she was looking at him with amusement, her eyes flicking lazily across his face. He coloured, glancing away.

She laughed. 'You're trying a bit too hard, aren't you?'

'What do you mean?' He tried to keep the defensiveness out of his voice.

Her hands skimmed the space between them. 'Can you walk on water?'

He looked at her, wondering. 'No . . .'

'Then you must leave me alone. This very instant.'

'What kind of logic is that?'

She didn't reply. Instead, she reached across to her left shoulder where the fraying strap had finally snapped. With practised ease she tied the two ends into a knotted tongue. Then, noticing that he was watching, she said evenly, 'Why did you come here anyway? You'll never be a part of this mindless scatter.'

'Why are you telling me this?'

She looked past him and surveyed the room. 'Because you know that I know.'

That stumped him again. 'What do you know?'

'That you're tired of this business. It's in your eyes.'

Before he could think of an adequate counter, she had ducked past him again and moved swiftly to the other side of the room. He watched her leave, making no attempt to follow this time. She walked out of the room without a backward glance.

Elemér, who'd obviously been following the exchange, called out: 'Don't let her play with you like that. She's playing with you, can't you see that? Women always do.'

András acknowledged this with a non-committal smile. He walked over to the windows overlooking the courtyard. Lighting a cigarette, he drew on it deeply. He wished he could leave but he knew that he would have to stay a while longer to avoid appearing impolite. Below him, the courtyard was deserted, and he could hear a cello playing somewhere on the northern side. In the street beyond the courtyard, the van with the painted butterfly had been moved to one end of a pillared portico. There was a straggle of bicycles in front of it. András couldn't see the driver although his marionettes were still arrayed along the pavement.

About to turn away, András stopped suddenly, a movement on the far side of the van attracting his attention. It was a glitter of silver, ascending and descending in a regular arc. At first he couldn't quite make out what it was. He leaned out of the window and craned his neck to see better. Then he started, the colour draining from his face. The silver glitter was the light of the sun on a metal club. At the receiving end was the driver: he was lying motionless on the ground, his prone form encircled by a group of men.

As András watched, horrified, one of the men unleashed a brutal kick, his boot ploughing into the still figure on the ground. A second man followed, and then a third. The man on the ground rolled to one side, his arm jerking limply. Then the cycle was repeated, the violence inflicted with systematic and chilling precision. Meanwhile, a fourth man, a leather-clad skinhead, was spray-painting *GYPSIES OUT!* across the side of the van.

It was at that point that András found his voice. He yelled with a mixture of outrage and fear. Startled, the men looked up. One of them, the skinhead, saluted him mockingly with a clenched fist. The others began to retreat slowly. They seemed to have all the time in the world.

András was the first to run down to the street, but when he reached the van the men had disappeared. By the time the police arrived, a crowd had gathered. A middle-aged woman was frantically trying to erase the *GYPSIES OUT!* sign from the van's paintwork. A teenager joined her, using the sleeves of his jacket to wipe out the scrawl. An ambulance streaked in silently, the monitor on its roof blazing like a wild, blind eye. It slid to a stop, its doors yawning open, a voice from inside rapping out a command. In a matter of minutes, the wounded man had been laid out on a stretcher and whisked inside, the doors slamming shut, the ambulance backing out of the courtyard.

A priest in a blue cassock crossed over to the site of the assault and sprinkled a few drops of water on the ground. He murmured a blessing, his lips moving as András looked on. A brightly coloured television-news van swung into the street.

Beside him, András could hear Elemér's laboured breathing as he leaned against a pillar, his head slumped on his chest; he had a heart condition. He turned to András, his face very pale. 'Look at these people crowding around. They want to show concern, but it's only morbid fascination.' He glanced distractedly at the sky. 'And I think it's going to rain, on top of everything!' He looked at András again. 'Time to go back in?'

Behind them, a familiar drawl cut through the silence: 'Why not? It's all over now. No point in crowding around.'

It was Clio, the dark-haired girl.

'They'll never catch them. They always show up too late.' She glanced at him. 'You look like you could use a drink.'

András shrugged. 'Thanks . . . but I'm all right.'

She nodded over her shoulder, 'I have a car. It's parked out in the street. Let's go.'

'No, thanks.'

'Oh, come on!'

'I thought you wanted to be left alone,' András said, surprised. 'Why the sudden change of heart?'

'That was inside the room. I got claustrophobic.'

Beside him, András sensed Elemér detaching himself from the pillar and moving away. He felt suddenly irritated. Trying to control himself, he addressed the girl, 'You're pretty intrusive, you know? And why do you think I should go with you?'

'Because you will.'

'Look, Miss –'

She interrupted him, suddenly earnest, 'Try the comfort of strangers.'

András winced at the cliché and glanced down. The girl's left hand was resting on the crook of her arm. It was missing a middle finger. He looked at her. 'How old are you?'

'What's that got to do with anything?'

'Go home, Clio.'

She took a step back, colouring. 'You think I'm playing games, don't you?' she retorted. 'You're very patronizing, you know. You sounded so pompous when you were speaking, that's why I had to ask you what I did. All those empty theories when all one ought to do is write. I compared your words to your eyes and you seemed like a man on the verge of drowning. That's why I wanted to prick your bubble and find out what was really inside. Listen –' she hurried on, seeing that he was turning to leave, 'I'm not with a newspaper. I don't deal with that kind of swarm. And I'm not some snotty college student looking to write you up for a term paper. I'm simply someone who likes to read and I've read all your books. Besides, I'm leaving the country soon and I'm never coming back and I know I'm someone you could talk to without fear or any of that bullshit, so . . .' Her voice tapered off.

'Where are you going?' András asked, in spite of himself.

'America.'

'America? Is that where the accent comes from?'

'No, that's from Paris.'

'You don't live here?'

'I spent my childhood here, but I'm visiting now.'

'And you're leaving for America soon?'

'Yup. I'm heading for the West Coast.'

'You get around.'

She shrugged. 'I have a friend in America, in a place called Eugene, Oregon. She's older than me. She's an artist, she makes icons. She's the one who introduced me to your books. She really likes them. That's how I first found out about you and I've been waiting to meet you ever since.'

'Oh?' He looked at her curiously. 'And why was it so important to meet me?'

'Because of the woman in red.'

'I'm afraid I don't see the connection.'

She made a swift, breathless gesture. 'I lived across the street, Mr Tfirst. I knew her when I was a child.'

92

'Her?'

'Immanuele . . . Immanuele Emperházy.'

András took a step back, involuntarily glancing up at the sky. He looked around the courtyard, not saying anything.

'We were neighbours,' the girl went on. 'In fact, I might even have seen you visiting, but it was a long time ago and I can't be certain.'

András decided to confine his query to an abstraction. 'Why do you think I should be interested in what you have to say?'

She looked surprised. 'It has to do with your past . . .'

'So what?'

'You mean you don't care?' Her voice began to rise.

'I mean I might no longer be interested.'

'Perhaps, but can the past be forgotten that easily?' She sounded triumphant, even a touch malicious.

'What do you mean?' he asked.

'I have a diary written by her.'

'A diary?'

'Yes. I think you would find the contents immensely interesting.'

He stared at her suspiciously. 'And how did you come across this diary?'

'After she disappeared, I found it in her room.'

He looked at her in amazement. 'You *stole* her diary?'

She hurried on, cutting him off before he could go any further, 'Don't misunderstand me. At the time I was too young to know what it was. I only wanted it as a keepsake.'

'A *keepsake*?'

'Yes, I wanted something to remember her by because I loved her.' She paused, adding, 'She was my friend.'

'And what did you do with this diary?'

'I hid it in a secret place in her house, a place that only I knew about, and that's where it's been all these years. It was only a couple of weeks ago, when I retrieved it, that I realized that you might want to take a look at it. I've been searching for you ever since.'

He stared at her without speaking.

She glanced away. 'It's just as well I got to it before anyone else did.'

93

'Did you read it?'

'Of course. That was what convinced me that you needed to see it.'

He considered this in silence. Then he asked, 'Where is it now?'

'In my car.' She gestured in the direction of the street.

'May I look at it?'

'Of course. In fact, I'll do better still . . . I'll give it to you to keep.'

'I suppose I should thank you –'

She interrupted him. 'I have one condition.'

He eyed her warily. 'And what is that?'

'I have some questions I'd like to ask you first.'

'Questions? What about?'

She met his eyes directly. 'Not here, if you don't mind.'

Suddenly making up his mind, he said, 'All right, wait here, I'm going to tell my hosts that I'm leaving.' He marched into the building without another word.

When he returned, she had put on a jacket. She shivered as he drew up. 'Come on,' he said, taking her arm, 'let's go.'

They reached her car, a battered yellow Trabant.

She opened the door for him. He looked at her, hesitating. 'Where's the diary?'

She motioned inside. 'Get in.'

There was a stack of long-playing records on the front seat, an ivory-handled clasp knife resting on top of them. András moved the records to the back seat and held up the knife. 'What's this for?'

'You saw what happened in the courtyard. I've learned to be careful of everything,' she added, 'and everyone.'

As he gazed at her, she asked, 'Where do you want to go?'

He ignored her question. 'You said you wanted to talk to me, didn't you? What about?'

'What happened to her. The mystery of her disappearance.'

'There's nothing to talk about.'

'Perhaps, but I still have a few questions. They won't take up too much of your time. After that, you can have the diary, I promise.'

András gazed at the street before them. Most of the onlookers had disappeared. A lone policeman loitered near the van, the street around him appearing very empty after the recent rush. 'All right,' he replied, 'talk.'

'Not here. What about Gellért Hill? I feel like heights.'

'That's fine.'

As they backed down the street into the main avenue, the sky, overcast moments earlier, turned ominously dark. They were still waiting for the traffic light to turn green when the first drops began to splatter on the windscreen.

The girl pounded angrily on the steering wheel. 'Damn!' she exploded, 'the wipers don't work!' Turning to him, she asked, 'Would you mind waiting? I can't drive in this rain.'

He pointed past her. 'It's stopping.'

'What's that?'

'I said it's not raining any more.'

She glanced askance at the street, and then she looked back at him with a grin. 'What do you know? A weather god!'

About ten minutes later they parked at the foot of Gellért Hill. Clio switched the ignition off and glanced at András. Neither of them made any move to leave the car. Instead, they sat in the silence and listened to the wind. Drops of rain pattered down from the trees, the residue of the recent downpour. Above the hill they could see the clouds in constant motion, now dark, now bright, their outlines stippled with rain.

'You're very reticent,' she ventured finally.

'That might have something to do with the circumstances of our meeting, don't you think?'

She gave a smile. She didn't seem in the least put off by the snub. 'I've been waiting to meet you for a while, you know. I suppose I'm just savouring the moment.' She stopped and contemplated him.

He didn't say anything. After a while, she opened the door on her side and stepped out. He followed her.

The western rampart of the citadel loomed above them. The air was crisp and cold, a high breeze cresting down the slopes in the direction of the river. The damp earth gave way under their heels, the grass springing back in their wake. They turned a corner and passed a fluttering flag, its contortions mirrored in a fragment of mirror lying on the ground.

András leaned down and picked up the shard. He gave it to Clio.

'Let's sit down,' she said. She pointed to the last bench at the end of the walk. Beyond it, the rampart limbered down in a cascade of furze and gorse. A flock of gulls was milling around the bench. They dispersed with loud calls as she ran towards them, their sleek white forms scattering like confetti.

She sat down first, taking off her jacket and letting it slide to the ground.

'I love sitting here by myself,' she said. She gestured at the river below them with a sudden vigour. 'And look at that! Isn't it beautiful?'

'You've been here recently?'

'Twice last week when it was raining and I knew there wasn't going to be anyone around.'

'You don't mind getting wet?'

'That's the whole point,' she laughed.

'And what do you think of Budapest?' He indicated the roofs of the city, dark with the rain.

She made a face. 'I returned here to get a sense of where I come from, but also to find out if I wanted to stay . . .'

'And you've decided it isn't worth it?'

'I've had enough. This is a land without fire. Life slips into a kind of *ennui* here, like living under water.'

'How long have you been here?'

'A few months.'

'And that's been long enough to make up your mind?'

'I know that may not seem long enough to you. But sometimes you just have to let go and move on, you know? Sometimes there's just no going back.'

She tossed the shard of mirror into the sky, the clouds reflecting brown and grey off its face. 'A piece of sky,' she said, catching it cleanly as it came down. Looking into it, she studied her face for a moment. Then she placed it carefully on the ground.

'Did you like living in Paris?' he asked.

'Paris? Did I like living there? I don't know if I'd quite put it that way. 'There was a time when everything I had was there.' She paused contemplatively. 'I loved the wide boulevards, the grey skies, the river, the glass-roofed arcades. I loved my cat. I had a cat named Monsieur, a white cat. I had a tiny apartment with a giant fireplace. A kitchen garden.'

'And what do you like about my books?'

She smiled wanly. 'You're jumping around a bit, aren't you? What do I like about your books? They're weird.'

'Of course. *Weird.* That would explain it.'

'I mean, they're so unlike real life.'

'Ah,' he raised an eyebrow, 'so unlike real life . . .'

'Stop being so condescending, András.'

'*András?* We're on first-name terms already?'

'Look, I could leave right now, if you like.'

There was an awkward pause. Finally, he broke the silence. 'No, I don't think you should leave.'

'Why?' she retorted challengingly. 'The diary?'

He didn't reply.

She nodded vigorously, almost to herself. 'One thing I can't understand, though, is why you lied to me.'

He stared at her uncomprehendingly. 'What about?'

'About the woman in red. About not knowing her.'

He studied the ground for a moment before replying, 'You don't give up easily, do you?'

'No, I don't. That's why I brought you here. I planned this carefully, don't you see? I was serving coffee at More Than Dust a week ago when I heard someone mention that you were giving a talk. I've been trying to locate you ever since I found the diary, you see, and here was my chance.'

'More Than Dust?' he asked.

'It's a café in the old town. It's a coffee-house during the week, and at weekends it transforms itself into a dance club called the Totalitarian Zone. It's a tiny place, but very trendy. I worked there for a while.'

'And what about the woman in red? Where does she fit into all this?'

'It's about Immanuele, don't you see? There are all these similarities.' She paused, considering. 'There's something peculiarly relentless about the way you keep returning to her in every book, as if you simply can't let go, simply can't get enough, even if she doesn't have a place in the narrative or anything. It's almost as if you're searching for something that you want to find and resolve once and for all. I mean, she'll just be there, standing under an awning when it is raining and you'll run into her, but then you'll force yourself to carry on because there is this other story that you are engaged in telling. It's clear to me, though, that you are as surprised as the reader to have found her there. There's such a sense of wonder in the way you write about her. That's when I decided I was going to attend your lecture and find out if I could meet you. Find out if you had the answers to my questions.' She stopped abruptly. 'I'm sorry, I don't suppose I'm being too coherent.' Suddenly self-conscious, she noticed that he was staring at her hands. She drew her fingers into the hollows of her fists.

'What, in your opinion,' he asked carefully, 'would I want to find and resolve once and for all?'

'Oh, I don't know . . .' She gave him a troubled look. 'If my hypothesis is correct and the woman in red *is* Immanuele, then one could understand that as some kind of way to assuage guilt over the way things turned out, don't you think? You were the one who talked about it this morning. How did you put it? That guilt is usually an individual matter rather than a collective one.'

'That wasn't quite the context in which I meant it –' András began, his voice deep with anger, but the girl interjected before he could carry on. 'Look –' she said awkwardly, 'I'm sure I'm reading a lot into this. You shouldn't take everything that I say too seriously or we'll both be going around in circles. The reason I wanted to talk to you about Immanuele's disappearance was so that you could make things clearer for me, not more confused.'

'And who else are you talking to about this besides me?'

'Who else?' she faltered, the question taking her aback. 'There's one other person I have in mind . . .'

'Who is he?'

'I'd rather not say.' She pursed her lips, looking both uncomfortable and determined.

András contemplated her with distaste. 'This is a convenient arrangement, isn't it?' he said cuttingly. 'You get to ask all the questions, but retain the option of censoring your answers. You said you planned this meeting. How did you know I would agree to talk to you?'

She hesitated. 'I had my reasons.'

'Of course, the inducement of the diary.'

'I have as much right to that diary as you do,' she retorted.

'Oh? And how's that?'

She avoided his eye. 'For me it's this link to Immanuele, and through her to my childhood and my past. A link far more faithful than the blubber of my memories. Can you understand that?'

András didn't reply.

She gazed at the windward slope and carried on, her voice sounding strangely imploring. 'I worshipped her as a little girl, you know? I loved her completely and unconditionally, as only a child can.' She shook her head. 'So much of my childhood is locked away in the world that she dwelt in. I keep wanting to go back to find out how much of that is responsible for the way I am now.'

She drew a deep breath, collecting herself. 'My parents were going through a nasty divorce, there was always banging and screaming going on at home and the silence at Immanuele's served as a much-needed solace.' She looked at András with curiously empty eyes. 'That's why I need to rediscover that world in order to try to understand myself. It's why I returned to Budapest.'

'You gave me an inkling of that world,' she continued, after a pause. 'In your books I found what I was looking for, I found Immanuele in the woman in red, I found my childhood places in your settings. You opened the door to the forgotten places in my mind. But I need to know more now, I need to know about Immanuele herself, and about what happened to her. The reason she was taken away from me so suddenly.' She looked at him with a curious kind of expectancy. 'Will you help me?'

He glanced at her thoughtfully. Then he stood up abruptly and held out his hand. 'The diary, please.'

She stared at him, surprised at this sudden turn. 'What do you mean? I thought we had an agreement.'

He remained standing, his hand still outstretched.

99

She stood up as well, frowning. 'Well, goodbye, then. There's no point in my staying around.'

He hesitated for a moment, looking at her with a remote kind of interest. Then he said gravely, 'Goodbye.'

She gathered up her jacket and began to walk away.

She had nearly reached the flagstaff when he stirred himself, stepping forward and breaking into a run. 'Clio!' he called out.

She watched him as he raced over.

He panted to a halt.

She contemplated him with a critical eye. 'You're out of shape.'

'Well?' he asked, a trifle uncertainly.

'I thought you'd had enough.' There was a lilt in her voice.

'I've changed my mind.'

They returned to the bench.

She sat down, grinning. 'That was a stupid trick and you fell for it! I wasn't going anywhere.'

'You knew I'd come after you?'

'Of course.'

He motioned vaguely, 'I don't think I understand any of this.'

'I told you earlier, you're trying too hard. All I want is some information.'

'What exactly do you want to know?'

'I want to know what happened to Immanuele.'

'What do you know about it so far?'

'What the newspapers reported at the time. They said that she disappeared from her house one night. I must have read those reports a hundred times.'

'And you don't believe them?'

'No, I don't. It was obvious to me they were a load of crap. Just like that stuff you've been feeding me about the woman in red.'

He tensed and dug his heels into the ground. Dislodging a fragment of earth, he bent over and picked it up. Examining it closely, he replied, 'You're right about that, I did lie to you. The woman in red is Immanuele.'

'That much is obvious. Why the need to keep lying?'

He replied stonily, 'It's private.'

He looked away. After a while, he lit a cigarette and gazed down at the river.

'How old were you when you left Budapest?' he asked.

'I was six. My parents had just divorced, and I accompanied my mother to Paris. It was supposed to be a holiday, but she decided not to return.' She shrugged. 'But I've been wanting to come back here for a very long time.'

'It's like a sense of folly, isn't it? The need to go back to where we come from?'

She turned to look at him. It was clear that she knew exactly what he meant. 'It was partly that,' she replied, 'but I was also driven by the need to find out what had happened to Immanuele. She was my friend at a critical time in my life, she took me under her wing and gave me the refuge I needed. I even used to go back to her place after she'd disappeared. I'd sneak in and wait for her, convinced that she would return, that there had been some kind of misunderstanding.'

After a prolonged pause, she resumed speaking. 'When I finally stood in front of her house a few weeks ago, it all just seemed to come back to me. It was late in the evening, I was willing myself to go in, wondering if I could. I didn't want to feel like an intruder.'

András interrupted her. 'Do you know who lives there now?'

She glanced at him with an element of confusion. 'You mean you don't know either?'

He flushed. 'No . . . I haven't been there for years.'

To his surprise, she gave a shiver, her face suddenly pinched. She leaned away from him. Her lips were trembling.

He eyed her with concern. 'Is something the matter?'

She didn't reply.

'Would you mind telling me what's going on?' he asked.

There was a moment of uncertainty during which she appeared to be fighting for composure. Then she lifted her head, her face pale and set. 'It's nothing,' she said calmly, looking him in the eye.

Mystified, he spread his hands. A bit diffidently, he offered, 'It takes time to mourn.'

She ducked her head, her shoulders swivelling. She began to

101

say something but then checked herself and looked down. 'God, these platitudes! Mourning – is that what you really think I'm doing?'

'I don't know. I think that's what it is, but I could be mistaken.'

She shook her head tiredly. 'Maybe you're right. Maybe it is a question of time. If I could just get to the root of all this, if I could pull that off, then everything could go back to the riddle that began a long time ago. And then I could narrow it down to a practical problem.'

'The problem of Immanuele's disappearance?'

'Primarily that. I know that at first I refused to acknowledge it, I was too young. And I've refused to accept it ever since. Everything I've ever done has been conditioned by this peculiar consideration of the past.'

'But you must have been very young when all of this happened?'

'I was . . . why do you ask?'

He tried to put it as gently as he could: 'To want to comprehend the past like this is a bit unusual, isn't it?'

'Is it?' She paused, reflecting. 'When I was young I used to believe that one day the dead would return from their secret musings and we would have to answer to them. Maybe that's why I used to pray every day that I would be allowed to die and my life be assigned to someone else.' She drew into herself. 'There's this conviction inside me, you see, that one day there'll be a judgement, an answering to some kind of tribunal. That's why I need explanations – not just any explanations but the ones that matter, the ones that make the difference.' She looked at him with a strange kind of longing.

He decided not to reply, sensing there was nothing he could say. Instead, he stretched himself and fixed his gaze on a clump of trees in the distance. 'Memory . . .' he said, almost to himself, 'a fickle thing . . .'

She stood up in response, beginning to pace up and down. Then, as if making up her mind, she extended a hand to him. 'Come on,' she said.

He looked at her in surprise. 'Where to?'

'Back to the car.'

'And then?'

'Margit Island.'

'Why?'

'It has to do with what you said in your lecture about memory and its resuscitation.'

'I don't understand.'

'You will, trust me.'

He followed her down the hill. It began to rain again, a light drizzle that cast a surface sheen on everything. They ran the last few steps to the car. As András waited for her to open the door, the rain began drumming impatiently on the car. Then the door swung open and he slipped in thankfully.

She looked at him as he settled back into the seat. Reaching into the glove compartment, she took out a thick manila envelope tied up with string. She handed it to him without saying anything. He untied it and took out a worn beige journal. Glancing inside, he recognized Immanuele's handwriting. Then he shut the journal and put it away.

'Well?' she said. 'What do you think? Time to go?'

They drove slowly in the direction of the river, the road widening gradually before curving down. By the time they reached the water, the rain had let up, fronds of pale green light spilling out of the clouds. A brisk breeze followed in the wake of the light. It tossed the surface waves into a fine spray that lashed the concrete embankments lining the Promenade.

They strolled down to the island. She led him to a stone bench. He sat down while she took a couple of steps to the river's edge, her back to him as she contemplated the water.

'What would you do if Immanuele came back?' she asked.

He gazed at her silently, not trusting himself to speak.

'You wouldn't know what to do,' she said. 'Isn't that right?'

'I saw a man beaten senseless today,' he replied, choosing not to answer her question. 'We both did. For all I know, he might already be dead. He was a puppeteer setting up a show for local kids, but he was also a gypsy and that was his mistake. The punks who beat him up walked away laughing.'

She shrugged. 'Those weren't punks, they were skinheads. There is a difference.'

She turned to look at him. 'Tell me more about Immanuele,' she said, with a meaningful glance at the manila envelope in his hand. 'Why she was so reclusive? What happened to make her like that?'

'She kicked a hole in the sky.'

'It had to do with the Gabriel Club, didn't it?'

'As a matter of fact, it didn't,' András said curtly. 'It preceded that.'

From across the river a church bell began ringing the hour. András waited for the reverberations to die down before he carried on. 'Before she founded the Gabriel Club,' he said, 'Immanuele was studying to be a conductor at the Academy, an orchestral conductor. She was one of their most promising students, as well as being quite unique in that she was a woman. There were rumours of apprenticeships with Karel Ančerl in Prague, Rozhdestvensky in Moscow, possibly Kondrashin – they were all very high profile. And then, one day, she was forced to give it all up. From a kind of celebrity she became an outcast overnight. On the eve of the Haraszti trial, she signed a petition demanding his release. Professionally, it was a suicidal move, and the directors of the Academy called her aside and advised her to withdraw her signature. They said that things had deteriorated in the wake of events in Prague, that they had little room to manoeuvre, and that anything that smacked of unorthodoxy threatened the very survival of the Academy. They said that she'd set a bad example for the other students. They said a true artist must be above ideology, and that art must separate itself from the real world and stand apart. Of course, she disagreed with them. She said that they were completely wrong in their lack of principles, and that she would never recant. It was stubborn and impractical of her, but that was the way she was – convinced that certain things in life were not worth compromising. They expelled her as a result, their best pupil in years. It was all hushed up, of course, like everything else at the time. But she never performed in public again. Simply dropped out of sight and restricted herself to playing music within the confines of her house, and that too in almost complete isolation.'

'Is that when you came into the picture?'

'Around then,' he replied.

'And the Club?'

'That followed with time.'

'Did you spend a lot of time with her?'

Despite himself, András found himself reddening. She must have sensed his discomfort because she reached out and touched his arm. 'Why don't you tell me about her music instead?' she asked.

'What about it? I'm not a musician. I wouldn't know what to say.'

'If it was that important to her, why did she give it up?'

'She didn't quite give it up,' András replied, bemused by the artlessness of the question. 'There were days,' he said, 'when she would practise for hours on end, day after day, day in, day out, as if the conventions of time and space had no meaning for her. On other days she would stop playing entirely, she couldn't bear to hear a single note, didn't want to have anything to do with music or with anything else. For a while, she even nailed down the lid of her piano. She took up writing instead, but I don't think it was ever an adequate replacement, not for the way she felt about music. It was the air she breathed in, her true medium of existence. She rarely talked about it, but she did mention once, just in passing, that for her making music was akin to the creation of life. It was the only effective way to counter her disappointments, she said, the only way to hold them back.'

'Did she play for you?'

'Sometimes,' he said briefly, 'but not often.'

'The music never goes, you know.'

'No . . . the music never goes,' he said in agreement.

'And what about her writing? Did she let you read any of it?'

'A few things . . .'

She looked at him, surprised. 'Did she publish anything?'

'Not really.' He hesitated. 'Life got in the way.'

'Not even in *samizdat*?'

'No, not even in *samizdat*. In any case, I don't think that that was her intention. To her it was a completely solitary enterprise. She could be intensely, even obsessively, private. I recall my telling her once that her privacy made her a difficult person to understand.'

'Was it pride on her part, do you think?'

'Pride? No, I think it was more a question of trust. Look –' he leaned forward, 'I don't want to give you the wrong impression. She could also be quite the opposite. When we met, for instance, it was she who first told me about herself. She said that her music had taken up all of her time and emotional space, that it hadn't really left her room for anything else, and, in any case, she was convinced she wasn't made for much else. A bit later, though, she said she wouldn't mind having children; she spoke of the wonder of small voices, of their inspiring amazement. But she questioned the efficacy of marriage and referred to her parents to support her case. She said that her mother's biggest error in life had been to marry the man she had. That was why it was so important to make the proper choices: to choose the right vocation, find the right person. To her, it was all a question of orientation. Proper orientation was the only way to overcome love, that forever formless and shifting maze. Only out of that quest could emerge truth, beauty, order, and the sense of what was good and right. And yet the question of love exhausted her. She said that for her, love meant a complete losing of self and that was why she could never contemplate it. But she continued to be attracted by it; it was the only way she thought the tediousness of her reality might be alleviated now that her music was spent.'

'She believed that love was a losing of self?'

'That was the way she described it to me, yes.'

'Did you agree with her?'

'I don't know; everything she said was important to me whether I agreed with her or not.'

Clio stared at him, and then she turned away. András offered her a cigarette and she accepted it, lighting it pensively. She waited for a moment. 'Will you tell me about the first time you met her?' she asked.

'What's the point? It's all buried in sand now.'

'I don't believe it can all have been for nothing. I don't believe it was meant to be buried in sand.'

'That's easy enough for you to say.' Struggling to hold himself in check, he said, 'Sometimes I don't know if the memory of her has been my lifeline or the rope I've hung myself with.'

She gazed at him with a strange kind of comprehension.

'Memory's messy work,' she said.

'Ah, yes . . . memory again.'

'What would you do if she came back?'

He looked at her in surprise. 'You've asked me that already. It's a pointless question.'

'Yes – but what if?'

'I can't answer that. I've stopped dealing in possibilities.'

She turned away when he said that, picking up her jacket and bringing out a photograph. 'Here –' she gestured, 'take a look at this.'

It was a sepia print, all grainy and discoloured. It showed a woman on a terrace leaning against a stone balustrade. In one corner there was an enigmatic explosion of white. It meandered to the centre of the picture and spilled over the woman's face.

He tapped the photograph. 'Who is it?'

'You don't know?'

'I can't tell.'

'It was my first camera. She showed me how to take the picture. I've carried it around with me ever since, that figure without a face.'

He returned the photograph to her. She held it in her hand and looked at it for a moment, as if making up her mind. Then she took out a pen and scribbled across the back of it. 'Here's the number you can reach me at tonight,' she said. 'If you want to, that is.'

She held out the photograph to him. 'And this is for you. I want you to keep it.'

'Why?'

'Consider it a restoration. It ought to belong to you, along with the diary.'

He remained silent, but he took the photograph.

She attempted a smile. 'András . . .' she said, hesitating. There was an altered timbre in her voice, a barely noticeable displacement. 'For a long time,' she said, 'I hurt myself by refusing to allow a question into my life.'

'And what was that question?'

'The question of what happened to Immanuele. Real, living people simply don't disappear into thin air, least of all someone that vital. And I think it's time someone did something about it.'

He looked at her as if he hadn't heard her properly.

'You think I haven't tried?'

'I think you gave up too easily.'

He restrained himself, remembering that he owed her for the gift of Immanuele's journal. Instead, he said, 'Please forgive me if I sound bitter, but sometimes you have to play the hand you've been dealt.'

She stared at him in disbelief. 'And you're satisfied with that?'

'Of course I'm not *satisfied* with that. But in this case satisfaction has had to take second place to survival.'

'Survival?'

'Yes, survival. The simple act of existence.' He carried on, his voice scathing, 'But I suppose you're far too young to understand that. Not all of us were fortunate enough to live in Paris when things here were falling to pieces.'

She blanched visibly. '*I* would have done everything in my power to find out what happened to her. I would have stopped at nothing.'

He gazed at her in amazement. 'And what do you think I did?'

'Not enough.'

To her surprise, he burst into laughter, his teeth glinting in the light.

She felt suddenly defensive. 'Why are you laughing?'

He simply shook his head from side to side and refused to comment.

A sudden gust blew her hair across her face. She tossed it back angrily and stood up. 'I think it's time for me to leave, Mr Tfirst. There's not much else to be said.'

'You're dying to resurrect, Clio,' he replied, 'and that can be dangerous.'

She didn't say anything. Instead, she slung her jacket over her shoulder. With her eyes still on him, she began to retreat slowly, her strides lengthening as she put distance between them. When she was about a dozen paces from him, she glanced back, but very swiftly, and he couldn't make out her expression. Then she carried on her way, not towards the bridge, as he'd expected, but in the direction of some pine trees, their low-hanging branches parting to make way for her before springing back again.

András gazed at the manila envelope she had left with him. He unfastened its clasp and took out Immanuele's journal. He held it in his hand for an instant before opening it on a page of closely written text. He stared at it, his head strangely heavy. Then he snapped the notebook shut and replaced it in the envelope, his fingers stiffly wrapping the string back around it. Stuffing the bundle into his jacket, he hunched forward and stared at the river, his eyes wide open but seeing nothing.

He had no idea how long he'd been sitting there when he felt a gentle tug on his shoulder. Startled, he turned around. It was a little girl, no more than about four or five years of age. A fairy princess, dressed from head to toe in gold sequins and white brocade. She had a cardboard star pasted on her forehead and diaphanous paper wings.

She regarded him gravely. 'Mister,' she said, 'would you like a toffee?'

She held out a sticky toffee to him.

'And who might you be?' he asked.

She took a step backwards, rolling her eyes and slapping her forehead. 'Why, silly! – I'm your fairy godmother, of course!' She considered him with reproach, then glanced away, distracted by the seagulls flapping over the river. She directed his attention to them. 'Baby geese!' she said.

He looked at the birds. 'No, those aren't baby geese,' he said, 'They're seagulls.'

She sounded it out: 'S-e-e-g-a-w-l-s?'

He corrected her again. Pleased, she stuck out a grubby little hand.

'You're nice,' she announced. 'I'm Quackie.'

Before he could respond, András heard a stentorian voice call out from the distance: 'Quackie! Come back here at once, child! How many times have I told you to stay away from strangers?'

András turned around. An elderly woman, probably the grandmother, was shaking a cane in their direction. He waved in reassurance, but the child, deciding not to brave her formidable guardian's wrath, dropped the toffees on his lap and hurried back. She ran past a group of brown-clad monks, her feet flying frantically up and down. A rush of wind from the river followed her.

Making up his mind in that instant, András stood up and looked across at the causeway where Clio's yellow Trabant was parked. He decided to walk over and wait for her to return. This time, he determined, he had a few questions of his own that warranted answering.

As he neared the car, he noticed a young woman leaning against it, but it wasn't Clio. She was staring in the opposite direction so that he couldn't make out her face. She was small and very thin, with sloping shoulders and a clean-shaven head. She had a bar code tattooed on the back of her neck. She turned at the sound of his footsteps, her eyes huge and dark. She regarded him silently as he approached. Her hands, he noticed, were trembling.

András cleared his throat, a bit uncertain. 'Excuse me . . . but I'm looking for the woman who drives this car . . .'

She stared at him with undisguised wariness.

'She's about this height . . .' he made a gesture. 'With dark hair.'

She shook her head. 'Go away,' she said, her words slurring. Her voice was hoarse and indistinct. She seemed to be having difficulty breathing.

He hesitated. 'I asked you a question . . .'

She lowered her head in response. She looked ashen and exhausted, her charcoal eyes in absurd contrast to the pallor of her face.

András was about to turn away when she stopped him with a gesture and pointed down. Around her feet was a scatter of broken glass. He glanced back at her, puzzled.

She avoided looking him in the eye. 'If it's Clio you're looking for,' she murmured, 'she's on the island.'

'Oh, you do know her, then? The island? But I've just come from there –'

She started, obviously surprised. 'You've come from the pier?'

'The pier?' He stared at her. 'No . . . I was sitting with her on a bench . . .'

110

She relaxed visibly. She seemed enormously relieved, although she drew away from him. Her voice dropping again, she said, 'Look for her by the pier. You'll find her there.'

'What pier? Which one?'

She was already turning away. She paused and appeared to gather herself in. She coughed, a stricken sound. Then she raised her hand and pointed very deliberately to the place he'd seen Clio entering the pine grove. 'There's a path,' she said slowly, taking great care to enunciate her words. 'The pier's at the end of it, at the edge of a clearing. You'll find a circle of roses there.'

'A circle of roses?' he repeated, not certain he'd heard her correctly.

She turned away in silence.

He left, aware that she was watching him. Feeling strangely irresolute, he returned the way he had come, his steps leading him down the causeway and back to the island. Following her directions, he turned towards the pines, their slender branches held aslant.

He found a path through the trees. It was winding and dark, the sunlight consumed by leaves braiding thickly down. Sections were paved with stones, the rest concealed under thick and wiry undergrowth. To the right, glimpses of the river glinted through the trees; to the left, the canopy of leaves closed over completely, a thick black silence shaping through everything.

With his hands held out before him, András edged onwards, surprised at how wild the place was. He ducked under branches and stepped over stagnant pools, surrounded by a damp smell, the swamp scent of decaying vegetation and silt. Eventually, ahead of him, closer to the river and at a slight elevation above the path, he glimpsed an open meadow. He hurried towards it, the late afternoon light turning yellow and then a bright golden.

As he emerged into the clearing, he slowed down, filled with a curious sense of foreboding. The place was a beehive of activity, overrun with uniformed policemen. At the far end of it, through the thick of the crowd, he noticed a pier reaching over the water.

He stepped forward, his feet sinking deep into the wet grass

111

and mud. One of the policemen noticed him, his eyes glancing up dourly before he went back to taping together what had once been a child's teddy bear.

András stopped in front of him.

'You the poor sod who knew her?' the policeman asked.

András stared at him. 'Knew whom?'

'Why, the woman, of course . . .' The man pointed to a dug-up area encircled with yellow tape and partly covered with planks. 'The one that was buried there. We're expecting some-one who's supposed to have known her.'

'There was a woman buried there?'

The man hesitated. 'Well, not exactly a woman, but a life-sized replica of one. We found her floating in the river –' he pointed, 'by that pier. Made of wax, but all stained with earth and moss. Made me quite sick to look at her, I can tell you, because that's the way *she* looked, beautiful and sick, with a circle of red roses crowning her head. But you're not the one that knew her?'

András began to tense. 'No,' he replied, 'I don't think so.'

'She must have been a looker, though. I thought I'd seen everything, but this was something else altogether. The wax-work was so uncannily true to life. She must have been buried . . . oh, only a few days ago, at most. Very bizarre.'

András walked over to the edge of the opening, his shoes sink-ing into the mud and adding to the confused welter of footprints. The dank smell of wet mud permeated the place. Leaning over the taped-off barrier, he looked down. At the bottom of the pit was an elongated wooden box. It took him a moment to realize that he was staring into a coffin, its insides lined with a dark blue cloth.

From somewhere behind him, he heard a man shout. He turned: a workman was preparing to prise out the coffin. Moving out of his way, András watched him prop a winch against a tree.

The policeman he'd spoken to earlier came over and stood next to him. 'That's where she was buried,' he said, indicating the dug-out.

András tried to keep his voice even. 'You speak of her as if she were a real person.'

'Oh, she was real all right, didn't I say? The Inspector

112

recognized her. A case from a long time ago, he said. It made him go all brooding and silent.'

'And where is this waxwork now?'

'Oh, they took it to the station, something about it not being quite right.'

'Who found it?'

'Ah, that's another story altogether. She was found by a seven-year-old boy who'd given his guardians the slip. How he found her we'll probably never know, seeing as he's not quite right in the head. Not very pleasant, not very pleasant at all. But I mustn't say more, I'm not allowed . . . Lucky the Inspector was around to put two and two together. Surprised us when he described the case, not the kind of thing you'd forget in a hurry.' He spat on the ground. 'He's a good sort, is the Inspector. Been on the force long enough, God knows.'

Feeling slightly overwhelmed, András decided to interject. 'Actually,' he said, 'I came here looking for a young woman. She has long black hair. It's very distinctive. I was wondering if you'd seen her.'

'No, I don't think so. Not as far as I can remember, but I've been very busy. But I can see the Sergeant and he's not going to be too pleased with me shooting my mouth off. You'd better be moving along.' With a shrug of his shoulders, he walked away, past a man in a black coat who was gazing intently at András.

The man was tall and thin, with a faintly lugubrious cast to his face. András had no idea how long he'd been standing there. Catching his eye, the man walked over. 'Mr Tfirst, isn't it?' he asked, his tone neutral.

András stared at him in surprise. 'How do you know my name?'

The man extricated a card. 'Réti, Ede Réti, Sergeant,' he said, with a quick, disingenuous smile. He held the card in the air long enough for András to read it, and then he replaced it in his wallet. 'We've been waiting for you for a while now. The girl said you were on your way.'

'The girl?'

'The one that sent you here.'

'Excuse me?'

113

'You're here to identify the body, aren't you?'

'The body?'

'The waxwork, you know what I mean.'

András considered this with a growing sense of unreality.

'Are you sure I'm the person you're looking for?' he asked.

'Well, naturally.'

András decided to try again. 'Let me understand this, Sergeant –'

'Réti, Ede Réti.'

'You want me to identify the waxwork of a person apparently known to me?'

'That was the original intention, but it's too late now; we had to get it out of here before the place became a bloody circus.' He nodded at the growing crowd of onlookers.

András looked around. 'And where is the girl who is supposed to have sent me here?'

The policeman glanced at him sharply. 'How do I know? All we got was a telephone call.'

Increasingly uneasy, András forced himself to concentrate. 'Sergeant, can you tell me the identity of the woman whose waxwork was buried here?'

The other began to look slightly baffled. 'I don't understand . . .'

András took a step forward, trying to keep calm. 'Look, I know that an Inspector identified her. One of your men just told me that. So why don't you just tell me who it was?'

The policeman shifted from one foot to the other, appearing to give the matter consideration. Then he held out his hand, his mind made up. 'I'm sorry, Mr Tfirst,' he said impersonally, 'but you're going to have to wait for the Inspector. He'll be in touch with you shortly. His name's Szegedy, Andor Szegedy. He'll tell you where things stand.'

'You'd better leave now,' he continued, his tone brooking no further discussion. 'There's work to be done here.'

Back on Margit Bridge, András stopped and looked carefully around. Darkness was falling, a flicker of lights illuminating the bridge. There was no sign of the yellow Trabant, no sign of Clio or the shaven-headed girl. On a sudden impulse, András turned

114

around and raced back to the island, making for the clearing with the coffin and the policemen. When he reached it, the Sergeant had gone. He accosted the nearest policeman, grabbing him by the arm. 'Can you please tell me the name of the woman who was buried here?'

The man looked at him strangely.

'You mean the waxwork? Why? Are you from the papers?'

'Just tell me, won't you?'

The other held back. 'I don't know if I can . . .'

'Please!'

'Look, I really don't know. I don't know if there's been a positive identification, and even if I did, I wouldn't be at liberty to tell you. There are procedures that must be followed.'

◆

'Hello?'

'Is Clio there?'

'Who?'

'Clio.'

'Clio? There's no one by that name here.'

'She gave me this number.'

'Is this some kind of a joke? It's three o'clock in the morning!'

'Are you sure? She said she could be reached here . . .'

'Of course I'm sure! I live here! We're respectable people! Look! – who is this? Hello? Hello?'

Chapter Two

Still Life with Water

By the time Szegedy had pulled the car over to the side of the road, a cloud-white clay of fog had already overtaken the dawn. It swamped everything with its formless, opaque sheen, drops of water condensing on hidden branches and falling to the ground. Visibility was too poor to risk driving and he decided to walk down to the river until the weather cleared.

It took him a while to find the path, and he had to be careful not to venture too close to the cliff. Above him, above the slopes worn down by rain and groundslide, the sharp morning light was melting into the fog. He tried to keep ahead of it, his feet hurrying over wet clumps of grass and heather. Variations of grey replaced one another endlessly, a damp and immaterial swirl now rising, now falling, the silence permeated by the sound of dripping water.

Where the path levelled out, a finger of clear light separated the riverbank from the water. There were already boats out on the river: he could hear the fishermen's voices echoing as they laid their nets and traps; occasionally he could catch the sound of their laughter. Kicking off his shoes, he stretched back on the rocks, watching the sky that was at once dark and luminous. Morning was coming, but slowly, the storm still a distinct memory preceding the dawn. In the city, in the room with the scabbed and peeling walls, that storm had been a distant sound between gouging bouts of rapture. It had been a strange night, culpable and steeped with desire. He'd been moved to the point of embarrassment at times, marvelling at the facile movements of his own body in the dark, and of its swift, cathartic emissions. And then to venture into the storm as he had.

The next time she'd ask him for more money, he was sure of that.

He recalled the smell of her soft blonde hair, her knees bunching up as he entered, her eyes wide like a child, but with that certain edge of despair, desperation. He'd asked her to hit him, but she'd refused. He'd grasped her breasts then, squeezing the nipples hard, her skin clammy and cold, her eyes listless and cold, and cold her probing fingers. She had ended up hurting him as much as he had managed to hurt her. But that was how it ought to be, pain in careful measure of pain, pleasure for immeasurable pleasure.

Shivering, he sat up. Something about the fog reminded him of her skin, it had that same cramped texture. Imagining the other men in her life – there were bound to be others – he felt a hot flush wash over him, his stomach knotting into a cramp.

He wondered if he were jealous.

Unbuttoning his trousers, he decided he was definitely not jealous. The novelty was what was preoccupying him, that was all. He'd simply have to be less skittish about it. There was nothing perverted in what he had done, nothing abnormal. After all, she had given in to everything he'd asked. Or could it have been the other way around?

Perhaps he could take her to the cinema to make up.

Some cheap, unambiguous film about love.

Stepping out of his trousers, he lay back on the rocks, wondering if he could be seen. Although it wasn't warm, he could feel the drops of sweat on his skin and the knobbed contours of the rocks pressing against him. Raising his head he surveyed himself, his lips pursing involuntarily. She'd used her teeth on him, he could see the marks on his skin. Reaching down with a sudden, awkward motion, he gathered himself with one hand, rolling back his foreskin in order to see better. The skin was a distinct brownish-purple running to red, the scrotum shading to black where she'd bitten him, a thin and wrinkled line separating the scrotal sacks. Grimacing angrily, he let go of himself; sometimes it could be inordinately difficult to get them to comprehend exactly what it was that he wanted. Not quite an epiphany – God alone knew he had given up on that long ago – but at the very least something approximating pleasure, like a mood, or an instant of rapture.

He stood up and stepped over to the river. He tested the water with an outstretched foot. The river was cold and dark, its boundaries hidden in the fog. It parted with a silver sheen as he waded in, the texture like molten glass. As he slipped below the surface, he opened his eyes and looked around, the sky receding into an inverted bowl filled with light. Below, where the river ran through subterranean channels, he could see dark grooves in a bed of solvent brown. Thoroughly invigorated, he surfaced to catch his breath, squinting at the sky before he turned and headed back towards the bank.

He pulled himself out of the water. The sun had carved a corridor of light through the fog, the momentary dazzle enough to make him recall that the forecast for the day had been marvellous. A crimson swathe ran across the sky, the river transforming into a thick band of the same colour, then the water turned a dark red, like wine, the waves lighting up with sparkles that spread to the narrow beach and its congeries of sandstrewn rocks. Further upstream, the fog merged with pockets of grey and darker coloured rocks, its substance rapidly absorbed by the trees and the drying grass and sand. The sun lit up what was left of the residue, driving it closer to the ground, stray strands dissolving in the growing light.

In the car, he changed into his business clothes. Arrayed in a stylish trench coat, sporting an elegant silk tie and a carefully cultivated air of distinction, he was a portrait in grey and black – black shoes, black trousers, grey jacket tailored in the latest mode – the epitome of conservative *élan*. He slicked his wet hair back and sprayed his wrists with cologne, the sharp creases of his cotton shirt caressing his skin as he flexed his arms and shoulders. He stuck a cigarette into his mouth and shut the lid of the cigarette case with a snap. Pouring himself some coffee from a thermos, he took out a map from the dashboard compartment and studied the directions written along the margin. He realized he had quite a way to go before he reached his destination. Folding the map and replacing it, he adjusted the rearview mirror and looked at himself, baring his teeth in the semblance of a smile. Then he softened his features, putting on a modest and unassuming expression, one that belied his position and reputation. 'Hello, András,' he said softly, 'it's been a while.' He repeated it several times, retracting and extending his hand in accompaniment to the words, stopping only when he was satisfied. Then he put on a pair of mirrored glasses, turned the key in the ignition, and pulled away.

Finding the bridge turned out to be easier than he had anticipated. A sign warned that it was scheduled for repairs and barred, as a result, to heavy traffic. Below the bridge, the river coiled through the valley in a listless skein. The road that followed its winding course looped in wide curves along the cliffside, its asphalt surface reflecting the sun. Elsewhere, all was rock, black rock and bleakness, the windswept faces reflecting both the sky and the turbid and near-motionless river.

The bridge itself was ancient. Steep parapets ran along its entire length, and at the northern end, a pile of rubble was all that remained of what must once have been a massive wooden gate. A stone tablet impressed upon a sconce attributed the construction of both the bridge and the gate to the 'Raven King'. Where the sconce was embedded into the side of the bridge, the masonry had broken loose to reveal the stonework beneath, the massive individual blocks wedged firmly together. The façade was regular and precise: dove-tailed blocks working their way along the length and culminating in the wooden gate with its ruined machicolations and towers.

The man in the car eyed the bridge with wonder. Parking in the shadow of the wooden gate, he stepped out into the bright sunlight, his shiny black shoes stirring up dust. Ahead of him, the bridge curved down a sinuous central spine, the hillsides sweeping back beyond it in an eruption of height. There – when he shaded his eyes against the sun – he could see a densely wooded crest, the vegetation flaring up in leafy explosions.

A cough attracted his attention. It was followed almost immediately by a faint rustle from a stairwell adjoining the wooden gate and leading down to the river. He walked over and peered down the shaft. He couldn't make out what had produced the noise, but he saw that the steps descended in a perilous corkscrew that plunged almost vertically down to the river.

With a sense of disquiet, he glanced over to the barren and rocky banks of the river. Abandoning the warmth of the sun, he began to descend the staircase, gingerly testing his footing with each step. When he reached the bottom, he turned and made for a bare and rocky promontory of land jutting into the river. A man was sitting with his back to him. He walked up to him and coughed to attract his attention. When the other turned around, he extended his hand in a formal greeting. 'Hello, András,' he said, 'it's been a while.' He waited for a reply, and when he sensed none was forthcoming, he sat down, taking off his jacket and spreading it on the ground.

'You know, András,' he said, breathing heavily from his recent exertions, 'the more I think about this business with the wax-work, the more I'm convinced that the only way we can find out what's going on now is to go right back to the past, to the matter of Immanuele's disappearance.'

Goaded by the other man's silence, he carried on, 'I still don't have the faintest idea what to make of the waxwork, but whichever way one looks at it, it doesn't make any sense.'

András leaned down and took off his shoes and socks. He stood up and glanced at the river while studiously ignoring the policeman. Wading into the water, he stopped when he was up to his knees, the ripples tracing out his submerged feet and calves with silver. He stood there for a while, looking down.

Szegedy spoke again, his voice both resigned and indignant. 'Look, András,' he said, 'I can understand your reluctance to speak to me, but this is about the waxwork, not about anything that might have occurred between us in the past.'

The man in the water stirred. 'Are you completely shameless?' he asked.

'What do you mean?'

'What do you think?'

There was a moment of silence. Then Szegedy said bitterly, 'It's easy to be judgemental, isn't it?'

'Sometimes it is. Remarkably easy.'

'My past makes me automatically suspect? Permanently compromised?'

'Do you want me to laud you instead?'

Szegedy coloured. 'No . . .' he said slowly, 'I don't want your applause. All I'm trying to tell you is to forget what happened between us and deal with the matter at hand. Is that too much to ask? I'm not going to apologize for my past. I've made mistakes and I've admitted to them in the proper circles. Now I'd like to get on with my life, to forget all that, put it behind me and carry on.'

'What a privilege, Inspector, to be able to put such things behind you and look forward to a rosy future.'

'I was part of a system,' Szegedy replied defensively, 'and part of the system that worked. It's absurd to insist that the whole thing was an aberration, that over the span of forty years absolutely nothing good was done. I'm not going to pander to that kind of self-flagellation. We were a public service, nothing more. We were interested in active criminals, potential law-breakers, political trouble-makers. We left law-abiding citizens alone.'

He stole a glance at András, who was staring impenetrably at the water. 'It was a strange period for all of us. Perhaps I didn't ask the right questions at the time, but to me that was beside the point. I was a technician, not an ideologue. I did my job. I wasn't responsible for the nature of my work. I simply obeyed political directives. If something appeared ethically questionable or problematic, I accepted it as the psychology of the time, the way things functioned. It was policy, how could I have thought otherwise?'

A fly buzzed past his face, distracting him. He swatted it away in irritation. 'But things are very different now,' he carried on, 'for better or for worse, and I'm in a different department, with different problems, different responsibilities, different crimes. I deal with ordinary police work – hangings, stabbings, beatings, things like that. Case in point: the present investigation, a riddle whose origins go way back into the past, and whose circumstances, such as they are, involve both you and me. Add to that the background of your relationship with my poor dead brother, and the difficulty is compounded.' He paused, controlling himself and slowing down. 'Believe me, I am not here by choice. I would rather be doing something else altogether. But I've managed to recognize that neither one of us can help the past and that we're both responsible for the resolution of the present investigation. That's all I'm asking of you, that you put your animosity behind you and deal with the situation from an objective standpoint.' He lowered his voice, his tone turning suddenly caustic. 'And in any case, I don't have to keep justifying myself to you. I'm merely doing it out of courtesy.'

András turned to look at him with a steely eye. He remained silent.

Sighing perceptibly, Szegedy leaned to one side, his weight resting on his left arm. It was beginning to get warm, the sun soaking into the rocks. He unfastened his collar and loosened his tie. Fishing into a pocket, he fumbled for a cigarette, putting it in his mouth without lighting it.

A shadow fell across the path just then, causing him to look up. It was a black-backed gull, its bright eyes scanning the river. It swooped low as he watched, its wings opening and closing in untidy bursts. Then it dived under the bridge and emerged on the other side, its streamlined shape ascending in tight circles and rapidly gaining height. Below the bridge, the water shimmered over an outcrop of stones, the eddies catching the sun.

Watching the silent András, Szegedy wondered how he could engage him in anything resembling a constructive discussion. 'You know,' he offered conciliatorily, 'I realize this must be very difficult for you to deal with, so much of the past being brought back in this manner . . .' He paused to assess the effect of his words. Although he couldn't be certain, he thought he detected a gratifying tension on the other's part.

András turned to look at him with a hard, mocking stare. 'Don't patronize me, Inspector.'

Szegedy decided not to react. 'I'm sorry about losing my temper over the phone last night.'

András shrugged ambivalently and returned to his contemplation of the river.

Trying to contain his exasperation, Szegedy carried on, 'You weren't exactly being cooperative.'

'I had no desire to speak to you.'

'I don't normally lose my composure like that.'

After a while, with his back still turned, András asked, 'When can I see this wax figure?'

'I don't have an answer for you right now. We've got people examining it. It won't be pleasant.'

There was a slight delay before András replied, his voice without resonance: 'I would like to take a look at it as soon as possible.'

'Of course, I understand. To be perfectly frank, though, it may well have been fortuitous that you didn't get to look at it that day on the island. It would probably have come as too much of a shock.'

András spoke again, his voice strained, 'What about the boy who dug her up?'

Szegedy grimaced. 'He was seven years old, and more than a little deranged. When we found him on the island, he was wearing a newspaper wrapped around his head like a turban. It was covered with his excrement.'

'Where is he now?'

'His family took him back to Rome. There was very little we could do about it. He's the son of the Italian Consul; it would have caused a major diplomatic embarrassment.'

'You questioned him?'

'To a degree. He's mentally retarded.'

'And what did you find out?'

'How he'd stumbled upon the figure and dragged it out . . .'

'Dragged it out of the ground? A seven-year-old?'

'That's what he mimed. We had to depend on his mother's interpretation. I'm told people like that can be awfully strong when they put their minds to it. But we also have another theory. We think the person who made the figure deliberately placed it in the open grave, intending it to be found. It was pure chance that led the boy to it. He probably fell into it, discovered the waxwork, and dragged it out.'

'Where is the mother now?'

'Back in Rome with her son. We were told they were considering treatment to help him deal with the trauma. Of course, we took down her statement before they left. We couldn't find out how he got the waxwork to the river. We assume he used the rotted planks from the coffin to lever it around. There was a trail of planks to the pier.'

'There were no witnesses to any of this?'

'No witnesses at all. It took place in the dead of night.'

His face tense and white, András turned to survey his informant.

Szegedy glanced at him in concern. 'Are you all right?'

András frowned and swayed slightly in the water. 'Yes,' he said, his voice sounding muffled, 'Please carry on.'

Szegedy resumed, a trifle reluctantly, 'There's not much else to tell. He was lurking around the pier when he was spotted by the policeman who then found the waxwork and sounded the alarm.' He paused and looked at András who was staring at the water again, preoccupied. Apparently oblivious to the policeman, he made a circle with his hands and looked through it to where the sun had broken up the surface of the river. The ripples glittered back at him. He hunched over and held his breath. He'd discovered that if he narrowed his eyes, he could make out hundreds of tiny mirrors reflecting off the face of the

◆

water. He turned to point that out. 'Look at that, Immanuele,' he said, screwing up his eyes to see better. 'From a certain angle, the surface of the water acts just like a prism.'

She didn't reply. She was lying on the riverbank, her face screened from him by the overhanging branch of a willow tree. She had languidly cast back one arm, the back of it resting on the ground. The other hand rested on her belly, gently following its rise and fall.

124

At length, she turned and looked at him through half-open eyes. 'I wonder if the Madonna liked gazing at the sun.'

'The Madonna?' He looked at her, surprised. 'Why?'

'Oh, I'm sure she did. Things like that must have made her who she was.'

'Does this have anything to do with what I said about the river?'

'It could have, I don't know, I suppose I was contemplating something else. I was thinking about the slings and traps that have punctuated my life and the sunlight that keeps flooding through the crossroads regardless.'

'Why think about that now?'

'Because I'm feeling hopeless.'

'Hopeless? Why?'

She smiled. Then she sat up and stretched. 'Come here.'

He waded through the water and stopped when he reached her. Trying to read her mood, he asked, 'Why such black thoughts?'

'I don't know,' she replied, gripping his arm with a surprising strength. 'I'm feeling melancholic.' She turned her face away from him. 'Is there anything you're keeping from me?'

He stared at her. 'No,' he replied carefully.

She sat up, straight-backed, her brows furrowing. 'I can't sleep any more.' She gazed past him, her hand still holding on to his arm, her eyes restlessly scanning the river. 'I feel as if the entire impetus for our relationship is coming from me. The time that we spend together . . . everything has become so burdensome.'

'What do you mean?'

'I mean that I can see no vision for our future. No space for me to find my way into your life.'

'It's been a difficult time for both of us. It will pass.'

'It wasn't supposed to be like this. I work just as hard as you, but it's never that exclusive. It's almost as if your work is a ruse to maintain your distance, and your books nothing but an escape from the reality of our life. I know this must sound mad, but it's true. And it wasn't like this in the beginning. In the beginning you needed me, you sought me out. What's happened since humiliates me.' She let go of his arm. 'I know that you'll tell me none of this is true, that I'm imagining things, but it's the way I feel, almost as if I'm dealing with a different side of you.'

She looked down. 'When will your work be done? I want a simple answer: when?'

He tried to keep the weariness out of his voice. 'You said you would understand. You were the one who made the analogy with music, remember? You wanted to provide that kind of space for me, you were the only one to recognize that need.'

She shrugged her shoulders. 'It's different with you, André. I can do that for the others: for János, for instance, or for Stefán. Their need is primarily intellectual, not emotional. But you . . . we were supposed to be different. We were supposed to lose ourselves in each other. Entirely.'

'We had an arrangement, Immanuele.'

'An arrangement!' She smiled. 'Of course.'

He softened immediately. 'That's not the way I meant it, it just came out like that . . .'

She turned away from him. A bee flew past her face and alighted on a neighbouring rock. A glint of sunlight fell on it, catching its wings and turning them into glitter. 'I don't want to stand in the way,' she replied.

'But you don't! How can you say that? I feel safe with you, I feel secure.'

'This isn't about safety, André, it's about something else.'

'Something else? What else? Is it about love? Is that what it's about? I don't know anything about that. Every time I begin to express myself, I find myself running out of words.'

She considered him sardonically. 'And you're the writer . . .'

He flushed, reaching out to touch her face. Her skin felt warm. She bit her lips. 'I'm beginning to despair, André. I'm depressed and exhausted. My mind refuses to think. It's as if I'm drowning. I can't even speak any more. To you or to anyone else.'

'It could be the lack of sleep . . .'

Her eyes flashed as she gave him a glance swift with fury.

'How *can* you sleep?'

'Look, I do love you. You must believe that. I love you very much. It's just that . . .'

126

'What?'

He shook his head.

She sighed and turned away. 'There's something here you're refusing to acknowledge. Something that's making it that much more difficult for us to communicate. You've replaced your life with an idea, and your fealty to that idea is getting in the way of your admitting to our failure. I wish it were different for your sake, if not for my own. But there's still some honesty left in me.'

He tried to reason with her but it was no use. She remained adamant and he found himself losing patience. There was no alternative but for him to get up and leave, which he did, reluctantly, disappointed when she made no move to stay his departure.

On the bridge, he stopped his bicycle to turn around and look at her. She'd moved into the shadow of the tree. He gave up trying to make sense of the situation, pedalling resignedly across the bridge and into the distance.

When he returned the next evening, she was already there, writing her journal. She put it away as he approached, making room for him to sit beside her.

'Are you still angry with me?' he asked.

She smiled. 'Of course not.' Sitting up suddenly, she pulled his face towards hers, her breath warm and moist. On the point of kissing him, she stopped, her hands grasping his arms tightly just as they had the previous day. Lying back on the ground, she pulled him down beside her. 'In response to what you said yesterday, André, I feel safe with you too, but I can't depend on you. Which is good in a way, I suppose. At least there's no pretending.'

Something in the way she said that, her curious choice of words, perhaps, made him uncomfortable. He sought out her eyes but she was looking away. To compensate, he tried to embrace her but she moved away. He contented himself by resting his hand gently against her shoulder, but she removed that as well. That was when he began to sense that in some fundamental way she had abandoned him. He wondered if he should get up and leave again, whether she would even notice. Instead, he lay still, feeling the slow weight of the earth on his shoulders, his world threatened by dissolution.

He was still staring at the sky when he felt her stir beside him. Sitting up, she turned her face towards him. After a moment's hesitation, she said: 'I need to ask you a question. And I need you to be completely honest.'

'What's the question?'

'What did they do to you in prison?'

Almost immediately, his head began to pound the way it always did when he thought about the incarceration. He closed his eyes, shutting everything out. She began to say something but stopped as soon as she noticed his pallor. Her murmured apology was still ringing in his ears when he collapsed against her and blacked out.

When he came to, his face was wet. She had soaked a handkerchief in the river and used it to cool his lips and his forehead. She stroked his hair as he opened his eyes. Her face was white and drawn.

He glanced around; they were under the willow tree now. He tried to sit up but she held him back, the handkerchief sliding off his face, drops of water trickling into his mouth. 'How are you feeling?' she asked. He didn't reply, continuing to look at her. She turned away from him.

'No . . .' he whispered, reaching out to stop her.

'Do you remember anything?' she asked quietly.

'No. What happened?'

'It was just like the other times. You fainted.' Her eyes began to cloud and she stood up abruptly. Her shadow fell across his face, the sun directly behind her head. 'What did they do to you, André?' she said. 'What have they done?'

He tried to sit up, but there was a weight inside his chest, and he fell back, despondent.

'Don't strain yourself,' she said, a clear touch of irony in her voice. With her head inclined, she stepped past him, moving with the extraordinary grace so characteristic of her.

He let his head drop, a defeated expression on his face. 'Maybe you're right, I should probably see a doctor.'

'Do what you want. But don't do me any favours, please.'

'Why are you angry with me?'

'Because you won't let me help you,' she replied.

Suddenly she walked straight off, and into the river. Stretching out her arms, she flung herself into the water.

'Why does it have to keep coming to this point?' he shouted after her.

She surfaced in a circle of foam.

'You know I want you!' he yelled. 'You know I want you!'

She turned on her back and floated on the water, her skirt spreading out in a fan around her.

He sat up, his head reeling.

She waded out of the river, the water streaming off her clothes.

'You're not ready,' she said. 'It's as simple as that.'

He glared at her. 'Let me be the judge of that. I want you now! I want you here and now, under this sun!'

'No!' She stood next to him. 'Please stop, you're embarrassing yourself.'

He sat back, hating himself. 'Tell me what I should do.'

'Will you go to a doctor?'

'What good will that do?'

'Then I'm not the one you should be talking to.'

He checked himself. 'I'm sorry.'

She regarded him calmly. 'You're going to see a doctor, André, I'll arrange for an appointment.' Reaching down, she grasped his shoulders. 'It's going to be all right, do you hear me? It's going to be all right.'

He moved restlessly, freeing himself. 'One day I'll grow old. One day I'll grow withered. One day you'll wish we'd never met.'

'Don't be ridiculous.'

His mouth set in a sullen line. 'What's the use of going on like this? I feel so powerless, can't you understand that?'

'These are just words.'

'Words are all I have! They're all that's left!'

Her eyes glinted. She opened her mouth as if to say something, and then, appearing to think better of it, she said, almost casually, 'Give me your hands.'

He extended them towards her.

129

'Hold them in the air.'

He did as she directed.

She leaned forward and touched his face. 'How easily we lose the moral compass of things. How easily we lose ourselves, our visions . . .'

She touched his lips.

Then, with mocking tenderness, she said: 'I wonder how many mouths these lips have singed . . .'

He began to lower his arms when she stopped him:

'No – keep them in the air. Your hands – how still can you make them?'

He made them still.

'Now: clench your fists.'

'Like this?'

'Yes. How fierce can you make them, André?'

He clenched them tightly, the veins standing out on his wrists.

'Good. Now tell me, what do you want from me?'

He considered that for a moment before answering: 'From you, everything.'

She stared at him intently, watching every movement of his eyes. 'And what do you want from life? What are you looking for?'

'Absolution.'

'Absolution?'

'Yes, absolution. Absolution from the present as well as from the past.'

'Do you really believe the past can be expunged?'

'If I can find something to expunge it with.' He hesitated. 'Or someone I can surrender myself to.'

'Why? Why would you want to surrender that responsibility?'

'You already know the answer to that, Immanuele.'

'Explain it to me again.'

'No . . .' he looked at her, resigned, 'it's impossible.'

'Then it's a question of abrogation, isn't it? Not absolution.'

'No, you don't understand. I don't want to abrogate, I want to forget. I want to forget everything and give myself up.'

'And how will you do that?'

'By living in truth. By getting inside –'

130

'– inside another person?'

'– inside another life, perhaps.'

'That's impossible, absurd!'

He laughed softly. 'Impossible! How we keep throwing that word back and forth. Everything seems impossible now. Flight – impossible. Freedom – impossible. Union, transcendence – all impossible. We tremble at how impossible the world has become, this meagre thing, this world that we promised to overcome!'

She pulled away from him and let go of his hands.

He scrambled to his feet and began to pace up and down, his fainting spell forgotten. 'And what about you? What are you seeking?'

'At this point, a bit of relief, that's all.'

'Relief from what?'

'From what you've become,' she said in resignation. 'From the toll it's taken on us.'

'But we've been through so much!'

'Perhaps, but experience is never finite, is it? What would I give to be able to return to some sense of normality. Normal: an alien word. I think about the rolling plains I used to visit with my mother when I was a child: the wandering rivers, the rambling old houses in forgotten towns, the crooked little lanes encircled with comfort. What I would give to be able to return to those places, to stand alone in the twilight by the banks of the rivers and gaze at the sky, waiting for the stars to come out . . .' She gave an ironic smile. 'And then I think about the reality of my childhood . . . oh, nothing very dramatic, just the little things that could have been different, and I know I can never go back.'

She looked away. 'So all that's left is the here and now. Above me, this dazzling sunlight . . . around me, the square blue sky . . . before me, you sitting by the water, your head held down. You: the man I love, your head filled with ideals, your mind filled with confusion. You ask to be allowed to surrender to me, you look for relief as much as I do, yet without any inkling of what that means. Don't you understand that love was never meant to be simple? Don't you understand that things must be very different for us to survive? It's about life, André, a strange thing, both dead and alive, but filled with dreaming, a gateway to flight. And a strange thing, that flight: impossible, infinite. If I could only tell you how much living means to me. If you could breathe as I breathe, dream as I dream. If you could only believe as I do . . .'

She stopped abruptly. A faint line of moisture had formed above her lips. The light from the water gave her face a pale sheen. He studied her hands as they rested on her knees.

After a moment of silence, he asked, 'If you were a painter, if that were your chosen vocation and you were to paint this thing you call love exactly as it appears to you, what would you paint?'

'What would I paint?' She looked at him for a long time, as if making up her mind whether or not to answer the question. Then she turned around and pointed at the river. 'Look at that river as it flows swiftly past that bridge. I would paint it exactly like that – as a still life with water.'

Later on, when he'd propped himself up on one elbow and looked past her reclining form at the river, he was surprised once more by the extent to which it did resemble a painting, precisely as she had described it, a still life, a still life with

♦

water. He heard an impatient cough beside him: Szegedy was watching him. 'What are you thinking about?' the policeman asked, giving up the attempt to restrain himself.

'Every time I stand here, in this place, I see her face.'

'Whose face? Immanuele's?'

'Sometimes Immanuele's, sometimes –'

'Sometimes?'

'Close your eyes. What do you see?'

Wondering, Szegedy shut his eyes. 'A grid of intersecting lines,' he replied, 'mostly yellow, against a black background, and behind that –'

'This river reminds me of her. It always has. I see her face in it.'

Szegedy opened his eyes. 'Just like that?'

'And then I open my eyes and look down at the water and I see her face.'

Szegedy glanced at the water and said irritably, 'It would help if you explained yourself a bit. I'm finding some of this difficult to follow. The case is complicated enough as it is, and it's not just the passage of years, or the fact that people keep appearing and disappearing. It's important that I maintain objectivity.'

András smiled drily. 'Objectivity?'

'That's what I said.'

'And where was your objectivity twenty years ago?'

Szegedy ignored the barb. Instead, he said, 'I've been meaning to ask you why you decided to meet me here, of all places?'

'Why not?'

'It's not very convenient, for one.'

'It was Immanuele's favourite rendezvous.'

'*This*?' Szegedy looked around, trying to keep the surprise out of his voice.

'Why, Inspector? What's wrong with it?'

'It's so *lifeless*.'

'That depends on your perspective, doesn't it?'

'Did she come here a lot?'

'Enough.'

'How did she get here? It's a bit of a distance from the city, isn't it?'

'She walked.'

'It's so lonely, so isolated.'

András smiled. 'Yes,' he said, 'that was precisely the attraction.' He nodded at the slope behind them. 'It used to be very different. There was a wood there with lots of undergrowth and brush. You couldn't see the path from here. A thick wood flanked it on either side. Now all that's left are the cliffs. Bare rocks tumbling into water.'

Szegedy shook his head, bemused. 'Why did she come here, though?'

'I thought I'd explained that. She loved the solitude, it's as simple as that. And she loved to swim. The river used to be much

133

cleaner. You could see right down to the riverbed. She would wade into it and let it flow into her.'

'She sought the river?'

'It reassured her.'

'Did you accompany her?'

'Sometimes.'

'You swam with her?'

'No, I mostly kept to dry land.'

Szegedy considered this carefully. Something about the conversation was beginning to puzzle him. Something like a lingering, twisting sense of desperation.

He felt compelled to say, 'I think I'm going to have to go through those last few years of her life with you again. There are too many disjunctions.'

András acknowledged this with a barely perceptible shrug.

Szegedy felt the need to reiterate. 'I want to go through the sequence of events right up to the time that she disappeared. Take the events one by one. Trace their links.'

The man in the river turned bright, reflective eyes on him. 'Why don't you consult your files?' he asked quietly.

Szegedy swallowed, regretting the action almost immediately. 'Files aren't everything,' he replied, 'and, in any case, their analysis dates. That's why I need your help to explore all the possibilities.'

'Your own point of view, for instance?'

Szegedy stiffened. 'What do you mean?'

'Oh, I was only recalling what you said a long time ago.'

'And what was that?'

'Your opinion, publicly expressed, that it was Immanuele who drove your brother to his death.'

Szegedy bristled. 'Why bring János into this?'

'Why not?'

'Because I was being rather emotional when I expressed that sentiment. I realize now it wasn't very professional.'

'Is that why you refused to treat her subsequent disappearance with the seriousness it deserved?'

'No, of course not! I resent that insinuation. I did everything that could possibly be done under the circumstances to find out what happened to her!' He waved his hand emphatically. 'A woman lives all alone in a great big house. By any standards, she leads an enigmatic, possibly dissolute existence. There are rumours, all kinds of rumours. And then one fine night she vanishes without a trace.' He paused. 'I tried my best. I did all that could be done. But I'm a detective, not a magician.'

'And here you are again, seventeen years after the event.'

'Yes, here I am.'

'Detective or magician?'

'If I had known things would resurface the way they have . . .'

'Yes, it must be rather inconvenient.'

'What's that supposed to mean?'

'We all have our motives, Inspector.'

Szegedy eyed him sardonically. 'And what wouldn't we all give for the delicate luxury of hindsight, András.'

'That's your speciality, isn't it?'

The policeman flushed angrily. 'Look, András, all I'm trying to do is find out what happened!' He glowered at the other man and then turned away and subsided into a sullen silence. Behind him, he heard András moving away, the gravel crunching under his feet. A sudden gust of wind sent ripples across the water. He felt the breeze on his face and shivered, surprised at how cold it had become. He picked up his jacket and draped it across his shoulders, absent-mindedly running his finger along the rim of the collar, the stale taste of tobacco in his mouth. He wondered if the morning fog was about to return. He studied the river, watching the play of light and shade on the water.

Behind him, András coughed, interrupting his reverie.

'It always surprises me,' he was saying, 'how different you are from János.'

Szegedy started, not certain he'd heard correctly. 'I wasn't very close to my brother –' he began, but stopped short, wondering what could have prompted him to volunteer that information. It irritated him that he'd let his guard down. There could be no denying, though, that he'd been thinking about János. Everything about this meeting reminded him of János. The place, the man next to him, the missing woman, that entire absent world.

A slow, golden light spread across the river as he ruminated. It softened the broken-backed trajectory of the riverbanks, making the rocks more visible and white. But the water remained dark and impervious.

'Why is the river so sluggish here?' he asked.

'Quicksand,' András replied.

'Excuse me?'

'Quicksand,' András repeated. 'That's why the place is deserted. It used to be notorious in the years immediately following the war. There was a warning sign on the bridge.'

'But I thought you said Immanuele swam here.'

'Yes, I did. What of it?'

'The quicksand didn't bother her?'

András smiled briefly, and then he waded further into the water. 'She took her chances.'

'And what about you? What are you doing in the water now?'

'Taking my chances. Losing myself.'

'Losing yourself . . . what does that mean?'

'Use your imagination.'

'Why don't you tell me instead?'

'I'm a writer, Inspector. I'm a writer, tied to my characters, bound by their words. At any one point, I carry at least a dozen people in my head, and the germs of at least a dozen more. Losing yourself in that maze can be pretty confusing.'

Szegedy bridled. 'Is that a threat?'

'A threat? No. Simply a word of caution for someone with a poor sense of direction.'

'Look –' Szegedy spread his hands placatingly, 'why are you being so difficult? You can help me find out what is going on. The important thing is clarity, and that's where you come in, don't you understand?'

'A distance of seventeen years would render any kind of clarity impossible.'

'Fine,' Szegedy replied shortly, 'I just thought it best to let you know where things stand.' He turned away, his hands working the gravel around him. When it was perfectly smooth and flat, he turned back to András. 'Tell me about the Gabriel Club.'

'There's nothing to tell.'

'You make it sound mysterious.'

'It was anything but.'

'Nothing is as simple as it seems.'

'And nothing is as mysterious.'

'What was it about?'

'You know what it was about.'

'Tell me again.'

'It was a literary society.'

'Was that all it was?'

'What else could it be?'

'A gathering of friends?'

'Perhaps.'

'Perhaps? Of intellectuals, then?'

'If you like.'

'What were you after? The usual revolution?'

'No, we didn't seek revolution, we sought retreat.'

Szegedy considered this with scepticism. Then he burst out: 'Intellectuals! Those magic circles guarding against the incompetencies of the rest of us! Bring us all to grief in the end!' He struggled to contain himself. After a moment, he carried on, 'So . . . what really went on?'

András responded gently. 'You're wasting your time.'

Rebuffed, Szegedy turned away. Keeping his voice neutral, he said, 'I'm not quite as ignorant about your club as you might think.'

The other smiled bitterly. 'After all the surveillance that your people subjected us to, you'd have to be a complete idiot to claim ignorance. We've met on this turf before, or don't you recall? It was a long time ago, I admit, but still, the memories!'

Szegedy eyed him carefully. 'Are you referring to the investigation into her disappearance?'

'No, I am referring, as you put it so delicately, to the earlier incidents. My arrest in 1974, for instance.'

'Oh, but that was different! There'd been reports of unusual activities. People had sent in complaints and we were duty-bound to investigate. We couldn't just ignore what was going on.'

'And what did you think was going on?'

The policeman pursed his lips and recited as if by rote: 'A concerted attempt to write works against the state and circulate them by means of a home lithograph.'

'And that explains the illegal surveillance?'

'Not surveillance, but observation. That made it perfectly legal.'

'What's the difference?'

'A matter of procedure – significant, but to the layman, ambiguous.'

'Please explain.'

'That's impossible, unfortunately. You see, any literal explanation that tries to describe the exact technical procedures, must, by definition, fall short of the crucial legal aspects, and thereby be forced to fall back on imprecise metaphors and analogies that are more misleading than explanatory.'

'These careful distinctions must come from long years of experience?'

'Of course. We were careful about not infringing rights.'

'Then how do you explain what happened during my interrogation?'

Szegedy met András's gaze, deadpan. 'That,' he replied, 'was unfortunate. And the actual procedure had nothing to do with me.'

András gave a wry smile. 'Quite a learning experience, that procedure.'

Szegedy looked away.

András smiled again, the corners of his eyes turning down. 'To hold the interrogation inside a church was an original idea, I grant you. It gave the proceedings a fittingly surreal aspect.'

'The church was abandoned. We needed a quiet space.'

'They've restored the interior of the church recently, did you know that? I go there sometimes. It's still pretty deserted, with the same grey light through the windows of the cloister, the same stone flags on the floors, the same uncanny impression of distance. And the street still sounds a world away.'

'I wouldn't know,' Szegedy replied uncomfortably, 'I haven't been back.'

'Conscience acting up?'

138

'No. I'm a practising Catholic now. I've earned my absolution, I've confessed. I've made peace with my past.'

'There are still stains on the floor, though, and scratches and scuff marks.'

'Look, let's leave that behind us, shall we? It was a long time ago. There's no point in bringing it all up again.'

'– although I might be reading into that –'

'This isn't going to get us anywhere –'

'– but I still wake up sometimes in the middle of the night.'

'– I'd rather you didn't go on.'

'Why?'

'Is there to be no common ground?'

'What do you think?'

'I'm trying my best, you must see that! Do you think this is any easier for me than it is for you? We're at a complete stalemate here! What do you want me to do?'

'Why don't you tell me about your brother?'

'Why must you keep bringing him into this?'

'As a point of reference, perhaps.'

Szegedy slumped back, his shoulders sagging. 'What do you want to know?'

'Everything.'

'That's not possible.'

'Because of what you did to him?'

Szegedy straightened and looked at András with sudden malice. He raised a hand, clenching it into a fist and holding it in the air. András watched him carefully, his thin face intent. They held each other's gaze, their expressions hardening. Then Szegedy relaxed, his face breaking into a peculiar smile, teeth as sharp and expressive as a knife. 'Very well,' he said softly, 'I won't tell you about János but I'll tell you about Immanuele. Really took to me, she did. I was quick and simple, not like the rest of you clever buggers. Things weren't complicated with me. I knew what I wanted from life.'

He grinned again, spitting at the ground. 'So why don't you be done with it and get back to telling me about your Club?'

András flashed him a fierce look. 'The Gabriel Club,' he said flatly, 'dissolved when your brother blew himself up in a car parked down the street from Immanuele's house. In the note he left behind, he held you responsible for driving him to despair. That is the sum and substance of the matter.'

Szegedy blanched. He turned his head away and hunched forward. 'Why are you trying to provoke me?' he muttered.

'You seem rather easily provoked by the memory of a brother who didn't mean much to you.'

'My brother was a boor! He drank far too much and he had no comprehension of the real world!'

'Indeed?'

Szegedy glanced down, and then he spread his hands in a conciliatory gesture. 'Look, let's get on with the present, shall we?'

'Do you really believe the past can be forgotten?'

'Why must you keep bringing that up?'

'Because this whole business is about the past. Because something very funny is going on here, and you know that as well as I do.'

'Do you think I'm trying to forget the past?'

'Only you can answer that, but I don't trust you, and never will.'

Szegedy stood up suddenly, exasperated. 'But you don't really have a choice in the matter, do you?' he demanded. 'I happen to be the one in charge here, and this is a police investigation, and your pointless reticence is beginning to infuriate me. You were ostensibly close to the missing woman. I assume you have an interest in finding out what happened to her. You should have everything to gain by helping me.'

András stared at him with contempt. 'Surely even you cannot believe that I'm simply going to sit here and confide in you, of all people?'

'Why not?' Szegedy retorted belligerently.

'Because you're on the wrong side of the fence, Inspector. People like you made life very difficult for people like Immanuele and me. It was the likes of you that sent us under. And it doesn't really matter that your masters have changed now. To me you'll always be representative of a particularly odious kind of animal.'

'I was simply following orders!'

'Precisely, and that's the whole wretched problem. I don't even know if you remember this, but those were your exact words when I tried to get you to help me seventeen years ago.'

'I didn't realize what was going on at the time. I had other things on my mind.'

'You refused to even discuss the matter with me. When I pleaded with you not to let your people end their investigation prematurely, your only response was that they had their priorities.'

'I had my orders. You have no idea how things were at the time.'

'Fine. I'm sure you have your defence fully worked out. Your kind always does. But I couldn't trust you after that even if I tried.'

Szegedy leaned forward and tried to sound reasonable. 'You're free to go ahead and judge me as you will for what happened at that time. But allow me to make amends. My interest in the present case is genuine, and the means at my disposal now are infinitely more powerful than they were in the past.'

András refused to be drawn.

Frustrated, Szegedy picked up a stone and threw it into the river. András watched it sink. In the sky above him, the seagull was back, soaring in slow circles. Shading his eyes, he fixed them on the bird, pinning it flat against the sun, its outline dissolving into an amorphous blur of light. Then even that disappeared and only the sun stared back at him. Seconds later, a sound like a gunshot echoed through the valley. The gull had cannoned into the river, surfacing moments later, water coursing from its wings. Startled, András stared at it, watching it struggle to rise, an enormous silver fish flapping from its beak. He felt suddenly dizzy. Behind him, he thought he heard a shout, but he couldn't be certain because the world was spinning around him: river, cliffs, bridge, sky, river, cliffs, bridge, sky . . .

♦

river, cliffs, bridge, sky, river . . .

Immanuele caught him as he fell.

141

He started laughing. He felt completely light-headed. 'Like a miracle,' he whispered, 'like a bloody miracle!'

He heard her ask, 'What are you laughing at?'

'What did you say?'

'I said, what are you laughing at –'

'I was staring at the gull. Or at least I thought I saw a gull but it's not there any more. Then the world started spinning around me and here I am, I must have lost my footing, the rocks are pretty slippery . . .'

'What gull? I don't see any gulls.'

'It was there a moment ago, believe me. But I don't know, I must be losing my mind. Losing my mind over you.'

'Well, that's all right then. Nothing abnormal. At least you know what the matter is.'

She pulled him out of the water with a smile.

'Faster than your heart, Immanuele,' he said, 'I'd like to strike you faster than your heart. Change your uncertainty to a certain fire.'

'Yes, yes, André . . . Oh, you've hurt your arm!'

'It's nothing, just a scratch.' He stood up. She was still smiling at him. 'The liquid dreams are the first to fall,' he said.

'What?'

'Oh, nothing, I was talking to myself.'

'I wish you wouldn't do that.'

'Why? I'm confused enough as it is. Sometimes I hear my voice and it's exactly as if I can see into the future.'

'I do wish you wouldn't brood so much. All this introspection, what good does it do? No, don't tell me, I don't want to know. Live in the present, I say, and the rest will take care of itself.'

'And what about the shadows? What about those shadows creeping out of the past, their whispers endlessly echoing?'

'Leave well enough alone is my advice. Think about the present, think about us, it's all that matters.'

They sat down side by side on the riverbank. She'd brought a bottle of lemonade with her. They took turns sipping the translucent yellow liquid through a straw.

'Tell me how I can believe in us,' he asked.

'It's a question of faith, I keep telling you that.'

'If I ever lose faith in you . . .'

'Don't worry,' she sounded suddenly serious, 'that will never happen.'

'And where do you find the strength for that conviction?'

'In a rather simple belief, André: in the belief that a love like ours holds the promise of perfection.'

'That is a truly terrifying prospect,' he said moodily.

'You're such a sceptic, Mr Tfirst.'

'No, I am not a sceptic. I'm a realist. There is a difference.'

'*This* is different.'

'Anything you say.'

She laughed in response. 'Proximity scares you. Admit it.'

From somewhere on the bridge, a herd of passing sheep bleated noisily in affirmation. Listening to them, András smiled. He lay back on the ground. He felt his eyes closing, a warm sense of well-being suffusing him, the river and the day beginning to fade away.

A raucous sound startled both of them, and András sat up hastily. A large black Soviet-made sedan was snarling across the bridge, its steel fenders glinting. He watched it accelerate into the gap between the hills and race off towards the city. Beside him, he sensed Immanuele shiver. The car made a sharp right-hand turn when it reached the end of the valley, and then it revved its engines and sped out of sight.

András felt a sour taste in his mouth. Grimacing, he glanced at Immanuele. Her face was taut.

Above them, a solitary black-backed gull floated over the river. Spotting it, András nudged her, whispering, 'Look, there's the gull.' They watched it sail over the bridge and disappear behind the ruined gateway, only its reflection appearing intermittently on the water.

She began writing across his back, using her forefinger as a quill.

'What are you writing?' he asked.

'I can't explain.'

'Is it a letter?'

'No . . . it's a poem.'

András sat still for a moment and tried to figure it out. 'I can't make out what you're writing,' he said, finally, 'but what does that matter? There's no future in words anyway.'

She turned to face him and her dark eyes grew darker still. 'Let me show you what words mean.'

'But what is the future of meaning?'

'The writing of words . . . the representation of songs, signs, feelings . . .'

'But *they* are limiting the word, and the world along with it . . . everything cancels everything out.'

'Only if we let it.'

'But they're destroying everything, don't you understand? And, in the end, we'll go hungry. Starved! They've reduced everything to the utility of things.'

'Not everything, André, not the imagination, *that* survives. The books that await the writing – there lies our salvation.'

'Literature! You must be joking! How can you say that? Look at me: I'm supposed to be a writer and here I am, writing in silence. Who reads what I write? Who cares? When survival is made into a matter of material necessity and nothing else, what can be left but a slow and painful asphyxiation?'

'The point of writing is to break that silence, André, and you know that as well as anyone. That's why *we* exist . . . in full consciousness of that fact. That's why we can't escape reality the way so many of our compatriots have. *That* would be the greatest defeat. And that is why you must keep on writing. That is why there is hope for us, despite everything.'

He kept his eyes on her face.

'And the Spirit entered into me,' he said softly, 'and took me by the hand and made me

◆

stand upright.'

Szegedy cleared his throat, breaking in: 'You were telling me about the Club and then you fell silent . . .'

'I was remembering a quotation from the Scriptures.'

'The *Scriptures*?'

'Yes.' András opened his eyes. 'Ezekiel. Book Two.'

144

'I didn't know you were religious.'

'I'm not. It serves as a distraction.'

'A distraction?'

'An interesting endeavour in an agnostic life.'

Szegedy regarded him balefully. 'Do you believe in anything at all?'

András smiled. 'What do you think?'

'Was the Gabriel Club a distraction as well?'

'I don't know,' András contemplated aloud. 'God only knows we needed it, if it was.'

Szegedy rubbed his hands suddenly and blew on them as if he were cold. He stood up and restlessly stretched his legs, looking up and down the riverbank. 'What fascinates me,' he remarked, 'is the *trompe-l'œil* character of that distraction. I mean, what was it all about? A group of young people shutting themselves up inside a decaying old house and playing at make-believe.'

'Mind you,' he added, 'I'd be the first to admit that the house was eminently suited to the purpose. Those vast shadowy depths, the sudden surprising recesses, the cellars, the turrets, and, of course, the owner herself, the mistress of all mysteries.'

He paused at the edge of the river. 'The entire set-up *was* Immanuele's doing, wasn't it?'

András glanced at him distractedly. 'What did you say?'

'I asked you if the Club was about Immanuele.'

'Immanuele?' András smiled. 'No, not at all.'

Szegedy considered this with decreasing confidence. 'Are you sure?'

András replied with a sudden irritation, 'What is this obsession with Immanuele?'

'She's the missing link to everything,' Szegedy responded mildly, 'the reason for this investigation.'

'Perhaps it was about her, then!' András snapped. 'Perhaps I've lost the capacity to discern over the years!'

Szegedy eyed him quizzically. 'Never mind. I'll let it go if you don't want to talk about it.' He flexed his wrists. 'Why don't you tell me about Ami instead.'

'No.'

'No?' Szegedy asked softly, 'Ami is not for discussion? Some things must be kept sacrosanct?'

'Yes.'

'All right. Have it your way. Let's move on to something else, then. Did the Club have a plan?'

'What do you mean?'

'Did it have a purpose?'

'Did we have a purpose? Like a manifesto? The point at which Stavrogin walked in and the time of troubles began? Yes . . .' András drawled out mockingly, 'I suppose we did have a plan. We started out trying to restore meaning to our world. Meaning that had been stripped away by your scavenging lot. That was our purpose, that was who we were, a bunch of fugitive dreamers shackled to a bastard regime. Incapable of absolutes, we resorted to believing in humbler things, mostly in ourselves.'

Szegedy saw an opening and seized it without hesitation: 'But all that was before my brother blew himself up and Immanuele became a recluse and everyone in the sanctuary ended up incurably sick, wasn't it?' He leaned forward belligerently and spat out the words: 'And then Immanuele disappeared, only to turn up as some kind of tasteless joke seventeen years later and we've come full circle in our idealized existence, haven't we?'

Caught off guard, András looked up with a halting, stricken expression. It was quite out of character and completely revealing in its fleeting passage. He stepped out of the river and deliberately gathered up his socks and shoes. Finally, he said slowly, 'Yes, we've come full circle now. So, Inspector, what do you think? What's it going to be this time? Detective, or magician?'

Szegedy studied him for a moment, and lit a cigarette. 'Alchemy, magic, metaphysics . . .' he said contemplatively, 'what's the use of any of that when you eventually go down?' He drew deeply on the cigarette. 'I can only tell you that I live in a world of conscious fact, a world where instinct must be tempered with cold logic and hard work. There's no room for metaphysics or fiction. No room for that at all.'

'Not a world of make-believe, then?'

'Definitely not a world of make-believe.'

'No magic?'

'None.'

'But *I* live in a world of magic, Inspector. And it's all inside my head. Are you certain that's what you want to lose yourself in?'

Szegedy grinned fiercely. 'Try me, said the logician to the magician.'

András regarded him for a moment with understated irony before carrying on, 'As always, the honest investigator, stolidly carrying out your tasks.'

'I am not here by choice.'

'No, you've made that much quite clear.' He contemplated the policeman. Their eyes met and Szegedy glanced away. He picked up a stone and sent it skimming across the water. Then András turned and walked over to the willow tree, sitting down with his back to the trunk.

Szegedy stepped away from the water. 'I'd like to meet Stefán Vajda,' he said casually. 'Do you have any idea where I might find him?'

András glanced at him in surprise. 'I don't have the faintest notion where Stefán is. I haven't seen him for years.'

'You have no idea where he lives now?'

'He used to live on the outskirts of Pest, in an artist's cooperative near the railroad tracks, a reclaimed warehouse, but the building burned down in the mid-eighties. For a while after that he lived in the metro.'

'He lived in the *metro*?'

'Yes, he spent his days taking a train to one station, then changing over and travelling in the opposite direction, intermittently changing from one line to another. At night he slept on a siding at one of the stations. No one questioned him. There was no reason to. He was simply one of many itinerants.'

'How long did this go on?'

'I don't know. There were rumours of his inheriting an apartment in the city, and I think he stopped being a vagabond after that.'

'You weren't interested in finding out what was going on in his life?'

'No, I wasn't.'

Szegedy examined his cigarette. 'And this was one of your

closest friends at one time? Your literary collaborator, your underground companion, things like that? It must have something to do with your Club? Something that happened to that community of trust?'

András looked away. 'A long time ago,' he said, 'Stefán and I parted ways. I left Budapest and went away. *His* spirit, as fire, consumed him.'

'Is that also from the Scriptures?'

'What do you think?'

'Ezekiel again?'

'No. It's a corruption of Isaiah thirty-three.'

Szegedy glanced at András uncertainly, then decided to change tack. 'Stefán still writes, doesn't he?'

'I don't believe he has written anything in a while.'

'And what did you think of what he wrote?'

'His calligraphy was impeccable.'

Szegedy smiled thinly. 'You people must share epigrams,' he said. 'A long time ago, when I had modest literary aspirations of my own, I showed Stefán a poem I'd been working on for forty days and his only response was to compliment me on my penmanship.' He shrugged. 'But you say you haven't seen him in years?'

András glanced up and airily extended his arms to embrace the sky. 'On the contrary,' he announced, 'I meet him, in a manner of speaking, every morning, afternoon and night.'

'But you said –'

'You misunderstood me.' András closed his eyes. 'As a matter of fact, at this very moment, he's lurking inside that ruined tower on the bridge and watching our every movement. But don't turn around or you'll alert him.'

The policeman stiffened. 'What are you talking about?'

'You heard me.'

'But why should he be here? No one else knows about this meeting!'

'That's immaterial. Stefán's been following me on and off for years.'

'What?'

'Yes – that's just the way it's been between us.'

Szegedy gazed at him in confusion. 'But why?' he demanded, while at the same time turning his head to glance at the bridge.

'I told you not to look round!' András said sharply.

Szegedy glared back at him. 'How do I know this isn't a trick?'

'Ah, but I'm afraid there is no way of finding that out.'

'Then it *is* a trick!'

'It's hard to say. It could well be. Or it could be a photograph or a memory even.'

'A photograph?'

'Certainly, a psychological portrait.'

'Jesus!'

'What, Comrade? Appeals to the Almighty?'

'Don't call me a fucking comrade!'

'Of course! Enter the Inspector, well-armed with invective.'

'Listen, you're trying my patience! I demand to know if there's really someone inside that tower!'

András gave him a laconic glance in response. 'Look,' he said instead, one hand pointing to the sky, 'our fine-feathered friend, the seagull, is back.'

'I don't give a damn about the seagull!' Szegedy retorted angrily. Before him, he could sense András enjoying his predicament. As he gazed at him helplessly, András turned his head, shooting

♦

a sidelong glance at his companion.

'My God!' Stefán was saying as he looked around the valley in admiration, 'this place is beautiful! I didn't even know the Danube had a tributary here.'

They stood side by side on the bridge, the three of them, gazing down at the river and at its banks sloping sharply past the trees clinging to the cliffs. András caught Immanuele's eye and smiled, feeling immensely grateful to her for suggesting they bring Stefán. Ever since his poetry had been banned, Stefán had fallen into a deep depression. Nothing had seemed to help until

Immanuele had persuaded him to come along with them earlier that morning. 'Trust me,' she'd wryly confided to András, 'even barren rocks and stunted trees can have a wonderfully bracing effect after what he's had to deal with recently.'

Stefán turned to them and gestured at the ruined gateway and the tower. 'How did you discover this place?'

Immanuele smiled. 'Completely by chance,' she replied. 'I read about it in an old book in my grandfather's library. There was a painting of the bridge, a watercolour, not very well done, but attractive enough to interest me in finding out if it was still around. So I bought a map and walked here one morning, and I've been back almost every weekend since. Sometimes I bring André with me as well, and sometimes he comes alone.'

Stefán pointed to the crater in front of the ruined gate. 'What happened there?'

'The Germans tried to blow it up during the war,' András replied.

Stefán made a cryptic sound. Then he turned suddenly to Immanuele. 'I haven't slept for days,' he said. 'I can't publish any more. Did André tell you what happened?'

'Yes, he did.'

Stefán turned away. 'I'm sorry, I don't suppose there's any point in bringing it up again.'

'I know what it's like,' she replied quietly.

He kicked at a loose piece of mortar. 'It's just that . . . I feel completely overwhelmed, you know, completely defeated.' He kicked at the mortar again, scuffing his shoe in the process.

'You're not thinking of giving up?'

'Hypothetically I suppose I must have considered it. But that would be too easy, I think.' He smiled ironically, his eyes creasing. 'Besides, I've always been too much of a masochist for my own good.'

She nodded, silent.

'But it was good of the two of you to bring me here. I'd forgotten what it could be like to get away from it all.' He looked at them. 'Shall we go down to the river?'

They walked over to the spiral staircase, Stefán hesitating at the top and looking down. 'It's a bit steep, isn't it?' Noticing

Immanuele's questioning glance, he hastened to explain, 'I get vertigo . . .'

She held her hand out to him. They descended in single file, András leading. On reaching the river's edge, Immanuele announced she was going for a walk. As they watched her leave, Stefán let out a sigh of admiration. 'My God, André! What a fascinating creature she is!'

They looked on as Immanuele navigated the riverbank, her bare feet crunching over the gravel and the sandbars, her shoes slung over her shoulders. She was wearing a long-sleeved white shirt and a thin blue cotton skirt with yellow flowers along the hem. A slight breeze contoured the skirt around her legs. Beyond her, against the sky, the bridge appeared to be resting on air.

As if aware that they were watching her, Immanuele turned and waved to them. András waved back while Stefán coughed uneasily and looked down.

When she finally returned, she had collected red and black blooms from a bush at the foot of the bridge. She gave the black blooms to Stefán, the red to András. They sat there for a while, faces turned to the sun. Then Immanuele caught Stefán's eye and gestured towards the bridge. 'Look at those arches, they're perfect ellipses. Only the Romans would know how to build them like that.'

They looked at the arches supporting the bridge, the columns rearing out of the water and joining in ellipses high above the river.

'Now lie back on the ground,' she suggested, 'and look at the top of the arches again.' They followed her instructions, the ellipses sloping into sharp gothic points as they did.

András chuckled. 'An interesting comment on the origins of Christianity, isn't it? The pagan transmuting into the gothic.' He turned to gauge Stefán's reaction. He was staring at Immanuele with a strange kind of infatuation. Noticing András watching him, he blushed and shook his head imperceptibly.

András turned away, aware that Immanuele had noticed their subtle exchange. She smiled silently. Then she stood up. 'I'm going into the water,' she announced. Walking over to a point about half-way to the bridge, she started to take off her clothes.

Stefán shifted uncomfortably and cleared his throat. 'I say, André, what's going on?'

'You heard her, she said she was going for a swim.'

'I mean, should we look away?'

'My dear Stefán . . .' András murmured drily, 'such discretion . . .'

They watched her wade into the river and sink up to her waist. The water was warm, she called out, beckoning to them. She began splashing around with her hands, her legs skimming underwater. Her wet hair clung to her like skin. She turned a somersault in the water. Then she began swimming towards the opposite bank where the water, András knew, was deeper than the rest of the river.

András was about to say something when Stefán cut him off with a gesture. There was a fixed look in his eyes. He gave a gentle cough, an inarticulate sound. He began speaking to himself, his head moving from side to side as he began to shout and fling his clothes off: they flew around like birds, taking wing. Stark naked, he moved towards the river, heading for the deepest part.

András tried to get up but his limbs seemed paralysed.

By the time he finally struggled to his feet, Stefán had entered the river. András saw him hesitate; he knew Stefán couldn't swim. Immanuele, in the meantime, had noticed what was going on and had turned to head Stefán off. As she neared him, he fell to his knees and lowered his face, his voice breaking. 'Look!' he yelled, raising his hands, 'They've cut my hands off! There's nothing left to fight them with!' He waved his hands in the air and began laughing hysterically, his voice rising as Immanuele reached him and caught him as he crumpled at the waist and slumped into the water.

When András reached them, Immanuele had already dragged Stefán out of the river and on to higher ground. She gathered the prone man into her lap, her hands on his shoulders, his face buried in the sand. Glancing up, she noticed András. Anticipating his question, she said, 'Go away, André. Please go away for a while.'

On the opposite shore, there was an explosion of wings. A nesting gull, disturbed by the commotion, glided over and circled past them. Watching it, András sighed. He stood up in slow motion. Behind him, he heard Stefán whimper. He walked into the river without a backward glance and spread out his arms. The water embraced him. Leaves drifted past. Then branches, flotsam, densely propelled thoughts. He ducked his head under the water, a vein throbbing above his eyes. He felt his throat catch.

When he finally surfaced, everything had turned white under the sun. He sensed himself floating, the water around him strangely bright. Huge red and black petals surrounded him. Turning on his back, he gathered them up one by one and arranged them across himself. In the distance, by the river-bank, he saw Immanuele leave Stefán. She entered the water and began to strike out in his direction. An island of petals, he turned in the water and deliberately drifted away from her. Ahead of him: blue rocks, black water, all fading into the light. As if from a great distance, he heard Immanuele call out his name, her voice rising above the roaring in his ears. He raised his head to look at her. For an instant, her silhouette seemed to merge with the water, flowing into it and becoming one. Then the bridge loomed over him and enmeshed him in its shadows. He raised an arm, water streaming from his wrist. Arm still upraised, he slipped under the bridge, his shadow following him underwater. 'What am I going to do?' he wondered, 'Whatever am I going to

◆

do?' Szegedy was asking him urgently. He sounded obdurate, insistent. 'I refuse to sit here knowing I'm being watched!'

András began to laugh.

'What are you laughing at?' Szegedy demanded.

'Your discomfort, what else? It's a bit ironic, isn't it, considering that it was precisely in that capacity that you made your sorry career, watching people on the sly, recording their every move, waiting for them to slip up. How does it feel to be at the receiving end?' He waited to assess the impact of his words, and then he glanced in the direction of the tower. 'Time to put you out of your misery,' he murmured, 'he's no longer there.'

'Where did he go?'

'I have no idea.'

'How do you know he's gone?'

'Why don't you take a look for yourself?'

Szegedy stood up abruptly. He stalked over to the spiral staircase and disappeared into its depths.

He re-emerged about ten minutes later, his face a dusky shade of crimson. Reaching András, he squatted down and opened a fist. There were three or four cigarette butts in his hand, one of them still burning slightly. 'Someone was there,' he said, 'but they've gone now. This must have been your doing. How else could he have known that I would be here? You must have engineered this.'

'Why would I tell you about it if I had?'

'I don't know,' Szegedy replied dubiously. The presence of the third man had unsettled him. 'This whole thing is beginning to stink,' he muttered as he stared moodily at the river.

A spell of silence followed, neither man inclined to break it. They contemplated the valley, a bank of dark clouds enveloping it from the east and driving the sky to darkness.

Szegedy adjusted his jacket around his shoulders. 'This Club of yours . . . were there any drugs?'

For once, András appeared genuinely amused. 'My word, whatever will you think of next?'

Szegedy grimaced, recalling his visit to the house on E-Daj Street the previous morning. Expecting it to be deserted, he'd found, on the tiles of the terrace on the second floor, two slices of bacon on a chipped earthenware plate, a half-eaten piece of toast and a jar of marmalade. He'd wasted more than an hour waiting for the mysterious visitor to return. Within the house, as he'd bided his time, the intersecting shadows had formed a web. A web in which he realized that his own unravelling role must, of necessity, remain uncertain.

Turning to András, he asked, 'You weren't at the house on E-Daj Street yesterday, were you?'

'At Immanuele's? No, I wasn't. Why do you ask?'

'It's not important.' He paused. 'On a completely different tack, do you think you can recall that last address for Stefán?'

'The artists' cooperative?'

'Yes, the one that burned down.'

'What good would it do? I doubt there's anything left.'

'It doesn't matter, it's a serviceable lead, and it'll have to do until I can come up with something better.'

András had to think for a moment before he was able to give the policeman the approximate location. It was not an area Szegedy was familiar with. 'How long did he live there?' he asked.

'I'm not certain. Five years, maybe six . . .'

'And this was around the time of Immanuele's disappearance?'

'No, that was earlier.'

'And when was the last time you saw her?'

'Immanuele?' András looked at him, surprised. 'My last glimpse of Immanuele was at the Mátyás Church a few months before she disappeared. I don't remember why I was there, I didn't go often. But there were a lot of little girls there that day. They were dressed in ballet costumes. Immanuele was walking among them, adjusting their posture and giving them directions. They were rehearsing some kind of a children's production. The church was very dark. I left before I was noticed. The street outside was quiet and cold, the snow piled up by the banks of the river. I can still remember the hissing of the street-lamps as I walked home that evening.'

Szegedy scratched his chin. 'How old was Immanuele at the time?'

András considered him mockingly. 'How old was she? What is this? Food for the carrion crow?'

'No, no, I suppose I didn't express myself well. I'm just trying to understand what she must have meant to you.'

'Why is that pertinent?'

'A link between two individuals is always pertinent.'

'A *link*? Jesus!'

'You would prefer a stronger term?'

'My God, yes, I would prefer a stronger term! She was the world to me!'

'But it was no longer like that by the time you left her, was it?'

András gave him a look of great exhaustion. 'You know, I have to admit that you're very good at this. You wear a person down.'

Szegedy smiled, a bit self-effacingly. 'Oh, it's in the nature of the work. All I'm trying to do is to understand, which is not the easiest thing when one is dealing with someone as reticent as you.'

'I'm not exactly dying to unburden myself to you, Inspector.'

'Will you answer the question?'

'What question?'

'The question about your relationship with Immanuele.'

'My relationship with Immanuele,' András repeated contemplatively. 'We were what we were of our own free will, parts of a single whole that included both of us and existed through the very fibre of us. Only a complete misunderstanding could have set us up in opposition to each other.'

Szegedy's eyes glinted with satisfaction.

'And there was such a misunderstanding?'

András stood up and extended a firm hand.

Szegedy stared at him in surprise. 'What – our meeting's ended? Already?'

'Already? We've been here for hours, Inspector. In any case, I'm beginning to find your entire line of questioning more than a little –' he placed careful emphasis on the last word, drawing it out so that there could be no ambiguity, 'vulgar.'

Szegedy hadn't expected this. He was being dismissed. He decided to hold back and not ask any more questions, at least for the present. He stood up, his head hitting an overhanging branch of the willow tree. He gave the branch a jaundiced look. 'This tree is dying,' he said, 'like everything else here. It's a menace. Someone should cut it down.'

'It's alive, leave it be.'

'It ought to be removed.'

'It's a rare species of willow. Immanuele was very fond of it.'

'It's the ugliest thing I've ever seen.'

156

'Then it's a question of erasure, isn't it?'

'What nonsense! We're talking about dead wood here.'

'Not dead wood, but something infinitely more precious!'

'Got your wind up?'

'Only your ugly imagination –'

'Wouldn't you like to smash it in?'

'I don't destroy things.'

'Better to let them rot?'

András stepped back and clenched his fists.

Szegedy laughed, his voice rising. 'What's the matter, dreamkeeper? Left your anger in the past?'

András paled. 'Not all of us are that primitive.'

'That would explain a lot, wouldn't it?'

'It probably would, Inspector,' András retorted softly, 'but in ways you could never even imagine.'

He waited for Szegedy to put on his jacket. They walked over to the staircase, Szegedy lagging behind. Half-way up the steps, he dropped his cigarette and stubbed it out with his shoe. Sensing András gazing down at him, he looked up but couldn't make out his expression.

They emerged into a sudden wash of light. The stones on the bridge were hazy with iridescence. As they stopped beside the car, Szegedy turned uncomfortably to András. 'Are you going back to the city?' he asked.

'Yes, I am.'

'Would you like a ride?'

'No,' András replied.

Rebuffed, Szegedy got into the car. The interior was oppressively warm. Somewhere in the back a fly was buzzing. He ignored it and gripped the steering wheel, his hands instantly sticky with sweat. Looking around for his sunglasses, he realized he'd left them on the riverbank. Deciding against going back, he switched on the ignition, all too aware that he was being watched. Something about András's expression reminded him of the way he'd looked while describing his very last sighting of Immanuele. Was it wonder? Was it sadness? Was it resignation? The possibilities twisted round and round in his mind: helplessness? scorn? fear? emptiness?

He glanced at the sky. With an inexplicable sense of dissatisfaction, he lowered his window, letting the engine idle. 'Just one last question –' he said.

'What is it?'

'The woman who called us on the telephone, the one who told us you would be able to identify the waxwork, who is she?'

'Just an acquaintance. She has no part in this.'

'How did she find out about it?'

'She must have read it in the papers.'

'But the papers didn't find out till much later.'

'Then I must have told her about it.'

'You don't remember?'

'I'm afraid not.'

'And you don't find that intriguing?'

'No, I don't.'

Szegedy gave up. With a gesture of resignation, he reached over and took out an old-fashioned spool tape from the glove compartment. He held it out of the window. 'This belongs to you,' he said to András.

'What is it?'

'The transcript of the interview with you in 1974.'

András stared at him, his eyes narrowing. 'It wasn't an *interview*, Inspector, it was an *interrogation*. I was under arrest. You were one of the interrogating officers. There is a difference. Let's not revise history to that extent, shall we?'

He took the tape out of its plastic case and held it in his hand. 'Why are you giving me this?'

'To establish my goodwill.'

'I could choose to make this public.'

'I am aware of that.'

András handed the tape back. 'It's too late for that kind of gesture.'

Szegedy sat still for a moment, staring ahead of him. Then he accepted the tape and slowly replaced it in the glove compartment. Inside was a coil of rope, a cigarette lighter, a torch, a pair of pliers made of steel. He slipped the tape in next to the pliers, leant back and shut the compartment. He revved the engine for a couple of seconds. Then he rolled up the window and pressed his foot down on the accelerator, the man on the bridge receding into the distance.

Following Szegedy's departure, András returned to the river. At first he restricted himself to a walk, then he began to run, picking up speed until he reached the rocky outcrop. He leaned against the willow tree and made a tremendous effort to remain still, only the tremor of his hands betraying his tension. An unbearable pain overwhelmed him. It spread from his shoulders down to his chest. He felt his throat constricting. He closed his eyes and sat down. Then he stretched out full-length on the ground.

When he opened his eyes again, there was a purplish tinge to the sky. Caught in the half-light, the bridge stretched its white spine across the valley, only a single lamp casting a sepia glow over it.

He rose to his feet and walked slowly to the foot of the bridge where he had wedged his bicycle. He took it out, shouldering it, and climbed up the spiral staircase. By the time he reached the top, it had begun to drizzle. He set the bicycle down, the rain abruptly turning into a downpour. Caught by its force, he staggered to keep upright. Barely managing to hold on to the bicycle, he set off across the bridge, riding against the wind.

Presently, the hills gave way, the road curling gently down. Power lines reared straight into the sky, the rain sparking against them. A seeping, pallid stench warned of the city's approach, innumerable smokestacks belching fumes into the sky. They lit up the sky with their chemical tongues, their thick pall contaminating everything.

Soon a steeple loomed out of the grey, then a gable, gushing rain. A tram clattered past. The road widened into a square. The rain began to falter.

András walked the bicycle parallel to the river, the air impregnated with sweet, fresh scents. All around him, the city was untangling from the storm, the rooftops rearranging into a skyline. In the west, in the gathering darkness, the hills had begun to merge with the sky. A crescent of crimson clouds rose into the air. Against the burning husk of evening, the bloodshot sun flared into the horizon.

Deprived of its landscape, the day collapsed abruptly into night. The city transformed to black. As András got back on his bicycle, banks of streetlights began to flicker in the darkness. Rain-sodden trees thrust out bright, metallic arms, the lights of speeding cars reflecting off their branches. The night entered the trees and sank into their silhouettes in tangled patterns of black. Overhanging branches brushed against András as he pedalled uphill, splattering his face with rainwater.

It was late by the time he reached his apartment. The building almost always looked deserted, the façade a uniformly dirty shade of brown, parts of it covered with corrugated metal sheeting. The only contrast to this stark and overwhelming monochrome was a vestibule with small, round windows and a narrow, curtained entrance. As András wheeled his bicycle inside, a large woman in flowing robes brushed impatiently past him. She was speaking excitedly to a tiny, harassed-looking man. They were headed for the door, the woman explaining the meaning of 'this thing we modestly call life'. They hurried out of the building, oblivious to the car parked on the other side of the road. It was a grey sedan, its windows rolled up. Inside, its sole occupant scanned the building intently, his eyes fixed on a particular window on the second floor. In a matter of moments, his patience was rewarded, and the window lit up to reveal the silhouette of a man. The man crossed over to the window, drawing aside the curtains and flinging open the windows. It was András, and the stranger in the car sat bolt upright. He thought he saw a seated woman behind András, her head held down, but as he leaned forward to get a better look, András shifted, blocking out the woman and the rest of the room behind him. Disappointed, the watcher slumped back, his eyes following András as he began to pace to and fro inside the room. After a while, András stopped and appeared to pick up a book and sit down. Leaning out of the watcher's sight, he switched on a light. Then he stood up again, restlessly discarding the book. Although he repeatedly crossed in front of the seated woman, neither of them seemed to acknowledge the other's presence.

András returned to the window and lit a cigarette, his eyes

160

scanning the street, the cigarette glowing fiercely each time he inhaled. He stood there for a while, and then he ground out the cigarette on the windowsill, drawing the curtains shut and turning off the lights.

Unknown to the watcher outside, he returned almost immediately to the seated woman. Kneeling before her, he brought her hands together and pressed his lips to them. Then he stood up and unlocked the brake to her wheelchair, wheeling it into an adjoining room.

It was dark, and very spare, almost devoid of furniture save a single bed and a writing desk. Both the desk and the bed were made of metal and painted white, as were the walls. A pale cloud of light entered the room through drawn curtains, the half-open shutters impressing their shapes on the weave.

Expertly negotiating the darkness, András pushed the wheelchair to one side and gently lifted the woman on to the bed. He rearranged the sheets as he tucked her in. Carefully, he sat down on the bed and gathered her to him. He felt calmer every time she was in his arms again. It gave him a feeling of sharing in her dark and silent world. He felt her warm breath on his skin. Her eyes were wide open and she was staring past him at the shadows on the ceiling. He thought he detected a movement of her lips, but she was silent. For a moment, he imagined her gleaming eyes were focused on him. Then he turned away, repudiating the game he played with himself every evening. Moving sideways, he slipped his hands below her shoulders and lifted her into a sitting position. Holding her upright, he unbuttoned her dress. When he had slipped it off, he angled her gently back and drew the sheet to her chin. Sensing her eyelids becoming heavy, he lowered them with his fingertips and kissed her on the lips. Behind him, as he straightened up, he could feel the room filling up with shadows. The shadows, he thought wearily, that come back without fail every night. He placed her hands by her sides, leaning over and resting his head on her chest. Her breathing was thin and frosty, like mist. 'Good night, Ami,' he said softly as he stretched out beside her, an immense tiredness washing over him. The wages of sin, he thought to himself, the shadows from the past sinking in.

Chapter Three

Still Life with Air

'The trouble with you, András,' Szegedy was saying, 'is that you have absolutely no imagination.' He leaned back on his chair and surveyed the man sitting across from him. 'Because if you had any imagination,' he continued, 'you would realize that you only stand to improve your position by cooperating with me.'

They were sitting under an awning outside the Café Royal. From time to time, a car raced by, skirting the pavement and passing dangerously close. Every time that happened, Szegedy found himself leaning away involuntarily. But he didn't suggest going inside, and he didn't suggest changing the table. Instead, he went on, 'The file that I sent you on Immanuele's disappearance, did you get a chance to look at it?'

'Yes, I did.'

'What did you think?'

'It didn't say much that I didn't know already.'

'Why do you think I let you read it?'

'I really have no idea.'

Szegedy pursed his lips, choosing his words carefully. 'You know that I need your help with this investigation. It's extremely important if I am to get anywhere. I'd like to find some explanations to integrate the missing links, establish the connections . . .'

162

'That's your job,' András said, 'not mine.' He glanced away. 'Have you been to the house?' he asked.

'The house?'

'The house on E-Daj Street, Immanuele's house.'

'Yes, of course I have. There's nothing there. Since the estate lapsed to the state, a regular inventory's been maintained, and the health and sanitation inspectors go round once in a while. We've interviewed them, and the consensus seems to be that there's nothing there of relevance to the case.'

'The estate lapsed to the state? I wasn't aware of that.'

'It took place a few years ago. It's nothing unusual, it's what happens when there are no legal claimants. You should go there while you can, before the property is auctioned off.'

'I'm not interested.'

Szegedy glanced at him curiously.

At that moment, the lights came on inside the café, the harsh electric glare spilling out on to the pavement. Outside that bright circle, the shadows of buildings interspersed with the silhouettes of trees. Inside, a jazz band began to tune their instruments. About to resume speaking, Szegedy glanced past András, his face breaking into a smile. An attractive young woman was crossing the street, walking rapidly in their direction. She was evidently in a hurry, her blonde hair falling in wings on either side of her face. She wore a tailored blue dress with a blue scarf and a maroon beret. The outfit was in perfect taste, yet had a slight tell-tale shine that betrayed its age. As she came abreast of their table, Szegedy stood up and greeted her with a kiss, his hands resting on her hips with an unmistakable familiarity. She returned the kiss with a marked lack of enthusiasm. Szegedy turned to András in the meantime. 'András, meet Katalin. Katalin sings with the band here.' A crash of cymbals momentarily drowned him out, and he glanced sharply into the café, obviously annoyed. He waited for the noise to subside before turning back to the woman. 'This is András Tfirst, the writer. You must have heard of him?'

She looked askance at András. 'No . . .' she replied, her voice barely audible, 'I don't think so.'

'No? I'm surprised.'

'I don't read much.'

Szegedy looked pleased. 'That's all right. He's quite a star with people of my generation, but fame can be fleeting. Isn't that right, András?'

He turned to András with an expansive smile. 'Katalin's only recently arrived from the provinces, so you shouldn't take her ignorance too much to heart.' He gestured at her. 'Are you feeling unwell, my dear? You look a bit pale.'

She bit her lip. 'I'm all right,' she replied, with a tense little gesture of her hand. Her nails, András noticed, were bitten to the quick. She tried to move away, but Szegedy held her back. He offered her a cigarette, obviously in no hurry to end their exchange. When she declined, he gave her a furtive sidelong appraisal followed by a louche smile.

Suddenly angry, András decided to relieve the awkwardness of the situation. 'Look –' he addressed Szegedy, making no attempt to conceal the irritation in his voice, 'excuse me for questioning the spirit of this little tête-à-tête, but I am in a bit of a rush. Could we get on with it, or are we done?'

Szegedy flinched at being addressed like that. He turned brusquely to his companion and dismissed her. 'You can go,' he said, steely-voiced, 'I'll see you around.'

She inclined her head, her face expressionless as she glanced at András. Then she walked into the café.

András stood up as well. 'I'm leaving,' he said.

'Wait a moment, please.'

'Good night.'

'Sit down, André, sit down. What I have to tell you concerns you, but even more than that, it concerns Ami.'

András stopped in the act of turning. 'Ami? What about Ami?'

A fly alighted on the table, filling the space with a sleepy buzz. Watching it, Szegedy gave a satisfied smile and inserted a cigarette into his mouth. 'I see I have your attention now.' Pitching his voice as if he wanted to be overheard, he exclaimed, 'Now sit down and try to behave yourself.'

András sat down. 'What about Ami?'

Pleased to have gained a foothold, Szegedy hurried on, 'In order to answer that question I would have to bring up the Gabriel Club.'

164

András shook his head grimly. 'Do I have the option of refusing?'

Szegedy fussed over his cigarette. 'I only raise it because it's relevant,' he replied. 'Although I must confess that you've always held such a peculiar fascination for me, the four that led your mysterious Club. Everyone in the department knew about you, of course. The higher officials, the people in the field, the administrative staff, everyone. You were the literary heroes of the underground, the young Turks, the Trojans. It was partly the way you presented yourselves, I suppose. People talked about you, they were interested in you.' He gave András a meaningful glance. 'But your secrecy was seen as an unhealthy obsession. It made our people suspicious, as if there were something else going on. That's why they turned to me for information. After all, I was the brother of one of the four, perhaps I could become an accomplice or even a confidante. These things were commonplace, as you well know.'

He gave a pained smile. 'Little did they realize that I knew as little about the lot of you as they did, less even. After all, even when he was at home, János scarcely deigned to notice me. He never spoke to me about anything, he couldn't be bothered to waste his time on me, and he made that very clear. I was invisible to him – that was the full extent of our relationship – and I hated him for treating me like that, that supercilious younger brother of mine. I know he felt a tremendous sense of betrayal because my politics had turned out so differently from his. But he was always like that, impulsive and emotional, an absolute devil, wild and dangerous to be with, as well as completely unpredictable. He'd fly into these intolerant rages and leave the house for days on end, roaming the city and driving my poor parents out of their minds. There wasn't a docile bone in his body and in many ways he was hopelessly complicated and mad. My parents couldn't understand him; they could never fathom what was going on. What's the matter with him? they'd keep asking. What is he so angry about? I think they were very relieved that I turned out to be nothing like him. I was even-keeled and stable, and I had a steady job. I was the son they could rely on. When my father had a heart attack and could no longer work, I was the one who dropped out of school and picked up the slack. I hated my brother for it, and I knew he didn't give a damn!'

He stopped speaking and considered András, who had been listening to him without comment. András returned his stare. 'I presume that all this is leading up to some kind of explanation of your comment about Ami?' he asked.

'But naturally . . . it concerns the connections between the four of you.'

'The four of us?'

'I mean, of course, Immanuele, Ami, you, and Stefán.'

'And where does Ami come into this?'

'Oh, but Ami must come into this! Ami comes into everything!' Szegedy busily extracted a notebook from his pocket and scanned a page before reading it out loud. 'Refresh my memory with a few facts, will you? You first met Immanuele in the summer of '71?'

'Yes.'

'And the relationship lasted . . .'

'For a little more than three years. I've told you that before.'

'Till the end of 1974?'

'Yes.'

'And then no contact until the beginning of 1977?'

'That's correct.'

Szegedy tugged at his shirtsleeves in a fastidious manner. 'All in all, a rather drastic sundering of ties, wouldn't you say?'

András lit a cigarette. He didn't respond.

Szegedy carried on. 'And this final meeting was at Elemér Klein's house . . .' He studied his notebook again. 'An accidental meeting, as it transpired?' He didn't wait for András's reply. Instead, he made a casual gesture. 'Would you like something to drink?'

'No, thank you, I'm quite all right.'

Szegedy smiled easily. 'I suppose you will insist on making me out to be more inhospitable than I am. Very well,' he smoothed back his hair, 'perhaps you can tell me how well Stefán and Immanuele knew each other?'

'Stefán and Immanuele?' András stared at him, taken aback. 'As well as can be expected. As well as anyone else. Why?'

'Did Stefán know about your relationship with Immanuele?'

'Of course he did, we were friends.'

'Did he ever ask you about it?'

'He might have.'

'You don't remember?'

'That is not what I said. I wasn't in the habit of confiding in him. I preferred to keep my private life to myself. I still do. It's a failing of mine.'

Szegedy ignored the snub. 'Then it was perfectly apparent to the other members of the Club that you and Immanuele were romantically involved?'

'What is this leading to?'

'I'm trying to find out if Stefán might have been jealous of your privileges with Immanuele.'

'I introduced them to each other.'

'Are you being deliberately naive?'

'Do you want to know if Stefán was in love with Immanuele?'

'I suppose you could put it like that . . .'

'Everyone was in love with Immanuele. It was impossible to be otherwise.'

'That doesn't answer my question, András! Why this circumlocution? I'm trying to make this as easy for you as I can. You were my brother's best friend. I'm trying to spare you the rigours of a formal investigation. Surely that much must be obvious.'

'What precisely do you want to know?'

'How did Stefán react to Immanuele's disappearance?'

'He had a nervous breakdown, as I'm sure you know.'

Szegedy lit another cigarette. 'Was there any contact between you and Stefán after that?'

'We met sometimes.'

'Only sometimes? But you used to be such good friends.'

'Our lives diverged. It can happen to the best of friends, Inspector.'

'I'm sure it can. It just seems a bit odd, that's all.'

'Events came between us. Your brother's suicide, for instance. Immanuele's disappearance. Something had to give in the end.'

'Immanuele's disappearance led to the dissolution of the club?'

'No, it took place well before that. After János's death,

everything began to come apart. Immanuele tried to keep things going for a while, but things gradually ground to a halt.'

'So I take it that the relations between the four of you were already strained by the end? János's death simply brought matters to a head?'

'That's what I said.'

'That was when you and Immanuele separated as well?'

'Yes.'

'You left the city after that and went away to Eger. How long were you away?'

'For the rest of the year. I returned to Budapest in January 1976.'

'Where was Stefán during this period?'

'In Budapest.'

'Did he and Immanuele keep in touch?'

András placed his hands flat on the table. 'They didn't sleep together, if that's what you want to know.'

Szegedy raised his eyebrows but he kept his eyes fixed on the table. 'That's not what I asked.' He examined his fingernails. 'Stefán's father died in a uranium mill in the fifties, didn't he?'

András looked surprised. 'I didn't know that.'

'Are you sure you wouldn't like something to drink?'

'No, thanks.'

'What about Ami and Immanuele?'

András looked at him carefully. 'What about them?'

'How did they meet?'

'They met when I was away teaching at Eger.'

His eyes still on the table, Szegedy ventured, 'Ah yes, Eger . . . I presume you introduced Ami to Immanuele before you left?'

'No, they met afterwards. They hadn't known each other before then.'

'They became close friends, didn't they?'

'They did, yes.'

'Ami lived with Immanuele for a while, didn't she?'

'For a while, yes.'

'For how long?'

'About a year.'

'And when you came back from Eger, she left Immanuele's?'

'No, she'd already moved out by the time I returned.'

'And would you say they parted on amicable terms?'

'Of course they did.'

'Interesting, interesting . . .' Szegedy scratched his head. In the background, there was a roll of drums from inside the café, accompanied by some desultory clapping. Then a woman's hoarse and beautifully dissonant voice broke into song: '*The way you held me. The way you looked at me. The comfort of you. My God, all I have left are words. Life reduces, life reduces. I didn't want to love you. I didn't want to fall in love. Tell me, where did I go wrong?*'

Szegedy broke into a beatific smile.

'Katalin . . .' he remarked, to no one in particular. 'What a voice!' He turned to András. 'Do you like jazz? I tell you, that woman makes the fifties come back to life! The way she marks out space demands a more poetic homage than this place allows.' He gestured around. 'I'm going to get her out of here, set her up in style. One of those new nightclubs, that's what she deserves, somewhere they'll appreciate what she's about.'

The interior of the café was beginning to fill up, the air thick with smoke ebbing and flowing with the song: '*And what about yourself? How do you sleep at night? And what about yourself? Are you still as blind, blind, blind?*'

Listening to the music, András suddenly felt depressed. Opposite him, Szegedy leaned forward to make himself heard. 'A slightly unrelated question this time. Tell me, why do all your stories revolve around death?'

Without turning his head, András replied evenly, 'All my stories do not revolve around death.'

'Many of them, then.'

'Hardly that many. I write about love and I write about death. What else is there?' He paused and glanced at Szegedy with a tired smile. 'Are we moving on to literature now?'

Szegedy sucked in his cheeks. A strand of hair fell across his forehead. He brushed it back irritably and glanced at András. 'Why are you smiling at me like that?'

'I was merely reflecting upon the irony of our situation.'

'And what might that be?'

'The fact that despite the sea change in political circumstances, I am still obliged to answer your questions.'

'There can be no comparison, the two situations are very different.'

'Naturally, and therein lies the irony.'

Szegedy's expression became guarded. 'What do you mean? There've been infractions of the law . . .'

András mimicked him, 'Naturally, there've been infractions of the law, disturbances of the peace and so on. Naturally, strong measures are called for.'

Szegedy gazed back stolidly. 'I was a policeman in the past,' he said, 'I am a policeman now.'

'Ah, but you're not just any policeman, Inspector. You've managed to save your skin, unlike many others. You've done quite well for yourself.'

Szegedy broke into a sudden grin. 'I'm not going to deny that. That's why I find it entertaining that you should be the one who's amused. You see, the real irony in the situation lies in the fact that I'm the one who's been able to make the adjustment from the old order to the new. You, on the other hand, were the misfit then and are the misfit now. No, don't contradict me, I've read some of your interviews in the papers. At least in the past you could call yourself a dissident or what have you and claim the moral high ground. But now? Now that the changes have taken place you're like a fish out of water – purposeless, anchorless, rudderless. Useless. You've lost something vital that informed your identity. Meanwhile, it's business as usual everywhere, my friend, and the people know that. That's why, in a way, I suspect you even miss the old ways. You needed the repression, didn't you? It gave you reason to survive.'

András restrained himself to a single word: 'Bullshit.'

Szegedy flushed angrily. 'So we're back to being hostile?'

'Right. We're back to being realistic about this interaction.'

'Look, I apologize . . . I got a bit carried away . . .'

'Why apologize? You were being honest for a change.'

'Come, András, surely we can drop the antagonism?'

'And how would you propose to begin, Inspector?'

'Well, for one, it makes me uncomfortable to hear you keep

calling me Inspector like that. It sounds so unnatural, given that we've known each other for so long. Call me Andor. Would that be too much to ask?'

'Whatever you say, Inspector.'

'Why must you insist?'

'Because I'd rather not deceive myself.'

'Still no common ground?'

'None.'

'Very well, then.'

They studied each other for a moment. Behind them, sad-voiced Katalin was singing again, a reworking of a traditional song about watching the Danube flow, a deeper male voice scatting in the background, the two voices weaving in and out. Listening to the words, Szegedy lowered his head and toyed with the ashtray. 'I'd like to ask you something else that's been on my mind. Have you noticed any connection between Immanuele's disappearance and Ami's advent in Budapest?'

András tensed, listening without answering.

'No response?' Szegedy paused. 'You know, in my line of work, what is remembered and what is forgotten is always such a revelation.'

András chose to remain silent.

Szegedy smiled pleasantly. 'Now, let's talk about Ami, shall we?'

'No,' András snapped, 'I'm not here to talk about her. It's not relevant to your investigation. I've said that before. She's out of bounds.'

Szegedy picked up the ashtray on the table and tapped it contemplatively. 'And you're the one that decides?' He leaned over to a neighbouring table and picked up a couple of ashtrays from there as well, proceeding to arrange and rearrange them in different configurations. 'The chaos of space,' he observed, with a sidelong glance, 'or so I've heard, is the true medium of architecture, and the practitioner must unscramble that chaotic jumble in order to make sense of the matter at hand. The same, in a slightly different way, could be said to apply to the work of a criminal investigator, except that the latter studies motives while the architect studies lines in space. In an investigation, motives are everything, and what matters is not so much the constituent elements as their interconnections in space and time. What results from these interconnections is the systematic arrangement of facts.' He swept the ashtrays aside. 'Eventually, therefore, a good investigator, much like an architect, manipulates the given elements to come up with an architectonic, a composition that makes sense. Such an architectonic requires a peculiar vision, because every little piece of information is relevant. So I'm going to ask you again, can we introduce Ami into the picture?'

'No. She's not part of this.'

Szegedy shrugged and leaned back, his face impassive. 'Immanuele disappeared in March 1977, didn't she?' He closed his eyes. 'I can recall that time quite clearly. A cold, bleak winter, I was snowed under at work . . .' He opened his eyes suddenly. 'You were quite persistent in your efforts to get in touch with me. Where was Ami then?'

'Around.'

'Around . . . I see.' He placed his hands on the table, very deliberately. 'Yesterday I dropped by Stefán's old haunt,' he said, 'the artists' cooperative. I hadn't realized the fire had caused quite so much damage.' He watched András closely. 'Apparently Ami was living in that same warehouse at the time of Immanuele's disappearance . . .' He looked at András with mock reproach. 'You never told me that.'

András stared back at him, his eyes steadily holding the other man's. 'Why should it be of interest?' he asked.

'Because it adds yet another overlap to the existing architectonic.'

'A coincidence.'

'One more of the many coming to light.'

András remained silent.

'*Quidquid luce fuit, tenebris agitur*, André . . . what occurs in the light goes on in the dark.'

'Evidently,' András said drily. 'I'm glad you're enjoying your architectonics.'

Szegedy turned away, his hands tapping at the table. 'When did Ami move out of this warehouse and into your apartment?'

172

'Later that year.'

'The year that Immanuele disappeared?'

'Yes.'

'And you lived together in Budapest until 1984 when you left for Abrahámhegy?'

'That's correct.'

'You were in Abrahámhegy for ten years.' He gave András a sidelong smile. 'Ten years of peace and quiet for everyone concerned. Then you show up again and the next thing we know we're dealing with this wax effigy . . .' He paused, adjusting his tie. 'Tell me, how does one explain that kind of coincidence?'

Before András could reply, prolonged applause sounded at the end of a song. A man came dancing out of the café with a broad smile on his face, his hands raised above his head. He turned a full circle, clicking his fingers, before going back in again. When the commotion had died down, Szegedy continued. 'By whose standards?' he asked.

András stared at him, nonplussed. 'Excuse me?'

'Didn't you just say that Stefán had something to do with it?'

'No, of course not. What are you talking about?'

'Oh, never mind, I must have misheard you. The noise around us . . .' He glanced down, eyeing his waistline. 'Do you think I'm putting on weight?'

'What? I don't know. I have no idea how thin you used to be. Look –'

Szegedy cut him off, 'It doesn't matter.' He gestured wearily. 'My wife keeps telling me I'm putting on weight. So, I'm not getting any younger. Where's the motivation?'

'Why are you telling me this? What does it have to do with Immanuele or Ami or with anything else?'

'Ami . . .' Szegedy leaned forward suddenly. 'Why must you be so damned suspicious, András?'

'Force of habit, Inspector.'

'Force of habit!'

'Yes. It comes from long years of practice with dealing with the likes of you. But you're sweating. Rattled?'

'Rattled!' Szegedy grimaced, his voice rising. 'Listen, I'm tired of suspicion.'

'Really? You don't say . . .'

'Are you being deliberately obtuse?'

'Perhaps.'

'Damn you, then! Do you have any idea what it's like to be constantly eyed with suspicion? With fear? With revulsion, even?'

András found himself shaking his head, bemused. 'You will always be compromised, however much you try to present yourself as reformed. There are too many recognizable traits. And these little games . . . even they are familiar.'

'You patronizing bastard!' Szegedy lumbered to his feet, his face shadowed by the overhang of the awning. He leaned his weight against the table, his jaw jutting forward.

András thought he looked ridiculous. 'Does your wife know?' he asked.

'Does my wife know about what?'

'Does she know about Katalin?'

'What are you talking about?'

'I'm a writer, remember? I can play these games just as well as you can.'

Szegedy scanned the other's face, wondering whether to believe him. Then he bent over suddenly, picking up one of the ashtrays and throwing it with vicious force into the street. András watched it land, shattering against the cobblestones. There was a lull around them as people turned to stare. A waiter began to hurry across but slowed down when he noticed that Szegedy was involved. A moment later, the conversation picked up again as if nothing had happened.

Szegedy turned to András. 'We're leaving,' he said abruptly, taking out his wallet and signalling to the waiter.

'We're done for the evening?'

'For the time being, yes,' Szegedy replied. 'Where are you heading?'

'I'm going home.'

'I'll walk with you for a bit. I'm taking the metro myself.'

Just before they left the café, Szegedy stopped in mid-stride. 'What's going on, András?'

'What do you mean?'

174

'Everything's slipping . . .'

'Slipping?'

'Never mind.' The policeman scuffed the ground with the toe of his carefully polished shoe.

'*Neminem laede, immo omnes, quantum potes, juva* . . .'

'What?'

András glanced down the street and studied it closely. 'Hurt no one,' he translated, 'rather, help everyone as much as you can.'

Szegedy didn't reply. A sudden breeze blew leaves and dust into the air. They began walking. Behind them, András could hear snatches of Katalin's broken-voiced crooning, then even that faded away.

They turned off into a narrow side-street. 'There's something about this case . . .' Szegedy remarked, 'that I can't put my finger on.' He thought he heard a laugh behind them, but when he turned his head there was no one there. He shook his head in exasperation and lengthened his strides to keep up with András. They plunged deeper into the shuttered street, the streetlights growing dim around them. Warm gusts of steam billowed out of grates, cantilevering over the kerbs. Stagnant clouds of steam gathered over open gutters, flowing around the men and following in their footsteps.

They turned a corner and the street gave way to a wider tree-lined boulevard. Brightly lit shops crested the pavements, many of them selling shiny new electronic goods, expensive textiles, perfumes. Given the late hour, the shops were all closed, but from deep within their darkened interiors fluorescent lights danced in graceful and continuous motion. Pointing to one of the windows, Szegedy was just about to say something to András when a small shape lung ed out of the shadows, reed-thin hands grabbing at his pockets. Swearing, Szegedy managed to swat the child away, his fist connecting with a doughy white face as the tiny pickpocket jumped backwards and melted into the darkness. Szegedy made as if to chase him but stopped short, cursing furiously and clutching his left hand, the palm dripping blood where he'd been slashed with a razor.

The entire episode couldn't have lasted more than a few seconds.

175

Szegedy broke the silence first, his voice shaking with anger. 'What are you staring at?' he snapped at András as he searched through his pockets and pulled out a handkerchief. Crumpling it around his hand and stemming the flow of blood, he struggled to regain his composure. 'That little gypsy shit!' he swore as he held up the injured hand and examined it in the neon glow of the shop window. The gash was long and jagged, and he tightened the handkerchief around it.

Gritting his teeth, he turned to András. 'I'm very close to a solution,' he said. 'I want you to know that.' He looked at his hand again. 'That little shit!' he repeated. Then he turned and marched away towards the entrance to the metro station. On the verge of descending the steps, he swivelled around and walked swiftly back to András. Planting his feet belligerently apart, he said, 'Listen to me, and listen carefully. I took this case of my own volition and I intend to see it through to the end. I have no new angles on the past, no exciting theories or conjectures. An investigation's normal sense of purpose requires that certain things be considered dead, and I don't intend to get lost in the fog of what happened seventeen years ago. But what's going on now is very different. This is an entirely separate matter, and I'm going to find out what it's all about. Someone's playing around with the past, and I'm going to find out why.'

He paused for a moment before resuming, his voice cold and precise. 'Which brings me to you, András. I've been patient in our conversations, I've tempered my questions with self-control. I've respected your public standing and made allowances for your reputation. But don't mistake my patience for uncertainty or for capitulation. I am not a sentimentalist and this is not an adventure of the heart. It's a matter, I am convinced, of the appropriation of reality, and the significance, the transparency, and the emptiness of the past. There's a very complex puzzle inside my head, and it's resolving itself piece by piece, as it always does. And when I've put all the pieces together, when I've satisfied myself that they fit snug and tight, that's when I'll go after whoever's responsible, and bring them to book. And if it's you, then I'll come after you, you can be sure of that!' He raised his hand in the air, barely able to contain his anger, and then turned on his heels and stalked off.

◆

The house on E-Daj Street was very different from the way András remembered it. It was still surrounded by a tall wrought-iron fence, with arrowheads that cast serrated shadows across the street. But someone had torn down entire sections and replaced them with crudely made wooden palings. Through a gap, András glimpsed the familiar path leading up to the house, its borders hemmed in on either side by a cavalcade of dead trees. Surrounded by those trees, the once vibrant garden had transformed into a marsh, stagnant pools of water interspersed with coarse grass and weeds. Lifeless bushes stood abandoned amid the waterlogged expanse, an anaemic light speckling through their midst. At the very centre, an elevated Greek fountain was crowned with a marble statue of the hunter Actæon, but his hounds had long since left him, their shattered torsos strewn along the ground.

The house stood about a hundred yards away from the street, its bright yellow façade discoloured to brown, its terrace and gabled roof a play of light and dust-coloured shade. Most of the windows had been boarded up, although some had their shutters tied together. A section of the roof had fallen in.

A thick, damp carpet of leaves lined the path to the front door. They made a whispering sound as András stepped on them. He found the door propped open with a brick. Stepping past it, he entered a dark L-shaped passageway, the creaking floorboards betraying his every step. The passageway led into a small room that had once served as the antechamber. Here, a dilapidated grand piano, a French-made Érard, stood angled across the room. Walking over to it, András lifted the lid and pressed down on the keys. They made a bony, clicking sound. He replaced the lid, stepping back and contemplating the dead instrument. He recalled the first time he'd heard Immanuele play it. It had been after they'd returned from her mother's grave one evening. She had played Scriabin's Eighth Sonata, going over it again and again. She'd still been playing it when he had left her that night.

A pair of large glass doors opened out from the antechamber into an enormous domed hall, its lofty cupola rising a full three floors. This was the largest room in the house, the walls punctuated by blue marble columns that supported the ceiling. The spaces between the columns had once been inset with painted panels, but most of the paint had flaked off now. The rest of the hall was gloomy and dark, with only a few shadowy slivers of light probing in through cracks in the shuttered windows, revealing the extent to which the room had been stripped: even the walls had been pillaged, pale squares and rectangles outlining absent paintings and photographs.

With his hands clasped tightly behind his back, András walked through the hall, stray objects catching his eye. He sat down in one corner and willed himself to remember the place the way it had been. Rooms in isolation: that was all that was left. Walls stripped down, exposed, laid bare. Beams spilling out in unflinching testimony to deterioration. Nothing left that was even remotely intimate or connected to the past. History as an accident, a completely futile thing.

With his head in his hands András contemplated the trespass of time around him. It seemed like a dream, almost a cry of despair. In anguished flashbacks, he reviewed episodes in Immanuele's life and in his own. Mired in the complexities of his own background, he hadn't recognized, until it was too late, her extraordinary courage and compassion – and as a result he'd never accepted her love for him. That kind of vitality and endurance – he'd had so very little to give her in return.

He remembered the last time he'd been here. A dark and gusty day, it had been raining outside. Immanuele had returned from the clinic three hours late. The door had opened and she'd walked in, completely drenched. He'd rushed to greet her but had stopped as soon as he'd seen her expression. He'd waited for her to speak, and when she remained silent, he'd turned away.

'It's done, André,' was the very first thing she'd said.

178

Her hair was soaked, the ends curling into points and turning inwards. She looked pale and fragile, her eyes listless. He didn't say anything, extending his hand and taking her coat instead. She glanced around the room, then out of the windows at the rooftops. He took off her wet shoes; she let him.

He'd walked over to the kitchen and put on some water for tea. In the next room, he could hear her walking back and forth, her footsteps slow and exhausted. Then she entered the kitchen and came and stood behind him. She placed her hands on his back and rested her chin on his shoulder. They watched the water boil, its surface sheen crumpling.

'He's gone, André . . . our possible child. Now there can be no going back. Not even thoughts of it.'

The water boiled. He removed the tea leaves and stirred in milk and sugar, his hands automatically pouring the liquid into two cups. She reached around him and searched for her cup, finding it and lifting it to her lips. The bones on her wrist stood out. There was a fresh scar. He heard porcelain cup touch porcelain teeth. She ran a hand through her hair and gazed down at her feet.

He was waiting for her to finish drinking when she put the cup down and gently pulled at his sleeve. They walked back to the neighbouring room and sat down.

'Turn on the lights, André,' she said.

He looked at her. 'They're already on, Immanuele.'

'Oh! I . . . it's very dark in here . . .'

'It must be the sedative . . .'

Her lips parted anxiously, and then they slackened. 'They said it was going to be like this for the next few days.'

He raised his hand as if to touch her shoulder, but withdrew it at once when he sensed her draw away.

'I wasn't entirely prepared,' she whispered.

'I shouldn't have let you, I should have insisted . . .'

'There's no need to go over it again. It's done. Finished.'

'I couldn't sleep last night,' he said, wearily. 'I must have dozed off early in the morning. When I woke up it was dark again.'

'I remember the instruments more than anything else. Shiny steel instruments.'

179

He turned away and lowered his head.

She pointed to the photograph he'd been looking at when she'd walked in. 'What's that on the table?' she asked. She sensed his hesitation. 'What is it?'

His reply was muffled. 'It's a photograph.'

She stood up and walked over to it, her eyes straining to see. Picking it up, she turned to him. 'Who is she?'

'That's America.'

'Oh,' she said, a catch in her voice. 'So *this* is Ami.'

She turned her back to him. 'Strange name . . .' he heard her say, 'strange name. And a piece of you I've never seen . . .'

She went down on her knees and stared intently at the photograph. He reached for it but she pulled away from him. 'Where is she now?'

'In Berlin. She used to live in Vienna, but now she's in Berlin.'

'What does she do?'

'She's a painter.'

She looked at the photograph in silence.

He glanced at the floor. 'What is happening to us?'

'We need time, André. Time to think things out.'

'Do you . . . oh, God! You must despise me!'

'No . . .' she replied deliberately. 'Why should I? There's no reason to.' She held out her hand. 'Tell me about Ami.'

'This is hardly the time!'

'Please – distract me.'

'What is there to tell?'

'Anything.'

'But why now, of all times, why *now*?'

She gazed at him steadily, her eyes bright. 'Please.'

Giving in, he replied with some reluctance: 'She's different.'

'Different?' She tried to smile. 'Of course . . .'

'It's not as you think.'

'Do you write to each other?'

'No, I'm not much of a correspondent.'

'Does she mind?'

'I don't know. She probably does.' He turned away. 'Sometimes I wonder if she's not more present in my imagination than in reality.'

'What is she like?'

'There's a part of her that's like a very young girl, almost a child. And yet she's astonishingly mature and wise. When we were young, she was always the leader. She's still much more assertive than I am. She's searching for something, I think.'

'And what do you think she's searching for?'

'Herself . . . the meaning of freedom . . . true love . . . who knows?'

'True love,' she smiled gently. 'When is she coming to Budapest?'

'I don't know.'

'Am I ever going to meet her?'

'Look, must we talk about her? Tell me how you're feeling, for God's sake!'

She looked young and tremendously vulnerable.

'I don't want to talk about it,' she said.

He took the photograph from her and replaced it in his wallet. She watched him closely.

He leaned over suddenly and touched her on the lips. 'What happened? Please tell me. I can't take this any more.'

She stood up and walked across the room to a sofa. Sitting down on it, she gazed out of the window. 'Look outside,' she said. 'Can you see the sky? Can you see how dark it is, how murky? It reminds me of the ocean. The waters cresting the wind, the waves appearing, disappearing. Last night I dreamt I saw the ocean bleeding. And flowers . . . many, many flowers . . .' she paused. 'There was a church in the middle of the ocean . . . very large, like a cathedral. Inside was a great hall, painted white and filled with horses. Snow was falling. Great big flakes, soft. There was a fire in the centre of the hall and it melted the snow as it fell. The horses ran past the fire from one side of the hall to the other. They were white, probably Lipizzaners. But there was something wrong with them. They couldn't stop running. They kept smashing against the walls, reeling back from the impact each time, bloodying the paint with great ghastly smears. At last, they rolled over one by one and lay very still. Their flanks trembled. Their breath rattled deep inside their chests. Then, one by one, they fell silent.'

She looked at him. 'And now the day is nearly done, André. We must return to the living.'

'I can't. I haven't got your strength.'

'But it's not strength, don't you see?'

'What is it, then?'

'I don't know. But I do need you to know that I'm not afraid.'

'You don't need to tell me that!' He walked up to her and reached for her hands.

'I tried to embrace you last night,' she said, 'forgetting that you weren't there.'

He knelt before her. 'Will you let me come and see you sometimes?'

She kissed him on the mouth. 'Perhaps I will, one day.'

He held on to her until she pulled away. 'Will you go now?' she asked gently.

'I don't want to, Immanuele.'

'You must, you promised.'

'What can I do? If there is anything I can do, anything at all . . .'

'No. Nothing. You've done enough.'

'Is there no hope?'

'Go.'

'Please be careful, please . . .'

She was already looking away. 'I will,' she said. She stood up and walked away from him. She stopped in front of a window and stared out into the night.

He was about to leave when she flung the window open, the violence of the action arresting him.

She raised her hands, her voice suddenly urgent. '*András* –'

He crossed the room swiftly and grasped her by the shoulders. 'What's the matter? Immanuele, what is it?'

'Look out of the window . . .' her voice began to quaver and break, 'look there . . . in the street . . .'

A car had burst into flames. A man was standing beside its fiery exoskeleton, an open book in his hand. He raised it high above his head, as if in acknowledgement of their presence. He stood there for a moment, long enough for András to recognize him. Then he crumpled backwards into the burning vehicle, the flames engulfing him.

They ran out blindly, screaming his name.

'*János!*'

It had been raining outside.

That's what it had been like in this room that night. Black rain outside; darkness within.

András resumed his pacing, his footsteps guiding him to the massive staircase that led upstairs. He ascended slowly, counting the steps as he climbed, the sound of his footsteps rendering the silence even more dense around him. At the top there was a recessed alcove that had once held Immanuele's favourite painting, a watercolour depicting a small girl reaching into the crystal-clear waters of a pond towards a small boy, the moment caught precisely at the point at which it became impossible to determine whether she was pulling the boy out or being pulled in by him. Like so much else in the house now, the painting was missing.

To the left of the alcove stood the door to Immanuele's room. A bank of tattered lace curtains hung across it, surprising András with their survival. He brushed past them into the room. To his right, a row of bay windows opened out on to the terrace, their clear glass panes looking over the city and the river running through it. Adjoining the windows was a huge four-poster bed, a protective white sheet draped over it. András stared at the bed, bemused that it was still there. It was enormous, and it dominated the room like a great beached galleon, its bulk further emphasized by a mirror on the wall facing it. The mirror was cracked and spotted with age. A faded inscription – sandwiched between cavorting marble intaglios of nymphs – announced that the mirror had been a gift to Maddalena, the Serene Princess Emperházy, from his Imperial Majesty Rudolph Habsburg, Crown Prince of Austria and Apostolic Prince of Hungary.

András walked away from the mirror, crossing the room and standing in front of the door to the terrace. From here he could see the high ground slope gently down over a sea of rooftops to the banks of the Danube. In the sky above, a white vortex of clouds was advancing towards the city. They escorted the sun in an orderly procession, their thick white fleece lifting and floating high in the air.

Turning away from the view, András walked into the adjoining room. It had been Immanuele's grandfather's study. Pale impressions made by long-gone bookcases now lined the walls from the floor to the ceiling. A leather armchair slumped sullenly against a wall, its dirt-blackened exterior accentuating the desolation of its surroundings. Above the chair, the ceiling had fallen in, a ragged filigree of brick and mortar letting the sky dangle in.

More than any other part of the house, it was this room that most clearly testified to the circumstances that had overtaken it. Purposeless now, it surrounded András with its silence. There was no space for memory within it, no space for reflection. Only the visible dissolution of light and shade remained.

Shaken to the core, his history suddenly lacking evidence, András walked out of the room and abandoned it to its own forlorn devices. It was hot and unusually bright on the terrace. There wasn't even a semblance of breeze, only the glaze of the sun. He heard the voices of children from a nearby playground, their laughter shimmering across the roofs. A bevy of pigeons spilled from a nearby dovecot and ascended towards a steeple.

About to leave the terrace, András heard a sound from the study. It sounded like a footstep. Moving swiftly to the door, he scanned the room. There was no one there. Perplexed, he crossed over to Immanuele's room and looked in there as well. Then he glanced back at the terrace with a start, catching sight of something. He hurried across and picked it up. It was a metronome, and it hadn't been there seconds earlier. Flipping it open, he released the clasp. Next to the sliding weight on the pendulum was a minute inscription with Immanuele's name on it. There could be no doubt about it: he had given this metronome to Immanuele on her twenty-fifth birthday.

He stood there for a moment, pensive. Then he fastened the clasp and slipped the device into his pocket. On his guard now, he returned to the study. Through a door on the far side was a corridor which led into a large room, its interior dark. As András stepped in, the door behind him slammed shut, and he heard the sound of someone running in the direction of the study. He rushed back into the now-deserted corridor, and then into the study. Leaving nothing to chance, he turned and hurried through the terrace into Immanuele's room and down the steps. In the domed hall below, he called out: 'Clio?' He waited for a couple of seconds and then he called out again, a little less certainly: 'Stefán?' When there was no response, he ran out of the house and down the winding path into the street.

It was deserted there as well. Feeling defeated, he leaned against the gate. There were no sounds in the street, and the house he had left behind was equally silent. It made him wonder if he had imagined the entire thing. On the verge of reopening the gate and marching back in, he heard a cough from behind him. With a start, he turned around.

'Hello again,' Szegedy remarked, 'you don't seem to waste any time. What brings you here? A trip down memory lane? New material for a book?' He nodded at the house. 'Find anything interesting?' Misinterpreting András's rather distraught silence, he carried on, a trifle defensively, 'Things not quite as you expected them to be, I take it? It does need a bit of cleaning up –'

'A bit of cleaning up? The place has been ransacked! There's nothing left!'

Szegedy eyed him curiously. 'It's not what you think. With a very few exceptions, everything is in storage. In any case, what did you expect? The place hasn't been lived in for years.'

'When did you get here?'

'Just now. My car's parked around the corner by the square.' He glanced at András. 'Why? Is something the matter?'

'There's someone in the house,' András replied.

Szegedy appeared to mull over what he'd just heard. Then he nodded briefly, a hint of excitement in his voice. 'Shall we go inside?'

They emerged almost half an hour later. Szegedy stood at the front door, lighting a cigarette and looking around. 'I'm going to post a man here for the next few days,' he said, 'or at least until I've found out what's going on.'

He stepped away from the door. 'Well, there's no point in my waiting around. There's no one in the house now.'

'I'm going to stay,' András replied, turning and staring at the house with a fixed expression. Sensing his distress, Szegedy decided not to say anything.

They walked down the path without a word. When they reached the street, Szegedy said, 'Personally, I think you're wasting your time. Whoever was in there isn't going to be back for a while.'

András nodded, preoccupied.

Szegedy hesitated. 'While I'm here,' he added, 'is there anything else you'd like to tell me?'

András studied the deserted street. 'No,' he replied, 'nothing else comes to mind.' He turned his back to Szegedy and pushed the gate open, walking back towards the house.

He returned to the terrace. Behind him, the sun glinted off the windows in Immanuele's room. He glanced down at the street, but it was deserted, the policeman gone.

The man in the grey sedan thought he saw him there when he drove by that evening. Following his instructions, he parked the car across from the house. The street was dimly lit and flanked by trees, the streetlights shading it to a softer hue that was almost blue, like moonlight. A thick, dark hedge interspersed the trees. The leaves gathered along the pavement in a shifting constellation, the street itself appearing to sway when the wind swept through them.

Outside the car, a single raindrop splattered on the windscreen and coursed down a groove to the bottom of the glass. Another drop followed, and then the rain began sliding down the windows with a feverish hum. It flapped over the car in a thick-fingered web, trying to squeeze in. The windows began to mist up. A sudden wind whipped through the trees and scattered the rain into corners. Then the downpour ceased as suddenly as it had begun, the streetlights revealing the houses on either side of the street. The rows of trees resumed their sentinel vigil, water dripping off their leaves.

From inside the car, the man scanned the house opposite. All seemed calm until someone suddenly came out of the front gates. It was Szegedy, his face pinched with frustration and lack of sleep. Climbing into the car, he slammed the door shut. The

186

man inside the car held out his hand, pointing towards the terrace: 'He's *still* in there?' Szegedy made a sour face, not bothering to reply. Instead, he lowered his window, watching the rain resume. 'Bloody rain!' he snapped, rolling the window up again. With a gesture, he indicated they should move on. The car swung into the street. As the sound of its engine faded away, a match flared up on the terrace of the house. There was a trail of white smoke, and a face moved towards the flame, a cigarette lighting up. It was Clio, her features angular and pale, her eyes fierce in concentration.

◆

András was watching from the street when Clio left the house that night. He remained concealed in the shadows, holding himself back until she reached the end of the street. Once she turned the corner, he set off at a brisk pace, following at a safe distance. She was walking swiftly, and in a while it became clear she was headed in the direction of the river and Margit Bridge.

A thick grey fog was rising over the Danube. Softer than the shadows, it slid across the water in thick columns, its very formlessness threatening to dissolve the river into its insidious screen. The bridge was silent, the night chilly, and the river below András smelt of petrol. Fearing that he'd lost Clio, he was about to break into a run when he caught sight of her near the causeway that led down to Margit Island. She was standing under a lamp-post across which someone had scrawled: '*Ich werde es zerreißen!*' As he debated whether or not to go forward, she stepped out of the shadows and stood directly in his path, her eyes challenging him.

Realizing that he'd been discovered, he raised a hand in greeting, but she swivelled around and set off rapidly in the direction they'd come from, her footsteps retracing themselves. At the end of the bridge, she hurried across the avenue and turned down a narrow side-street.

Surprised, András rushed after her, a sudden, sharp chill

reminding him that he was completely soaked. She must have been drenched as well, he saw her draw her jacket around herself. She stopped once, bending to take off her shoes. The lights of a passing van lit her up, then a passing car, a grey sedan. It skirted the pavement, splashing her as it swerved past. She watched it turn the corner and then she straightened up and hurried on, her bare feet flashing over the slick black shadow of the street.

She entered a street in the Castle district, one of the many that wound their way up the slope of the hill. She headed towards a boarded-up house, running down a flight of steps that led to a door below the level of the street. András watched her slip inside, and quickly followed.

A sign above the door identified the place as the Totalitarian Zone. A black and white poster on the door advertised a concert by a band called the Gypsy Destroyers Guard Regiment. András looked at the poster for a moment, taken aback by its explicitness. Then he pulled the door open and walked in.

He was in a cellar, spacious and dimly lit. There were mirrors on the walls, and small cages filled with candles hung at the four corners of the room. Most of the tables had chairs inverted on them; it looked as if the place were ready to close for the night.

A man sitting at a table to the right of the door looked up as András walked in. He was quietly strumming a guitar. There was only one other occupied table at the far end of the room. There was no sign of Clio. Intrigued, András glanced across to the table at the far end and the four men who were sitting there with their backs to him. All four were dressed in black, with knee-length leather chaps and aviator jackets.

He studied the rest of the room, wondering at its strangeness. A strip of mirrored glass ran above the bar, the frame surrounded by plaster casts of mutilated cars, their red-painted innards spilling out like guts. Next to the mirror, a naked, life-sized plaster mannequin hung upside down from the ceiling. Its torso was skewered on a pole, and one hand listlessly held a sign that read 'No Exit.' There didn't seem to be anyone behind the bar, and András walked over to the group of four with the intention of asking if they had seen Clio.

He approached the man nearest him but another raised a gloved finger to his lips. Confused, András turned to the rest of the table, but they only stared expressionlessly back at him. The first man got up from the table and walked past András, his eyes fixed on the mannequin. When he was directly below it, he swung a fist through the head, separating it from the rest of the torso. With an abrupt underhand movement, he raised the head high above him while at the same time turning to András and wailing in a falsetto: *'La muerte entra y sale de la taberna!'*

András backed away, aware of the scraping of chairs as the others rose to their feet. About to turn around and beat a hasty retreat, he heard a woman's muted laugh. Glancing over his shoulder, he was just in time to see a familiar figure walk rapidly out of the room. He turned to follow her, the men at the table breaking into a fierce hissing.

Outside, a red light flashed on and then off in a darkened house across the street. A car swerved past András, its wheels coming dangerously close. It was a grey sedan, and as it swept down the street, its headlights alighted on a slight figure dressed in black. Recognizing her, András set off immediately, realizing that she was walking back in the direction of Margit Bridge. She ducked into an alley as he hurried to catch up. He started running, but by the time he turned the corner it was already too late; she was nowhere to be seen.

◆

Determined to find Clio, András returned the next morning to the house on E-Daj Street. He was about to unlatch the gate when he noticed a man sitting on a folding chair on the path to the house. It was the Sergeant András had met on Margit Island the evening of the discovery of the waxwork. Reluctant to venture inside the house with the policeman there, András watched him as he slowly leafed through the pages of a magazine. Acknowledging the futility of waiting for him to leave, András walked hesitantly away.

189

He wandered all the way down to the river. Sitting at a table at an open-air restaurant, he gazed at the water and at the hill cresting the opposite bank. It was a warm and humid day, the sky peppered with clouds, the sun a blaze on the water. Rows of barges drifted past, flocks of seagulls circling listlessly in their wake. Some of the gulls skimmed the water's surface, others made wide circles in the air as they ascended. A group of children ran after the birds, their voices excitedly trilling across the promenade. One gull, especially, seemed to be holding their attention. It would hover motionlessly for a while, then plunge into a corkscrew of erratic flight. As András watched, the bird climbed sluggishly into the sky, its wings straining. In the shadow of the clouds, it cartwheeled, plummeting and gathering speed, wings splaying as it hurtled into the river with an explosive splash.

András looked around in consternation. Others had noticed as well, their voices rising wordlessly in alarm. A man opened a window in the distance and pointed at the river. The driver of a passing van slowed down in confusion. Together, they stared mesmerized as the dying bird contorted from side to side, its lungs throttled by water. Great waves rolled over its heart, constricting it. Wing tip by wing tip, it sailed the brown depths of the water, a film clouding its eyes. Then the river closed over it.

'Would you care for an aperitif, sir?'

It was a familiar voice, laughter lacing through it.

András started, looking up. '*Dénes*! You startled me! Did you see what just happened?'

'Do you mean that bird? Yes, I did. Very strange . . .'

'It just killed itself. Deliberately! Drowned itself in cold blood.'

'Yes, it's been known to happen . . .'

'But that's the second time I've seen it in as many weeks! What's the matter with these birds?'

Dénes shrugged glumly.

András collected himself. 'But what are *you* doing here?'

'What does it look like? I work here.'

'You work here?'

'That's right. I've a joint stake in the business with my father-in-law.'

András stared at him in confusion. 'Since when?'

'It's been a couple of months now. Things have been really hectic here, that's why I haven't been in touch.' His voice sounded strangely muted.

András looked baffled. 'I don't understand . . .'

Dénes glanced away. 'What is there to understand? I know what you're thinking but I've killed the captain of my ambitions, André. It hurt like hell in the beginning. But the money . . . It's better than translating, and the poetry just wasn't paying enough. One has to survive, pay the rent, things like that. I'm not getting any younger, you know – I have a family, a wife and two kids. I can't take the risks I used to.' He looked resigned. 'In any case, the meaning's all in materialism now. Everyone's after money, people no longer have the time for verse. There've been too many changes too fast, and it's all one can do to keep up. I'm working so much I don't even have time to think. Now all I'm looking forward to is to make enough to build a house with a garden in Szilvásvárad, in the heart of the Bükk mountains. Once that's done, I'm leaving all this behind. I'm sick of city life, I'm tired of this treadmill.'

András cut him off. 'Maybe I'm totally out of touch. Maybe I haven't been following developments closely enough, but you were one of the best poets of our generation, Dénes. You and Stefán. And now you, of all people, say that the meaning is in materialism?'

'It's simple enough to wax indignant when you've managed to make a living out of literature, but I'm running out of time. I gave poetry the best years of my life and I have little to show for it. Believe me, André, I've travelled that road, it's time for me to move on to something else. I'm tired of living in a hole. I'm tired of living a life without conclusions.'

'I heard of a job translating Breton . . .'

Dénes looked away. 'Breton . . .' Changing the subject very deliberately, he carried on, 'How are you liking Budapest, now that you're back?'

'I haven't really noticed, Dénes, there've been other things on my mind.'

191

Dénes looked suddenly contrite. 'Ah, yes . . . Immanuele . . . the whole wretched business with the waxwork . . . I heard. I'm sorry, André.' He glanced away. 'Oh, look, some customers! I have to go. Hold on, will you? I'll send someone over to take your order.'

He hastened off as András watched, disappearing into the gaudily decorated interior of the restaurant. He emerged a few moments later with a bottle of wine and placed it with a flourish before András. 'My compliments! Red wine from Sopron, your favourite!' He uncorked the bottle with a twist and smiled. 'The next time I'll take you to my other place. You may have heard of it, it's called the Café Royal.'

András sat up. 'You own the Café Royal?'

'You seem surprised –'

András recalled his meeting with Szegedy, and the contretemps with the jazz singer, Katalin. 'It's just that I was there recently,' he replied.

Pleased, Dénes smiled. 'You've read the reviews then?'

Before András could think of a response, Dénes had to excuse himself again to take a phone call.

While they had been speaking, a group of tuxedoed cellists had arranged themselves in a circle at one end of the promenade. András thought he recognized some of the musicians. As they struck up the opening chords of a popular dance suite by Bartók, another seagull began circling out of the sky, picking up speed as it lost height. It hurtled past Castle Hill before turning upside down, its wings shredding through the last few metres before it smashed into the concrete at the exact centre of the musician's circle. The music came skidding to a halt.

No one moved.

Next to András, a young girl in a shawl crossed herself. 'It's bad luck,' she said. Someone else whispered, 'I saw an identical thing happen at the dockyards in Fiume in '65 . . .'

A rotund man wearing tortoiseshell glasses hurried up to the bird. 'It's all right, it's all right,' he said, 'I'm a vet . . .'

Everyone waited, silent and tense.

After a while, pointing to the bird's gullet, his voice rising with the verdict, the man in the tortoiseshell glasses declared,

'Lead poisoning!' He stood up and shook his head in distress.

The girl in the shawl crossed herself again, 'I don't like this. Something bad's going to happen. There've been all kinds of signs. The river froze over in the middle of the day a couple of weeks ago. And the water's much colder now than it ever was. They say it's entirely saturated with chemicals.'

The crowd dispersed in a subdued mass after that, the cellists calling it a day and packing up their instruments. 'Same time, same place, tomorrow . . . please come back . . .' their leader called out disconsolately after the rapidly departing backs.

András watched them leave.

A waiter placed a glass of water on his table. It glittered in the sun.

A torn sheet of newspaper drifted across the promenade, landing on top of the dead bird. In seconds, the paper was soaked through with bright crimson. It slid away from the dead bird and moved in wind-driven bursts towards the river. András watched it land on the water, a coppery residue flushing through the headlines.

In the sky above, the sun slid behind a bank of clouds.

A solitary mandolin player strolled across the promenade. He stopped for a moment to look at the dead bird. András gazed absently at him, thinking about the deaths he had just witnessed. Two deaths on the Danube. Two fierce and beautiful deaths on the Danube. Committed by laughing birds.

Grimacing, he reached into his pocket, taking out and reading, once again, the note that he'd found in his letterbox that morning:

My Dear André,

Forgive this typewritten note. What we lose in epistolary aesthetics we gain in the preservation of meaning. You know what I mean.

This may strike you as a strange letter, but I'm sending it before I begin to edit

out the irrational parts. You will
probably be amused to see me chasing my
tail like this, but please understand
that I am completely serious. I have to see
you, we need to talk. I should probably
explain, but I'd rather do that in person.
It's about recent events, and about events
of the past.

Please, will you agree to meet me? If your
answer is yes, and I suspect it will be,
ask Elemér Klein for directions. He's the
only true friend.

Stefán

Chapter Four

The Gabriel Club

They had arranged to meet at Szabadság Square at seven o'clock in the morning. The hour was at Stefán's insistence: to avoid the rush-hour crowds, he'd said. András arrived early, and he settled down to wait under the natural scaffolding of an oak tree. The square was deserted, the dawn light just beginning to creep through the streets. A cool, dry breeze rustled through the trees and swept past the pillared façade of the Magyar Television building. It had rained the previous night but now the puddles were drying up on the asphalt. András had brought a magazine with him; he leafed distractedly through it, glancing at the pictures but not really reading it.

Stefán was almost an hour late. He was wearing a black military greatcoat at least two sizes too large for him. He crossed the square swiftly – tall, stooped, falcon-like – walking with a pronounced and unfamiliar limp. Cutting through a flock of pigeons idling on the ground, he hurried up to András. 'I'm sorry I'm late,' he said, his eyes scanning the square, the greatcoat flapping around him.

András held out his hand formally. 'It's been a while, Stefán.'

'Thank you for agreeing to meet me.'

'Don't mention it.'

Stefán raised a hand and ran it through his hair. There were dark circles under his eyes, and his face looked puffy and slack

195

with fatigue. When he turned his head, András saw a scab on one side of his face, below the eye. It was raw around the edges.

He had altered enormously.

Stefán smiled grimly when he noticed András studying him. 'I've been followed these past few days, André,' he said, 'so you'll forgive me if I seem a bit on edge.'

'Who is following you?'

Stefán squared his shoulders awkwardly. 'It's a long story,' he said, 'and I'll tell you everything, but not here. Let's go to my place. It's safer there.'

They walked in silence, Stefán turning around from time to time to make sure that there was no one behind them. They crossed the square and entered a shaded street. Stefán's apartment was located in a massive grey building at the end of it. As András glanced up to take it in, his eyes met those of a little boy staring at him. A young woman appeared at the window just then, her face peering down. She looked at András suspiciously, and then she reached out and yanked the boy in.

Stefán lived on the third floor, but the lift wasn't working. The stairway was narrow and dimly lit, the walls covered with mildew and graffiti. Grimy lamps flickered on alternate floors, lighting up stacks of rubbish and exposed plumbing.

After walking down what seemed like an endless corridor, they entered Stefán's apartment. As András hesitated, his eyes adjusting to the gloom, Stefán crossed the room and opened a door at the opposite end – a rank and putrid smell assailing András as he did. Determined to ignore it, he made to follow, but Stefán shut the door behind him, leaving András marooned in the darkness. There was a sound of windows being unfastened, and then Stefán came out again, a bright beam of sunlight spilling over his shoulder. It took only a few seconds after that for the fresh air to banish the mustiness.

The room András was in was wedge-shaped, with the narrower end behind him. To his left was a single casement window, which Stefán was in the process of unlatching. In the middle of the room was a hard-backed wooden chair with a dilapidated couch facing it. A dusty stack of canvases leaned against the back of the chair.

It was what occupied the walls on either side of the room, however, that arrested András's attention. Diagonally opposite him, in the right-hand corner, there was a life-size blue male nude painted on the wall. The artist had captured the figure in mid-motion with only half the torso and the back of the head visible, almost as if it were strolling through the wall to the other side. The effect was eerie, and it was only after staring at it for a moment that András turned to look in the other direction, a shock of recognition shooting through him. At the exact centre of the peeling wall, a framed portrait of a young woman stared directly back at him. She held animal (or human?) entrails between delicately bared teeth, her eyes gleaming from behind translucent lids. Framed by a mass of glowing amber curls, her face was a perfect oval, the forehead pale and pronounced, the cheekbones high and distinct, the nose thin and slightly upraised.

Stepping back involuntarily, András closed his eyes, a familiar voice going off inside his head: *'Have you ever wondered what it's like, André, to live on the edge like this? Have you ever wondered what we'll have to accomplish to exchange skin for skin, to slip out and slip in whenever the whim takes over and pulls us in? Me for you and you for me, Ami for András, András for Ami. Your eyes for mine, your lips for my lips, nothing to be left separate in the mix. And when it rains and the small of your back fills up with water like an oasis, there'll be mysterious caravans streaming out of the Sahara and gathering around us to drink . . . arks moving across the desert, their shadows shimmying down the sandskin dunes that are your hips. I must have all of that. We must be joined together, merged together, each completely lost in each . . .'*

A hand touched his elbow.

Startled, András swung around.

Stefán was extending a pack of cigarettes towards him. 'Cigarette?'

'No, thanks,' András replied, collecting himself, 'I have my own.'

Stefán nodded at the portrait. 'Ami catch your eye? What do you think?'

András hesitated for a moment before replying. 'It's completely tasteless.'

197

'Tasteless?'

'Those eyes, that red mess trailing down the chin.'

'The eyes? What about them?'

'They're dead, like eyes of the night.'

'It's one person's insight, André.'

'Bullshit. It's cheap, and it's offensive.'

'You could choose not to look at it.'

'It's a bit difficult to ignore, isn't it, given its prominence?'

'I could take it down, if you like . . .'

'And replace it when I go? No, you'd better leave it as it is. When did you do it?'

'I didn't. Ami did.'

András stiffened. 'Ami? Ami painted *that*?'

Stefán turned away so that András couldn't make out his expression. 'It was one of the last things she did,' Stefán said. 'A self-portrait. She meant it to be a representation of Astarte. She got the idea from an exhibition on Greek and Assyrian deities. You know how she felt about the exotic, and this was bizarre enough to be that much more fulfilling.' He gestured briefly. 'I'd intended this apartment to double as her studio. I'd just moved in and wanted her to be able to live and work here with me. You were in Eger at the time and it didn't make sense that she should be living by herself. Of course, everything collapsed before that could happen. I loved her, you know; I wanted her so much, but she wouldn't have me.' He paused and stared at the painting. 'That portrait was the only one she did of herself when she was living at the warehouse. There were dozens of other things: masks, paintings, photographs, all kinds of eccentricities.' He paused, holding his hands before his face. His fingers were long and slender, the tips stained brown with nicotine. 'I got rid of most of them,' he said, his voice distant. 'One day, I simply lost the inclination to look at them. Something snapped in me. I stopped using the room after that. That portrait is one of the few things that remain; I couldn't bring myself to part with it.'

András looked around. 'Where are the rest of them now?'

'I gave some to a gallery, so I've lost track of those. The remainder . . .' he nodded at the canvases stacked against the

chair, 'are right there.' He glanced at András. 'I'm sorry I gave
the others away but they were reminders of her. I couldn't take it
any more, I couldn't take the guilt.'

András pointed to the nude on the wall. 'Did she do that as
well?'

'Yes, she did. It started off as an allegory of Adam, and then it
mutated. The blue was my idea, although by that time she'd lost
interest and I don't really think it mattered. Male love as self-love
is what she wanted to convey.'

András winced. He couldn't help it.

Stefán bent over, his hands fumbling with a shoelace that had
come undone. 'Look, André,' he said, his tone measured, 'I know
that this must be difficult for you. I realize the associations must
be distasteful. But Ami meant the world to me. You must believe
me when I say that.'

'Do I have a choice?'

'I don't know. But nothing I can say now can bring back the
past.'

András felt the hostility flood back. 'Look,' he replied tersely,
'this isn't why I'm supposed to be here. I didn't ask to come.'

'Of course, I'm sorry. It's just that we haven't met since . . .'
Stefán cleared his throat, suddenly formal. 'Would you like some
tea, András . . . André?'

'Yes, I would like that very much, please.'

Stefán left the room.

There was a sound of running water, then the sound of a kettle
being filled. András tried to think, but it was no use, the splash of
water drowning out everything else. Giving up the effort, he
closed his eyes.

He heard Stefán calling out to him: 'I'm going to suck you
into this like quicksand, André, bit by bit.'

Moments later, he returned with a cup of tea.

András stared at him. 'I beg your pardon?'

'What for?'

'I thought I heard you speak to me from the other room.
Something about quicksand . . .'

'No, I'm afraid I didn't say anything.'

The tea was scalding and András put it down carefully on the floor. They lit cigarettes, each holding the stem in the horizontal 'missionary position' so popular during their days in college, the lighted end cupped by the palm and pointing inward. It was a badge of common identity.

It was Stefán who broke the silence first. 'It's such a relief just to be able to talk to you,' he said. 'Do you know how long it's actually been?'

'I haven't kept track.'

'Ten years at least, maybe eleven . . .'

'As long as that?'

'As long as that. Strange, isn't it?' Stefán hesitated. 'What made you decide to see me? I half-expected you to ignore my plea. After everything between us . . .'

'It was your letter that did it,' András observed drily. 'The contents were a bit too mysterious to ignore, even by your standards.'

'My standards . . .' Stefán coloured. 'I suppose I might have taken offence at that at one time, but I'll let it pass now. So much has happened since.'

There was a brief silence, and then Stefán said, 'We'll stay in this room, if you don't mind.' Clearly committed to pursuing his own line of thought, he went on, 'Besides this room, there's only that one over there, behind me.' He paused and glanced at András emphatically. 'If you need anything at all, I will get it for you. You are free to walk around this room, naturally. You are also free to leave, if you so desire. But if I hold your attention for the next few hours, as I believe I will, and I say this through conviction, and not through any mistaken sense of self-importance, I'd really rather you didn't go into the other room. That's my only request.'

András heard out this curious speech without response. He sat down on the couch. 'Where are your books?' he asked, looking around. 'In the other room?'

'No. I got rid of them.'

'All of them? You had a lot of books.'

'Ah, yes, I suppose I did, didn't I? I had to sell them for food – Kafka for cabbage, Chekhov for potatoes – rather appropriate, don't you think? The ones that I couldn't sell I used as note-books. I wrote some of my best verse on pages of Tolstoy and

200

Dostoevsky.' He stopped speaking abruptly, and stood up. 'Is it cold in here? Are you cold? It can get very damp . . .'

It was very cold.

'No, it's not cold,' András replied.

'Well, then . . .' Stefán said, sitting down again. To his right, the bright light from the window cascaded into the room. András narrowed his eyes, creating an impression of looking at a dazzling stage at the same level as himself, with the curtains half-drawn and an actor sitting across from him preparing to recite his lines.

'Well, André . . .' Stefán began, his voice a bit uncertain.

'Well, Stefán?'

'Here we are now, all that's left of the Club. Just like old times.'

András had to correct him. He wasn't here to pretend. 'No,' he retorted, 'it's not just like old times. This is very different.'

Stefán looked at him in surprise. He tried to affect an air of indifference but it was too transparent and he sat back, his shoulders slumping. 'Yes, of course,' he replied wearily, 'you're quite right. Thank you for making that correction. It was good of you to point that out. This is obviously very different from old times. How could it not be?' Then, in a savage voice, he burst out, 'Just look at the state I'm in!'

András responded evenly, 'What about it?'

Stefán's voice rose: 'What about it? What about it?' He appeared to be at a loss for words. 'What about it?' he repeated. Then he calmed down, shaking his head and speaking almost to himself. 'What you see in front of you,' he said, 'is not all there is to see.'

'Fine,' András replied, 'I'll take your word for it.'

Stefán hesitated. 'Why are you being so hostile?'

'There are good reasons for that, wouldn't you agree?'

'What reasons?'

'The way you've been shadowing me over the years, for instance –'

Stefán ducked his head, as if to avoid a blow. He spread his hands and made a sign of acknowledgement.

'You have nothing to say?' András demanded. 'No explanation for that kind of surveillance?'

Stefán flushed. 'Yes, I followed you, I freely admit it. But it wasn't neurotic or anything like that. It was just that I desperately needed to talk to you, I desperately needed to make amends, driven as I was by guilt. Of course, the immutability of our past kept defeating me every time I approached you. I had no idea how to overcome it. That's why I kept following you around, like a dog. I just couldn't bring myself to walk up to you.'

András wondered if he ought to argue. He averted his face. 'You weren't very good at hiding yourself,' he said. 'You stuck out for miles.'

'It was a mistake,' Stefán said. 'In so many ways you had become a creature of my own making, once my dearest friend, now a combination of fact and fantasy. I don't know whether you'll understand it, but I suspect that the idea I had developed of our relationship had become far too complicated to translate into reality. That is why, at some point, I found that I simply couldn't walk out of the shadows and present my case to you, at least with any degree of coherence.'

He swallowed and shifted to the edge of his chair. 'I've been exhausted for a long time now, my life fragmented beyond belief.'

'So you followed me from street to street –'

'I knew it wasn't right, but I couldn't help myself.'

'Like a dog, you said.'

'My predicament constricted me.'

'What predicament?'

'The past, André! I've become a prisoner of the past. Can't you tell?'

András looked away impatiently.

'You don't understand!' Stefán said, his tone suddenly sharp. 'You've never understood anything! Do you think this is easy? Well, it isn't. You might've been able to put the past behind you, but I haven't. It's a skill I've never been able to master. The past haunts me like nothing else. I have to live with it every day of my life. But what's the use of telling you that? I've always lacked your resilience, your inhuman resilience. You always knew your mind. Your nerves were unshakeable. You never made mistakes. That's why I've always envied your ability to get on with living.'

'That still doesn't explain why you followed me.'

Stefán sank back. 'I can't tell you any more than I already have,' he replied. 'I've run out of words.'

'What did you hope to get from me?'

'Grace . . . salvation . . . a way out of this . . . labyrinth.'

'What did you find?'

'Nothing.'

'And what about yourself? Where was your own strength?'

'Strength wears itself out.'

András pursed his lips, clearly displeased. Stefán waited for a moment, and then he carried on, determined to make his point. 'In any case, this no longer matters. I stopped following you a year ago, around the time that I realized there was little to be gained. All of my life I'd been searching for a vessel for communion, a grail, or a medium, at the very least. And all of my life I'd been searching for that in externals and in others: in poetry, in János, in you and Immanuele and Ami. I'd been scouring the outside world for answers, and all the time they were contained within me.'

András smiled with a sudden irony. 'I told Andor Szegedy you were clandestinely watching a meeting between us at the Raven King's Bridge last week. I don't suppose you were there?'

'At the Raven King's Bridge?' Stefán stared at him, taken aback. 'No . . . I haven't been back there for years.'

'I thought as much. I've a good idea who was, though.'

'But I don't understand. Why did you bring me into your conversation with Szegedy?'

'I didn't bring you into it,' András said, a bit on the defensive. 'He did. He wanted to know your whereabouts.'

'But to tell him I was watching you! Why did you tell him that?'

András looked away. After a lengthy pause, he said, 'It had to do with the construction of signs. The construction of meanings, implications, identities.' He smiled again, humourlessly. 'What does it matter now, in any case? We're obviously in the same boat.'

Stefán looked down and appeared to draw himself in. He closed his eyes and hunched his shoulders, as if arriving at some internal conclusion. Then he opened his eyes and shook his head.

'I'm afraid we're no longer in the same boat, André,' he said slowly, 'or even on the same journey.'

András glanced pointedly at his watch. 'I'm sure that would provide the grist for another fascinating conversation between us, Stefán,' he said in an especially dry voice, 'but it doesn't explain why you've brought me here. I expect it would help if you . . . if you would get straight to the point.'

Stefán stood up restlessly, and then sat down again. If he felt offended by the other's abrupt interjection, he didn't show it. 'Yes, of course . . . the point and nothing but . . . vintage András. All right, have it your way, I'll do my best to be succinct.' He took off his overcoat and draped it with studied deliberation over the back of his chair.

'Do you recall the questions you used to ask, way back in the past, about image and reality? I was thinking about that today before I came to meet you. I was wondering how to explain everything that's happened.' He hesitated for an instant, and then he took out a battered blue notebook from his pocket and held it out to András. 'This is a journal that Immanuele appeared to have kept in the weeks before her disappearance,' he said. 'Someone slipped it under my door last week when I was out on a walk one evening.'

He paused for effect. 'Of course, what made things particularly interesting was the visit, the following day, by a police officer who claimed they'd discovered a waxwork of Immanuele on Margit Island. He said that after all these years they were reopening the case of her disappearance, and that the investigating officers would be very interested in knowing what I thought. I listened to what he had to say, but I didn't tell him about the journal. I preferred to keep it to myself, and I'm glad that I did, given what's gone on since.'

He sat up, morning street-sounds creeping into the room from the outside. Clearing his throat, he said, 'If I've caught you off guard, my apologies. I suggest we continue after breakfast. I'll go and warm the food up, it's already prepared. Why don't you relax in the meantime? The journal's yours to keep, of course. I don't have any use for it.' He stopped and looked at András. 'You've gone very quiet,' he said. He waited for a response, and when none was forthcoming, he shrugged and disappeared into the adjoining room, closing the door behind him.

András stared at the notebook in his hand. It made him instantly tired. Scanning through its pages, he realized that it covered the period following the entries in the diary that Clio had given him. He thought about the way in which he and Stefán had come into possession of the journals, right down to the similarity of their meetings with the police. The conclusion was inescapable. It was obvious that Clio had targeted the two people she'd identified as being closest to Immanuele.

His mouth set in a grim line, he wondered what could have inspired Stefán to confide in him. Not a sense of kinship, surely; there was too much between them for that. Nothing had transpired over the last few years to alter their mutual antipathy. That was what made this entire meeting intriguing.

He glanced around the shabby little room, his attention drawn to the stack of canvases leaning against Stefán's chair. He stood up and walked over to take a look. There were about a dozen of them, all depicting the clear surface of a river or a sea. One of them was markedly different from the others. It showed a white-haired man suspended just below the water. He was frozen in mid-stroke, his arms stretched out like wings. It was difficult to make out his features, but it was obvious that he was drowning, if not already dead.

The door between the rooms swung open and Stefán walked in with a plate of food. Setting it down, he said, 'Eat up.'

András began stacking away the canvases.

'I didn't know you had these,' he said. 'I've always wondered what happened to them.'

Stefán shrugged. 'I don't think Ami liked them very much. But you're welcome to them, I've already told you that. '

András picked up the plate of food. 'I like to keep track of her work,' he said.

'Of course, I can understand that.'

'There wasn't too much left by the end.'

'No, probably not. She gave most of it away. She didn't like the idea of selling it.'

205

'She wasn't very organized,' András said, 'she didn't keep catalogues or anything.'

'No, I don't suppose she did.'

'I really don't care either way. I want you to know that.'

'If I'd known that you wanted the paintings, André, I would've given them to you a long time ago. They mean nothing to me.' He hesitated. 'I also have her letters, but I intend to keep those. I read them almost every day. The writing's so faded she seems to be whispering.'

András refrained from saying anything. He watched as the other man walked over to the window.

Stefán nodded at the view. 'Ami used to stand here for hours on end. She liked to watch the gulls soaring. Way out over the river they would fly, sometimes south, sometimes north towards Esztergom. She loved the cathedral there.' He straightened unconsciously, his back erect. 'I remember everything about her,' he said. 'Her voice, the colour and substance of her words, the sensations she caused in me.' He smiled sadly, the sun throwing a criss-cross of light and shadow around him. When a cloud passed over the face of the sun, the light at the window diffused, and Stefán stepped away and returned to his chair. It was as if a shade had been pulled over his eyes.

'Is it any good?' he asked, indicating the food.

'Yes,' András replied, sounding more terse than he'd intended. In an attempt to compensate, he asked, 'What about you? Not eating?'

Stefán made an absent-minded gesture. 'No appetite . . . one of those things . . . perhaps a bit later.' He turned to leave the room. 'Let me fetch you some water.'

'Are you glad you came, André?' he called out.

'Glad? I don't know. No, I wouldn't say that.'

Stefán returned with the glass of water. 'I suppose not. I'm very grateful, though, for this opportunity to talk to you. I've been meaning to for a long time.'

András put his plate down and picked up the glass of water. 'Shouldn't we be getting back down to the matter of the waxwork?' he said. 'You were telling me about the detective who visited you the day after you discovered Immanuele's journal.'

'The detective,' Stefán began, 'was from the criminal investigation department. His name was Wagner, and when I asked him for identification, he showed me his papers. He said he'd come about a waxwork resembling Immanuele that they'd found on Margit Island. When I looked at him for clarification, he said there was reason to believe that I could help in making an identification.

I accompanied him to the police station. I was told there'd be a slight delay before the Inspector arrived. I was directed to a long table in one corner of the room with a group of people around it. As I took a seat, I noticed a girl sitting across from me. She was soaking wet, and she kept breaking into shivering fits. She looked at me as I sat down and gave a start, as if she recognized me. It was very odd; she kept staring at me after that, so that I was forced to look away.

Men in uniform sauntered in and out of the room, looking at our table and conferring in low voices. They kept glancing at the girl, she seemed to be the centre of their attention. One of them walked up to her and tried to talk to her, but she wouldn't answer him. The crackling sound of an intercom pierced through the room every few seconds. Somewhere else, I could hear a loud voice arguing on the telephone.

Someone tapped me on the shoulder. It was a policewoman, holding a form I'd filled out earlier. Handing it to me, she pointed out that I hadn't signed it. She waited while I scribbled. Then she addressed the girl. 'Clio . . .' she said dolefully, 'Clio . . . what will your father say when he finds out?'

I heard the wailing of police cars in the distance. Soon the station was inundated by the sound. It ceased abruptly just as a large man in uniform walked through the door and headed in my direction. I recognized him immediately: it was Andor Szegedy, János's older brother.

I stood up to greet him but he ignored me and rapidly crossed the room. He was walking purposefully towards the girl named Clio. There was a disdainful look on her face.

Szegedy approached her briskly but just before he reached her he hesitated and went down on his knees. He appeared to be praying. Then he stood up and signalled to the waiting police-men. They led her out of the room while he followed slowly behind.

I turned in surprise to the policewoman and she shook her head gloomily. 'That was the Inspector's daughter,' she said, in a low voice. 'There'll be all kinds of trouble now.'

Szegedy re-entered the room at that moment, giving me no time to react to what I had just heard. He walked directly over to where I was sitting, his face immensely troubled. Sitting down at the table, he looked past me, his mind obviously elsewhere. Then he pulled himself together, apologizing for having made me wait.

'I assume you know why you are here,' he began. 'We've found a waxwork resembling Immanuele Emperházy on Margit Island. I know it sounds strange, but we'd like some help from you. I'd planned to sit down with you tonight, but something else has come up. There's no point in wasting your time, so I'm arranging to have you taken back home. I'm afraid you're going to have to return here early tomorrow morning.' He waited for a moment in case I had any response. Then he stood up, excused himself and left the room.

That was it. The briefest of encounters, with no more ques-tions asked or information given, and I found myself being driven home in an unmarked police car. The driver was courte-ous and silent, and I was content to look out of the windows at the passing streets – I had quite enough to think about.

When we reached my apartment, I got out of the car and waited for it to leave, but the driver pulled over and parked on the other side of the street. Surprised, I hesitated for a moment before turning around and entering my building. As usual, the lift was out of order, and I had to take the stairs. The corridor to my apartment was dark – the lights had gone out – and as I fumbled for the keys, someone struck a match at my shoulder. Startled, I swung around. A man in a black overcoat was standing behind me. It was Wagner, the policeman who'd taken me to the station earlier that evening. 'I'll wake you in the morning,' he said smoothly. 'Have a good night.' I smiled uncertainly, not knowing what to say. I entered my apartment and shut the door firmly behind me.

The sound of my neighbour yelling at her ten-year-old son woke me the next morning. I got up and walked over to the windows. It was raining and very dark. As I stood there, collecting my thoughts, I heard footsteps. They stopped in front of my apartment. Anticipating the knock, I walked over to the door and opened it. It was the ubiquitous Wagner. He shouldered past me, heading for the telephone. He seemed to know exactly where it was. Picking it up, he dialled a number. 'I'm calling the station to find out what time you need to go over,' he explained. He spoke rapidly into the receiver. Then he replaced it and turned to me. 'Please get dressed,' he said. 'I'll wait for you in the lobby downstairs.'

Szegedy looked very different from the picture of disquiet he'd presented the previous night. He was wearing a business suit with an elegant blue tie. He looked up as I entered and motioned me to sit down. 'I used to read your work when I was younger,' he remarked. 'A pity you stopped writing. You ought to consider taking it up again.' He tore out a page from a pad in front of him and scribbled rapidly across it. Then he asked if I would like some coffee. I replied that I would.

While he poured the coffee, I examined my surroundings. The office was spartan. A single bookcase stood behind Szegedy's desk. Next to it there was a cabinet heaped with files, and above it a large street map of the city. A lopsided poster on the wall celebrated the virtues of summer holidays at Lake Balaton.

There was an open window behind the desk, looking out on to a derelict warehouse. The roof of the warehouse was wet with rain and it reflected a red neon street sign that alternately flashed '*kávé*', '*tea*' and '*kakaó*'.

Szegedy interrupted my thoughts: 'Now to the work of the day. Some paperwork, some procedural documents and, of course, the identification. Nothing unduly taxing.'

He passed over three sheets of typewritten paper from a folder. They contained a comprehensive description of the events surrounding the discovery of the waxwork. When I had finished reading, I returned the sheets to him. 'The waxwork's downstairs,' he said. 'I'd like you to identify it.'

I shook my head. 'I don't know if I want to.'

He studied me for a moment; he appeared more amused than not by my reticence. 'You're not even curious?'

'No, I'm not curious.'

'I'm afraid you don't have a choice. There are certain requirements that must be satisfied.' Before I could object, he reached down and pressed a bell below his desk. A large man walked into the room. Szegedy nodded a greeting, and then he turned to me, 'Sergeant Réti will take you to the waxwork. A necessary evil, but we'll try to keep it brief.'

Making it clear that I was unhappy with the situation, I followed the Sergeant out. We walked down a short flight of steps. On the way, he turned to me and asked, 'Do you juggle?'

'Excuse me?'

'Do you juggle? You know . . . throw things into the air and keep them there?'

'I'm afraid not,' I replied, baffled.

'Pity . . .' he said, 'you have the build.'

The room where the waxwork was turned out to be tiny and freezing cold. There was a flat-topped stainless steel table in the middle, a blue plastic sheet draped over the shape lying on it. A trolley stood beside the table, rows of plastic bottles dangling over its sides.

The Sergeant pointed at the table. 'I don't know what to say. I've never seen anything quite like this. It gives me the creeps.' He paused. 'If you feel sick or anything, feel free to step out.'

I nodded tensely, anxious to be done and out of there.

He fiddled with the buttons fastening the plastic sheet to the tabletop and moved out of the way. I walked forward, feeling ill, my throat parched and tight. The room suddenly felt deserted, the light hard and flat. Making an effort to control myself, I stared at the waxwork.

I pulled the sheet back . . . pulled it down to her knees.

It made a rustling sound.

I felt myself swaying on my feet.

There could be no mistaking . . .

210

I brushed away a loose fragment of wax.

There was a thin slit across her forehead . . .

It was like a precise surgical incision.

I pulled the plastic sheet over the waxwork and covered it. Clearing my throat, I said: 'I'm done.' Then I took the form that the Sergeant had placed on the table and signed it.

The policeman's voice was faint, 'Did you . . . recognize?' Without waiting for a reply, he took the form and signed his own name below mine. We left the room.

He walked beside me with long strides. 'Whoever did that should be put away,' he said with feeling.

I interrupted him. 'I'd rather not talk about it.'

'Of course,' he said, 'I'm sorry.'

Szegedy was leaning back on his chair, staring out of the window. He got up as we entered. Taking off his glasses, he looked inquiringly at the Sergeant, who handed him the form.

'So – it was a positive identification? Very well, Réti, thank you. I'll see you in the morning.' The Sergeant nodded and left the room.

Szegedy wrote in the margin of the form. 'We'll return to this tomorrow. I need to take you to Margit Island to establish a few facts . . . ask a few questions.'

I stared at him. 'I thought we were done. Why do I need to go to the island?'

'I'd like to show you where the waxwork was found.'

'Why's that relevant?'

'That's for me to decide, don't you think?'

I turned to leave, and then I stopped. 'I take it that you've already spoken to András Tfirst about this?'

'Yes,' he replied, curtly, 'I have.'

'Has he seen the waxwork?'

'No, he hasn't. I decided to spare him that. I think he has enough on his mind as it is. That's why I needed you to take a look at it. It had to be someone who knew her intimately, someone who could establish identity at a glance.' He hesitated for a moment, appearing to make up his mind. 'As a matter of fact,' he said, 'that's why I want to see you tomorrow. I want to talk to you about the Gabriel Club.' He gave me a smile faintly tempered with condescension. 'And that'll be the end of our association, I promise.'

The ride home was uneventful. The police car dropped me off and went over and parked across the street, as it had the previous evening. But there was a different policeman stationed in front of my apartment. He was younger, fair and tall. His name was Brander, he said, looking thoroughly bored with his assignment. He watched me as I unlocked my door and walked away without comment.

I spent the rest of the day trying to keep my mind off the morning's events. My strategy for distracting myself proved to be of little use, however, and the evening found me lying down with my eyes wide open, brooding.

It must have been nearly midnight when my sleepless ruminations were interrupted by a knock on the door. I walked over and opened it to find Brander standing outside. 'I wanted to make sure that things were all right,' he said, evading my outstretched arm and stepping into the apartment. Looking around, he carried on, 'What we have here, Mr Stefán, is a situation that entails our keeping an eye on you.' He smiled pleasantly at me. 'It's nothing to worry about,' he said. 'We're simply looking after your best interests.' He strolled back to where I stood watching him, skirting past me and shutting the door behind him.

◆

'You don't look too happy, André,' Stefán broke in. 'You look pensive, almost sad.'

'I'm listening to your voice and thinking.'

'About the past?'

András gave a dry smile. 'No. Not about the past. I haven't become that much of a sentimentalist.'

'What's wrong with being a sentimentalist?'

'It gets in the way of things.' András glanced around the room. 'And it gets in the way of life, doesn't it?'

Colouring, Stefán replied, 'I'm glad you've worked things out

for yourself so very differently. I've been happy for all your successes, pleased that one of us at least will have lived out his life
with honour and integrity.'

'Do I detect a trace of sarcasm there?'

'No, I'm being quite sincere, believe me. Perhaps I ought to
be sarcastic. Maybe that's what's called for, but I don't have the
energy. Nor do I think any point would be served by it. What's
obvious to me, though, is how much you've changed since we
knew each other before. There's a coldness to you now.'

'I'm sorry you find me cold, whatever that means.'

'You're guarded, wary. It's in your eyes. You weren't always this
controlled. Years ago you were quite different. You were volatile
and you spoke your mind to the point where I feared for your
safety. I hope you've grown out of that because it was impossible
to be with you when you were like that.'

'Impossible –' András observed wryly. 'Why?'

'Because you made me nervous. The whole business of dissidence was such a fix to you, that's why it was both so attractive
and at the same time such a dangerous undertaking. There had
to be something wrong with that kind of single-mindedness. I
used to wonder if you felt emotion like the rest of us. I know that
the others found it wonderful and stimulating but then again
they were a mad bunch themselves. János was definitely over the
top, and there wasn't too much that was right with Immanuele by
the end. Of course, when things went well, being with all of you
was absolutely exhilarating. The kind of fidelity you demanded
from life was uncanny. When you live life like that, everything
becomes an obsession. Everything has to be excessive, like a neu-
rosis. And you loved that, you clung to it. It was your mode of
survival, to challenge the dreariness that surrounded you with the
substance of your imaginings. But I wasn't made for that, I had
no appetite for it. For me, being with the three of you could be
nightmarish.'

'Why did you stay?' András said sharply. 'No one forced you.
You could have left at any time.'

'I wanted to serve you,' Stefán replied. 'But also to save you.'

András raised an eyebrow. 'How so?'

'Oh, I deluded myself into believing that I could safeguard the lot of you from your own crazy undertakings. Have you forgotten the things you used to come up with? Immanuele's plan to blindfold the Statue of Liberty on May Day. János's scheme to project film footage of the 1956 uprising on to the façade of Parliament on the eve of that Soviet minister's visit. You can't deny that I was the one who dissuaded you from these things, usually at the last possible moment. You wouldn't be sitting here now if I hadn't stepped in the way I did.'

'Then you think you did us a favour?'

'I don't know about that. All I wanted was to hold up mirrors to all of you, to show you how you had become such fragments of your own fictions, bizarre and out-of-control and eccentric. So much abstraction that in the end it left no room for any form of objectivity. That's why the Club went so wrong; it had become masochistic, fetishistic – nihilistic. But that was in the nature of the beast you'd created. When you think like that, you can fit in for a while but ultimately it's addictive. It takes over and when it's done there's very little room left to breathe and to carry on with the living. That's what happened to János, he burned out at both ends, he had no energy left to survive, he'd forgotten how to exist. And to a large degree, it's also what happened to Immanuele. But you were the champion, André, you surpassed all of them. It was as if there were some place inside your head that had gone completely insane. I kept wishing you'd calm down a bit, if only for the sake of our collective sanity. I longed for us to cultivate some other way to deal with our condition, something like an ironic detachment, even a sense of humour. But in the end it was the very intensity of our fire that consumed us. Or, at least, I know that it consumed me. How could I carry on after that without breaking down? My nerves were shot to bits.'

'Why didn't you try to leave the country if things were that unbearable?'

'Of course, you would ask me that! The question of exile, that eternal whore! Oh – but I did think about it – I agonized endlessly. But tell me, where would I have gone? Munich, Vienna, Lisbon, Rio? Australia, Canada, London, Mexico?' He pulled a face. 'Ami was so convinced New York was the answer. It was the world to her, she couldn't hear enough about it. Central Park,

Broadway, Fifth Avenue, Times Square. Heaven knows I would love it there! Rib-cage inside a steel-cage under an alien sky! A poet from Hungary, here I am, give me a new life, a job, a fantasy. What would I be? An astronaut? A car salesman? A guest lecturer? A doormat? Open a vending stand, drive a taxi-cab? Run an émigré journal, invent a community? Constantly homesick, constantly heartsick, increasingly distanced, scrabbling for funds! From social engineering to cold, hard cash! From Leviathan to damned Mammon! Hardly any kind of –' he searched for the right word, 'solution. And I didn't want to leave here, despite everything. I didn't want to go away even if staying meant the sky would always be out of reach. I knew the language of exile was simply not one I would be comfortable with. Where's the logic in that, you might ask? There was none, you see. When it came down to the bottom line, the cost-benefit analysis just didn't add up for me. I didn't want to leave, I didn't want to run away. I love this stupid country and not because of patriotism, not that at all. It was much more than that, or so I wanted to believe . . .'

He stood up and began walking around slowly, the thick brew of mid-morning light pouring in from the window. 'János, in a similar state of mind, once confided to me that the brute resolution would be to simply give up and give in. Accept the way things were, learn to live within narrowly defined limits. But he also said that was a resolution denied to people like us. He claimed that as intellectuals we had a larger role to play, a larger responsibility. I don't recall his exact words, but they made sense under the circumstances. But then he went ahead and blew himself up in that car. What a meaningless end! It was so inconsistent with the way he'd spoken about things, it suggested that that kind of passion could never really coexist with the banalities of day-to-day living.'

He stopped pacing and faced András. 'But then again, you proved to be the biggest surprise of all. I was resigned to your fate, do you know that? Every day I waited for the news of your demise. After János died, I counted the days it would take for you to crack. After Immanuele disappeared, it could only be a matter of time before they did you in. But you survived it all. Of the four of us, you, of all people, kept your head above water. There's no

215

explaining it. Looking at you now I marvel at that and I also feel tremendously tired because I don't know how you did it. I'd like to say that I know you too well to be taken in by your façade. I'd like to say that what I see before me is precisely that – a façade – but I can't, and that unsettles me. I look at you now and acknowledge that perhaps I didn't know you at all, and perhaps none of us did. I have no idea how your mind works. I wonder if I ever did.'

András stirred testily. 'What are you implying?'

'The implication's clear, isn't it?'

'Not to me, it isn't.'

There was an edge to Stefán's voice as he replied, 'You were stronger than any of us, André. You were the fulcrum, we the outposts. That's why you shouldn't have stopped writing. You shouldn't have stopped the way you did.' He hurried on when he saw András about to interrupt. 'I know you had your reasons, but the writing should've risen above everything else, it should've been the last refuge, despite Immanuele, despite Ami. That kind of intellectual fierceness, that kind of fiendish integrity – it gave people hope, they looked up to you, there was no one else to turn to after you quit. You were their inspiration, and that inspiration abandoned was a terrible thing.'

András made a dismissive gesture. 'I can't be held responsible for the world.'

'Once you were filled with dreams.'

'Even dreams bear their own kind of responsibility.'

'But dreams nevertheless? Dreams of a world without walls, without barriers, armies, boundaries!'

'Immaculate dreams –' András retorted witheringly, 'assertive and pure, lures for private relief.'

'In demeaning yourself, you demean the whole Club.'

There was a tense moment of silence, and then András replied with less acerbity, 'It wasn't my intention to demean anyone. I was commenting on myself, that's all. I don't think the two should be confused. And as for the Club, that was an entirely different matter. We made signals in the forest for others to follow. We planted hopes like flags. That was our legacy. It's the way I'd like to look back on us. We did more than most. We did more than enough.'

'Perhaps that's true,' Stefán persisted, 'but consider the rest of us: where are we all now? Where are we who promised to ignite new revolutions with the tinderboxes of our scripts? Where are all the books that were supposed to have been written? Those rumours of manuscripts hidden in drawers, those epics that would forever alter the way things were perceived? No, no, André, we know better now. Our spirits are finished – we're the ones destined for the rubbish heap of history!'

'That may be so,' András responded drily, 'but you keep forgetting one thing.'

'And what is that?'

'You invited me here for a very specific purpose, to tell me about the events surrounding the discovery of the waxwork.'

Stefán didn't answer immediately. He looked away, a hint of sadness in his face, but also bewilderment, as if he were wondering what else he could say to make his visitor less remote. With a stiff gait, he walked over to Ami's portrait on the wall and studied it. Behind him, he heard András shift. For a moment, he entertained the idea of giving up and asking him to leave. Then he dismissed the notion as unrealistic. Instead, he turned around and said softly, 'I must be the only one left who still believes in dreams.' He looked at András very deliberately. 'And you? You were once a sanctuary, but now you've become a fortress: defensive, transfixed.'

'That's beside the point,' András replied evenly. 'I am not a fortress, and this is not a game, or even a battlefield.'

'No, this is not a game,' Stefán concurred, with a frigid smile, 'or at least, not one worth playing. But we are already well into it.'

'Your move, then, I take it?'

◆

'The telephone rang at seven the next morning,' Stefán resumed. 'It was Szegedy. He apologized for calling me so early, but he wanted to change the time of our meeting to five that afternoon.

217

He said that he hoped it wouldn't inconvenience me, and hung up.

Having stayed up most of the night, I tried to sleep through the rest of the day. When I left the apartment that evening, the unmarked police car was parked across the street as usual, and I was driven directly to Margit Bridge where Szegedy, I was told, was waiting for me. We arrived at the bridge at the same time as he did. I asked him why it had been necessary to post policemen outside my apartment but he brushed the question aside.

We walked down from the bridge to the island. Following a path through the trees we came to an embankment that sloped down to the water. A row of slatted wooden benches ran along it. Szegedy walked over and invited me to sit down.

'I love this river,' he said. 'Look how slow it is here. It almost seems placid enough to swim in. And yet there are whirlpools along its course that can take a ship down.' He paused contemplatively. 'My father was a deck-hand on the Dunakanyar steamer route. He used to tell me there was nothing more treacherous than those whirlpools, not even women. He was very disappointed when I didn't follow in his footsteps. He said it took a real man to work the river. Only a real man, he believed, could battle its moods and tame its waters.'

He picked up a stone and threw it into the river. We watched it break the surface of the water, and then Szegedy stood up and pointed in the direction of a distant pier. 'We should be moving on before it gets any darker . . .'

A straight line of trees cut across the path, hiding our destination from us. As we approached the trees, Szegedy began speaking again. He seemed to be in a very introspective mood. 'Look at that wall of aspen trees. There's something so melancholic about them, don't you think? They remind me of a poem by a Prague poet describing a walk through the woods with his father. They are walking towards a group of aspens just like the one before us, when one of the trees suddenly and inexplicably begins to shiver. There is no wind around them, the atmosphere is completely still, and neither can find any explanation for the tree's strange behaviour. The poet turns to his father and is touched by a strange premonition. He notices that his father has

218

turned deathly pale, that he appears to be in mortal fear. Without a word exchanged between them, they turn on their heels and walk away from the tree, their hearts heavy with apprehension. In an afterword to the poem, the poet notes his father's death only a few days later.'

'Why are you telling me this?'

'I don't know,' Szegedy replied. 'Must there be a reason for everything?'

We approached the trees and walked through them without slowing down. We left the path we'd been walking on and made towards the pier. Dusk was rapidly encroaching, and there were dark shadows in the water.

Szegedy walked down a flight of steps to the pier. 'This is where they found the waxwork,' he said.

I joined him on the pier. The water was brown and dark and choked with weeds.

'I've seen a lot of strange things in my life,' he carried on, 'but this was the strangest yet. When we first hauled it out I thought it was some kind of bizarre and especially tasteless prank. And when we turned it over, I noticed how exact the resemblance was, and the surface discolourations that looked like bruises.' He sat down on the pier and picked at a splinter. 'It caused quite a sensation among the men.'

'The report you let me read stated that the waxwork must have been found during the night. Have you established an exact time?'

'We're estimating it was around the same time the boy was reported missing.'

'And you believe that it was this boy who dragged the waxwork out of the coffin and into the river?'

'We can only assume that's what happened. Of course, a number of things must have transpired between the time of its discovery and its subsequent despatch into the river. But that's only one of many possible hypotheses.'

'There are others?'

'There are always others.'

'Such as?'

He looked around carefully before replying. 'Have you ever been to a nightclub called the Totalitarian Zone?'

I gazed at him, mystified. 'the Totalitarian Zone? Where is it?'

'It's in the old city.'

'Why do you ask? Is it pertinent?'

'Naturally. Everything is pertinent. This nightclub also alternates as a café and a performance space. The people who gather there are very peculiar. And there are some pretty strange sculptures in there as well. Sculptures made of wax. There's even one hanging from the ceiling.'

'I don't think I follow –'

'There's a mirror in that café, also made of wax.'

'A mirror made of wax?'

'Yes.' He edged towards me and dropped his voice: 'In a small room curtained off from the rest of the space, there is an exquisite rococo statue of an angel.'

'An angel, in a nightclub?'

'Not just any angel. The archangel Gabriel.' He paused and lit a cigarette. 'The first time I saw it, I thought it was so gorgeously incongruous. But it's typical of the place.'

He leaned forward confidentially. 'I went there a couple of nights ago. We'd received reports of some very funny going-ons so we decided to find out for ourselves. What we saw there wasn't pleasant.' He paused, lost in contemplation. 'Very, very nasty, this skinhead resurgence,' he added. 'It makes one wonder what's really been happening over the past forty years . . .'

He turned to me with a faint glitter in his eyes. 'But the important thing is, what information can *you* give me about the place?'

'I have no idea what you're talking about.'

He stood up and pressed his hands down on my shoulders. Leaning the full weight of his body on me, he said, 'What are you hiding? What are you concealing? Who are you trying to protect?'

I controlled myself and looked at him coldly. 'I'm afraid I have no idea what you mean, Andor. Incidentally, you're beginning to hurt me. I have a bad back.'

He gazed at me for a few seconds, all traces of his former conviviality gone. When he resumed speaking, it was with an air of studied indifference. 'Get yourself a good lawyer.'

'Get myself a lawyer?'

'That's what I said.'

'Why should I? What does any of this have to do with me?'

'Perhaps nothing at all, but it's always good to cover all eventualities. I wouldn't want you to feel that you hadn't done enough to protect yourself.'

'Protect myself? From what?'

He looked at me, deadpan. 'Possibilities.'

'Possibilities? I have no idea what you mean.'

'I'm talking about something black, I'm talking about what happened that night in March seventeen years ago.'

I shook my head. 'I'm not following any of this. There must be a mistake.'

He gave me a quick smile. 'Oh, I wish it were a mistake, but it isn't, and you must treat it with the utmost seriousness. You do understand, don't you, that unless you're open with me, we're simply going to talk right past each other?' When I kept silent, he walked in a circle around me and planted himself in front of me so that I would have to look him in the eye. 'Tell me about the Gabriel Club,' he said.

'I was wondering when you'd get round to that. Why the need to digress?'

'I'd like to be the one who asks the questions here, if you please. Now, why don't you go on ahead and tell me what the Club was about.'

I considered him in exasperation. Then I said: 'It was about hunger.'

'Hunger?'

'The hunger of the spirit.'

'What spirit?'

'The compass of the universe.'

'And in slightly less abstract terms?'

'The counter to impoverishment.'

'How so?'

'Through the shared experience of words. Words to fight the hunger with.'

'And what did you seek to propagate?'

'The freedom of the individual. The rights of man.'

221

'Freedom – a nebulous concept.'

'To you, perhaps.'

'And did you feel as strongly about free will?'

'Yes, of course.'

'The common good?'

'No. Not that. Not that at all.' I looked at him sardonically. 'We left that to the likes of you. How could we possibly have been so presumptuous?'

'Then it was about the narrowest kind of self-interest?'

'Self-interest?' I had to smile. 'No, I don't think so.'

'What did you seek, then?'

'Rapture.'

'Rapture?'

'The death of grief. The birth of grace.'

'Ah, it was about passion, then?'

'Perhaps.'

'And what about death? Did you see death as voluptuous?'

I turned away and glanced at the river. 'What a strange light on the water,' I remarked.

'Is there, Stefán? And what about my question?'

'I have nothing more to say.'

'Nothing? Nothing at all? You've thought carefully about this? Very well, no more questions.' He glanced at me with a disconcerting mix of curiosity and indifference. Then he tilted his head, suddenly formal. 'Thank you for your time. I sincerely wish we could've met under more fortunate circumstances, but be that as it may . . .' He gave me his hand and pulled me to my feet.

We walked rapidly back through the trees. Night was falling, fleet and dark, and there were blue shadows across the path. Emerging into the open, we turned towards the bridge. Szegedy said briskly, 'There will be a car waiting for you on the bridge, a white sedan. You shouldn't have any problems finding it.' He shook my hand. 'Good evening.'

It was getting colder and I drew my collar up. Moving into the shadow of a tree, I watched him walk away. Presently, he was joined by a couple of men who appeared from the vicinity of Margit Bridge. As he addressed them, they turned and looked in my direction. Then they all moved away.

Stefán looked at András with a tired smile. 'Some more tea now, André . . . or, later, perhaps?'

'Now's fine, Stefán,' András drawled, feeling inexplicably drowsy. He watched Stefán make for the adjoining room and shut the door behind himself. Wondering at his secretiveness, András picked up his glass of water. Raising it to his face, he pressed it against his cheek. He held it before his eyes and looked through it at the portrait of Ami on the wall. Tilting the glass to one side, he dissolved her into bubbles.

A gaggle of voices floated in from the street.

'It's my birthday tomorrow,' he said, for no particular reason, when Stefán returned.

'Congratulations, André!' Stefán replied, surprised. He placed the cup of tea on the floor by András. 'Heartfelt congratulations! God! I wish I had some wine –'

András pointed to the tea. 'This will do.'

Stefán perched himself on the edge of his chair and closed his eyes. He sat motionless for a moment. Then he gave a wan smile. 'You know, André,' he said, 'it's funny to hear myself go on like this. I'm talking so much I'm beginning to feel like a fool, especially in comparison to you. They say you didn't speak at all for four years after Ami's accident. Not a word. I can understand that. I went a little crazy myself. But life's like that, wouldn't you say? I mean, look at us now. We used to have such an amazing rapport. Nothing was secret between us. We were brothers in all but name. You were my idol, I saw in your quest my own desire for freedom. That was the meaning of the fierce circle you created with Immanuele. To me, proximity to the two of you was like living in a vortex, sucked in one moment and left for dead, ejected into a dazzling cosmos the next. I'm sure János felt the same way. Because the rest was madness. It had to be; madness to try and defeat reality and attempt to transmute it into some semblance of self-respect.' He smiled mirthlessly. 'That's why, after what happened to Ami, I had to get away from you. There was no other way for me. I had to lose myself in the city. Become a face in the crowd. No more free fall. None of that pain. Now that I think back on it, I feel ashamed. I can't look you in the eye. I qualify my statements so many times. Where is the justice in this world? That's why I don't know any more. I don't know who you are, I don't know the world, and I don't know myself. There's no breaking through this wall of time.'

He sat perfectly still, his face turned to the window. Somewhere in the building a door rattled in the draught and he lifted his head to listen. He seemed to have become quite oblivious of András. 'I had so much to offer,' he said with a catch in his voice, 'so much to give – what went wrong?'

He stood up and walked over to the window and lit a cigarette.

András stood up as well. He reached into his jacket and took out the two cigars he'd brought along. He offered one to Stefán. 'From Cuba,' he said. 'Quite an experience. To your health,' he added.

Stefán accepted the cigar and examined it. 'Ah, the fruits of success! You know, André, I have to admit there've been times when I've wondered whether I should envy you your success, but I never have.' He caught András gazing at him and said, 'Thanks for the cigar.'

He patted András awkwardly on the shoulder. 'How is Ami, by the way? I've been meaning to ask.' Sensing the other tense, he instantly regretted his question. 'You needn't reply,' he muttered under his breath. 'It was stupid of me to ask.'

András looked at him as if he hadn't heard. 'Ami is the same,' he said.

'No change at all?'

'None expected.'

Stefán looked away. Then he turned around abruptly and left the room. After a while, András heard him call out: 'Do you know, I have a splendid picture of her somewhere. Would you like to see it? Yes, of course you would!' He hurried back into the room, fishing into a canvas satchel and taking out a photograph. He held it out to András, who took it carefully, as if it were made of glass. They looked at each other for a moment, then Stefán backed slowly out of the room and shut the door again.

Ami . . .

She was wearing her skin like a white dress. The photographer had used a filter to dissolve the outlines into the surrounding snow. Only her head rose out of that oblique haze, her hair cascading down on either side of her face.

András closed his eyes.

Hello, Ami.

Hello, André.

Feels strange, doesn't it?

She smiled at him, her mouth half-open, lips shaping her words:

Strange? Why?

You can hardly expect me to be comfortable in this situation.

Things change, André.

Her hair fell across her eyes.

He brushed it back. An old habit. It made her smile.

You're just like winter, André.

What do you mean?

You're so cold. Your voice. Your touch. Everything.

It feels so very strange, being here, like this, the three of us . . .

Yes, but you're the one. You are my king. You know that.

Ami, I . . .

Stefán walked back into the room. 'You know, André,' he said, 'when I was young, I used to believe, with an obscure prescience, that time would resolve everything. Now, of course, the knowledge – even eternity has an end . . .' He broke off, regarding András with an expectant air.

'What's the matter?' András asked uneasily.

'Ah . . . it's just that . . . is there to be no going back, André?'

'What do you mean?'

'Is there to be no forgiveness?'

András's face drained of colour.

'One can either be completely faithful to one's resolutions or not at all,' he said, his voice clipped. 'There is no room for half-measures in my world. By that standard I can never forgive you. There can be no forgetting, no going back.'

Stefán looked down at his hands. 'I'm sorry, André . . .'

András considered him without sympathy. 'You're mad to

225

believe that I could forgive you,' he carried on. 'How could you expect it? Every single day I live with the consequences of what was done. Every day, do you know what that means?' He struggled to recover his composure.

Stefán sank deeper into his chair. 'It was an accident,' he said, his voice hollow. 'It was an accident.'

A silence fell in the room. Somewhere in the background a tap began to drip. Stefán wiped his forehead feverishly. 'I'm sorry, André,' he said again. 'I should have known better than to make that appeal.'

Before András could say anything, Stefán hurried on, 'Tell me, though, what could I have done differently? What would you have done in my position?'

'How can you look to me, of all people, for an answer to that question?'

'I don't know.' Stefán glanced away hopelessly. 'I don't know any more. Maybe it's time to let go.'

'I have no palliatives for you, Stefán, if that is what you're asking for. I told you that years ago. There's been no reason to change my mind since.'

'Of course,' Stefán said, with a rush of bitterness. 'But have you ever wondered how I've lived with the guilt?'

'There are some things I'd rather not know about,' András retorted.

'You might have wondered,' Stefán answered. He wiped his hands furiously on his shirt. 'But there's no moving you. All I was trying to do was to ask you for your help. For your sake as much as for Ami's.'

'I didn't know you had either of our interests at heart. It's going to take me a while to get used to this renewed concern.'

Stefán's voice rose, 'Do you think it's been easy to live the way I have? What do you think I've been trying to tell you all this time? It's just that I've always believed in the eventual resolution of things. But I also realize that I'm very good at fooling myself. Believe me, every time I stand before a mirror, I ask: Why me? Why did this have to happen to me? I look at myself – these bluish veins, growing darker with age, these uncertain eyes, this scar, here, below the chin, the fact of this inadequate fate – and I

226

ask, how could suicide be anything but the right thing after all that has gone on, how could it be anything but the right decision? And what does that matter even, the issue of what is *right* . . . the moral question, the ethics of the thing? I mean, who cares when it's all over and done with? Once I'm dead and planted deep under the ground, people will simply dismiss it as yet another easy escape: label it, reduce it, condemn it. And why even care about that anyway? Since what happened to Ami, I've had no desire to live. I've truly wanted to put an end to it. Perhaps not a very convincing reason, but better than to try to carry on when the object of my love no longer existed.'

András held the teacup to his lips, his eyes meditating along its rim. When he started speaking, his voice was very tired. 'The object of love, if I may use your expression, will *always* fall short of the expectations imposed upon it. It will *always* be compromised by itself. The faculty of feeling that we term love is sustained by an idea, an abstraction that is quite independent of the object that initially inspires it. From that point of departure, everything – desire, respect, hope, trust – becomes a matter of the imagination. And it's only when the imagination dies that life truly ends. Anything else is a sham. And as for the matter of suicide,' he added drily, 'my own belief is that if one were truly capable of killing oneself, one would no longer have to carry it out. The knowledge of that capability would be enough to make the act itself irrelevant.'

Stefán's face darkened. 'Are you calling me a coward?'

'No, I'm not calling you a coward. I am simply wondering aloud at your ability to simplify things.'

'Maybe I *am* crying out for a resolution of things! Unlike you, I've never been able to suppress my feelings. I mean, look at me, barely surviving from day to day, and all because I can't even hide inside my own skin!'

'That's hardly logical, Stefán, and you ought to know that – you more than anyone.'

Stefán gave an exasperated smile. '*Life* is not logical, André,' he replied. 'Why must death be so? Or love, for that matter? To strive for the impossible, to attempt to achieve that, one must first, quite literally, go insane.'

227

'Or surrender to the imagination,' András countered. 'It's a matter of perspective, I know, but one that makes a significant difference.'

Stefán shook his head in disagreement. 'It's in the eye of the beholder, isn't it?'

He paused, contemplative. 'In any case, let's move on to something else. Something a lot less complex and much more pleasant. There's some cognac on the floor behind the couch. Feel free to help yourself.'

András stood up and surveyed the floor. 'Stefán,' he said, 'there's no cognac here . . .'

'What? Oh, well, I suppose I must have drunk it. Look under the couch, though. There's a bouquet of flowers there. I bought them yesterday from the vendor across the street. A bouquet of roses. I'd like you to give them to Ami. Write my name on the card. Will you promise me that?'

'Of course.'

'It would mean a lot to me.'

'I'll give her the bouquet.'

András looked under the couch. He couldn't see any flowers. He eyed Stefán dubiously. 'What's going on? There are no flowers here.'

'Of course there are. They're blood-red and lying on the floor, partly wrapped up in paper. Take another look, please.'

András went down on his hands and knees and searched under the couch. Then he stood up, his face heavy with irritation. 'No, there's nothing here. There are no flowers under the couch or anywhere else in this room. See for yourself if you don't believe me.'

Stefán looked at him enigmatically. Then he gave a strangely satisfied smile, looking much more animated. 'But there *are* flowers there, András! Only you can't see them! Just as you couldn't see the cognac either. You see, they're a part of my reality, not yours. So much for surrendering to the imagination.' Evidently pleased with himself, he turned his back on András. Then he turned around again and said: 'Watch this.' His hand slipped out from the shadows surrounding him and sank towards the floor. He left it there, suspended above the floorboards. 'Now, André,' he asked, 'what do you see?'

'I see your hand suspended above the floor.'

'Wrong, you see my hand picking up a fistful of earth from a ploughed field, and here –' he raised his fist, a fresh red rose nestling inside it, '– you see a flower.'

'What's your point?' András snapped.

'My point is that the virtues of your precious imagination are hardly as absolute as you would choose to believe; on the contrary, they're not only relative but quite dangerous.'

'Dangerous? Why?'

'Because what you term the imagination is nothing but an extreme form of self-delusion. Madness, really.'

'Madness?'

'Yes, it's exactly like madness. It has that same peculiar clarity: sharp and jittery. And somewhere in there one can sense a tensing, a tautening, a breaking down of things. An unravelling, like insomnia on the verge of waking.'

'And what does *that* mean?'

'It's the death wish.'

'I'm not sure I understand.'

'No? I'm not surprised, André. I'm not at all surprised. I didn't think you would.' He smiled morosely. 'When I used to write poetry, I'd spend days on end obsessing over a single word. I'd select it carefully and hold it in my head. Consider it for hours, lay it out, turn it around, hold it upside down, listen to it whisper, listen to it breathe. I'd imagine the sounds it made; silently, in the mind, as well as what it would sound like when read out loud. And then I'd say to myself: No! this it too flat! It has no life! It must be done differently! And I'd carry on like that endlessly. What is that if it's not madness? When one finds oneself preferring the company of words to the reality of experience, life has already become a delusion and a mistake. That's why Mr Kafka had the right idea: one must burn it all. Either that, or produce the book of perfect poetry, never again to be surpassed, a book with nothing written on it, page after page of pristine white emptiness. Nothing to speak to the reader but the wide-eyed silence of the pages. *C'est le commencement de la fin.*'

András set his jaw in a stubborn line. 'That is neither coherent nor logical, Stefán.' He shrugged irritably. 'And what is more –

and I hate to draw your attention to this just as you're getting into the thick of things – there's a smell in this room, as if something's rotting, and I'm beginning to find it hard to ignore.'

Stefán sat back on his chair, visibly annoyed at the digression. 'A smell? I don't know,' he muttered, 'it could be the drains . . .' He looked around. 'There should be a few incense sticks in that box with Ami's paint-brushes. I'll light one.'

The air filled with a sickly sweet aroma.

Stefán walked back to his chair, his head held down. The midday sun caught his face as he passed the window. He seemed very tense as he sat down, restlessly crossing and uncrossing his feet. His hand touched his throat and then he turned and looked towards the room behind him. The door was still firmly shut. With a sidelong glance at András, he lit a cigarette. 'What are you looking at?' he asked.

'The play of shadows across your walls,' András replied.

'They are shadow spirits, André. Their meaning's in their mystery.'

'Our meeting's a bit like that, isn't it?'

'What are you implying?'

András hesitated, measuring his response. At length, he said, 'I'm not very good with shadow-plays, Stefán. Especially when everything – even the most minute detail of all this – is beginning to appear carefully staged.'

'Staged?' Stefán repeated quietly. 'Is that what you think? I suppose I ought to take umbrage, but don't worry, I'm not put out. I'll guide you through the shadows as I go on.'

◆

'Darkness had fallen,' Stefán said, 'by the time I walked back to Margit Bridge. There was only one car there, a grey sedan, not white, as Szegedy had described. As I hesitated, a man called out from inside: 'Please! Your car! – the other one had a mechanical problem.' Reassured, I began walking towards the car when I noticed that it had three other occupants. They were all quite young and pleasant-looking, but there was something about them that wasn't quite right. Disguising my uneasiness, I leaned in through the window and explained that I felt like walking. I thought I could take the tram home. Two of the men got out and smilingly blocked my way. One of them had a clip-board in his hand. He handed it to me, explaining that I would have to fill out the attached form. The Inspector had given them strict instructions to escort me home. It was all a matter of procedure, he explained. He smiled apologetically, the door to the car yawning open behind him. Recognizing that further argument was futile, I folded my wings and squeezed in.

We drove quickly across the bridge and headed west. I looked at my companions in surprise. 'Excuse me,' I said, trying to keep my voice steady, 'but we seem to be going the wrong way.'

They turned to me and smiled, appearing to find what I'd said amusing. The man to the right of me laughed. He explained that they were only making a slight detour before dropping me off. Familiar landmarks flashed past as I watched helplessly. We passed Eagle Hill. We passed a graveyard lit with candles. We drove for long stretches without houses or streetlights. The sky was overcast, and there was a strange, fugitive excitement inside the car. My temples began to throb, I felt claustrophobic and sick. Turning to my companions, I insisted that I be let out because I was feeling ill.

They looked at each other and then one of them turned to me and said, 'Is that so, Mr Stefán?' He turned and addressed one of his companions. 'Here?'

'Yes.' The man sitting to my left spoke for the first time, his face in shadow. 'This will do. Stop the car.'

The car slowed down and pulled over. The man on my left opened the door and climbed out, motioning me to follow him. We walked over to a deep ditch separating the road from a field. I was about to turn around when I felt a knuckled fist press into the back of my neck. Softly, mockingly, his voice dancing with a strange irony, the man behind me said, 'We don't really want to hurt you, you do realize that, don't you?' He hit me sharply on the back of the head. 'But we don't pretend, Stefán. This isn't a game with us.'

I tried to protest but he hit me again. 'Don't interrupt me. I don't like being interrupted. Now listen carefully. What do you know about the waxwork? Who's behind this ridiculous charade?'

I remained silent.

His voice hardened, 'Very well. It's going to be like that, is it? Get down on your knees.'

I knelt down. 'What are you going to do to me now?'

'Now? Why, now I'll show you the instruments, my friend. Put your feet together. Don't try to move or turn around.'

It was at that point, quite incongruously, that I saw a couple of shadowy forms rise to their feet and detach themselves from the darkness ahead of us. I saw one of the forms fumbling and then a torch switched on and pointed straight at us. Behind its dazzling glare, I made out a young couple, the boy holding on to the girl's hand and looking quite irritated. I heard him ask what was going on, his voice pitched high, while his companion laughed nervously.

The man behind me began to curse, the words following hard and fast below his breath. He spat furiously on the ground, and I heard his footsteps shuffling slowly backwards. There was a moment of silence, and then he broke into a run. Someone called out and I heard a car door slam. An engine coughed to life and the grey sedan swerved off into the night.

I rose to my feet. I saw the couple with the torch step forward and a feminine voice asked me anxiously if I was all right. The boy seemed much more put out by the rude interruption of their love-making and I heard him mutter an obscenity. But I was far too relieved to take his comments personally. I scrambled out of the ditch. I heard the boy snicker as I slipped on a piece of wet turf and lurched forward, but I was in no mood to quibble. Elated by my improbable escape, I hastened away from the field.

The road I found myself on had large houses on either side of it, their black bulks merging into one another. I followed its contours until it banked upwards and opened into a large deserted square. I spotted a tram, its generator purring. With a silent word of thanks, I hurried up to it and clambered in.

As I settled into my seat, the man opposite me stared at my

face. He asked me if I knew that my forehead was bleeding. I stood up and looked in the mirror next to the running board. There was a gash just below my hairline. I accepted the handkerchief the man offered me and kept it pressed to my forehead for the rest of the trip.

♦

Stefán stopped speaking and gazed at András with concern. 'You look pale,' he said. 'Are you feeling all right?'

'I have a bit of a headache,' András replied, stirring slowly.

'I'll bring you some more tea. It might help.'

András hesitated. Impatient at the delay, Stefán stood up, the afternoon sun visible through the window behind him. It made his head appear transparent, the light flooding through a forest of veins and arteries. Dazzled, András looked away. 'Look –' Stefán prompted, 'I'll get you the tea, it'll do you good.' He hurried out of the room, returning with a steaming cup. He set it down beside András. 'You'd better taste it.'

'It tastes fine,' András replied. 'Thank you for asking.'

'If it's bitter, it's because I've added apricot brandy.'

'It's fine,' András replied, 'I don't think I can taste the brandy.'

In the silence that followed, Stefán walked over to the window and looked out to where the sun had gone behind a bank of clouds. It grew dark swiftly, an extremely warm and sunny day turning suddenly black. From far away they heard the crack of thunder. Lightning flashed. A fine rain began to fall, swiftly and steadily. In the distance, the sky separated into three distinct bands: a light grey over the city shading into a darker grey and then into black.

Stefán turned away from the window. 'It's strange, isn't it, the way the sky changes colour with the onset of rain?' He walked to the corner of the room where he retrieved a small black umbrella. He opened it above his head. 'One day, André, you'll remember all this,' he said, with a fleeting smile.

András smiled back without irony; the umbrella reminded him

of high school, for some reason, of rain-drenched afternoons spent tinkering with brightly coloured models of atoms and molecules, all his attention devoted to attracting the prettiest girls in chemistry lab. He told Stefán, who broke into a laugh, his teeth flashing with a ghostly tint. 'Associations . . .' he said, sounding a bit strained, 'How can you explain them? It's like looking into a mirror, isn't it? Like looking into a mirror expecting to see one's face and what appears instead are the most nightmarish fragments from one's personal history.'

András leaned forward. '*That* would depend on the eye of the beholder, wouldn't it?'

'Perhaps, but what if the mirror *is* the eye? What if the mirror reveals precisely that which the eye has sought to conceal?'

'Is that what's going on here between us?'

'You can be the judge of that, André. And you can be the jury.'

◆

'It was very dark in the apartment,' said Stefán, 'when I returned home that night. There was a musky smell in the room and the air felt thick and dank. As I reached for the light, the telephone began to ring. I walked over to pick it up, my hands fumbling in the darkness, but it fell silent again. The mouthpiece was warm and clammy. Something scuttled away from the receiver as I set it down. I turned on the light just in time to see a large brown rat scurrying across the floor. It disappeared into a hole, a trail of dust looping into the room behind it.

With a distinct feeling that something was amiss, I walked into the other room. A man was stretched out on the floor. It was Brander, the police guard from two nights earlier. He was pallid and still, his mouth wrenched open in a silent scream. As I stared at him in bewilderment, he shielded his eyes from the light and sat up. For a moment, he simply sat there, blinking at me. Then he stood up and smiled vacantly. 'Welcome home, Mr Stefán,' he slurred, swaying unsteadily on his feet. He waved a languid hand to embrace the space of the room.

234

'What are you doing here?' I asked, trying to keep my voice steady.

'Oh, visiting, just visiting . . . feeling a little crazy . . . you know how that can be . . .' He hesitated. 'I liked your room the last time we met . . . I liked the feeling . . . that naked man painted into the corner . . . very . . . very warm . . . emanating . . .'

'Well, thank you, but I'm really very tired. I'm afraid I'm going to have to ask you to leave.' I took a step back and pointed to the door.

He smiled again, ignoring me. 'And where have you been? I was worried. You've got to have a sense of responsibility, you know . . . you've got to be responsible to those who're responsible for your well-being . . .' He brought his face close to mine. I could smell the alcohol on his breath. I stepped back, not bothering to conceal my distaste. He swung his head from side to side, his hair falling across his forehead. 'My head . . . my head is killing me . . . I get these cluster headaches . . . blame it on the heartbreak . . . I trained to be a dancer, you know . . . but to survive all this *shit* . . .' He staggered forward and touched my face. 'Do you realize you're a very attra . . . attractive man, Stefán?' He bent his torso, his muscles rippling under his skin. He watched my changing expressions with amusement. 'Yes . . . very attractive . . . did you know that?' His voice dropped to a whisper. 'Humour me . . .' he said, speaking so low I could hardly hear him. 'Tell me, please . . . do you like . . . me? Could you . . . like . . . me? Would you consider?' He clasped my hand and moved it downwards. 'Do you like . . . this?'

Touching.

'Unlock this door, my friend,' he said, very quietly, 'and all the material wonders of the world . . .'

I stepped back and hit him hard with my free hand. As he went down on one knee, I stepped over him and smashed my fist into his face.

He scrambled to his feet and wiped the blood from his mouth. Glancing at his hand, he gave a strange laugh, clenching and unclenching his fist. His head flopped to one side, then snapped back again, rigid. 'Bad mistake, Stefán,' he murmured, 'bad mistake, old son.' Mouth falling open in a sidelong grin, he ran his fingertips down his chest. Then he pivoted on his heels and came straight at me.

He was like a battering ram. I didn't stand a chance. I felt myself being lifted and flung to the ground. I crumpled, half-blinded with pain, while he leapt across to the door and locked it from the inside. Leaning against it, he gave me a look filled with contempt. 'Welcome back, Comrade Poet . . .' he said grimly. 'Welcome back to your own sweet perdition.' I tried to crawl away but he walked over and placed his foot on my chest and pinned me down. Kneeling, he pressed his hands flat on my face and whispered: 'I've always believed that a man who hasn't been to war is a man who hasn't made love.'

He removed his hands from my face and patted my shoulder.

'So let's find out if you're man enough,' he said. 'Let's find out if you're a man.'

♦

A jagged sound cracked through the air. Stefán had bitten right through the rim of his glass. A thin red trickle ran from his lips. Splinters of glass clung to his mouth. He exhaled sharply through his teeth. András scrambled up and rushed across to where he was leaning against the door, but Stefán tackled him, propelling him back towards the couch. They fell in a heap on top of each other. 'What's the matter with you?' András exclaimed. 'This is ridiculous!'

Stefán stood up hastily. 'I'm sorry, André,' he said, the blood flowing from his mouth in a stream. 'I'm really sorry, but I don't want you near that room. I thought I'd already explained that. Are you hurt? Did I hurt you? Are you sure? I'll go in and wash, then. Please don't leave or anything.' He gave András a hand and pulled him to his feet.

Seething, András asked sharply. 'What *is* that smell in the other room?'

Hunkering down like a boulder, Stefán looked at him carefully. 'What smell?' he asked. Behind him, a fly buzzed across the adjoining room, alighting on the window pane. Its delicate, transparent wings quivered against the glass as András replied, 'A decaying smell, like something decomposing . . .'

Stefán stared back, wary. 'I don't know what you're talking about,' he replied. He wiped his mouth with the back of his hand. It came away sticky with blood. 'I'm going in to wash my face,' he announced. He closed the door firmly behind him.

András returned to his couch. There was little else to be done.

Stefán came back moments later.

◆

'Have you ever felt a clenched fist connect against bone, André?' Stefán asked. 'It's like a brick wall collapsing. You feel like touching your face constantly to see if it's still there. Everything splinters and fractures, the bones pulverizing into fragments . . . you can feel the gristle, flesh, blood . . . everything . . .

When I regained my senses that night, my eyes were already open. There were no lights in the room, only a single, dull beam from the streetlight streaming in through the windows and filling the room with shadows. I was lying face down on the floor. I tried to move, but stopped immediately, arrested by a sharp and stabbing pain, my rib-cage stiff and sore as if it were gripped in a vice. I let my head fall and rolled over until I lay on my back, my face to the ceiling. It was as if the entire weight of the room were pressing down on me, making it impossible to breathe. Slowly, and very carefully, I raised my head and looked down at myself. My shirt was torn open and there were bruises all over my chest. There was a dark serrated line running diagonally down from my shoulder and right across my groin. I propped myself up on my elbows, craning my head to see. I stared at myself in disbelief.

I sank to the floor after that, my mind suddenly empty. In all of my wildest nightmares, I could never have imagined this. I tried to stretch out my legs but an unbelievable pain shot through me. I realized I was about to lose consciousness again. I think my head must have hit the floor after that, because everything clouded over and came crashing down on me.

♦

András looked at him incredulously.

'Wait a moment! Have you told the police about this?'

Stefán's eyes widened in surprise. 'Haven't you been listening to me? He *was* the police!'

'Stefán,' András replied, trying to keep his voice steady, 'this is absolute nonsense. Where is your telephone?'

Stefán leaned back and closed his eyes, his tension manifest. 'Ah, but I don't have that option any longer, André.'

'Where is your telephone?' András repeated. He looked around, struggling to master an overwhelming tiredness.

Stefán raised a warning finger in reply, his voice suddenly steely, 'Please don't do anything foolish.'

'That's up to me, isn't it?'

Stefán went white. He thrust his hands deep into his trouser pockets. 'You've already attributed cause and effect, haven't you?' he said. There was a clear touch of irony in his voice.

András tried to grasp what he meant.

'Well –?' Stefán prompted.

Filled with confusion, András began to speak but Stefán seemed so on edge that he stopped without finishing.

Stefán made an impatient gesture. 'Will you hear me out?'

'What is there to hear out? What will that achieve?'

'I've been devastated these past few days, don't you understand? There's no other way to put it. The only person I could turn to after that, the only person who could make sense of any of this was you, my sometime friend. That's why I wrote to you; that's why I walked over and stuffed that note in your letter box. Then I returned home and waited for you to respond, as I knew you would, despite everything.'

'What sense can I possibly make of this?'

238

'Perfect sense. It's a race before they get me, don't you see?'

'What do you mean?'

'What is this, André?' Stefán snapped with a sudden irritability. 'What's the point of playing the fool like this? I've spent hours trying to work this out. I've analysed it from every possible angle, believe me.' He hesitated for a moment. 'You see, I think they need a scapegoat for what happened seventeen years ago, and I'm the most convenient target, the one least able to resist. Why else would they harass me like this? They need someone they can pin Immanuele's disappearance on, and that's why they've been trying to bludgeon a confession out of me.'

'You're crazy!'

'Crazy? Perhaps I am. Not my place to question a random word. But truth, now, that's an altogether different kettle of fish. Much more difficult. And justice, that's the really dangerous one. That's the one that pretends it's always around and just when you've let your guard down –' He broke off and looked at the floor.

'But I don't understand! I simply don't understand! How do you know they suspect you? You haven't been accused of anything.'

'Oh, I know that, but those are mere formalities. It's only a matter of time before they do me in. They'll grasp at any pretext, and I have nothing to fall back on. And now it's too late for me!'

'But there must be some answers!'

'Sometimes there are no answers,' Stefán replied, 'only ambiguities. No form, no substance to the shape of things, only similarities.' He gave András a sharp, anguished look. His mouth had paled and there were dark furrows across his forehead. 'And in any case,' he carried on softly, 'why should I torment myself? I don't have much longer to live.'

András guessed rather than heard what was said. Something stuck in his throat. With an effort, his legs giving a little at the knees, he rose to his feet. He shook his head; he seemed to have a great deal of difficulty in standing. He glanced in Stefán's direction in confusion, only to find the other man studying him closely. 'Sluggish, eh?' Stefán said quietly. 'It's probably fatigue. Why don't you try walking around the room for a bit? You've been sitting still for a long time.'

A sudden shout from the street startled both of them. It was followed by another, and then the entire street seemed to erupt into a cacophony. Stefán stood up instantly and walked over to the window. He looked out, his back to András, who'd just taken a step towards him. 'Stefán –' András whispered, 'I think I'm going to be sick.'

'What was that?' Stefán replied, still distracted by the commotion outside.

With a sudden groan, András crumpled abruptly to his knees, his frame bent double, his head reeling. He hit the ground with his shoulder as Stefán turned around. He had a momentary glimpse of Stefán moving towards him.

'André –?' Stefán called out, but András was already stretched out on the floor. He lay there, disorientated, waiting for the room to stop spinning. He tried to move his limbs, but it was no use. It was as if they had completely frozen over. Bewildered, he watched his hands grope along the floor and then grow still. He addressed Stefán in alarm: 'What's the matter with me?'

'Are you feeling cold?' Stefán asked. 'Would you say you feel frozen?'

He knelt beside András, watching him intently. If he was feeling any emotion, he didn't show it, his eyes increasingly remote and hooded. Only his clear, carefully controlled voice betrayed his tension. With a quick movement, he hoisted András up by the shoulders and dragged him back to the couch, propping him up against it. His voice fell, his tone gentle and persuasive. 'I think it's time,' he said calmly.

'Time?' András whispered. 'Time for what?'

'Time to end the play-acting.'

'The play-acting?'

Stefán made a sudden gesture, his face dry and quivering with nervous energy. 'No offence meant,' he said, 'but the line between being earnest and being disingenuous is very thin and I wouldn't like to . . .' he drew out the words, 'stretch it.'

András felt a curious sense of weightlessness. His vision began to blur. 'I can't see you very well,' he said. 'Everything's dimming . . .'

Stefán stood very still. His head seemed to have expanded

240

into an inordinately large globe that scarcely moved at all. It compressed abruptly as András stared, floating across the room and hovering above him.

'More tea, André?'

In the middle of trying to struggle up from the couch, András stopped and looked up in horror, comprehension dawning on him. 'My God! –' he said in a strangled voice, 'it was the tea, wasn't it?'

Stefán tapped him on the forehead in reply. 'This head's only so much ballast now,' he said laconically.

'What did you put in it?'

'A necessary ally, André. Fact this time, not fiction, unfortunately.'

'You said it was apricot brandy!'

'I lied . . . my apologies.'

'You must be joking!'

Stefán straightened up, his voice filled with asperity. 'What?' he snapped, 'Would I be joking at a time like this? Would I?'

'But why? For God's sake, why –?'

'Because I can't let you interfere. I'll have no heroics here. No attempts to save me from myself or anything like that. You've ingested a mild sedative that'll incapacitate you for a few hours. Unfortunately, it appears to be taking effect well before I intended it to so I guess I'll have to hurry things up a bit.'

For several seconds, András felt his mind go completely empty. He sensed Stefán's hand on his shoulder and looked up to meet his gaze, expectant and fixed on him. He opened his mouth to speak but broke into a coughing fit.

'André?'

Mechanically, András raised his hands and dropped them again. He attempted to find words but was overwhelmed by nausea. Gagging, he slumped back on the couch.

Stefán looked at him with glittering eyes, his cheeks and temples sunken. His lips moved but he didn't say anything.

At length, András gasped, his voice making a hoarse, sucking sound, 'What have you done?'

Stefán turned away sharply, as if from a blow. He made to leave the room but then he appeared to stop himself. Speaking

241

softly and clearly, he said, 'At first all I felt was guilt, naturally, but that passed soon enough and what was left in its place was a tremendous weariness and indifference. That, and the need to end this, to get it all over and done with. Do you know what I mean?' He gazed at András without expression. 'You don't believe I mean you harm, do you?' he asked, his voice very quiet.

András tried to speak but couldn't utter a word. He began to shiver. He felt himself veering in and out of consciousness.

Stefán looked at him through narrowed eyes and then his face relaxed into something resembling peace. 'How shall we comfort ourselves, André?' he said. 'We, who gave the best years of our lives to the struggle?'

He turned away from the drugged man and walked over to the window. Outside, it had stopped raining; in the hollow between the river and the hills, the city was filling with tiny buds of light. It would be dusk soon.

He leaned against the glass, the setting sun directly behind him, its airborne sinews muscling into the room and holding him upright. For a moment, he looked like a formless statue, filled with shadow and light. 'Gold and silver and sparkling finery,' he murmured, 'these are the currency of the day. We who fought for freedom in the largest sense . . . we're nothing but a sideshow now.'

He gazed out. 'Freedom . . .' he repeated sadly, 'and in the end, what was the point of it all? Tell me, what was the point?'

He hesitated, his voice gaining strength. 'And yet – we could have ruled this land. Our kind. The alchemists, the poets, the painters, the playwrights. It was our birthright to rearrange the days. One that we'd fought long and hard to earn. A pity nothing came of it in the end.

'But if you really think about it,' he said, 'none of this will matter in the end. And neither of us will matter. People like you and me. The people with nothing left but the queries, the confusions, the questions –

'Because they are replacing us with machines, André. Look around you, all these machines: a million politicians, bankers, soldiers . . . billions of cosmic scientists even. Frenetic. Mephitic.

'Headless.'

He stopped to consider András with melancholy eyes.

'Where are we going? What is going to happen to us? What are we doing to ourselves? There's no time left to ask these questions. No one left to do the asking. And, eventually, when we have all perished, only that dark mirror – that black river – will still be alive, oblivious to our passing. Because fate is impervious. And blood dies quicker than water in the end.'

He held his hands behind his back and began to walk slowly around the room, the sliding altercation between his silhouette and the sun casting blood-red shadows on the walls. 'I've just been so wrong about everything –' he said, speaking intently. 'Oh, in 1989, I celebrated like everyone else. That euphoria, a once-in-a-lifetime experience! Were my expectations unrealistic? I don't know, and I don't suppose I ever will. But the possibilities, the possibilities that should have opened up to me! The world was at our feet! Can you remember what it was like? I'm sure you can. Can you remember that banner on Erzsébet Bridge? The one that said, "Today the Berlin Wall, Tomorrow infinity!" That said it all for me. I remember walking around the city on wings, hugging strangers, laughing, crying. But after the initial headiness, after those first few days, there was nothing left to fall back on, just a feeling of the most complete and uncomfortably familiar emptiness. It's been one of life's many ironies, hasn't it? To look forward to a grand liberation and then realize that within the greater scheme of things a few people are completely out of sync. At first I tried to deny it. I tried to tell myself that I was free, that that was the important thing, at last we were free! It took me two or three months after that to realize that for me, at least, nothing had changed. I began asking myself, What did this freedom mean? Why was I having so much trouble understanding it? And how could I be free when I found my own personality constricting me? That was the paradox. Unlike everyone else, I just couldn't seem to slough off the past like dead skin. Or even to make the necessary adjustments. If ambition is the ability to single-handedly pursue things, then I simply didn't seem to have it in me, though *that* caught me off guard in the beginning. I had dozens of notebooks filled with

243

essays and verses and things. Oh, I had written it all down, my experience of the dark ages. Twenty years of work, carefully compiled and ordered for posterity. The same kind of stuff that saw me banned in the first place – what János used to call my anti-epics. I sent them off to the new magazines, the new publishing houses, the new young editors. And, of course, they sent them straight back. "Not quite right for the market," they said. "Not quite the thing."'

He gave a tight smile. 'One of them even went so far as to try to make me see that there was no commercial value to what I was doing. He said I should try my hand at bestsellers and get back to him. It's back to normal now, he advised me, there's no more room for these angst-ridden masterpieces, their time is past, the world you write about is behind us and people don't want to be reminded of it. Those exact words! What blissful self-confidence! The definitive expression of a truly sublime stupidity, or a truly stupid malevolence!' He gave his collar a savage tug. 'So where was the place for me in the new order of things? The answer was bloody obvious, though at first I didn't quite understand its magnitude. But when I finally did, I sat down quite calmly and reduced my manuscripts to smoking heaps. For me there was no longer a present, only the shifting, swirling consciousness of freedom and the emptiness it had brought with it. After that, it was all downhill. For me there could be no such thing as making the *necessary* adjustments because I simply couldn't adapt. Something in me had snapped a long time ago. My terminological confusion was complete.'

He made a weary gesture. 'Wittgenstein was mistaken. The world is not all that is the case. If it were, then the temptation to exist would be far simpler than it actually is. It's not enough to simply live life, one must always exceed it. To determine one's fate, one must throw oneself, body and soul, into the making of one's destiny. Anyone with the slightest sense of ideals would find anything else completely unsatisfactory. There's nothing in the temporal world that can substitute for the life of the spirit, no words or theorems that can suffice. Because the world that surrounds us, this relentlessly materialistic world, is a world in delirium tremens. It is heedless, it is heartless. There is no silence

244

in it, no truth or harmony. It's a world that treats humans as raw material, as fodder for commerce, as expendable currency. It's a world populated by people immersed in themselves, a world where all freedom falls through an empty space, and life sinks into dead routine.'

He stopped pacing and turned to face András. A shadow crossed his face. 'But enough of me and the spoor of my life –' he muttered. 'What's left of it all in the end? And what's left of me in the end? A clenched fist? A confused tangle of words? The fleeting reality of existence? Look around you: there's nothing left but rage and rust. What a waste. What a *waste!*'

His mouth contorting suddenly, he limped over to where András lay sagged on the couch. 'Don't look so agonized. This is for justice, you understand? A grim idea, not just another word. Now that I'm nearly dead, it's up to me to square my accounts. What goes around comes around.'

He knelt before András and ran a hand through his hair. 'Now, listen to me,' he said, his breath stale and tense, 'and listen carefully. In a matter of moments you will find out what today's been all about. And when you do, think of what I've done and why I did it. There can be no more running away for me. They've second-guessed me at every point and read into my intentions even, but you don't want them to do that to you. Think ahead of them, keep ahead of them. It's their survival against ours, and they're well aware of it. And there are many more of them than there are of us and that's what gives them the edge. They're very good at what they do, you can take my word for it. It can only be a matter of time before they come after you.'

He stood up and cast a quick glance around. Then he left the room, shutting the door, as always, behind him. Moments later, the door reopened and he came back in. There was a sense of finality to his movements. 'You'll understand my need for caution soon enough,' he said, 'so don't worry. Think kindly of all this when you look back on it. I had to exert all of my sadly flagging ingenuity to come up with it.' He patted András gently on the cheek. When he spoke again, his voice was pitched so low that András had to strain to hear him: 'And so, in the end, everything must be forgiven . . .'

245

Without another word, he walked into the other room, this time leaving the door wide open. András heard him turn on the tap, draw the shades over the windows. The apartment grew dark. Only the lights from the street vented a dim blue glow as Stefán paced up and down next door, his shadow sliding ceaselessly along the walls. He must have walked for miles while András waited, the paralysis overtaking his body. He wanted to call out, but he couldn't even move his lips. He weakly attempted to turn on his side. Finally, he slid to the floor, his head hitting the wooden chair and knocking into the pile of canvases. They collapsed in an untidy heap. Dragging himself away from the couch, András began to crawl forward, his voice screaming soundlessly: 'Stefán! Don't do it!' His words crashed against the wall of silence surrounding him: 'Don't be insane, Stefán! Don't do it! *Please!*'

He tried to stand up. He heard himself making strangled sounds, inarticulate words getting in the way. Increasingly desperate, he lurched sideways, knocking over a can filled with paintbrushes. They scattered over the floor. Sliding after them, he stretched full length on the ground. He saw Stefán's silhouette opposite him. He was kneeling down. He looked as if he were praying.

That was when he heard the gunshot.

A single gunshot . . .

'*Stefán!*'

He fell back on the floor.

With a herculean effort, he began pulling himself forward. He slid through the open door. Stefán was stretched out beside it, his fingers convulsively clasping a gun. András crawled over to him and turned him over. Stefán was warm to the touch. A thin, dark trickle ran down to the open book in his hand. András stared at the pages, they were empty and white. He flipped through it, and then he thrust it aside. It was Stefán's volume of perfect poetry, flecked with his blood. Picking up a half-empty glass of water, András flung it at the wall. The water splattered and streamed down to the floor. It ran across the room to an object lying in the shadows of the furthest corner.

András stared at it, finding it increasingly difficult to breathe.

It was a plastic body-bag, the ends carefully sealed with wax.

András shook his head in disbelief. With nausea flooding through him again, he stumbled towards it. He reached the bag and rolled it over, struggling to tear open the plastic. There was a ripping sound. Something flesh-like spilled out. Something grey, something squalid.

He had found Brander.

The room reeled away from him.

♦

Night.

András heard a loud banging on the door. There was an interval of silence, and then a convulsive crash. András tried to prop himself up on his elbows. He heard whispers, voices rising in excitement, shouts. Someone knelt next to him. He forced his eyes open and looked around. To his surprise, the room was beginning to fill up with leaves. And the leaves – they were gleaming. They were grains of sand. They were pieces of glass. They were fragments of mirrors. Sharp reflecting shards. They piled up around him, steadily filling the room, the floor disappearing, the body in the bag disappearing, Stefán disappearing, his feet disappearing, his legs disappearing, his hands disappearing, millions of tiny particles climbing past his face, his eyes on a stone slab, his head on a stone bench, then a sudden silence, Stefán looking back at him, shining back at him, soaking into him, freefalling, freefalling, freefalling . . .

♦

Someone was standing in the middle of the room. It was a man. He was pressing a handkerchief to his mouth and gagging at the stench. He leaned over and picked up András's head, breaking it off from the rest of him.

András cried out in pain. The man flipped open his skull and looked into the flux. Speaking very slowly, as if to a child, he asked, 'Are you all right?' His eyes waited for a reply. Then he forced some water into András's mouth. It tasted bitter. Coughing, András spat it out.

'What did he give you?'

'It was in the tea . . .'

The man found the cup and held it to his nostrils. He grimaced and put it down. He signalled to someone. Indistinct shadows waded through the haze, heads protruding into the darkness. A huddle of men gathered in the middle of the room. One of them drew a shape on the floor with a piece of white chalk. Someone else tried to help András to his feet. He struggled, striking out with his hands.

'It's all right, it's all right . . .'

They brought a stretcher into the room.

András heard himself slur: 'Water . . .'

There was a horrified shout. 'Oh God, it's Brander . . . he's dead . . . his head's been smashed in!'

Someone began taking photographs, the flashlight painting mirrors on the walls. There was a brighter, frantic flare, then a quick dying out.

There were others in the room now, hazy figures, blurred lights. In their swimming glow, András glimpsed a man dressed entirely in white, and, standing behind him, like a shadow, another, shrouded in black.

Someone shone a torch into his eyes. 'Relax now, I'm a doctor . . .'

He leaned close to András. 'Listen, we're moving you out of here . . .'

'Doctor,' András whispered, his voice rising, 'I can't remember . . . I can't remember a thing . . .'

The physician misunderstood him. 'It's all right,' he said, 'it doesn't matter . . . you've been through a terrible experience.' He cleared his throat. 'You must rest now. You're too distraught. Just rest.'

They heaved András on to a stretcher and carried him into the next room. He glanced around in confusion. There was an empty space on the couch where the blue notebook should have been. He turned to the doctor, pointing. 'Who took the journal? Where is Immanuele's journal?' The doctor patted his hand. 'No one has taken anything,' he replied in carefully measured tones. 'Try to rest now.'

András looked around again, his eyes desperately searching the room. There could be no mistaking it. Someone had taken it.

Immanuele's journal was missing.

Chapter Five

The Transubstantiation

A very bright light –
        'He's coming to . . .'
    'Hello, Mr Tfirst . . . Can you see me? Mr Tfirst?'
    'Ask him if he can hear you . . .'
    'Can you hear me? You're in a hospital now. I'm a doctor. No, don't move away. What is it? Do you need something?'
    'Ami . . .'
    'What was that? Did anyone catch that? Mr Tfirst . . . can you hear me? There's no need to worry. You've suffered a severe shock. A severe trauma, do you understand?'
    'The diary . . .'
    'What was that? Listen, I want you to relax. Pretend you're floating on a sea of clouds . . .'
    'No . . .'
    'Mr Tfirst, I'm going to have to . . .'
    'Here, let me . . . András, this is Andor Szegedy. Can you hear me? András? András . . .'

♦

András opened his eyes.
    It was late in the afternoon. A rich, golden light was streaming

250

into the room. Outside, there was a scent of rain. Further outside, there was a smell of river. Inside, there was a scent of flowers; a smell of perfume. Further inside, there was a scent of dream. He drew a deep breath, the outside and the inside flooding into his lungs.

He looked around, focusing sleep-blurred eyes. Next to the bed there was a table with a book. A glass of water rested on it, holding the pages down. He picked up the glass and tilted it against his cheek. The water ran down his skin. Pressing his knees together, he made a lake. He drew his knees apart and the dam burst, the lake dying down to a trickle.

Above his head a handwritten card announced Ami's thoughts: '*Carpe diem*, András!' The writing looped and plunged in giant whorls.

He sat up and called out her name.

There was no reply.

He called out again.

The wind whispered back.

She must be by the riverside.

Down by the waterline.

◆

He climbed out of bed, walking over to the window and gazing down at the river. The air outside was very still. It was probably going to rain. The sapling that Ami had planted three months ago had bent over again. It had a habit of doing that every time there was going to be a storm. He leaned against the windowframe, its airless gape separating the room from the garden. Picking up the curtain by its corner, he wrapped it around himself.

The city was a maze in the distance.

He wandered back into the room, looking for something to wear. A shadow crossed the floor before him and made him look up. A woman was standing outside the window looking in. She held a bouquet of red roses in her hands. She broke off a stem and threw it in. 'Give me a day just to kiss you,' she said. He looked at her in surprise. 'Don't misunderstand me,' she said. 'You're probably too young to know what I mean. I was taking these flowers to my baby. He died last month. But I saw you here and you looked so forlorn, so I thought I'd give them to you instead . . .' She hesitated for a moment and looked sadly at him. Then she turned around and walked away, leaving him alone again. Alarmed, he cried out: 'Maman, there was a strange lady here . . .' Maman didn't answer his call, but Ami did. She hesitated at the door and gazed at him curiously. Then she walked over, moving slowly.

In the distance, he could see a ship, its masts curling out of the strip between the river and the horizon . . .

Maman died that year.

It was very sudden.

He remembered running with Ami along the banks of the river one evening when, without warning, she froze in mid-stride, a look of great fear on her face. 'Maman!' she cried, her eyes searching the sky. She didn't have to tell him what it was, he was already scrambling through the snow-strewn woods towards the house. He fell down, noticing that the leaves were ice-cold, that they had turned to stone.

Uncle Iván was already there. He was standing by the door. His cap was in his hand and he was twisting it round and round. He looked lost and helpless. András could hear his father crying inside, great, broken-hearted, breathless sounds: 'Why, Aida, why?' Someone saw them running towards the house and shouted: 'Don't let the children into the house! Don't let them see! Don't, for God's sake, let them in!' Beside him, András heard Ami scream. He'd never heard her do that before. She flung herself right past him at the closing door, banging her head against it. She wouldn't stop, just kept on banging her head. That's when Uncle Iván picked her up. Her forehead was bruised and red; it began to swell. Uncle Iván looked at her and burst into tears. He sat down and folded her into his lap. They held on to each other, Ami hanging limply from his neck. András sat down on the steps next to them. He didn't know what to do with his hands or with anything else. All he could feel was this huge stone stuck inside his throat. Where had it come from?

After a while, the door opened and they were let inside.

The coals were still burning on the grate where András had seen Maman stoke them that morning. Father was sitting at the table, his head resting on his hands. András could hear him breathing deeply: he was sleeping. Someone said something about a sedative. What did that mean?

Maman's little sister, Aunt Zsuzsanna, knelt down in front of them. She was wearing a black dress with black flowers sewn into the hem. Her eyes were very bright. In a calm voice, she explained that she would be their Maman now. András had never heard her sound like that. So old. Like that.

The next evening Aunt Zsuzsanna took them to the river. She said that Maman had left behind a message for them on her tape-recorder. She said that it was a private message and that they were to listen to it with all seriousness. She said that she would come back after that and take them home. For some reason, that made András feel grown-up. And thrilled. Until he heard Maman's voice, that is. Then he broke down and cried. He simply couldn't help it.

The message was short and it was strange. First Maman spoke to Ami. She said, 'My baby, take care of your brother. Give him a little kiss sometimes.' Then she said, 'Be careful of him, Ami.' To András, she said, 'My baby, take good care of your Ami. Give her a little kiss sometimes.' Then she said, 'Be careful of her, André.'

There was static on the tape following her voice. Then it shut down.

Aunt Zsuzsanna hurried back after that. Her face was very pale. They knew that she had been listening, that she had heard Maman's words. She held both of them close to her and told them not to worry about anything. She was breathing very fast, almost gasping. Later on, inside the house, Ami heard her telling Uncle Iván, 'Whatever could Aida have been thinking of? She couldn't have been in full possession of her senses during those last few hours. It must have been terrible for her, but what a thing to leave behind for the children!'

Ami called it the killing song.
She said she could hear it playing inside her head.
She asked András to make it go away.
But that was when they were both older.
Much older.

♦

Uncle Iván and Aunt Zsuzsanna lived in a cottage on the banks of the Danube. It was large and airy, with a balcony overhanging the river and a massive arboretum. Uncle Iván was an architect and had once been the editor of the prestigious European journal, *Space and Form*. As if to attest to this, his vocabulary was liberally peppered with architectural jargon. As András was to learn later on, he had once been one of the most influential practitioners of his discipline until he'd fallen out with Imre Perényi, the Soviet-trained architectural tsar. The famous Sztálinváros Steelworks and the Vocational School for Farmers at Várpalota were both based on his designs.

Aunt Zsuzsanna was a Modernist painter who'd been a student of the Bauhaus visionary, László Moholy-Nagy. In a public gathering in 1953, she'd dared to criticize the powerful Minister of Culture, József Révai, for his 'neanderthal aesthetics'. Ever since then she had become a non-person condemned to internal exile. Only Uncle Iván's Party connections had saved her from a harsher retribution.

The night Maman died, before putting them to bed, Aunt Zsuzsanna repeated to them: 'I will be your Maman now. Nothing bad will ever happen to you again!' András fell asleep dreaming of Maman, though, *his* Maman, but then, at some point during the dream, Maman turned into that strange lady with the red roses. This time she was wearing a red dress with red chains and tresses. She led him to her house. It was a very large house, much larger than theirs. Holding him by the hand, she guided him up a tall stairway, carved and fashioned like a spiralling tree. Together, they entered a large room, dark, like

254

the sea. There was a baby resting inside, sleeping peacefully. The lady knelt down next to him and whispered into András's ears: 'He's my son, my only child. Isn't he pretty?' András thought he was very small, actually. He looked like a wizened fruit; his head was tiny.

There was a mosquito net over the bed. As András looked on, the net turned red. It was bleeding. That scared him and he wanted to leave but the strange lady had turned her back to him. He watched as she took off all her clothes, a warm light emanating from under her skin. She walked over and kissed him on the forehead. Her lips were very soft, they felt like air. Then she went down on her knees and knelt before him. In one hand, she held a single red rose on a single stem. She gave it to him. He walked home after that, the rose clutched in his fist.

The next day, he took Ami to the sand-pit that was their place for private confidences. Drawing her aside, he told her about the dream, or at least the parts that he could clearly recollect. After listening to him carefully, Ami asked if the lady had been pretty. What a strange question! András told her so. 'No,' she explained, 'what I meant was . . . was she prettier than Maman?' No, of course not, he said. No one was prettier than Maman, not even Aunt Zsuzsanna. 'Was she prettier than me, then?' András got very cross and stalked away. Behind him, he could hear Ami calling out plaintively: 'Don't leave like that, André! Please don't ever leave like that!'

But he ignored her pleas and left her to her own devices.

A metal dog was chained to his dream that night.

But this time around, he decided not to tell Ami about it.

The following day, András overheard Father talking to Uncle Iván. He heard him say: 'I just can't do it, Iván! Every time I look at them, I see her face. I just can't help it! I have to go away. I have to leave Budapest.' He said that he was thinking of going to Szekszárd, or to some other place that was even further away.

Aunt Zsuzsanna came in to tell them that their father was leaving them for a while. But they already knew. András had told Ami. They listened to Aunt Zsuzsanna's explanation in silence.

Later that same morning, András heard Uncle Iván say: 'That man has no loyalty to his children, no feelings. They're only seven years old, for God's sake! He should have considered that when he decided to leave.'

Feelings. It was what they all said he lacked. All of them, even Ami.

Father left without saying goodbye. They stood at the window, straining to see the train in the distance. Ami pointed out a faint brush-stroke of smoke on the horizon. Was that his train? There was no way of telling.

Father never came back. One day, Aunt Zsuzsanna, for once not bothering to conceal her anger, told them that he had gone away to a place called Canada. A town called Vancouver. 'Vancopúver . . .' András said wonderingly, rolling the syllables around on his tongue. 'Now where on earth is that?' 'It's across the ocean, dummy,' Ami replied irritably. Near India. And where was that? Ami refused to answer his question and rolled her eyes in exasperation instead.

Father never did come back.

Their Maman would never have done that.

♦

Maman had been Hungary's most famous opera singer. They heard people say that she had 'transformed the operatic world'. She'd travelled all over the world and Hungaroton issued recordings by her every season. *Der Spiegel* called her 'the divine Aida – a rare flame, truly incandescent!' *Le Monde* termed her death 'an international tragedy'. *Magyar Hírlap* mourned 'a loss of incomparable proportions to the nation'. Aunt Zsuzsanna called her a dreamer, a revolutionary, a sensualist. Uncle Iván remained silent, but his face said it all.

Once he described one of her concerts to them, his eyes shining like fire. They listened to him in wonder, spellbound. Later, Ami said she was sure that Uncle Iván had been in love with Maman. Madly in love, she insisted.

András remembered one of Maman's opening nights. They'd been seated in a box of their own and had been instructed to be

256

perfectly still. Father hadn't been able to come, as usual. He was attending a conference on global modelling or something like that, in Krakow, in Poland.

The box, a dark little room with plush velvet curtains, felt quite overwhelming. A faint smell of perfume adhered to everything. Ami inhaled the smell with slightly dilated nostrils, trying to act all grown-up and calm. András tried the same trick but broke into a sneezing fit. Greatly embarrassed, Ami told him to behave himself. He wrinkled his nose in response and made a funny face. That was all it took for her to forget where she was and stick out her tongue at him and wiggle it in the way only she could: sideways.

Their seats were so soft that they sank in completely. Trying to sit on them was a bit like swimming. They flailed around for a while, enjoying the unexpected treat. Then Ami started giggling, the way she did when they tickled each other at home, playing hide and seek under Maman's bed. Or in the dining room, under the table with the broken leg. But once Maman started singing, they both fell silent and forgot everything else. Even though they were used to hearing her practise at home every morning – when they woke up in their room with the sun pouring in – she had never quite sounded like *that*! It was over-powering! Her voice soared into the sky, bracing against the ceiling, the notes falling back into the audience, each one separate and distinct. And she seemed to know exactly where Ami and András were sitting because she kept turning and smiling at them. It was almost as if out of those hundreds and hundreds of people, she were singing only for the two of them. That was when András heard himself whisper, awestruck: 'Maman!'

Ami said that if he closed his eyes when Maman sang, he'd be able to see shining birds and angels with wings. She was right. And once when Maman held her voice on a single note for a very long time, the lady in the box next to them broke down and began to weep. Why did she do that? Maman probably didn't even know her. And she was very kind-hearted, she would never have wanted to make anyone cry like that.

During the interval, a lady who seemed to know Maman walked into their box. She was wearing furs and lots of perfume. She

257

seemed very excited, she kept flapping her hands around like a duck. 'Isn't Aida simply amazing?' she exclaimed. She introduced them to the big, stiff man by her side. 'This is Party Secretary Kovács, children. Say hello to him.' Ami curtsied prettily. András shook his hand instead, the way his father had taught him.

The lady had brought them something to eat. 'And where is your father tonight?' she asked. Before András could say anything, his mouth being stuffed with cake, he heard Ami reply quite gravely, 'He's gone to a *big* meeting, Ma'am, on globular masturbutating.'

For some reason, the lady went very pale and clutched on to her companion, who had turned red and was trying desperately to hold back his laughter. They heard the lady ask him in a scandalized whisper, 'Where did she learn that w-o-r-d?' The man broke into a wide-open grin and tweaked Ami's cheeks. 'Kids!' he chortled, 'Kids these days!'

At that point Ami politely asked him why he had three brows on his face. She was like that, always asking questions. He didn't understand her. 'Well,' she continued, explaining, 'You have two eyebrows and a mouthbrow . . .' He still looked confused. He was obviously not too bright. 'I think she means your *moustache*, dear,' the lady said, a bit tartly. The man started guffawing at that, opening his mouth wide so that András could look straight inside and see gristly globs gleaming within. But since the interval had just ended, and the lights had dimmed, and everyone else was being very quiet and still, the sound made quite a commotion and people began turning around and staring at them. Mortified, the lady and the gentleman hurriedly took their leave and left Ami and András alone again.

'What strange friends Maman has,' András remarked to Ami. She nodded her head in agreement, 'They have dis . . . discombobulated minds.' András looked at her. What did that mean? She was using a *new word* again. One that she knew he wouldn't understand. He'd told her not to do that a million times! He turned his back to her in a huff just as she sank into her side of the sofa, the resulting swell knocking him off his end.

♦

Ami liked skiing in the woods behind their house in a thin T-shirt and cotton trousers and nothing else. She'd ski so fast that she'd work up a sweat and be more warm than cold when she came back indoors. She'd beaten down a meandering track that led deep into the woods and then doubled back on itself. She liked skiing at night best. Mostly she went out when Maman was on one of her tours and the old maid who looked after them had fallen asleep. András went with her sometimes, but she usually liked to be on her own, with the moon shining brightly on the snow and the trees stretching into the distance. He would try to stay awake until she came back, but most of the time he'd fall asleep. When she came back, though, he'd wake up instantly and watch her as she stripped down to the skin. She was immensely proud of her prowess with skis and what it was doing to her physique. 'One day,' she would tell him as she glanced at herself in the mirror, 'One day, when I'm much older, I'd like to ski at night, every night, stark naked!'

One night, she challenged him to a race. Since he couldn't ski half as well as she could, she told him she'd go at a much reduced speed. At first he hesitated, but then he gave in and strapped on his skis.

It was a moonless night and very cold. In the middle of the race, he stopped suddenly, out of breath. Sensing his distress, Ami slowed down as well. He sat down on the snow, his breath clouding up the air. Kneeling beside him, she held her face close to his, not saying anything. Their eyes locking, they looked at each other in silence. Then she stood up and dug her skis into the ground, taking off in a mad rush. He watched her disappear into the trees, her hair tossing wildly in the breeze. He waited for a few seconds to see if she would turn around and return to him. Then he rose to his feet and staggered home, his lungs rasping noisily inside him.

The year after Maman died, Ami and András spent the summer at their grandmother's house in Martonvásár. Grandma Lesznai was their father's mother but they liked her all the same. She was very old, and Cousin György, their father's oldest brother's youngest son, lived with her, looking after the house. He was hunchbacked, but nice.

Grandma Lesznai may have been very old but she had all her wits about her. She knew exactly what she wanted from life. If something happened that didn't please her, she would look the offender straight in the eye and say, 'So you thought you could get away with it, did you, that the old woman wouldn't find out? Well, you're mistaken! I may be old but I am *not* senile!' She used to do that a lot with the grown-ups. They would then become quite contrite, just like little kids. But with children she was gentle and kind.

When Ami and András arrived, she hugged them for a long time, cried a little, and called their father a coward. Then she asked them if they were hungry. They were, they said. 'You should be! You look skinny to me. Doesn't Zsuzsanna give you enough to eat? Growing boys must eat well. And growing girls as well . . .' She instructed Cousin György to kill a chicken for them. 'The big white one with the brown stripes on its breast.'

Grandma Lesznai had lots of chickens. They lived in a large wire coop outside. Cousin György took care of them. He gave the chickens names, but it was the roosters that were his pride and inspiration. There were three roosters: Socrates, Vladimir Stupovich and Ashkenazy. Vladimir Stupovich and Ashkenazy were from Russia, but Socrates, Cousin György said, was a gypsy and therefore really tricky.

Ami and András asked permission to stay and watch the killing: 'We could wash up later, please, is that OK? Please, please, *please?*'

Cousin György said, What did he care? It was all the same to him.

They sat next to each other on the wooden porch facing the

courtyard while Cousin György brought the chicken out of the coop. It was big and fat, Cousin György's hands disappearing into the feathers on its breast and its back. It had a red toupee and a bright yellow beak that glinted sharply in the sunlight. Taking care to avoid the beak, Cousin György picked the bird up, sliding one hand from the breast to the neck. The chicken made a clucking sound (a bit like Grandma, actually).

Ami slipped her hand into András's. Her palms were hot and sweaty. András turned to stare at her but she was looking away – at a field of sunflowers in the distance. Suddenly, Cousin György gave a powerful shout and heaved the chicken into the air by its neck. He called out to them while swinging the bird around his head. Ami jumped; András could feel her trembling. Her hand was like ice. Bothered by her distress, he took his hand away.

The chicken began screaming even though Cousin György had one large fist clamped tightly around its neck and mouth. There was a muffled crack. Then the bird flew off on a curve, spiralling across the courtyard. 'It's getting away!' András yelled to Ami: 'Look! It's flying away . . . that way!' She glanced to where he was pointing.

For some reason Cousin György was roaring with laughter. Wait till Grandma finds out about this, András thought.

The chicken landed on its feet. It was only then that András noticed it didn't have a head. He looked back: Cousin György was holding it in his hand, palm open to show them.

Blood was spurting out of the chicken's neck, but it seemed quite alive. András gaped at it incredulously. It was like a magic trick! How was it possible? Meanwhile, wings flapping, feet pounding, the bird raced up the incline of the porch and headed straight for the children. Ami scrambled behind András with a terrified squeak. He pushed her away, trying to laugh and show that he was not afraid. She fled from the porch, running pell-mell into the house.

In the meantime, still making an awful racket, the headless bird had slammed into a wall, smearing it with gore and falling over, feet in the air. Soon it lay very quiet. Cousin György picked it up and dunked it into a pot he'd filled with boiling water. The water made a hissing sound, steam pouring out of it. With a crooked finger, Cousin György called András over. András hastened to join him and peered into the cauldron. The water was red, the feathers fluffing out of the bird's skin, their follicles exposed and white. Cousin György dipped his hands in and pulled out soggy clumps. He grinned as he did it. 'City kids!' he said, looking at the boy. 'But you've got guts, André! You're all right.' András felt himself swell with pride.

The chicken, when Grandma cooked it, was fresh and soft. Much tastier than any that András had ever had.

But Ami refused to eat it. She looked away when it was served, opting for smelly cabbage stew instead.

And she refused to speak to András, maintaining a chilly and unforgiving silence.

◆

Later that year they went to Lake Balaton. They had both just recovered from an attack of chicken-pox. Uncle Iván said that András had given it to Ami. Aunt Zsuzsanna insisted that it was the other way around. The fact of the matter was that they both fell ill together, suffered together, and got well at about the same time. By the end of that period, they'd spent almost a month crawling around in bed, feeling completely trapped. That was why the waters of the lake were cathartic: crystal-clear and dreamlike.

They plunged in, screaming with anticipation. Ami won the first splashing fight. Then András sneaked in underwater and pulled her down. Ami climbed on his shoulders after that and they walked around in slow-motion, searching for fish.

Ami's legs were slick, she kept flicking water back with her toes into András's eyes. She was warm and wet. András began to feel that they were fused together. He sensed that Ami was feeling the same way, because she had suddenly fallen very quiet. They waded through the water as one person, breathing together. When she finally climbed down from his shoulders, they looked at each other for a long time. Neither of them made a sound. Then András leaned over and gave her a kiss on the tip of her nose. She made a tiny noise in response and buried her head into his neck. He swallowed hard, his breathing slowing down.

That night Aunt Zsuzsanna brought out her guitar and everyone sat around a campfire on the beach and listened to her sing. She had a sweet, high-pitched voice, not as powerful or as clear as Maman's, but it had a pleasant trill to it. Uncle Iván joined in from time to time as well, droning in a deep baritone. Every time he did that, Aunt Zsuzsanna would smile, her eyes glinting in the firelight. Soon other people gathered around. An old man with a huge dog kept time with a pair of wooden castanets. The dog was a snow-white German Shepherd with deep-blue eyes. Every time the old man played the castanets, the dog would bay in tune to the music.

Ami and András sat next to each other. He held Ami's hand. He heard Aunt Zsuzsanna whisper to Uncle Iván when she thought they weren't listening: 'Look at the children, Ivé . . . aren't they completely adorable?' Uncle Iván smiled. András snuggled closer to his sister. He felt happier than he had for a very long time. He wanted to jump up on to the folding camptable and break into song.

He didn't know why he felt like that.

That night they went to sleep inside their tent curled end to end. András tucked his face between Ami's legs; she placed him inside her mouth like a pacifier and fell instantly asleep. A stranger would have taken them to be one body, breathing together, their limbs wrapped around each other – a tight, compact oblong – dreaming faces flesh-warm and soft.

◆

A few months after the trip to Lake Balaton, Aunt Zsuzsanna left Uncle Iván and went to live in Vienna with another man. They'd been 'having difficulties with their marriage', Ami told András in an adult voice. But he wasn't too concerned about things until Uncle Iván and Aunt Zsuzsanna decided to divide their custody of the children. Ami was to leave for Vienna with Aunt Zsuzsanna while András remained behind.

Uncle Iván called him to his study to explain the matter. It was dark and gloomy inside the room, with the curtains pulled over the windows.

'Your aunt has decided she wants to live in Vienna,' Uncle Iván began. He turned his head away and stared at the ceiling, and then he turned back abruptly to survey András. Seemingly lost for words, he thumped his desk with his fist. 'I wish I knew how to explain this to you, André, but there's a man involved. I wish I knew how to explain it to myself.' There was a moment of awkward silence, and then he exclaimed: 'I hope the scoundrel breaks his neck!' A while after that, probably realizing he'd said the wrong thing, he composed himself and said, 'God help her soul!'

Aunt Zsuzsanna came to András later that day. 'I know your uncle has spoken to you,' she said gently. 'Sometimes things happen in life that are sudden and surprising. We don't expect them to turn out that way, but when they do we have to accept what's happened and make the best of it.' She gave him an unhappy look. 'When you're older, you'll understand what I mean.

'I'm taking Ami away with me,' she carried on. 'She'll be better off with me in Vienna, I've arranged for her to go to a good school and everything . . .' Her voice trailed off. She seemed unable to look András in the eye.

At length, she placed a hand on his shoulder. 'You'll be able to visit her as often as you wish, I promise. Your uncle and I have agreed on that much, at least.'

One bleak, black day he accompanied them to the train station. They had to hire two cabs because they had so many bags. Ami held on tightly to András until it was time for him to get off the train. He walked down the narrow corridor and descended the steps to the platform below. Ami was leaning out of the window and trying hard not to cry. He stood on the platform alone and watched the cars pull away one by one.

'Don't forget me,' he'd whispered to Ami just before their parting, 'Don't forget me, please,' she'd whispered to him, 'Don't forget me,' he'd whispered to her fiercely, 'Don't forget me, please,' she'd whispered to him, 'Don't forget me,' he'd whispered into her ear, 'Don't forget me, please,' she'd whispered to him, forlornly, 'Don't forget me, Ami,' he'd whispered to her, 'Don't forget me,' she'd whispered to him, brokenly, 'Don't forget me, please . . .'

The words going round and round and round inside his head.

◆

That night, he sat down at his desk and began his first journal.

'I am nine years old,' he wrote. 'My name is András Tfirst. I live with my Uncle Iván in a big house next to the river Danube. I am a student. He builds houses. We live by ourselves now. We are all alone.'

◆

He liked to hold his breath under water. It always seemed to him like proof of a special prowess. He'd puff up his chest and imagine the air filling up every nook and cranny inside him. It would drive Ami mad, she was so scared he would drown and sink into the depths of the river where no one would ever find him. Secretly, she was terrified he would suffer the same fate as Maman.

They'd been sitting by the river one evening when Ami had turned to him and said, 'You know . . . all one needs to do . . . in this place . . . is to close one's eyes and roll over the edge. I am often reminded of that when I think of Maman.

'Sometimes I think I can see her walking out of the river . . .' she'd carried on, 'over there, at that point . . . trailing leaves and weeds. She must have looked like that when they fished her out.

265

But as she nears, I realize she's made of water, like the rest of the river, and just before she reaches the banks closest to where I am, a giant wave breaks over her and dissolves her into itself.'

He'd glanced over the edge of the cliff. The river below had been murky. Opaque.

'You must miss Maman a lot . . .'

'Yes, I suppose I do. Don't you?'

Without waiting for an answer, she'd reached over and grasped his hand. He'd rolled it into a fist. She'd tried to pry it open. He'd relaxed his grip, allowing her to slip inside, their fingers entwining.

Later on, after Ami had left for Vienna, he found himself wondering at this proclivity of his to stay under water, especially after what had happened to Maman. It was like a dare, as if he were intent on proving something, although what that could possibly be was never very clear. He looked upon it as a challenge, albeit a private one, like Ami's skiing. If she didn't like it, she was welcome to go away and occupy herself. Play out her own death wish.

Perhaps it was the way things looked under water, all turquoise and translucent. And he liked the objects he found on the bed of the river. Once he found a brightly coloured wooden horse from a carousel. It must have been lying there for years, the wood rotted through and fragile, the bronze hoofs green with encrustations. He tried to pull it to the surface, but it kept breaking off, the pieces falling back to the bottom. Eventually he had to content himself with one of the hoofs, pulling it off and carrying it to the surface. In the light of day it had looked like an ordinary tin can, and a dirty one at that, and he'd realized with disappointment that there was really no point in keeping it.

One evening he dived into the river from a steep and rocky bank. He did it on a whim, or so he justified it to himself. He'd been strolling along the riverbank when he'd suddenly been overtaken by the urge to dive. Lightheaded and giddy, he'd stripped off and leaped over the cliffs at a place where he knew the water to be especially deep. He'd flown through the air and needled into the water. Instantly surrounded by darkness, he hadn't been able to see a thing, only the trail of white foam behind his wildly pummelling feet. It had taken him a second or so to realize that he had no idea where the surface was. His sense of orientation completely awry, he'd headed in one direction, only to find himself running out of breath. It was the first time in his life he'd felt blind panic. He'd broken into a fit of sobbing that had lasted well past the time he'd burst through the surface. He'd floundered on to dry land after that, a chastened, trembling, witless *thing*.

Yes – breathing under water, that had been his passion. Quite the opposite of his father, who'd dreaded the water and never learned to swim. The older he grew, the more András realized how fundamentally his father had failed them. It made him wonder what his mother could have seen in him in the first place, the shortcomings had always been so apparent. He swore to himself never to get married. He'd learn from all the mistakes his parents had made, learn never to repeat them. *Never*: how he'd loved that word. It had made the world seem so safe somehow, so definite and cleansed of error and accident. It was the only way he'd learned to rationalize the element of chance in his life. That, and, of course, the writing.

◆

One winter's day, when András was twelve, Uncle Iván put him on the magic train to Vienna. Ami and Aunt Zsuzsanna were waiting to receive him at the other end, at the Westbahnhof. Aunt Zsuzsanna held him tightly to her chest and sobbed all over his hastily lowered head. Ami, a little more reticent, gave him a peck on the cheek. András didn't really remember much else of that exciting first day, but the very next morning Ami took him to her school. She introduced him to all her friends. In an instant, András found himself completely surrounded. He had to answer many strange questions, most of them in his schoolboy German. Soon he became aware that one of Ami's classmates, older and taller than the rest, kept staring at her while asking him the most stupid things. It made it difficult for him to concentrate.

For one thing, the boy was awfully big. For another, he just couldn't seem to take his eyes off Ami.

András felt himself flushing. Unlike the others in the group, the boy didn't appear to know Ami too well and seemed incapable of going up and speaking to her directly. In fact, he couldn't seem to bring himself to get anywhere near her. András found himself secretly sneering at that kind of shyness.

An hour later, the boy came over to András again. Standing before him, he cleared his throat diffidently. When he spoke, his voice was gruff and self-conscious. 'Hello,' he said, 'Remember me? I'd like to ask you a question, please. That girl, over there, the really pretty one by the window, with the curls falling over her face – she is your sister?'

András replied, curtly, 'Yes, she's my twin.'

'Twin? But you two don't look at all alike –'

András stared at him, not saying anything. What was he, some kind of imbecile?

'Please, will you introduce me to her?'

'No,' András replied, tight-lipped, his mouth a thin cold line, crystalline.

'What?'

'No,' András repeated, with a whiplash smile, '*Nein.*'

'But perhaps you misunderstand me . . .'

András wanted to hit him in the eye. Instead, he controlled himself and looked away. 'No, I will not,' he repeated, his voice clipped, with a sharp ring to it.

The tall boy was crestfallen, his tone plaintive, 'But why?'

'She's already taken,' András lied. Then he walked away.

'You were very rude to that German boy,' Ami remarked later.

András became defensive; he couldn't help it. 'Was not!' he retorted. 'He was making a nuisance of himself!'

'You were rude!'

'Yeah! So maybe I was! So what? I caught him staring at you.'

'But that's not the real reason, is it?' She looked into his eyes, her voice surprisingly gentle.

András didn't say anything, biting his lip instead and looking away. He felt fiery and defiant and thoroughly mixed-up.

She took his hand, 'André . . . André . . . what are we going to do?' Then she added, almost as an afterthought, '. . . with you?'

She didn't say anything else, reaching up to his shoulder and patting him on his head. Then she stepped back and turned to leave. On the point of walking away, she stopped, suddenly swivelling around and kissing him full on the lips. She caught him off guard. At first, his lips were like stone. Then he let her tongue slide inside. He could feel her breath on his cheeks. His eyes began to water. She stopped as abruptly as she had begun, drawing sharply away. Looking down, she squeezed his hand and made a low sound before running out of the room.

He fell backwards into a chair. His tongue felt like fire. His lips tasted sweet and salty, like syrup. He felt very weak.

And dizzy.

Very dizzy.

◆

Ami crept into his room that night. With a finger to her lips, she beckoned him to follow her. They climbed up the winding staircase that led to the top of the house. By the time they reached the roof, András was completely out of breath. His heart was pounding and his breath burst from his throat in short, shallow gasps. Oblivious, Ami made him look over the ledge to the sheer drop below them. Peering down, András felt his head whirl and hastily stepped back, his legs unsteady. But Ami didn't notice, she didn't notice how thankfully he staggered back to where a water-tank made a natural seat from which he could safely view the prospect that so beguiled her. This was where she would like to ski, she told him. This, and on the windward side of the neighbouring building, where the snow on the ground tended to be even softer and thicker. When the snowfall was heavy, she said, it even formed a bluff that stretched down from the rooftop to the ground. As she turned to point it out, the moon emerged from behind a bank of clouds and dipped behind her shoulder. She said something to him, her eyes still surveying the houses and the outlying roofs, but he didn't hear her. He was far too preoccupied by her silhouette. He felt a catch in his throat. He thought he had never seen anything as beautiful as the curve of her shoulder against the moonlit sky.

♦

The very next night Ami interrupted him as he was engaged in the time-honoured tactic of counting sheep to fall asleep. He sensed her sit down at the edge of the bed and listen to him mumble. He screwed his eyes shut in a desperate attempt to maintain his concentration, but he gave up the effort after a couple of seconds and sent the sheep packing.

Ami was staring at him when he opened his eyes.

'I miss you all the time, André,' she said.

He didn't reply, pulling up beside her instead and hugging her hard. She held on to him equally tight. Then he loosened his grip in surprise. There was a strange new softness in the vicinity of her chest. He let go of her abruptly, not knowing what to say, his face hot with confusion. She switched on the bedside lamp, looking at him with an imperturbable air. Finally, he muttered, 'Are you hurt? Did I hurt you?'

'Breasts, André,' she said softly, 'I'm growing breasts.' She got up from the bed and walked over to the door, locking it from the inside. 'They're all asleep,' she said, turning around and smiling at him as he sat up and watched her with a mixture of trepidation and excitement. Walking back to him, she placed his palms flat against her breasts. 'See?' she murmured, 'They're soft because they're growing. The girls at school say they grow fastest at night but that's probably an old wives' tale. In any case, the only precaution I take is to rub vinegar on them to make them come out faster.'

She was casually unbuttoning her pyjama top by this time. Bereft of speech, András watched her slip it off and drop it on the bed. He didn't really know what to say. It didn't seem right to speak at that moment. Turning full face towards him, she slid out of her pyjama bottoms and stood suddenly revealed in her nakedness. There was a soft orange fuzz between her legs. She stared at him quizzically. 'What do you think? Do you find me pretty? Am I as pretty as that girl in school you wrote to me about?'

András decided to focus on her toes in response. Even they were pretty. 'Yes!' he found himself muttering, 'You're very pretty!'

'Look at me, silly! You needn't look so petrified. I want you to look at me.'

András glanced up at her. There were tiny beads of perspiration above her top lip.

'Am I prettier than Aunt Zsuzsanna?'

'Yes! Of course!'

'Prettier than Maman?'

He looked at her miserably, 'How can I say? I don't even remember.'

She hurried over and pressed his head against her breasts, instantly enveloping him in her warm, sweet femininity. 'My poor baby!' she whispered. 'Of course you don't remember. It doesn't matter. I will be your Maman. I will be your Maman and your Ami and your everything else!'

She took a couple of steps back and looked at him speculatively. Turning around, she asked him, 'Am I as pretty from behind as I am from the front?'

'Yes,' he managed, 'yes, I think . . .'

She stopped, turning around again and expertly tugging at his buttons. He let her, realizing that he was breathing a lot faster than usual. His hands were clenched, his fingers all bunched up and tense. She took off his trousers next. Below them, he was wearing his favourite blue and yellow polka-dotted underpants, the ones with the bright red stitching. Down they went to the floor as well, drawn by a force more inexorable than gravity. He watched them crumple with fascination. She took hold of his hand and whispered: 'Come and stand in front of the mirror with me. I want to compare.'

He did as she told him. They looked at their reflections gravely, András positioning his hands in front of *that* place.

'I'm almost two inches taller than you, Dré,' she announced, finally.

'Are not!'

271

'Yes I am. Take a look yourself.'

He glanced back at the mirror and made a much more precise estimate, taking care to sound all grown-up and casual. 'More like one inch, actually, or even less, if I straighten up, like this . . .'

'And why are you so scrawny? Even my shoulders are wider!'

'I'm not scrawny!' András protested weakly, the evidence staring him in the face and coolly contradicting his assertion. Remembering the huge German boy in her class, he suddenly felt miserable and puny. It must have shown on his face, or else she must have sensed it, as she always sensed everything. 'It's all right,' he heard her say, her reflection in the mirror smiling gently back at him. 'I like the rest of you.' She removed his strategically placed hands, '*That*, especially . . .'

'Ami!' It came out like a squeak.

'Scared?'

'O fourse not!'

'What?'

'I said . . . ah . . . I said . . . I'm not squared! Scared!'

'Lie down next to me.'

'Why?'

'André!'

'Oh, all right.'

'Do you know what these things are called?'

'No . . .'

She whispered in his ear. Her mouth was damp. 'See here . . .' she said, 'I have them, even . . .'

András glanced down at the wisps of shiny hair.

She took his hand in hers, 'There . . . run your hand through them . . .'

She looked intently at him. 'What do they feel like?'

'What do they feel like?'

'Yes.'

'Like a rug.'

'A *rug*?'

'Yes . . . like the rug Uncle Iván has in front of his fireplace . . .'

She cut him off crossly. 'You're a silly boy!' she said.

'Am not!' he contested hotly.

'You are too! Or else you'd know they felt just like silk!'

272

By this point, however, *that* region of his anatomy had begun to misbehave uncontrollably. And his famous mind-control system (devised especially for use during gymnastics at school) seemed to have deserted him. Mortified, he tried to turn away. She noticed and broke into a delighted smile, going down to give the matter a closer inspection. Picking it up, she held it in her hands, patting it, kneading it, rolling it around and playing with it. When she spoke again, her voice was hushed and muffled. 'André!' she whispered, 'Are all boys made like *this*?' Without waiting for his answer, she drew his foreskin back and gently bit down on him. Then she opened her mouth wide and took him in entirely. With an air of dazzling unreality, he watched her slip him in and out of her mouth as she whispered, her face hot and red: 'I'm going to get away from here and come back to Budapest and be with you, my baby . . . watch if I don't . . . watch if I don't . . .'

With a sense of the most complete wonder, András realized that she was crying. He began to tremble uncontrollably. He was just about to pull her up when he reared back, an electric shock shooting through his spine, his head suddenly on fire. He felt her tongue course through his veins. The floor of the room tilted towards the ceiling. Dazed and confused, he looked down at himself. A warm liquid was swimming out of him. And his twin was laughing and crying and swallowing, all at the same time. He closed his eyes, the world lapsing away, as if in a dream. Surveying the darkness within, he began to feel incredibly elated. 'I love you, Ami,' he heard himself whisper. He felt light-headed and giddy.

♦

Although neither of them could have predicted the delay, they wouldn't meet again until a full six years later when they'd just turned eighteen. It was the spring of 1968, in Germany, in Dresden. András was on leave from his studies in Budapest. Uncle Iván had sponsored the trip (a well-connected friend of his had arranged a scholarship). As he explained to András, it would be good for him to get away and get a taste of the outside world, even if it was only a few hours from Budapest. 'Of course, I would have liked you to have gone to Paris,' he'd continued, with a faint smile of regret. 'That was where I went when I was your age. But what with the way things are in Prague, with rumours of the Russians moving in, Dresden is the best I can do, I'm afraid.'

András's earliest impression of the East German city was that the smog there was even worse than in Budapest. The sky appeared perpetually dark and overcast, the streets choked with a thick brown haze. Even the sun seemed dirty and washed-out and filled with dust instead of radiance. At night, the rain came down in dust-stained dribbles; at dawn, the city greeted the light with smog from a hundred factories. And the rest of the time . . . but what was the point? Dresden depressed him and made him want to return to Budapest as soon as possible.

He had all but resigned himself to a miserable stay when, early one morning, he was woken up by a telephone call from Austria. A long-distance call, the concierge said grumpily, from a woman in Linz.

It was Ami. She was beside herself with excitement; she was arranging to come and see him in Dresden. But how had she found out where he was staying? And why didn't she wait until he returned to Budapest in a few weeks? It would be much more fun there, he had many more friends. He was a stranger in Dresden and was on a rigorous study programme, besides. In Budapest he'd be able to spend much more time with her, show her off to his friends. Budapest would really be the most sensible thing, he reiterated.

'Muxh!' she responded.

He asked her what that meant. She said it was a word she'd made up on the spur of the moment to tell him that he was wasting his breath. She did that sometimes – invented words that would only make sense to the two of them. She was still laughing at his objections when she hung up on him.

She arrived in Dresden less than a week later.

It took him some time to get used to her again. She wore a jacket made of razor blades sewn into a sort of chain-mail.

She wore leather gloves and a flowered silk mini-skirt that was ripped in places; her knee-high boots were hand-made in hell. What else? Oh, yes – she was training to be an anarchist, she said. András wasn't quite sure what she meant. He decided it must have something to do with the sensation she caused every time they ventured out of the hotel. Typically, Ami attributed the reactions to German provinciality and narrow-mindedness. They'd probably never seen anything like her in Dresden.

That very first evening they sat next to each other on the bed.

András couldn't think of anything to say. The room felt hot and airless, the ventilation system wasn't functioning again. Remembering her room in Vienna and the entire Western chic of that city, he felt suddenly embarrassed by his surroundings. It was a new feeling for him, this strange and inverse class consciousness. For the first time he realized how tatty the hotel must seem to her, how miserable his room, how utterly dismal and broken-down the bed. He knew that his spartan diet of bread, sausage and coffee would have to be changed for the duration of her stay.

As if to compensate for the poverty of his environment, he became dry and stiff in his mannerisms, uncharacteristically formal when he was in her presence. Miserably, he wondered if she could still understand him and sense what was going on inside him. But she seemed completely preoccupied with herself, especially by the effect that she was having on him, a trait that he found increasingly irritating.

'Not quite the way you expected me to look, eh, André?'

'What? No, it isn't that, it's just that it's been a while . . .'

'You're just going to have to get used to it.'

András bit his tongue and looked away. 'Why don't you tell me about yourself?' he said instead. 'What kind of music do you listen to, for instance?'

'Music? Oh, I don't know, lots of stuff.'

'I listen to Beethoven myself,' he began, adopting an unconsciously severe air. 'Mozart, Brahms, a little Schubert on the side . . . I suppose I am a bit of a classicist.'

She thought for a moment. Then she whipped out a small

tape-recorder, putting on a song. She clenched her fists as the cacophony came on. As he watched in amazement, she flung herself on the bed, drawing up her knees and laughing at the sheer anarchy of the sound. At the end of the song, which he found impossible to classify as music, she turned eagerly to him. 'What do you think?'

'Oh, I *loved* it.'

'Liar!' She kicked him on the shin.

He moved away from her, cringing at the bristles sticking out of the mattress.

'I also love small, fast sports cars!' she carried on, oblivious to his torment. 'I love going off by myself. I love roses. I love the colour red. I love rain. Rain affects me like nothing else! I love life lived on the brink: one little push, and, bam! – over the edge! And, incidentally, I *love* that shapeless *thing* on the wall . . .' She pointed to András's battered overcoat dangling from the end of a hook.

'*That*? You can have it,' he said, surprised.

'*Really*? I can have it?'

'It's a man's overcoat actually, an East German uniform, you can tell by the shoulders, by the way they're square-cut. But it's kind of battered, you know, it's seen a lot of wear . . .'

'That's exactly *why* I want it, stupid! It's original! That, and the fact that it's yours.'

She scrambled off the bed and put it on over her clothes. It dwarfed her, the ends trailing around her feet.

'How do I look?'

'It's a bit big for you, don't you think?'

'Oh, that's nothing! I can wear boots with heels to compensate.'

'Well, it's not exactly a sports car . . . more like a Trabant if you think about it.'

She made a face as she shrugged it off and returned to the bed. 'You're no fun!' she said. Lying down beside him, she ran her fingers over his face. Her hand was moist and warm; it smelt of deodorant and cigarettes. There was a tattoo in the middle of her wrist, a great fat sun with a drunken crimson face. András knew she had another one in the shape of a half-moon between her breasts. She'd written to him about it.

'You're growing a beard, André.'

'I've only just begun . . .'

'I can see that. It's still silky and soft, not rough like Uncle Iván's was. How is he, by the way?'

'Spoilt. His wife spoils him. She's very proper. She has two dogs called Lettuce and Paprika, and a cat named Jaime, Cardinal Sin.'

'You don't like her.'

'No, she gets on my nerves with all her affectations and airs. She used to work for some minister or other and it shows. I think she imagines a house ought to be organized along the lines of a secretariat. But she dotes on Iván, and that's probably what matters.'

She turned her back to him. 'Zsuzsanna's new husband is an art dealer. He's fat and comfortable and makes passes at me whenever he thinks she's not watching. But he's useful. Ever since I decided I wanted to work in the art business, he's been introducing me to all his clients.'

'Does Aunt Zsuzsanna know he's been bothering you?'

'Of course she knows! Why else do you think he's held off?'

'The pervert!'

'To each his own, André . . .' She turned to him and changed the subject. 'When you're alone,' she said, 'and maybe lying down like this in a darkened room, what do you think about?'

'Lots of things.'

'Do you think of me at all?'

'Sometimes. No, that's not right. I think of you quite often.'

'And what do you feel when you think about me?'

Instinctively, he knew what she was talking about.

'Sometimes I feel strange,' he replied.

'As if you're sick of *being*?'

'Yes, a bit like that. I feel an absence that I can never quite explain. An absence but also a sadness, a terrible endless sadness.'

'I feel the same way,' she sighed. 'Sometimes it's so painful I feel like screaming out. And then it's as if there's an echo travelling inside my head and trying to get out.'

'Like a yearning?'

'Yes, but it's also much more physical, like wanting to dance with a stranger inside my head. I get this mad urge to turn myself inside out. It's like having vertigo, only the torment is greater. My head starts spinning. I lose my sense of gravity and fall down. Then I get these dark and wretched-looking bruises, all red and purple. I crawl into a corner of the room to stop myself from falling down. I press myself against walls and try hemming myself in. I close my eyes and it's as if it's you that I'm pressing against. Sometimes I want to bang my head against the wall and reduce myself to a bloodburst, but mostly I just begin to sweat. I sweat profusely. It's like dissolving, being in a drowsy liquid state. It makes me want to go to sleep and never wake up again.'

'For me it's as if I can hear your voice.'

'In the room?'

'No, inside my head, like an echo, just like you said. And if the room is bright, everything goes dark and tires me out. It makes me wonder what's going on.'

'I get scared when that happens, you know? I have to force myself to think of something else to make the fear go away.'

'It's strange, that fear . . . like silence.'

'Like silence,' she assented.

'Or quicksand.'

'Quicksand?' she hesitated, thinking. 'Probably that too, in a way.'

There was a waiting smell in the room.

'André . . .' She reached out to hold his hand.

'What is it?' He turned to look at her. She was gazing contemplatively at him. She gave a hesitant smile. 'To be a woman, André, do you know what that's like? Do you know what it's like to feel the fluid trickle out of you and turn, in the cold, to silver?'

He shifted uneasily. 'Why do you bring that up?'

'Don't you know why?' She hesitated. 'André,' she said, 'I want to get inside.'

'What do you mean?'

She pressed his hand. 'I want to get inside us.'

He cleared his throat.

'André . . . did you hear what I said?'

'Yes . . . yes, of course I did . . .'

278

'Have you forgotten what it was like?'

'Well . . . not exactly . . .'

'How could you have forgotten?'

He stayed frozen, fixed to the bed. Chained.

'You're very quiet,' she persisted. 'Are you surprised? It doesn't matter. You don't have to reply. We'll think of some other way to connect.' She sat up. 'I have a new game for us to play.'

Relieved, he edged away. 'A game?' he said.

'Yes. I made it up only for us. It could be our game. Do you want to play?'

A curious sense of satisfaction filling him, he replied firmly: 'Yes.'

'Good. I knew you'd say that.'

'How do we play?'

'It's simple, really.'

'Show me . . .' His voice cracked. 'No, tell me,' he said.

'It's a simple game. It's all about changing places. About my becoming you and you becoming me.'

He laughed nervously. 'Just like that?'

'Just like that,' she said, slipping her shirt off over her head. It opened like a white flower and fell to the floor beside the bed. András felt her knees touch his. 'Just like that,' she said as she slid down between his legs. He swallowed and bent over double, pressing his face to the pillow to stop from crying out. He wanted desperately to touch her, to scream, or to suffocate himself. Controlling himself, he managed, 'And that's Ourgame?'

He heard her chortle. 'No, silly, that's not what it's called. It's not called Ourgame. Actually, I call it Mirroring. But you could call it Ourgame if you like. Maybe it's better that way . . .'

She raised herself beside him, a ring of wet encircling her palm. 'It looks like rain, doesn't it? It looks like snow, melting, driven . . .'

She ran the hand over her face and then over his. She touched his eyes, his cheeks, his lips. Her hand came to rest against his neck.

He gazed at her silently, feeling strangely reconciled with the world.

'It looks like snow . . .' she said, 'but colder, far colder . . . almost as cold as you are, André.'

She removed her hand, her eyes holding his.

'I've never loved anyone but you, my phallic bride,' she whispered. 'Some people would call that passion . . .' She glanced away. 'Some people would call it poison. But it's much more like a circle of reason, isn't it?'

She leaned over to kiss him on the mouth, her eyes withdrawn and sombre. 'Like a circle . . .' she murmured, 'spinning round and round until there's no reason left.'

She got up from the bed and walked over to the closet before tip-toeing back to him again. She switched on the huge orange lamp next to the bed. Holding on to his hand, she made him get up. He took a couple of steps forward. She made him turn sideways, leaning him backwards and raising his arms. She made him pirouette. Dug into her suitcase. Pulled out a sheer black dress. Walking across and holding it up against him, she made him undress. Next, she went to the bathroom and returned with a razor, a vessel filled with water, and some soap. Starting from his right ear, she worked the blade round the curve of his head down to his other ear, then down past his chin and up again. She did it again and again until there was no hair left, and then she rinsed off the lather. She dried his shaven scalp and face with a wash cloth and made him look at himself in a mirror. He looked pale and shorn and detached, as if he were already someone else. He closed his eyes and offered her the rest of him. She made him lie down on the floor, on a towel. He felt lighter than air, light-headed, liberated.

She dealt with the rest of his body. Made him contort, back to front, front to back. Shaved his back. Shaved his chest. Shaved under his arms. His legs.

He felt his skin turn finer, softer, imagined his hips filling out, his breasts . . .

She returned to her suitcase, that treasure chest. Pulling open a compartment, she scooped out a brassière. Sensible black cotton with supports. She made him take a deep breath, made him tuck his stomach in. He strapped on the bra. It was surprisingly soft. She took out matching black panties and made him put them on next. He put on her black garter belt. Then a thin cotton slip. Then the black chiffon dress. Stockings. Stilettoes.

280

Then the face. Foundation. Lipstick – the merest touch of gloss. Mascara. Pencil around the eyes. Perfume between the breasts.

He walked around the room and tested his balance. Moved his hands, softened his movements. Stared at the mirror from different angles, places. Returned to the mirror to make adjustments. Safety-pins here and there. Tightened his waistline with a belt. Raised his shoulders. Padded his breasts. Returned to the mirror again and again until he finally *became* the woman standing next to him . . .

He said, 'Hello, András . . .' exactly as she did, with that catch in her voice. He tried to be calm, but his lips began to tremble, the excitement of the subterfuge finally sinking in. He looked at the woman in the mirror, marvelling that it was really him: *she* tried to cover that up by taking refuge in the act of turning around. But it was too late, too revealing in all those little gestures that he knew so well: the gentle throbbing above the eyebrows, the slight pursing of the lips, the plucking motion . . . all those small self-revelations.

Crossing over to the window, he drew aside the curtains and gazed out through *her* eyes, silent.

Outside, the fog had started curling around blue-black leaves, sliding into each individual stem, branching,

as if in the throes of a fever, alien, the giant trees beginning to shiver and shake, eventually shattering

to pieces.

He returned to the centre of the room and determinedly faced his twin.

She cast an appraising look at him.

'Now it's my turn,' he said.

She smiled serenely. 'Yes.'

They fell on their knees, facing each other, his hands expertly reaching down. She gasped as he thrust hard against her and sealed the suture. He groaned out loud; she laughed, exultant. 'Oh, my sweet shared seed,' she whispered, 'my dark prince of indecision!'

'Kiss me, André,' she said.

He kissed her, smiling.

'You kiss like a murderer,' he said.

She turned away from him, her nostrils flaring. 'What an odd thing to say!' She looked around, a hand reaching up to her throat. 'I can't breathe, why is this room so stuffy?'

He pressed his lips to her neck, holding them there while he inhaled her fragrance. 'I don't know, Ami, I can't see . . . you're filling the room up, making it dense . . .'

She made a small sound and drew back with a grin, 'Flatterer!'

'No, it's not flattery, it's a fact.'

'Liar, then!' She looked around the room. 'Seriously, though, I'm breathing through a fug!'

'You mean *fog* . . .'

'No, I mean *fug*. F-u-g, fug!' she retorted, 'And it's *fogging* everything up, you included! Why is it happening?'

'Well, it could be due to any number of things. It could be the taller houses hemming us in. It could be the night draping down like a kiss. Or the chemicals in the fog, laminating. It could be that the season's changing. It could be all of our self-questioning. Or . . . even more terrible, it could be *both of us* . . . and finally, America and András discover, with a feeling of total panic, what they'd always suspected . . . that they are . . . oh God! . . . that they are *stuffy people*!'

'Oh, stop it!' She burst out laughing, her face lighting up. 'Sometimes you sound exactly like a dead writer's monologue!'

'André, I . . .'

'No, stop it! I'm getting completely confused between me and you! And these shoes hurt!'

'How could they? Your feet are smaller than mine!'

'They do, I'm telling you!'

'Patience! – it's just a matter of practice.'

She raised a hand, glancing at him quickly, 'André . . .'

'Yes?'

'Do you remember that part in one of your letters about needing to deal with your emotions for me before you could feel for someone else?'

'Yes, I do. Why do you ask?'

'And do you still think about me as often as you used to?'

'Often? My God! I think about you all the time! Why? – Why do you need to ask?'

She hesitated and turned her back to him. 'Because I've been wondering about what it would be like to live with you forever, that's why.'

He felt an inexplicable languor flood over him. Fingertips crinkling, he curled over to her side like a giant wing. Locking on to her eyes, he slid her gently backwards without once touching. Behind them, a single shadow spread over the wall. He lifted a hand in slow motion, letting it drift. She followed the motion. The hand detached in space, floating off . . . joined in an instant by his. Overwhelmed, he moved his face to one side. She followed him. He lowered his face, colouring. She did the same, merging. He looked into her eyes again. She drank him in. He swung his head from side to side, she replicated the movement. Her face broke into a smile, which spread in an instant to his. He turned round and round and round into her circles turning round and round and round into his circles . . . closing in. He closed his eyes and entered her blindside, exploring, while she . . . she sensed him part his lips, shaping the words as he said them. Her eyes flecked over, the light in them glowing. He looked down, his fingers instinctively following the intricate choreography of her dance. Reading her eyes, her hands, her lips, he leaned forward, touching, not daring to breathe, not daring to speak, nothing to explain, nothing to explain at all . . . A flash of pain, then a suspended calm, a sensation of falling. 'I can't see you,' he whispered, beads of sweat pouring down his forehead and his face and her forehead and her face as they went down on their knees and folded into the ritual rocking to and fro the words cascading out of them in a single stream enter me enter me enter me my andré enter me enter me enter me my ami enter me enter me enter me my andré . . .

Mirroring.

The angles and planes of the room slowed down, space flattening out, time standing still. They were children again, knowing nothing, sublime, infinite. They closed their eyes, looking down, their hands insinuating eels, entwining in a grotto of their own imagining. Dipping their heads, they descended among the rocks, plunging into the space between their arms.

They were lovers, they were hunters, they were Gemini stalking the murky waters, sensing the currents.

Let me in, Ami.

Falling into your arms.

Lying across an ocean . . .

He looked at his hand. It was wet. He rubbed it across his face, leaving a smear. Wet on his lips and wet on his face.

He broke away from her, turning away from that honey-coloured pelt and ending the masquerade. She watched him leave – watched him go back to the bed and lie down, the spell broken. He lit a cigarette and crossed his arms. He crossed his legs. He lay there and studied the fan rotating endlessly overhead.

At length, he sat up again. Returning to the mirror he stared at himself. His make-up was beginning to flake off, the blue shadows showing underneath. Mortified, he turned around and contemplated his twin. Her eyes met his gaze and then they dropped listlessly. She picked up a key-chain, moved a belt (his) to one side of the bed, then moved it back again. He looked away. With a swift and sudden resolution, he took off her belt. Took off her black dress. Took off the matching slip. The black panties. Matching brassière. Garter belt. Matching shoes. Matching stockings. Took off her face. Took off her lips. Took off her nails. Slipped off her breasts. Stepped out of her skin. Discarded her mannerisms. Stripped off her instincts. Shrugged off her sensuality. Washed off her perfume. Washed everything away. Returned to his own nakedness, returned to being himself. Replaced each article exactly as he'd found it. Walked back to the bed, smoothed back the sheets. Took one last lingering look at her before she stirred and stood up and walked over to the basin.

He contemplated her as she washed her face. By the light of the orange lamp, he watched her transform. He thought about how things between them would never be the same again. *Could* never be the same again.

She looked at him when she was done. 'Every man is the sum of his choices, André,' she said. He turned his face away; he didn't ask her to explain what she meant. She lay down beside him while he glanced around the room for one last time before turning off the lamp.

All that remained of Ourgame was that orange lamp.

That, and the absolute pitch of silence.

◆

Ami cut her visit short and flew out of Dresden the very next day. András accompanied her to the airport, but her flight was late, and she insisted that he shouldn't wait. He tried to resist but she cut through his feeble protests. They kissed half-heartedly, and then he saw her to the gate.

At a loss for what to do, he wandered around the city until late in the evening. He saw a dull movie, visited a dull museum, ate at a bad restaurant. When he finally returned to his hotel, a drunken man staggered into him on the steps and muttered under his breath: 'A stone is a stone is a stone and there's no mistaking it.'

Confused and miserable, and missing Ami more than ever now that she'd left, András entered his darkened room and flung himself hopelessly on the bed. As he curled up and lay in the darkness, the muted sound of the radio from the next room filtered in through the wall. It was a news report, the German commentator's voice dry and lifeless. At first András tried to ignore the voice as an unwanted intrusion. Then his neighbour turned up the volume and András had no option but to pull a pillow over his head.

He was still trying to stifle the sound when he heard the words 'Czechoslovakia' and 'peaceful intervention' and sat up, his own troubles instantly forgotten. Switching on the orange lamp, he ran across the room and pressed his ears to the wall to hear the news broadcast better. He'd just about begun to distinguish entire sentences when someone knocked rapidly on his door. Before he could answer, the door swung open and his neighbour, a Romanian student of philology, burst in. 'Have you heard?' he began excitedly. 'It's happened at last! The Prague

Spring is over. The Russians have invaded Czechoslovakia. History falls to pieces now! It's the end of all our hopes!'

♦

András returned to Budapest to a welter of confused impressions. Everyone else was preoccupied with the events in Prague but he was so relieved to have put Dresden behind him that he just wanted to lose himself under the vast blue skies of his native city. Caught up in the excitement of his return, he spent days roaming the streets with his head in the clouds, his mind revelling in the absence of confining walls, his pockets crammed with notes and ideas. In the evenings he went to the theatre and to concerts; at night he returned home in a fever of inspiration. An epiphany, this city I call home, he repeated over and over to himself.

He moved out of his uncle's house and rented a room in a hostel. The room was tiny, low-ceilinged and dark. The plumbing leaked, the doors had no locks, and the windows opened out on to a bare, brick wall. But there was a fresco painted on the ceiling, and the student next door sang arias from *La Traviata*, and the landlord was a cellist who'd played with Toscanini in New York.

His head filled with plans, he settled down to write. He wrote during the daytime at first, then the darker hours consumed him and kept him indoors. No flim-flam here, but page after page filled with purpose. Ideas flared up, then settled down, given form in words. Characters lived and died only to be retrieved and renewed, immortal. Sentences flowed into sentences; paragraphs and chapters formed from disconnected thoughts. And always he searched for connections, the empty pages charging him with a mad sense of mission. Mad? Yes, mad – he had to admit that that was the way it was, the search for the narrative stream, his major concern. Structure, process, motion, connections: strung out like a convoy of lights, these laws of his universe. Safe in his own world, learning from his own words, the quest for reality from within his own imagination.

Everything hurtled out of control after that, all the carefully conceived structures disintegrating with the passage of time. His mind on fire, he plunged repeatedly into his private sea, swimming with words. It was all he could do to put pen to paper to set it dancing. The images brimmed through his head.

♦

His first book was a novel, a portrait of an alcoholic and a madman. The second was a treatise on sadism and masochism that epitomized, in his view, the sickness of the time. The third book was rejected by the censors with an official warning. The fourth, set in an industrial town in the south, was his first book to be banned. Older now, his writing more mature, he learned to write faster, run faster, constantly keeping ahead of the censors. His fifth book – his first *samizdat* undertaking – was a collection of essays about a man with a hypodermic needle in his arm. He destroyed the manuscript of his next enterprise. He began his sixth book in 1979. A simple love story, he intended it to meld his world. Instead, it became the one that refused to be born, transforming instead into a collection of dreams, an unfathomable, unfamiliar mirage.

That was the way it was, his partly lived life. Each book a piece of him, for nine unforgettable years the confluence, the texture, the substance of his universe.

Yes, it had been that simple once. Shadow-dancing in deserted rooms. Boy turning into man, man turning into rock. Then the promise made to set himself free. *Then* that private sea, brimming over with words. At first, he'd put up his fists. Then he'd given up and plunged in, swimming, dancing. The most exquisite freedom, that journey inward. A bridge to another world.

But the seed to be a writer, when was that first planted? From the very beginning? No, that wasn't the way it was. In the beginning, he had wanted to join the opera like Maman, be a tenor, the world's greatest, a presence larger than life, a *star*. But it was Ami who'd shot that idea down, and quickly. Listen to me, André, she'd said, your ambition's a fickle thing, you can't sing, you don't have the voice, you simply can't sing! I'm saying this for your own good, you'd better think of some other occupation. Join a band – be my hero, play the guitar!

Instead, with typical mule-headedness (Ami's words), he'd abandoned Orpheus altogether, running away from music, taking off, in a manner of speaking, full tilt, never to look back.

No – the seed to be a writer was planted much later. There'd been nothing preconceived about it, no momentous revelations, no greater sense of purpose. One day he'd come face to face with a blank page and, before he knew it, a word had written itself down. It had made him nervous, to have it emerge out of him like that, an accident, unexpected and unprimed. But a trophy it certainly was, immaculate and fragile. There was nothing laboured about it, nothing self-conscious; it was calm and relaxed and completely natural. He'd wondered if there'd be any more like it – that very first word.

And then, when he was least expecting it, he'd found his first true moment of inspiration. There, by the river, the *idea* of becoming a writer, that first fleeting glimpse of the shape of things to come.

Or, at least, that was the way he'd explained it . . .

That was the way he'd explained it to Immanuele in a rare moment of divulgence. He'd surprised himself with his willingness to confide in her like that. It was the true beginning of their connectedness. In a fundamental way he sensed in her a shared passion, a fascination with the act of creation, that desire to harness the intellect to the divine. It brought them steadily closer, each seeking out the companionship of the other with new books, new ideas, new topics of conversation. The congruence was remarkable, her statements echoing his own ruminations.

It was a kind of intellectual companionship that neither one of them had experienced before. He had been too young to care or understand; she had been far too preoccupied with her musical passions. Once discovered, however, it served as an unerring source of strength for both of them, and they returned to it time and time again to slake their thirst. Both extremely reserved by nature, the liberation they experienced in each other's company could not have come as anything but a surprise.

It was completely different from what András had come to expect from his sister. With her he'd always felt the need to hold things back; there'd been no other way to demarcate his own sense of self. Until he met Immanuele, his had been a life defined entirely by an unsparing opposition to his twin, a life both bipolar and defensive, much of it spent doggedly digging in. It had made him precociously logical and dry, viewing reality with a permanently sardonic eye. Now that he was reeling under the impact of his emotions, he wasted little time in going to the opposite extreme, hopelessly idealizing Immanuele as the embodiment of all that was desirable.

That he found her breathtakingly beautiful served as an added impetus. It was a beauty that affected him profoundly, compelling him to strive to know her better. It was far from an inexplicable bewitching, as Ami would later choose to interpret it; on the contrary, it was Immanuele's acuity and perceptiveness that awakened him. She instilled a belief in the redemptive energies of art in him. It was as if her very existence filled him with faith in himself, her presence in his life a magnificent affirmation of his own convictions.

Their first meeting was at Elemér Klein's place. At the time, Immanuele was doing freelance work for underground publications. She also wrote poetry, but only for her own benefit and not for public consumption. She told him she'd studied orchestral conducting but that it hadn't quite worked out. It was the one thing she hardly talked about – that, and her childhood years.

She gave him some of her own prose to read. They were *feuilletons*, brief essays filled with a bleak, black humour. Her style was deliberately matter-of-fact and, in that, very different from his own passionate compositions. She already had an established reputation as a young dissident with a radically critical attitude towards the regime. In the public sphere she was completely fearless, her forthrightness attracting frequent official criticism. On a more serious note, there were rumours of a move to send her into exile. Elemér had revealed that to him, moving András enough to ask her if she was at all concerned about the dangers of her situation.

'Not at all,' she answered. 'I really don't care. The imperative is to end their farce. Turn their weapons against themselves.

Word against word. That's what they're most scared of. The power of words. Words are the most powerful force in nature, just like storms, or mountains.'

Yes, but what about the danger of exile? Of losing her voice entirely – what about that?

'Exile?' She'd smiled with more than a trace of bitterness. 'But that's an occupational hazard, isn't it? Anyone who's fool enough to play this game knows that. *Ought* to know that. In my world, *any* other alternative is to surrender and fall in with their dictates. Integrity, András, that's the crux. It's the one thing they can't take away from us.'

That first night they'd left Elemér's place together. András had offered to escort her home but she'd suggested a walk through a nearby park instead. It kept the thugs who followed her fit. She gave him a smile when she said that, a smile that had no humour in it at all. 'You probably shouldn't be seen with me,' she remarked. The way she said it made him shiver. In the face of her determined insouciance, it was all he could do to emulate her resolve. They sauntered through the park, Immanuele insisting on doubling back from time to time to surprise their watchers into revealing themselves. But their shadowers were either too wary or else too determined to maintain a safe distance, and they never allowed themselves to be caught off guard.

She lived by herself in a large and dilapidated house on E-Daj Street. Her room was packed with books and notepads and music scores. There was a thick coating of dust over everything. Every now and again she tried to restore some semblance of order to the place, but things inevitably returned to their habitual chaos.

More than once she'd thought about moving out, she confided. The place was simply too big for her and there were always things that needed to be done. But her grandfather had built the house, it was where she'd spent her whole life, and it was almost as if it had become a part of her. 'It's just like a song,' she said, 'with words that only I can remember and understand . . .' She smiled, a bit ruefully. 'I feel uneasy if I'm away from here for too long. I feel lost.'

It wasn't long after that first visit that András realized he was in love. After some degree of hesitation, occasioned by his own native diffidence, he decided to confess as much to her, only to learn that she didn't feel the same way about him. She liked his company, she said, she wanted them to be friends, but for her that was all there was to it. She'd had enough admirers in her time, she explained, to find that kind of attention distracting. She was being unusually candid and direct, she said, because she didn't want to keep anything from him. She valued his clear-headedness and she didn't want to lose him to any kind of foolishness.

Much to his dismay, he discovered that he didn't know how to handle her rejection. What made things worse was that she then decided to leave the city, giving him absolutely no hint of her destination. Elemér was the only person who knew where she was, but she'd sworn him to secrecy, and this time even András couldn't ferret the information out of him.

A couple of months passed with no news from her at all. With a twenty-one-year-old's bleak and exaggerated hyperbole, András began to question everything, not least his own possible role in her life, which he sadly concluded to be minimal. If the world up to that point had led him to believe in his own destiny, he was now convinced of quite the opposite: that his confidence in himself had been singularly misplaced, and that he really didn't amount to much. He tried not to think about it but it proved to be a constant preoccupation, a dark and niggling hazard.

His morale at its lowest ebb, he resigned himself to the inevitable. He tried to take refuge in writing but it was no use. He spent days locked in his room until the grey fog of countless cigarettes drove him outdoors. He wore out shoes walking endlessly in an attempt to drown out the sad-eyed acrobat of his soul. He bought himself a cheap guitar and, propped up in his bed, learnt to play. In the stumbling dark of a cinema, surrounded by rats and caved-in chairs, he broke down and admitted to himself that falling in love had made his life unbearable.

On the floor of his room, he wrote: '*I will cast my heart in bronze for you.*'

Across the bare expanse of his chest, he wrote: '*András, you fool!*'

And then, one slow and shimmering summer afternoon,

salvation tip-toed up to him in a yellow suit: it was Elemér, distributing fliers for a commemorative reading of Miklós Radnóti's poetry. 'I command you to come!' Elemér insisted. 'You'll never forgive yourself if you don't!' He held up a finger. 'No, don't ask me to say any more! Just call me the guardian angel who's going to turn your life around!'

♦

The reading was held in a lecture theatre at the College of Theatre and Film Arts. The room was packed to capacity and very dark. András met Elemér at the entrance. They had seats in the third row, next to some friend of Elemér's who was 'tremendously interesting and brilliant and a writer just like you!'

They stumbled down the dark aisle, moving slowly towards their seats. When they reached their row, Elemér bent over and tapped his friend on the shoulder and she turned around and looked up. Startled, András grabbed the back of a chair. Beside him, he heard Elemér chuckle. 'You mustn't mind him, Immanuele,' he laughed, 'you know what he's like.' She didn't say anything but stood up instead and smiled at András. Submerged in that smile, he slid into his seat, conscious only of the relief flooding through him. 'Where were you?' was all he could manage before she reached out and kissed him on the cheek. 'I was searching for wisdom,' she replied. 'And what about you?'

'Charting a strange course of heartbreak and thinking about you.'

She laughed out loud, her head surrounded by the blue haze of her cigarette. 'Elemér tells me you've finally finished your book. So, you're a fully fledged writer now, André?'

He made room for her question, carefully shaping his words. 'I *try* to write,' he said, 'there is a difference. I hear the words, I have to speak them out. I hear the words, I have to write them down.'

She waved away his qualifications. 'Will you let me read it? If you don't find it intrusive, that is . . .'

'Of course. But you might be disappointed.'

292

'Why do you say that?'

'I've been told my writing is peculiar.'

She smiled. '*Life* is peculiar.'

He looked at her, surprised.

She smiled again, 'I mean, shouldn't one be suspicious of any writing that makes sense in a world that obviously doesn't?'

Someone walked up to her, engaging her in conversation. She turned to András. 'Do you mind?'

'Of course not, please . . .'

He began to chat with Elemér, but found himself glancing at her surreptitiously, his eyes continuously straying to her face where the suspicion of a smile played faintly around her lips.

The room fell into darkness, an absolute silence descending as the audience arranged itself in a semi-circle around the elevated stage. A sole spot-light focused on the reader, who was sitting on a metal chair behind a small table. She was in her mid-fifties, with ash-coloured hair tied up in a severe bun. She looked just like a strict high-school teacher. When she started speaking, however, she was able to communicate an unusual degree of passion, her voice rising and falling with the lines and enthralling her listeners. She had a beautiful voice, cultivated especially for reciting poetry, the kind that breathed the words out loud and carefully nurtured each sound:

With your right arm beneath my neck I lay –
I'd ask you to hold my head, so hurt that day –
listening to your blood pulsing in the night . . .

The majority of the poems she had selected dated from the last war – some composed mere days before the poet's death – their discovery purely accidental. In 1946, in the process of exhuming a mass grave at Abda, a village in Western Hungary near the river Rába, a notebook filled with poetry had been found on one of the decomposed corpses (killed by a bullet to the head). The coroner's report stated that the corpse had been accompanied by 'a visiting card with the name Dr Miklós Radnóti printed on it, one small notebook, in the back pocket of the trousers, soaked in the juices of the body and blackened by the wet earth'.

András closed his eyes. The last entry in the notebook, dated
October 31, 1944:

Shot in the neck. You'll be finished off just like this –
I muttered to myself – so just lie still.
Patience flowers into death now.
Der springt noch auf, *spoken over me.*
Mud and blood drying on my ear.

András opened his eyes. Somewhere in the background there
was a smattering of applause. The reader closed her book and
left the stage, walking down the aisle and out of sight. Silence
followed her departure, the silence of loss. No one moved. The
air streamed soundlessly between the chairs, thick and still.
András closed his eyes again, his lids as heavy as stone. He
recalled the verses extricated from the clay and the decaying
flesh and bone – the red rusting of flesh on bone – each word
drying in the sun, deciphered one by one, each to each a
kingdom:

Death.   Desire.   Life.   Love.

He opened his eyes again in an attempt to ignore the very different presence to his right, the sense of something very bright
and sharply defined and *alive*. He tried to ignore the sudden rush
of blood to his head, the roaring sound that drove out everything
else and left only a single name. And the name roared with a
whisper louder than the entire world, slipping between the words
from a long-forgotten war and mixing everything up. And the
name formed a screen before his face, making him squirm and
shift as he struggled to get a grip on himself. In desperation, he
stared up at the ceiling and studied its blank expanse, filled with
a growing wisdom, yet ultimately ignorant.

He tried to concentrate. It was no use.

Driven by a force greater than the sum of all his inhibitions,
he burst out: 'Death and desire, Immanuele! That's what the
writing is all about! It's all that's left to us! The approximation of
the bone, not just a temporary fix to the wound!'

294

He could see heads rotating. Someone coughed. Someone else said crossly, 'Keep it down, please!'

Immanuele simply looked at him, her eyes glittering and bright. Her hands were clenched, her fingers white and tense. Tears were streaming down her face as she sat hunched to one side, motionless.

Immanuele.

In the middle of that room darkened by their collective hopelessness, how intoxicated he had become with that name!

Emperházy, Immanuele.

And yet . . .

about the only thing they had shared by the end was the pain.

That, and the midnight oxygen.

And somewhere in the midst of a mad blur of events, they almost made a child, a boy, Miklós. Their possible sun.

And András discovered the utility of mental blocks.

Or, how not to think about things . . .

Miklós. Immanuele had named him.

He was to have been her temple, her shrine, her altar.

Ami called him their sleeping star.

She had been in Vienna through that entire period.

Watching.

◆

That dream about running through open fields again, rain pounding down on him, the black night surrounding him. In the distance, he can see the lights of many campfires. The track winds down from an elevation, the ground opening up to a vast natural amphitheatre. Around the campfires he can hear the sound of many drums. They make the earth tremble beneath his feet as he runs on steadily. Turning his face to the sky and closing his eyes, he recalls a verse from a poet long dead and gone: '*Dark night, gods of light, a dense carpet of stars, ruled by the wind . . .*'

Immanuele waits for him within a circle of fire. Surrounded by flames, she asks, 'What do you have for me?'

He offers her his heart cast in bronze.

She casts it aside and asks, 'What do you have for me?'

He wakes up at that moment and tries to sit up, his hands scrabbling under the sheets. He is soaked in sweat. Why has he suddenly remembered that dream? Could it be the silence in the room? Senselessly empty, that silence. Parched and poisonous and filled with ghosts.

András turns his face to the wall.

Then he forces his head up from the bed, his eyes searching the room for reassurance. Beside his bed, there is a metal stand with row upon row of test-tubes filled with a bilious green solution. The light from the night-light filters through them and transforms them into glowing eyes.

He picks up a glass of water from the stand. It tastes like rain.

Sitting up, he looks out of the window to where the clouds are slowly moving over the river.

That river . . .

The river that belonged to Immanuele.

◆

'I wish I could get drunk,' he said suddenly.

Outside, the snow drifted silently past Petőfi's statue in the square, the flakes reflecting back through the windows, the room filling up with grey shadows. The city was tangling up in knots of white. It had been snowing steadily since the day before. The snow had piled up in thick drifts against the sides of the streets, covering the pavements with a thick slush.

'I wish I could get drunk,' he repeated.

Immanuele merely smiled.

'You couldn't get drunk even if you tried,' she said.

They were at the Prague Iguana, one of her favourite restaurants. It was a small place on the edge of Petőfi Square. It was cramped and dark and tucked away in one corner of an old insurance building. But it made up for that with an enormous bank of windows that overlooked the Danube. A massive glass tank containing a pair of iguanas stood behind the bar, lending the place its name and quirky ambience.

Immanuele selected her restaurants according to her moods, and this was a 'blue' kind of place. She told him that she liked its anonymity.

'So you don't think I can get drunk?' he persisted.

'No, I don't think you can. It's not in your nature.'

'That's probably true,' he admitted, 'but something has to give in the end.'

'What would you like, then?'

'A glass of wine, that's all.' He stood up, turning in the direction of the bar, 'And you?'

'Nothing,' she replied, 'I don't feel like drinking.'

He frowned slightly. 'You need something to warm you up.'

'There's warmth enough within.'

He studied her for a moment. Then he shrugged. 'Have it your own way,' he said, and made for the bar. He returned with his drink and put it down carefully. It made a wet ring on the table. Looking away, he lit a cigarette. 'I'm going through hell,' he said. 'I feel completely spent. Empty inside, like a shell. I haven't slept since we last met. I lie awake for hours on end.'

He brushed his hand against her wrist. 'How can I overcome the need to touch you?' he asked. 'To know you're in the same room as me, or lost in your own world but still nearby? To sit with you on your terrace and watch the river. To wake up as you slip into bed late at night. To wake before you in the morning and watch you struggle against the light . . .' He stopped, breaking into a coughing fit.

'What am I going to do, Immanuele?'

'The blind asking the deaf, András?'

He gave a self-deprecating smile. 'I've taken to writing letters to myself. I've been trying to write myself out of this impasse; that old strategy. A lexicon of words, of sights, sounds, impressions, all hopelessly misdirected.'

'Why are you telling me this?'

He grimaced. 'I feel lost to everything and everyone. I've tried to be honest with myself. I was glad when we decided to have some time apart. I was glad to be on my own again. I wrote like a maniac during the first few days. I was consumed by words, an avalanche of words, all swallowing me up. It was wonderful to experience that kind of freedom. And then . . .'

'And then?'

'I found myself looking for you everywhere. That sense of loss . . . a ravenous thing.'

'Didn't you realize that was inevitable?'

He ducked his head and avoided a direct answer. Instead, he said, 'I started asking myself why this had to happen.'

She smiled wanly. 'You told me you'd have to leave me because I lacked passion.'

András winced and picked up a napkin from the table. He crumpled it and pressed it to his nostrils. It smelt of cigarettes.

She moved his wineglass next to the candle, its flickering light soaking into the liquid with a luminous stain. Leaning her forehead against the window pane, she looked down at the street below them. In the cold flat air the smog was turning the snowflakes yellow. Flocks of bedraggled gulls huddled on the sidewalks. She watched them flap around. 'Why do cities always attract ugly birds?' she asked.

When he didn't reply, she leaned back on her chair and gazed at the captive iguanas, the green light of the tank webbing across her face. 'I've lost you, André,' she remarked softly.

'No!' He leaned forward. 'Don't say that, please!'

'It's the truth,' she said. 'Too much has happened since we parted. Too much that we can't even begin to admit to ourselves.'

'There's an explanation for everything . . .'

'I don't want to hear it.' Her voice was flat and final. She picked up his glass and nursed it in her hand. Then she drained what was left of his wine and looked around. 'I can't stand this place.'

He surveyed the gloomy interior. 'I thought you liked it here . . .'

'I don't any more.'

'Shall we go?'

'Yes,' she said. About to get up, she stopped suddenly, her face turning unnaturally pale. Startled, he followed her gaze. She was staring at the street outside where a scattering of rain had begun to fade into the sunset.

'What's the matter?' he asked. 'What is it?'

'It's nothing.'

'Immanuele! What's wrong? You've gone completely white.'

'Oh, I thought I saw someone.' She lowered her face. He heard her say, 'Got to get myself together.'

He leaned forward. 'What was that you said?'

'Nothing. It's nothing.'

In the background, a radio stuttered to life. András half-rose from his chair, leaning across the table and peering into the snow. Some of the snowflakes caught a draught and drifted upwards, brushing against the windows. Steam was pouring out of a vent in the pavement. Beyond the vent, a man was hurrying away, his coat billowing through the snowfall. He was too far away for András to make out his face.

Intrigued, András sat down and glanced at Immanuele. She had turned away from him, her knuckles pressed against the table.

He felt suddenly angry, the tension between them finally getting to him. 'Look,' he snapped, 'how can I know what's on your mind if you don't tell me?'

Her voice dropped to a whisper. 'Just let me be for a moment,' she said.

'Who was that outside?' he persisted.

She lowered her head, the lines of her mouth settling into a bitter cast.

He placed his hands carefully on the table in response, palms facing downward, fingers spread out. He must have pressed down with more force than he'd intended because the table tilted towards him and spilled her glass of water into his lap. As the water trickled over the side, he looked at her helplessly.

She was leaning across the table, her hands tightly gripping its sides. 'This kind of anxiety,' she said, 'I wouldn't wish it on anyone . . .'

A sudden splatter of hail set the window panes rattling and

made her pause. She glanced in despair around the room. 'I feel so trapped!' she exclaimed. 'I wish I could get away from all this! I wish I could get away!'

◆

The end of their relationship, when it finally did come, was uncannily precipitate. It happened one night when he was at her house. It was raining, a black storm surging through the city. There was a curious electricity in the air. He remembered racing through the rain, streaks of lightning flashing through the streets and providing a nervous illumination.

He found her in a very introspective mood. The lights went out as he took off his rain-soaked things. She lit a candle to compensate, placing it on the floor in the centre of the room from where it threw shadows over everything. She seemed melancholic and subdued. When she started speaking, however, there was a compelling resolution to her voice. 'The problem, André,' she began, 'is that even when you are with me, you always seem so far away, and I have no idea where that is. We talk about art, we talk about literature, we talk about politics, but I sense that your mind is never with me. We make love and I can sense your remoteness. You look away as we kiss. It's almost as if you've committed your soul to someone else. I don't even know if there is such a person or if I'm imagining all this. I know we've talked about this before, and I've believed you when you've denied all knowledge. But something holds you back from me and I don't know what it is and I resent it. It makes me constantly want to maintain my guard. It makes it difficult for me to trust you, and I have to keep reining myself in. And I don't think I am being paranoid when I say that. Nor am I calling you a liar. It's just that I can no longer tell who you are, or what your intentions are, and there's really no point in my saying this again because I'm simply going to start going round in circles.'

She stooped to shield the flickering candle and prevent it

from blowing out. 'Look at it like this . . .' she resumed, 'our love must be absolute and unconditional. It must be like a rope-bridge suspended over a chasm joining your rib-cage to mine . . .' To illustrate her point, she made a bridge with her hands crooking over the flame. 'And we are the people walking across that bridge . . .' She walked the fingers of her right hand over the left. The candle went out just then and they had to hunt around for matches before she could carry on. 'Of course, the bridge begins to show signs of age. It starts to creak and sway alarmingly, though it holds, just barely . . .' Her hands sagged dangerously close to the flame. 'But that's hardly the most serious problem. The most serious problem is that you, André, seem to hold a pair of scissors in one hand and a needle and thread in the other. Sometimes you slice through the ropes holding up the bridge; at other times, you decide to patch it up instead. There's no obvious rationale for your actions, at least none that I can find, they seem so contradictory. And the poor bridge gets confused, never quite certain what's being asked of it.' Her hands wrapped around each other and contorted. 'It has to keep trying to figure things out. But that only results in fur-ther trouble. One day, it will simply cartwheel and send us plunging off the edge and when that happens we will both . . .' – her hands parted in the middle – '. . . disintegrate.' She stretched out on the floor, moving closer to the candle. Her eyes staring into the flame, she whispered: 'Close to the fire, André . . . this close to the fire . . . too close, by far, and I falter still . . . each day growing smaller . . . and the smell of some-thing burning . . .'

She stood up, her hands darting around nervously. Her mouth grew drawn and tense. 'I can't pretend any more,' she said. 'I've got to give this a name, do you understand? I can't bear any more meetings like this.' She looked away. 'You'd better leave now. I've nothing left to say.'

She pointed to the door.

He stumbled to his feet. He wanted to say something but the words caught in his throat. He glanced at the candle on the floor, at its ravenous flame. 'You want me to leave in this rain?'

'What?' She looked at him abstractedly. 'Yes. Right now.'

As he staggered out of the room, he thought he glimpsed shadows in the corridor. The door swung shut behind him. He lengthened his strides, withdrawing from the silence he had left behind, running across the bridge, retreating over the chasm, running through the storm . . .

Let me in, Ami.

Let me in, let me in, letme in, letmein, letmeinletmeinletme

Falling into your arms.

Lying across an ocean.

◆

Ami moved to Budapest from Berlin in January 1975. The day before her arrival, she called András to tell him that she didn't want to be met at the station. She must have sensed his confusion because she hastened to explain that it was all part of a surprise she had planned for him. She wanted him to meet her in the basement of an abandoned house on one of the winding streets leading up to the Castle. The location was completely in keeping with her preference for the unusual, and András knew better than to question it, experience having taught him the virtues of compliance.

The house turned out to be at the very end of the steep and narrow street. A makeshift sign above the slatted wooden door announced the impending opening of the Auerbach Café. The door opened into a large room, painted white, with white tarpaulin sheets covering the floor and a stained-glass window that reached right up to the ceiling.

When András entered the room he realized that it was completely deserted; there was no sign of Ami or of anyone else. Intrigued, he walked around in a slow circle, pausing before the stained-glass window and gazing out at the street. He could make out the shapes of leafless boughs and the reflections from passing cars, while a muted blend of street sounds filtered in.

As he turned away from the window, a sudden vector of light shot out from one corner of the room. There was the whirring sound of a film projector, and the angular silhouette of a man

302

materialized on the wall opposite him. The man's face was concealed by a mask. He was standing in a large and airy room,
filled with strips of diaphanous white cloth draped from the
ceiling to the floor. Behind him, Ami sat on a shell-backed sofa,
dressed in strips of the same diaphanous cloth. She shrugged
them off as the man in the mask approached her. When he
reached her, he went down on his knees and placed his hands on
her strangely distended belly. She helped him take off his
clothes. They walked over to a sunken marble bath-tub at the far
end of the room. Ami stepped into it and the masked man followed her, standing behind her and holding on to her belly. She
began straining, her feet pressing against the sides of the bath-
tub. Her face turned red. Her legs parted as she whimpered,
beads of sweat glistening off her. Wisps of milky-red began slipping into the water. The water began to churn, something
emerging from her. First, the tip of a dome appeared, its smooth
and contoured curves catching the light and gleaming through
the water. Then crenellated walls slid out, their façades striped
with black and white, multicoloured flags fluttering about.
Finally, the entire mass squeezed out and descended into the
water. When it settled on the bottom of the tub, the man in the
mask clasped it with both hands and held it up to the light.
Turning to the exhausted Ami, he cried out aloud in ringing
tones: 'You have reason to be proud, my dear, it's an exact replica
of the Duomo in Siena!'

The screen went black, leaving András bewildered. He heard
a sound from behind him. The door to the room swung open
and he turned around. A woman stood silhouetted within the
space of the door. She paused momentarily to locate him in the
darkness. Then she walked into the room and greeted him with
a kiss.

It was Ami.

She took him by the hand.

They kissed again, András stepping back after that and holding her at arm's length. Her face was pale, but her eyes were
dark and glowing.

'Boyfriend –' she said, her voice exaggeratedly low-pitched
and seductive, 'say hello to your glitter girl!'

He shook his head in wonder and broke into a smile. 'Welcome back, Ami,' he said. 'Welcome back to Budapest!'

She gave him a playful punch on the shoulder. 'So –' she exclaimed, 'have you seen my surprise for you?'

'Do you mean the film?'

'No, silly boy! That was just a distraction. I'm talking about the wooden packing crate in the corner –'

'The crate?'

She gestured impatiently. 'There –'

András walked over and looked down at the crate. 'What's in it?'

She chuckled. 'It's filled with copies of your books. I snuck them in.'

He turned to her, completely at a loss. 'How did you manage to get it past the border guards?'

'There are ways, brother mine . . .' she said smoothly, looking immensely gratified by his reaction. 'There are avenues well worth exploring . . .'

◆

'Good day, everyone! Today's weather looks great, it's going to be a nice one out there . . . blue sky, twenty-five degrees, you're walking down the street and your sister is home at last! By evening there will be a slight change in atmospheric pressure as you go home to take that afternoon siesta. At seven-thirty there will be a chance of precipitation, about one forehead and two sweaty palms worth. This disturbance should be all over by midnight at which point you will be able to see the stars in all their glory . . .'

She laughed out loud as they stepped out of the Auerbach Café and into the street. 'I had a dream about you last night – this happens so rarely – it must have been in anticipation of our reunion today. We were in a place I've never been, a foreign country – France, perhaps? Let's say it was France, but there was a strong breeze blowing and a sky above the trees that was as clear as the centuries. You had just returned from somewhere, or you had never left, I don't remember which. But you were walking down the streets and looking for me when I found you. We stuck our heads in the door of a church, and then we were walking in the countryside, down dirt roads, and I was wearing a bottle of water on my foot . . .

'But enough of me or I won't stop talking! Tell me how you are, André.'

'What do you want to know?'

She took his hand as they walked down the street. 'Tell me about yourself. Tell me everything! It's been such a long time.'

'What is there to tell?' He gave her a dark look. 'What I have to say will only depress you and make you feel as I do. It's a struggle to survive. I find myself coming home exhausted every night. And then I try to stay up in order to write, but it isn't quite working out.'

'If money's the problem, what I have is yours.'

'That is not the point.'

'I have plenty . . .'

He took her arm. 'Let's go and sit down.'

They crossed the street and entered a restaurant, negotiating their way to a table in a corner. While they waited for a waitress, they studied one another, each seeing the other for the first time in years. To András it seemed that beneath her surface ebullience Ami was quieter than before. Quieter and more guarded somehow; there was something in her that was unmistakably grave. And there were shadows under her eyes that gave her a sharp, tired air.

She returned his gaze, breaking into a sudden smile that he recognized instantly. He relaxed and smiled back. She leaned towards him and patted him gently on the hand. '*Piu della mia m'è cara la tua vita* . . .' she murmured, 'Your life means more to me than my own . . .'

Maman had taught them Italian when they were young, and they had continued to use it even after she was gone because it made them feel closer to her and, therefore, to each other.

'You can talk to me, André,' she carried on, 'you know you can. You can talk to me about anything.' She stopped and looked

305

at him expectantly. It made him uncomfortable, that kind of scrutiny.

'Why are you staring at me like that?' he asked. 'Have I changed that much?'

'Have you changed? I don't know. You look much older, for one . . .'

'Lines on my face?'

'You look burnt-out, done in, ready to expire.'

He smiled, a bit self-consciously. 'Tell me about you,' he said.

'No! I asked you first!'

'Ami!'

'Oh, very well! I'll indulge you just this once. I've changed as well, as you can see. I've bleached my hair, for one thing.'

'You're like a conjurer's trick. Every time a different incarnation.'

'Incarnation . . . what a peculiar choice of word.' She waved a theatrical hand, her eyes constantly scanning the room in lively examination of their surroundings. 'It takes energy to keep up with trends, let me tell you. You need attitude, you know?'

'Well, you've got attitude, sister mine, with or without the hair.'

'Oh, I don't know about that. To cultivate the right attitude at the right time is a fine art. But the hair was Aunt Zsuzsanna's gift to me, actually.' She smiled at his scandalized expression, her red-painted lips catching the light. 'I just can't seem to stop smiling!' she burst out. 'What can I say? I am what I am and I'm back! You wouldn't believe me when I promised you that, but here I am.'

Then she glanced at him quizzically. 'I've just finished reading your latest book. It came out in Berlin a couple of months ago.' She gave him an off-centred look. 'This woman you keep introducing in your books, the woman in red, where does she come from?'

'She's not essential to the narrative.'

'Oh, I realized that! It's just that I don't understand her role.'

He replied, a bit defensively, 'And what did you think about the plot?'

'I found it a bit bloodless, to be honest. Some of it was

interesting, but it was all very morbid, like the rest of your work. But what do I know about literature? It keeps you afloat, so I'm not complaining.'

She took off her jacket to reveal a silk shirt with the arms scissored off. 'I'm here with an official permit, I'll have you know . . .'

'A *permit*? To do what?'

She smiled mischievously. 'Why, to ply my trade, of course.'

He must have looked confused because she hastened to clarify. 'Oh, André,' she giggled. 'Not *that* trade, sweetheart, although it's a thought. But I'm an independent artist now, a painter, and a businesswoman.'

She was going to find out about the local market, she explained; she wanted to explore the commercial options. The way she said it made him uncomfortable. He told her so, sounding a bit huffy, even to himself. She looked amused. 'But it *is* a crassly commercial proposition, dear heart. And it's always been that way. God only knows that that's what I've learnt from life. There's nothing left that could stand for high-art in your ideal sense. The Greeks, now, they were the ones, but they were also the first ones and so had an incomparable advantage over . . . oh, nearly everyone else, I suppose. Then the Romans copied them, and the barbarians copied the Romans, and so on . . . down to our very own culture of relentless imitation.'

She'd started her own gallery a while ago. She seemed eager to talk. 'I suppose you could call me successful, in a manner of speaking. I've never wanted for money, and heaven knows I've learnt to ask for little else. Though I had my ideals once – my heroic moments. You know what I mean: the usual thing, rebellion as ritual. Of course, I was also a pauper then, part of the nobler-than-thou *avant-garde*. Ah, Art, those golden years! Living on an empty stomach for days on end does bring up a certain kind of bile, doesn't it?' She laughed with only the slightest trace of bitterness, but even that could have been his imagination. 'But I picked up soon enough, you can be proud of me as far as *that's* concerned. One begins to miss the material comforts! One fine day I said goodbye to my starving friends and moved in with this businessman, a man with a particular kind of imagination, unabashedly mercenary and completely down-to-earth. He set me up in an apartment. I learnt a lot from him.' She made a face. 'By the time his wife found out I'd already made enough to move on.'

'Why did you leave Vienna?'

'No special reason, really. I suppose I was settling into a routine and I hated that. Routine is like death to me. I felt this restlessness setting in and knew I had to get out. I read somewhere it's the cross our generation bears . . .'

'Why Berlin?'

'Why not?' She gave him a sudden smile. 'I simply closed my eyes and pointed my finger at the map and Berlin just happened to be at the receiving end. But it was good to be there: so much more going on than in sleepy old Vienna. I decided to take a break from painting. For a while, I became the manager of a rock band, though that didn't quite work out. And then . . .' she stopped in mid-sentence, 'What is it? Why are you looking at me like that?'

András glanced away. 'It's just occurred to me how little we know each other. Somehow, I thought . . . it's just that . . . you've changed a lot, Ami.'

'Oh, I keep changing, Dré,' she smiled. 'Sometimes I think I am the ultimate chameleon, hiding my true nature behind my many façades.' She paused and stared pointedly at him. 'But then again, aren't we all, in our own very different ways?'

He looked at her guardedly. 'What *is* your true nature, then?'

'Don't ask me that, André, because I would have to return the favour and ask you about yours and I'm not certain you'd want to talk about it.'

He looked at her, surprised.

She gave him a caustic smile. 'Let's stick to art instead. It's much safer. Look – look at what I've brought.' She smiled again, taking the malice away from her words.

She was carrying a briefcase made of alligator skin. Unlatching the clasp, she brought out a glossy catalogue of her paintings. The first half of the catalogue featured a series of canvases covered with the word 'Blink' in different shapes, sizes and colours. The second half displayed endlessly repetitive reproductions of machine-guns and revolvers against monochromatic back-grounds. Despite the subject matter, András had to admit that her draughtsmanship was exquisite. She was obviously very talented and it made him wonder what could have transformed her into such a commercial Caliban. He wanted to ask her but remained silent, watching her morosely as she put away the catalogue. Sensing his discomfort, she asked, 'What's the matter, André?'

'People actually buy that stuff?'

She winced. He looked down, he hadn't intended to be that categorical. She said calmly, 'Sure, people buy that . . . *stuff*.' She bit her lip as if refusing to be drawn into an argument. Instead, she dipped into her briefcase again and pulled out another portfolio, a plain cardboard folder this time. She opened it and spread a series of pen and ink sketches out on the table. They were portraits she had done of him, and all from memory, he realized. They were amazingly lifelike, their shading reminding him of period sepia prints or daguerrotypes.

Raising his eyes from them, he gave her an appropriately penitent glance. She was watching him intently, a pronounced flush on her face. Rapping her knuckles sharply on the table to emphasize her point, she said, 'It's all a question of where you put your heart, André. I wouldn't sell these for the world.'

She continued speaking, though less animatedly now, her gaze fixed on the windows, which were misting up with rain. 'People do buy the stuff that I produce. That's what you called them, didn't you? *Stuff*? I don't mind; they sell, they keep me alive. I don't sell to museums, they're usually too strapped for cash. But private collectors, now they're a different matter altogether, those Maecenases from Monaco and Milano and Manhattan.'

She stubbed out her cigarette delicately, very droll. 'To those of us who predict the trends correctly,' she observed, 'here's to living in the material world.'

He sat back and sucked in his cheeks. He decided not to say anything.

'There's going to be time enough to readjust,' she continued evenly. 'Tomorrow I'm going to start searching for an apartment for us.'

'Oh?' He glanced at her in surprise. 'I didn't know it was going to be like that . . .'

'What do you mean? What else did you have in mind?'

His eyes fell. 'I don't know,' he replied. He felt strangely out of breath. 'I suppose I hadn't really thought about it,' he concluded lamely.

She nodded tersely. 'Look, we *are* going to live together, aren't we? I mean, isn't that why I came back? I don't know about you, André, but I'm getting extremely tired of these long separations.'

He was saved from a reply by the arrival of their food. The waitress had forgotten their knives and forks. Eyeing the glutinous mess on her plate, Ami sighed. 'I'm almost tempted to use my hands . . . I think I'll do just that. It's such a different aesthetic, isn't it?' She gave a little toss of her head. 'If I had lots of money,' she said, 'I'd spend it all on food. Thick, rich, sensuous food, enough to fill up an entire pond. Then I'd plunge naked into that pond. Sink into it, swim into it, fill myself with it. Oh, the luxury of *feeling*!'

'Have you heard of the village of Oia? In Santorini?'

'No, I haven't. What about it?'

'Picture this: it's summertime, you're sitting on a ledge overlooking the sea, the white village of Oia perched precariously behind you in the mist. There's a sharp, deep plunge before you, dark. They're selling these things out of handcarts, wheeling them up and down the narrow streets etched into the cliffsides. They call out to you in their rough and earthy voices. The food smells delicious, whatever it is they're selling, and you ask to take a look, your curiosity aroused. A wet cloth is pulled back to reveal a seductively glowing urn. Within, there are soft flesh-like chunks, still moving and alive. They show you where to bite in, how to snuff the life out with your teeth with a single snap. You hesitate, reluctant to display the animal in you, but you let yourself be persuaded and moisten your palette with wine, reaching for that first morsel beween your forefinger and thumb. You screw up your face in a huge grimace, anticipating the scrabbling horror inside your mouth. But nothing of the kind happens; there are no dying throes, not even the whispered awareness of a life slipping out. Instead: a slow, warm juice, fiery and pungent, with

310

the aftertaste of a kiss. You pause and savour it, wondering what it is that you've just had. Then you wash it down with the wine while everyone else around you smiles and applauds . . .' He spread his hands expressively. 'But I still remember the drifting mist more than anything else. Thick, blue-grey strands, the stuff of Jason's fleece. Mist from Atlantis . . .'

She glanced at him curiously. 'I never did get to Greece.' She leaned closer, her knees brushing against his. She touched his hand, her orange scarf slipping like a flame from her shoulders. 'It's very warm in here, isn't it?'

'I hadn't noticed.'

She nodded her head, 'It is, take my word for it.' She paused suddenly, as if struck by a thought. 'Would you like to bathe my breasts with warm milk and honey?' she asked.

'Excuse me?'

'Oh, come on, André, snap out of it and tell me what's going on in your head! Why were you so taken aback by the idea of our living together?'

He swallowed, remembering someone else.

'Well?' She forced a smile, suddenly less secure, her voice pitched a little higher. 'I've been looking forward to this, you know . . .' She hesitated, sensing his constraint, the smile disappearing from her face. Lowering her voice imperceptibly, she brushed his lips with her fingertips. 'André – what is it?'

He looked down, refusing to meet her eyes.

Her face became grave. 'András?' she asked again. 'What's the matter?'

He felt suddenly vexed. 'Why does everything have to be so physical with you? That film, our relationship, that reference to your breasts?'

'What's wrong with that?'

'It's unnatural, don't you see? That's what's wrong with it!'

'*Unnatural?*'

'We're *siblings*, Ami.'

'You poor fool!' She made a sweeping movement with her hand. 'We're not just *siblings*, the way you pronounce that word with such misery, we're twins, like to like, each a part of the other! It's always made us different from everyone else!'

'I'm not comfortable with that any more, Ami.'

'But I'm here now! I came back for you!'

'You never asked me how I might feel about it.'

'It didn't occur to me. How could it? To me it seemed like the most natural thing in the world.'

'I am not you.'

'You are a part of me.'

'Then I'm a stranger to myself, Ami.'

She stood up abruptly, pushing her chair back.

He stood up as well and grabbed her arm. 'Where are you going?'

She freed her arm from his grasp. 'There's another woman, isn't there? Don't ask me how I know, just tell me who it is.'

'Look – do we have to talk about this now?'

'André,' she said, trying to keep her voice level, 'if you don't tell me I'm going to punch you in front of all these people.'

He sat down.

'What do you want to know?'

'Everything! God only knows I've waited long enough.'

'Ami . . .'

'You are mine, André. *Mine*. The taste of you, the scent, the touch, all mine! You're not to be shared. Just get rid of her and we'll never mention this again.'

'Must you *always* simplify things?'

'So it's like that, is it? Very well, don't tell me her name. My only defence against her is to keep her nameless. Jealousy! This is what it is, isn't it? So what do you call her in bed? Sweet thing? Sweet! Tell me who she is. I won't break down . . .'

'It's a bit complicated,' he muttered, feeling inexplicably contrite.

'Who is it?'

'It's Immanuele.'

She blanched visibly. Her hand went up to her mouth. She appeared to be struggling to speak.

'Ami . . .'

She stared at him, her pupils jet-dark and numb.

'Make her go,' she said in a small voice.

'Ami, please . . .'

Her eyes filled up. 'Make her go away.'

He felt his shoulders slump. 'Oh, dear God!' he said hope-lessly. It came out as a groan.

Her eyes flashed, opening unusually wide. Keeping her voice carefully controlled, she said, 'Didn't you write . . . didn't you *swear* . . . never to have anything to do with her again? Isn't she the one who broke your heart? The one that threw you over, by your very own words?'

He gazed at her miserably. 'I only wish it were that simple, my love. She doesn't want to have anything more to do with me but I just can't seem to . . .' He ran his hand distractedly through his hair. She shook her head in response. Mistaking the gesture, he said softly, 'What can I say? I still love her, Ami.'

She turned her head sharply and looked out of the window, her eyes plunging down the streets of concrete and glass, past the tired red slogans, the mildewed placards, the obscure signs.

A cicada.

Small.

Lost in night-flight.

'You love her – isn't that what you said?' She spoke softly, her voice breaking with hurt. 'What is this thing you've mistaken as love? How can it ever compare to what we have?' She was crying freely by this time, tears streaming down her cheeks.

'I love you too, Ami!' he protested. 'But in a very different way!'

There was a pause while she considered this. Then she said with sudden resolution, 'I don't think you know what that word means, André. I don't think you have the faintest idea.'

He kept his head lowered. He didn't want to look at her. He didn't have the strength.

She put on her coat. 'Sooner or later you're going to have to make up your mind. You can't carry on like this forever. You're going to have to decide.' She hesitated, biting her lip and gazing down at him. 'I would be lying, André, if I didn't tell you that this has come as a complete surprise. But don't apologize, it doesn't suit you.' She turned around abruptly. 'Here's money for the food. I'm going back to my hotel now, if you don't mind. I wish you a splendid evening.'

313

She walked out briskly, turning up her collar and opening a large plastic umbrella. It was red and yellow, with black revolvers on it. She moved into the rain with long strides, her astrakhan coat flapping against the breeze. She stumbled once, then straightened up, holding her head high, shoulders drawn back. Above her, the evening sky was streaming to grey, night setting in, the day suddenly transformed to winter.

András turned away, feeling completely spent. He signalled for his bill and prepared to leave. Then he sat up in surprise, a thrill of recognition shooting through him. Immanuele had just walked in from the street. She wore an ox-blood jacket with a sleeveless crimson cloak. She squinted through the dense smoke, hesitantly trying to locate someone. As her eyes travelled around the room, they came to rest on him. She started. He watched her as she chose a table at a distance from his and sat down. Picking up the wine-list, she glanced at him for one last time. Then she looked away, her face in shadow.

András began to get up from his chair when Elemér Klein rushed in. He spotted András instantly and scrambled across the room, complaints trailing behind him. 'I'm so glad to find you here! What a day it's been! First the rain . . . then the subway breaking down . . . then the crowds on the pavement standing still like morons . . . then my glasses misting over . . . the resulting lack of breath . . . the resulting pain tearing through my sides . . . the resulting giddiness . . .'

He leaned over the table and grasped András by his shoulders, his eyes imploring him to listen to what he was saying. András looked over his shoulder, still distracted, but he could no longer see Immanuele. The table was deserted – she must have left just as Elemér rushed in. András gave him a despairing look. Misinterpreting, Elemér went down on his knees, dramatically clasping his hands together. András gave in and slumped back in his chair.

Pleased, Elemér draped his coat meticulously over the arm of a chair, then hurried over to the bar to get drinks. A crowd was jammed against the counter and he rapidly disappeared into it. Meanwhile, András couldn't help staring at his threadbare overcoat – the object of such loving attention – and comparing it to

Ami's expensive astrakhan. Hunching his shoulders, his thoughts increasingly black, he drew circles with his finger on the steaming window and glared at the street outside.

Elemér returned a few seconds later, blissfully oblivious to András's mood. He was about to sit down when András stood up. 'I think we should call it a day,' he said firmly. 'I'm sorry, but I don't feel well.'

They walked out together. Elemér paid for the drinks.

'And where are you off to now?' he asked.

'I'm on my way to find Ami.'

'America! Of course! When did she arrive?'

'Yesterday.'

'We're all looking forward to meeting her, you know . . .' He glanced at András with interest. 'It must be fascinating to have a twin. Is she anything like you?'

'No,' András replied, 'she's not. She's very different.'

They crossed the street and turned to go their separate ways. Elemér took the metro home. András sat on a bench to try and collect his thoughts.

A man walked past with a clutch of balloons and flowers. Sensing András watching him, he turned around and smiled, 'My daughter's birthday . . .'

An old woman slowly trudged across the street. She was carrying an empty shopping bag. Her eyes fell on András. She averted her face.

A young girl jogged down the pavement. Her T-shirt had a message hand-scrawled across the back: 'We are not sheep. Yet!' Rounding the corner, she slipped on something and went down on her hands and knees, turning her ankle.

András leaned back on the bench and gazed at the sky. He felt a gentle breeze on his face. All around him the night was crawling in, dense and saturated with clouds. Across the rainstained square, a poet, a dissident, sat down on a bench and composed a verse, intent on sending it to the West (that magic word). A white carrier pigeon alighted on his shoulder. The man rolled up the scrap of paper and inserted it into a metal canister under the bird. It took off instantly and joined a flock overhead. András counted the birds, following them with his eyes until they disappeared

315

behind a billboard jutting into the sky. Suddenly the billboard lit up and blazed its message into the night: 'Fly Malév for Comfort!'

It had resumed raining a while ago. András had just noticed.

And the city would survive, despite everything.

And one day . . . one day, perhaps, he would learn to stop the trembling.

He stood up and pointed himself in the direction of the hotel where Ami, he knew, was waiting for him.

He climbed the three floors to her room. He knocked on the door. It swung open at the second knock and he stepped in.

She was standing by the door.

There were tears in her eyes.

She stepped out of her robe.

She was naked.

She was smiling.

That night, as András walked back to his room through the deserted city streets, he was suddenly reminded of a small boy in a large house a long time ago. He was motionless in bed and fast asleep. He was very thin, his body inextricably wrapped around his twin.

He was following András in his dream.

◆

The next week András applied for a teaching post in the town of Eger.

It was a one-year appointment.

He left Budapest a few days later.

◆

Again and again, how precarious these memories . . .

Like a black dream. A dark and golden stain. The arc of a

photograph. The fragment of a face. Her precise nakedness. Night, dense night. The sacred and the profane. Again and again and again . . .

♦

András walked into the room just as someone switched on a gramophone. As the song came on, Stefán, his trade-mark black scarf wound tightly around his neck, stood up and cleared a space for himself between the tables and chairs. Everyone knew how much he loved dancing. Tonight, though, he seemed more than a little tipsy. He balanced cautiously on one foot and bent over with his arms outstretched on either side. With a severe face, he bowed to each member of his cheering audience. Even now, when he was drunk, there was something supremely dynamic and fluid in his movements. He raised his hands like a high-wire artist, a tremor of excitement running through the room. There was an anxious moment when he appeared to be on the brink of toppling over. Then someone ran up to him and balanced a bottle of beer on his head. With a roar of delight, he straightened up, tossing the bottle high into the air and towards the nearest wall. Then he broke into a wild jig, going down on his hands and knees and scuttling crab-like across the floor, a number of others joining in.

The gathering was at Elemér's place, a drawing together of friends. It was the winter of András's return from Eger. The room was small and crowded and choked with the grey fog of cigarettes. András waded in, the babel instantly overwhelming him, words floating past in a meaningless cacophony:

. . . the real wisdom lies with . . .

. . . Brezhnev's masseuse . . .

. . . it was all criss-cross after that, zigzag, helter-skelter . . .

. . . it's true, I do see better on Saturdays . . .

. . . one of the most important things to notice is . . .

. . . a banana peel . . .

317

. . . floating upwards in gradually expanding spirals . . .
    . . . like some rock star, can you *imagine* . . .
        . . . standing behind the lectern, lipstick all over his face . . .
    . . . looking very, very aggressive . . .
        . . . none other than János Kádár himself . . .
            . . . wearing some kind of see-through outfit . . .
. . . Galileo's trial, Sinyavsky's trial, Haraszti's trial . . .
        . . . if one is to have any moral validity, all one needs is . . .
            . . . a tender piece of meat . . .

Weaving through the crowd, András found himself sand-wiched into one corner of the room with Immanuele, Elemér and his girlfriend of the moment, Judit, the painter Tamás Betegh, the sculptors, Júlia Ambrus and Péter Ghymes, and two old friends from Prague. Immanuele looked wan and careworn. She glanced up as András perched himself on the arm of her chair, her eyes lighting up. She gave him a quick smile and then she stood up abruptly and drew him aside.

'I did something very strange yesterday.' She spoke into his ear to overcome the din. 'I wanted you to be the one to know.'

'What did you do?'

'I returned to the Raven King's bridge and spent a couple of hours there. And that's not all,' she carried on, a tremor in her voice, 'I conducted for the first time in five years.' She nodded emphatically. 'I played right through the Shostakovich Fifth. The entire thing.'

Not trusting himself to speak, he scanned her face carefully. Drawing closer to her, he asked, 'Are you taking up music again? Nothing would make me happier!'

She didn't answer him directly. Instead, she bit her lip and raised her voice. 'There was nothing there,' she said. 'It was so peaceful. There was nothing there but me and the Danube and the Allegro pounding down.' She smiled intently at him, her eyes filling. Then she turned away and returned to her chair, but she didn't sit down. Instead, she stood up on the chair and raised a hand, the conversation in the room coming to a scattered halt. She waited until everyone was quiet, and then she addressed them.

'My friends,' she began, 'Everything man-made – empires, ideologies, personalities – is finite.

'Only the imagination survives wars, earthquakes, inhibitions, great floods, plagues.

'And only illusions can reach into space.

'Yet, we are content to live inside carefully emptied minds.

'Please explain this.'

Her voice trailed off.

Someone called out from the back of the room: 'Look, you've only got one life. Why are you wasting away? Live in ignorance, like everyone else.'

In the back of the room, the poet Zoltán Kupper began singing a Beatles song, his voice slightly drunken, slightly off-key: 'All you need is love . . .' Soon everyone had taken it up, singing that single phrase over and over again, their mouths opening and closing, the space rocking with the sound.

Carried away, András started singing along. And when that song ended, there was another, and then another. By the time the chorus finally died down, the smoke in the room had thickened to smog. Breaking away from the crush, András looked around for Immanuele. Unable to spot her, he climbed on to the chair that she'd been standing on. Then he noticed Elemér gesticulating. He hurried across. 'She left a while earlier,' Elemér explained, 'but she gave me this note for you.' He turned his pockets inside out and retrieved a crumpled envelope. 'I'm worried about her, André,' he added. 'This is the first time she's been out in ages. She's shut herself up in that great big house and I can't tell what's going on with her any longer . . .' His voice tapered off. He backed away, trying not to look as András tore open the envelope with a sudden vehemence. '*My Dear André,*' she had written:

The Mistral is a cold and dry north wind that sweeps down from the high Alps and desiccates Europe.

The Ruagh is a south wind in the Old Testament that is under-stood by Spinoza to imply the Spirit of God in man. For instance – 'And the spirit entered into me, and made me stand

*on my feet.' (Ezekiel, ii, 2.) Or – 'A man in whom is the Spirit.'
(Numbers, xxvii, 18.)*

*You were born in winter, on the northern plains. You know
that I was born in the south, in Baranya, on one of my family's
tumbledown estates, since destroyed.*

*You were always a winter child, András, an orphan of the icy
Mistral.*

I, on the contrary, am a creature of the Spirit, wild and irrational.

*Whenever the Mistral collides with the Ruagh, only misfortune
can result. This much I have learnt from my life.*

*I knew that I would meet you here today. And I've known of
your attempts to get in touch with me, despite my appeals to the
contrary. I think I even glimpsed you one night from my terrace.
That is why I am addressing this final entreaty to you.*

*Too much has transpired in your absence. I am not going to
explain.*

*I want you to let go of me. I want you to let go of the memories.
To let go of the possibilities.*

*I want you to leave me alone. Because in a very short while, my
life will have run its natural course. Don't ask how I know this,
simply accept it. But please don't destroy this final peace I seek.*

Please don't destroy that, as you have destroyed everything else.

◆

András opened his eyes. It was very bright . . .
He was lying on his back on a flat steel surface. A hard and

320

metallic light was shining down on his face. It was very hot. He heard a voice in the background:

'He's well on his way to recovery. He should be out of here in a few days.'

A gloved hand pressed over his face. It smelled of formaldehyde.

'How do you feel?'

'Where am I?'

'It's all right. You're in a hospital. Everything's going to be fine. Don't try to speak. You're still very weak. No use in tiring yourself out.'

The hand moved away from his face and patted his cheeks.

'How are you feeling? Does it burn?'

'I don't know.'

'That's fine, then. You'll get better soon.'

'Who are you?'

'I'm a doctor.'

'Can you doctor the mind? Can you mend that kind of pain?'

'What was that?' The physician addressed someone else: 'Do you know what he's talking about? No? No idea? Listen, could you repeat what you just said?'

'I would like to be permitted to leave, Doctor.'

'Look, you need to rest . . . I'm turning off the lights.'

'I want to leave, Doctor, I have to leave . . .'

'Listen, you must try to get some sleep; we'll keep an eye on you through the night.'

All of the lights were turned off after that except the blue night-light in the corner. It cast a dim and diffused glow on the walls. András heard the voices retreating from the room. He thought he heard the sound of laughter.

He closed his eyes.

When he opened them again, a nurse in a peaked white cap was standing beside him, the night-light casting deep-blue shadows on her face. She smiled reassuringly at him. 'I'm going to turn you around,' she said, 'I need to take your temperature.' Her voice was low and monotonous; it reminded him of the ocean.

She leaned over him and adjusted the covers, patting them down. Then she smiled again. 'Here, take these tablets, they'll help you sleep.' She walked over to the windows as he watched, unfastening them and letting in fresh air. She left the room, her rubber heels whispering on the floor.

He lay in bed and stared through the open window. The air outside was limp and still. The moon was an explosion of silver against a bright wash of sky. He could hear the gentle hum of the river filtering in.

Shifting slightly to one side, he threw off the sheets and looked at himself. His skin was pale and blue, the epidermis wax-like and stiff. On the wall opposite him a clock ticked away steadily. Nothing disturbed the vast emptiness of the night except the occasional stirring of leaves, toneless rustlings in the dark.

A sudden explosion of light interrupted the silence.

András raised his hands and shielded his eyes.

It was the nurse again. She leaned over him and adjusted the sheets. 'I'm going to shut the window and turn off the night-light,' she said. 'You need to rest. Please try to rest.'

The room plunged into darkness. Only a distant light from the passage outside provided a vague illumination. The nurse gave András one last glance and closed the door behind her, leaving him alone with his thoughts once again.

Through the shuttered window, he could hear the wind densely whispering, the night pressing in. Feeling completely worn out, he closed his eyes. In the darkness inside his head he sensed their faces surrounding him one by one. They were all there, all four of them: János, Ami, Immanuele and Stefán. Their faces pale with exhaustion, they arranged themselves around him in their usual mysterious order, the men flanking the women, Stefán on the left, then Ami, then Immanuele, with János on the far right. Stefán's mouth was open, his face drawn and tight. His right hand was raised and clenched, he appeared on the brink of springing forward; only Ami's shoulder held him back. But she too had her hand up, her fingers firmly grasping a bottle or glass of some kind. She was staring past him, her eyes focused on an object in the distance. To the right of her: Immanuele, her cheeks gaunt and hollow, her head swathed, as always, in some kind of black gauze. And finally, a balding János, his face half in shadow, head held down at an angle and torso crouched so as almost to block Immanuele off.

322

Faces without dimensions, flesh without substance, they waited in a strange and deathly silence, their expressions expectant and taut. Then Immanuele began to speak, the same words dragging out in the same inarticulate stammer: 'My friend . . . my friend, my lover, my companion . . . my friends, my loved ones, my companions . . . my friends, my true friends, my compatriots . . . where did we go wrong? *Where did we go wrong?*'

◆

He was exhausted when he woke up again.

It was still dark outside.

He sat up in bed and, turning sideways, placed his feet carefully on the floor.

His legs felt heavy and leaden.

He took the steps one at a time.

Calm, slow, steady, calm, slow, steady . . .

Composing himself.

He imagined himself going home.

He imagined walking through the front door.

'Hello,' he said to himself.

There was no answer.

'Hello,' he said again.

He let his mind empty, fatigue and the darkness slowing down his thoughts.

Returning to the bed, he sat down. There was a glass of water on the floor, and next to it, a box of matches. He leaned over and picked up the box. Lighting a match, he held it in front of his eyes.

You and I are one person, André, that's what Maman said to me once. The only thing is, you refused to speak to me. You refused to speak. And I? – I didn't want to lie. In the end, I refused to lie. That's all.

The match went out.

He turned away and stared into the darkness. He rose from the bed and began walking slowly up and down. Four steps to the left, and then four to the right. He stopped in front of the window and looked out. It had begun to rain, blurry grey columns coming down at a slant. He listened to the sound of the rain, the rhythms constantly varying, the raindrops running down the window panes in broken lines. He pressed his face to the glass.

I'm giving up, he realized, I can't give up . . .

Hush. You should fall asleep like everybody else.

I've worn out sleep, Ami. There is no rest.

If only I could disabuse you . . .

How can you disabuse me? Can you compartmentalize grief? Can you contain it, pacify it, reify it? Can you tell me what to do when I long so desperately to return to the past? At night when I go to bed I feel as if I've been asleep for years. In the morning when I wake up I imagine I am back in the past. The memories are with me every night. Dreams of those days were once rare. Now they are with me every night.

Enough, enough, my love! Enough of this winter melancholy! No more seasonal bittersweet! All these silent reflections cannot possibly be healthy. You are right, it has been a long and difficult time. But we have crossed many thresholds, and now the night and the solitude await. Oh, I count the hours and rejoice that the sun will shine on us again one day. Kisses, sweet kisses, mi amor. And hands where they should be. And legs tangled in all. And dead limbs where they suffer the bliss of lying in embrace . . .

They've removed the bench I used to sit on to read the letters that you sent me from Vienna. The bench that was grey like the November sky, nestling in the shadows of a poplar. I will stand under that poplar even though they will accuse me of trampling the grass . . .

Più della mia m'è cara la tua vita, André. Sometimes I wondered if you read my letters and realized that I was crazy. Enough! Enough! – you would cry! Where does she come up with this piddle?

Piddle? Do you realize that now, after all these years, I miss you more than ever? Do you realize that? No response? – Oh silent one! No response?

András felt his head begin to spin. Turning around and staggering slightly, he leaned his head against the window and stared out into the night. Somewhere in that darkness he sensed the mud of perpetual sleep, but tonight, as on every other night, it managed to elude him.

Instead, the memories insisted on crowding in.

The memories? What memories?

The memories that massed around him and returned him to that night on the Fishermen's Bastion, with Stefán pacing agitatedly along the ramparts.

He swallowed to moisten the dryness in his throat.

He wondered if he should laugh.

Dreaming while he was wide awake: the imagination as an act of violence.

That had become his cross.

He considered Stefán, who pretended not to notice. Instead, he kept on pacing back and forth, his head down at his shoulders, his hands in the pockets of his trousers, his words coming thick and fast. 'I don't think I can agree with you on that, André,' he was saying, 'I don't think writing is a means of forgetting. On the contrary, I think it's precisely a means of remembering. That's what all the great writers have used it for, to remember what might otherwise be forgotten.'

To the right of them, Ami shifted restlessly. She was sitting in the shadow of a portal, her back to a pillar. It had been raining, and the stones of the Bastion had a damp smell, little pools of water shining in their corners. Watching Stefán pace, Ami laughed. 'André thinks just the opposite, Stefán,' she said. 'He uses his writing to forget – to retreat from the world. I don't think he could bear to write if it had anything to do with the preservation of memory.' She turned to András, her eyes gleaming. 'Isn't that right, André?'

Stefán was speaking again: 'But how can anyone retreat from this shit? It overwhelms everything! What is the point of writing unless you can throw yourself headlong into the world?'

András made a brief gesture that indicated clearly what he thought. Ami glanced at him and then she addressed Stefán. 'I don't think André writes for the public realm, Stefán. His writing is entirely for himself, it's a private enterprise. I've tried to tell him as much, of course. I've tried to tell him that to write as he does is to pretend to live, but I don't think he's too enamoured with that interpretation.'

'I simply don't understand how he can carry on,' Stefán replied. 'It's seems like such a compromise.'

'Oh, leave him be! It's his prerogative. What about you? What are you writing these days, my poet?'

'Dead verse. Simply more dead verse,' Stefán replied sadly. He turned his gaze towards András. 'That is why I think that those who have the gift – the blessings of the muse, so to speak – should use it to the fullest degree.'

'Oh, but André doesn't have the benefit of a muse! Isn't that right, András?'

András remained silent, fully aware that every inflection of his voice, every refutation, would instantly be subjected to analysis. Instead, he squeezed Ami's arm and rested his head on her shoulder.

'What? No answer, André?' She turned to survey her brother. 'My expert eye tells me that André prefers to remain silent,' she said mockingly. 'My expert eye tells me that André prefers the safety of silence to the danger of spoken words.'

'Silence is also the sound of absence, Ami,' András said softly, 'and sometimes the absence of words is more illuminating than their sound.'

A shadow flitted across her face. 'Who is absent?' she asked, her voice pitched low. 'Whose silence are you mourning? How much longer is this going to go on?'

Without waiting for his answer, she stood up and walked over to the edge of the ramparts. In a more normal tone of voice, she addressed him again: 'Do you know what this place reminds me of? It reminds me of the story you once told me about the island of Santorini in Greece, and the village of Oia at night. Do you remember that story? With the mist drifting up from the sea?' She peered over the crenellated walls of the Bastion. 'Except that instead of the sea below us, now there's the pitch-dark pit of the city.'

She turned to Stefán. 'When we were young, André and I were always planning to travel to exotic places. One time, I remember he promised to take me to Greece. He'd read about it in a magazine, and he said he would take me there.' She laughed. 'At twelve it was possible to believe in anything. But nowadays André doesn't care for that kind of fantasy. Nowadays he is content to keep to the feverish hours of the night, his mind filled with all kinds of morbid longings. He wants to be the perfect writer, you see, with nothing to occupy his mind but the most perfect metaphors. But do you know what I say to that, Stefán? I say: thank heaven for our imperfections!'

There was the rasping clang of an anchor chain from the river. Stirring slowly, András rose to his feet and walked up to Ami. In the distance, he could see the white caps riding the swell of the water. Beyond its black abyss, the lights of Pest drove a white wedge into the horizon.

He leaned over the battlement and gazed down at the sea of trees. A strong wind was getting up. It whipped through the shaggy tops of the trees, their branches parting like surf.

Drawing his attention with a gesture, Ami tugged at his sleeve. 'Well? – have you nothing to say?'

'What do you want me to say?' He lowered his voice. 'In any case, this is hardly the place . . .'

She smiled at him with a peculiarly capricious air. In an undertone that matched his and evaded Stefán's hearing, she murmured, 'When are you going to forget her?'

He drew away instantly. 'That isn't really your concern, is it?'

'You owe it to me to tell me what you feel!'

A look of irritation flitted across his face. 'I don't owe you anything.'

She surprised him with a wan smile, but didn't say anything. Instead, she watched him as he took a couple of steps away from her. Then she walked over to the embrasured wall and climbed nimbly on top of it. Spots of colour stood out on her cheeks, and her eyes were bright and feverish. 'God! –' she exclaimed. 'I'm so tired of all this stumbling around! I'm so tired of this kind of living! This constant struggle where everything is sodden with fear and there's no room left to breathe!'

'Try sitting down for a while,' András suggested curtly. 'Try keeping still.'

'That's all you can ever think of, isn't it? Keeping still?'

327

'But in this place, under the open space of the night, at least for a while, one can be free . . .' Stefán suggested hopefully.

'What open space?' Ami countered. 'All that I can see around me is miles and miles of land-locked earth. God! This illusion of freedom! This is struggle-city! What a trap!'

She jumped from one crenellation to the next. The stones echoed with the sound of her feet. 'I'm tired of the passivity,' she cried. 'I'm fed up with the way people here accept their captivity! It's impossible for me to live like this! I was meant for better things!'

András stirred uneasily. He drew his coat around him and shivered. 'Let's not talk about it, Ami.'

'You don't understand, do you?' She gestured angrily. 'How can you call yourself a writer? You never understand anything!'

'Look – if that's the way you feel, just leave me alone and we'll treat all that's happened as an intellectual exercise and forget about it.'

She drew in her breath sharply. 'Ah! – the life of the mind! How could I ever presume to impose upon that!'

'My mind is a cool and calm place, Ami. One of us has to be that way. One of us needs to think clearly.'

Stefán stepped between them. 'Look here, you two, break it up, please! It's a beautiful night, just look around you!'

'Oh, go away, Stefán!' Ami retorted angrily. 'Can't you see that this is the end? It's the end of everything!'

András sat down. He felt as though he were suffocating. 'Why are you always baiting me, Ami?' he asked wearily. 'What do you hope to gain?'

'I disappoint you terribly, don't I? I know that I disappoint you. How can I not? I come too close to your precious memories.'

'Of course you don't disappoint me.'

She flared up. 'There you go again, damn you! For once, can't you be a little less altruistic? I *know* that I disappoint you terribly! But know this, know only this, that deep inside of me I can hear your voice, I can hear your voice calling out to me from the backbone to the sea!'

328

She jumped up to the next crenellation, her feet slipping dangerously before they gained hold of the rough stone surface. 'You're afraid to admit it to me! Like everything else in your life, you're scared to come out and admit it!'

Stefán turned suddenly to András. 'André,' he said, his face pale and tense, 'tell her to stop, the masonry's coming loose! Tell her to get down. It's stupid and dangerous!'

András shrugged and buried his hands deep inside his coat. 'She's old enough,' he muttered, 'she knows what she's doing.'

'But she's too agitated, can't you see? She's not thinking straight. If she slips, it's a sheer drop to the rocks! Talk to her, damn it!'

Turning his back on him, András kept stubbornly silent. Behind him, he heard Ami laugh wildly. 'Do you see that, Stefán? He's content to remain silent. Silence is all that he's concerned with!'

Suddenly losing control, András shouted, 'We mourn those we love, Ami! We mourn their absence with our silence! It's the least we can do to maintain their memory!'

'What's this, André, the waiting sun of self-recognition? You don't mourn anyone! You've been inside yourself for too long! What do you know about love? It's alien to your very being!'

'Love is a silence! Love is a prayer! And that's all there is to it.'

'No, it's not! Love is a whore, a martyr, a fire, and you know nothing about its burn!'

'Stop it! Don't you dare tell me about my feelings!'

Stefán raised his hands imploringly, 'Come on, André, truce!' He grasped hold of András. 'Will you tell her to get down, please?'

András brushed him aside and strode away angrily. Behind him, he heard Ami call out, her voice beginning to quaver and rise: 'What do you want, André? What do you want from life? What *can* you want from life? You're so filled with dead things!'

András whirled around, his eyes taking on a slightly manic gleam. 'What do I want? I want solitude! Can you understand that? I want to isolate myself! Especially from you!'

329

There was a moment of stunned silence. Then Ami said in a faltering voice: 'And if you got your wish, do you really think you would be happy?'

'I *know* I would be happy!' András replied vehemently.

She recoiled from his words. Her voice broke: 'But you're all I have . . .' She sagged suddenly, her knees buckling. Stefán rushed forward, his hands reaching out to prevent her from falling. Oblivious, Ami straightened up abruptly and leaned over to correct her balance. Caught off guard by her sudden change of position, Stefán collided against her. She began turning around, a look of surprise on her face. Her hands went up in the air just as Stefán screamed. She toppled back slowly, Stefán lunging out in a last desperate attempt to grab on to her feet. For a few seconds – no more – András saw a bright white shape hurtling down the slope. Then the shape spread out and catapulted off the ground, the hands splayed uncannily like a seagull's wide wings. Black sky. White bird. Black sky. White bird. In the distance, Stefán's prolonged and unnatural scream . . .

♦

He opened his eyes.

He was lying in bed. The room was empty, cold and stark. There was a mirror on the wall, and he stared at it in despair. He looked sick and very pale; there were black smudges under his eyes. He felt old and shrunken; wasted, spent.

That was when he recalled why he was there.

And he recalled everything else as well, why Ami could no longer play Ourgame, why she wasn't there for him to reach out to her the way he always had, reach out and get under her skin, touch her from within . . .

No, there would be none of that.

Just before she'd slipped into the coma, she'd wanted to look at the sky one last time.

Why?

330

'All those butterflies in the sky . . .' she'd whispered, with a tired smile. 'Paralysed by butterflies . . .'

Screwing his eyes shut, he curled into a ball. With a savage force, he pressed his hands to his head, imagining he was inside Maman again, part of Ami again. Inside his mind, he could sense the swamp: lightless, lifeless, fenced off by pain.

Remembering everything, he wanted to scream out loud.

Instead, he merely stumbled out of bed, himself again, alone again.

Bereft.

BEREFT.

He called out her name: 'Ami!'

There was no reply.

He screamed it out: '*Ami*!'

The wind whispered back.

It was time to go down to the river again.

Down to the waterline.

Chapter Six

The Garden of Earthly Delights

Sunsetsilhouette. East of the setting sun, west of the horizon, a young boy walks slowly along the skyline. He is slender, naked, he raises each foot carefully and brings it down on the thin beam of the bridge, the wind whistling around him. After each step, he stops, the beam swaying and buckling under him. His hands grasp at the blue vacuum surrounding him. Against the pale white flesh of his chest, a million ribs stand out, flailed by the failing light of evening. Below him, metal wires mesh together and plunge down towards the city. Further below, at the bottom of the void, the Danube glistens.

Wide-eyed and deathly pale, the boy hesitates in mid-stride, looking back the way he has come, his hands running through his hair and plucking at his lips, uncertain. He turns around, parting the thickening curtain of dusk and carrying on. When he reaches the exact centre of the bridge, he lies down on his back, suspending his spine and letting his feet dangle down.

He closes his eyes.

He is waiting for the stars to come out.

And when they do . . .

Then.

◆

Sunsetsilhouette. West of the setting sun, east of the horizon, a girl, young, carries a rocking chair to the edge of a rooftop. She is naked, her dark hair cropped shoulder-short. She sits down on the chair, her arms resting lightly along its sides, first leaning it back, then rocking it forward. Her hips, where they cradle the chair, gleam pale against the woodwork.

Holding her head to one side, she closes her eyes, with every rocking motion edging closer to the sky. When the chair teeters at the brink, she stops moving, suddenly very still. She is shivering. She draws her feet up. Six floors below, a row of streetlights flare into the night. Their glow reaches up to where she huddles in a crouch. For a while, nothing moves on that black rooftop. Then she draws forward and leans over, looking down. She can feel the cool breeze on her face; she closes her eyes.

She is waiting for the stars to come out.

And when they do . . .

Then.

◆

Sunsetsilhouette. Between the east and the west, a man paces sleeplessly about his room. From time to time, he raises one of his hands in the air, as if in supplication, and then he lets it drop again, lifeless. A wide-circling seagull attracts his attention as he glances out at the sky. He follows its flight, hypnotized. First the gull passes the boy on the bridge. Then it glides past the girl on the rooftop. The man straightens up, suddenly focused, his neck craning forward. The gull raises its head, its spine cresting as it arches backward . . .

And then . . .

Then.

The first star appears in the sky.

It is Sirius, the dog star, blazebrightstumbling into the night.

333

The man narrows his eyes. In the distance, the girl on the rooftop opens hers. On the bridge, the boy opens his. For the briefest of intervals they all watch the ascent of that distant sun. Then the seagull sails between them and breaks the spell, its featherfingers splaying open. Suddenly heavier than air, it plummets to the ground.

They watch it fall.

The boy spreads his wings, preparing.

The girl spreads hers.

At that very moment, from deep within the city, a single handclap sounds, sharp, like a pistol-shot.

Silence follows. Sudden. Crisp. An interval. Unnatural.

A couple of feeble claps ring out: hesitant, stuttering, dying out.

Then a series of claps tears into the lull – muscular, powerful, and much more resonant. The sounds build up, hands slapping into hands and building into waves that cascade over the city. The boy on the bridge starts. Rearing back on the beam, he tries to locate its source. By this time, it is as if the entire city has exploded into sound. From every building the handclaps burst out – *Come on! Come on!* – their echoes sweeping up to where the boy lies waiting, urging him on. They run all over the bridge, drumming along the girders, supremely fleet and agile. Hard as nails, they tap insistently on his feet, knocking out his elbows, pushing against his knees. *Come on! Come on!* But he only edges away in response, leaning into the darkness and almost falling off. Shaking violently now, he crawls back the way he has come – hugging metal, concrete, plaster – careful not to look down. And still they try to trip him with tendrils full of sound. *Oh, Come on! Jump!*

Squinting through his tears, moaning through saliva like an old, old man, the boy finally reaches the ground. Doubled over with fear, he gropes for his clothes, the handclaps battering against his mouth. They slap his cheeks from side to side, drawing blood. They slap his chest, his hands, his heart. They slap each disc along the length of his spine, digging between the vertebrae, crying *Come on!*

They are still hitting him as he staggers into the darkness, choking, bleeding, breaking down.

And then . . .

Then.

They turn around, spiralling upwards and gathering around the girl on the rooftop.

They follow her down.

Separating from her chair, she picks up speed, her silhouette falling in and out of the skyline.

She hits
the ground.

The chair smashes into the asphalt.

The clapping reaches a crescendo now; it swells over the street like a shower.

And then . . .

Then.

It stops as abruptly as it had begun.

♦

In the room above the street, the man, suddenly cold, cries out, blocking the window with his hands and sagging to the ground. His head resounds with clapping sounds. He can hear his heart-beats pounding: hieroglyphs.

He tries to prop himself up.

He tries to remember . . .

a side-long silence, a look, a word, something about that
seagull
white seagull
plunging . . .

And a harbour
far, far away
in an inner sea
a bridge, a river
a shelter, an arbour . . .

A sound, a sound, a sound!

While over that distant bridge

And over that distant rooftop

And over those white-washed Danube walls
Night comes scribbling back to remove the essential strands.
Oh, Ami, my Ami, once again memory, that trailing round.

◆

The house on the hill was painted white. It stood on one of the
highest points, the area behind it a scraggly climb of boulders
and sand-blasted rock. On the heights beyond, clusters of bright
red poppies and lambent sunflowers frolicked against a cloud-
white canvas. There was a painterly, two-dimensional quality to
the day, and the stretching horizon was almost seamless.

A broad avenue of chestnut trees swept up to the house. They
were decorated with yellow bunting, and a filigree of roses grew
out of the elaborate wrought-iron trellis flanking the front door.
Instead of a doorknob, there was an embroidered leather strap.
As the visitor pulled it, he could hear a bell echoing inside, but he
had to ring again before the door swung open to reveal the
owner of the house.

Szegedy stared at András in surprise, automatically shading his
eyes from the glare. He was wearing a silk smoking jacket with a
tasselled belt, and a chequered white scarf around his neck.
There was a long silence before he found his voice. With a
slightly awkward air, he asked, 'Are you well enough to be walking around like this?'

'I'm as well as can be expected,' András replied.

'You look awfully pale.' Szegedy turned to survey the drive,
and then he glanced back at his visitor. 'It's not that I'm surprised at your turning up, but I must admit I hadn't expected you
quite as soon as this.'

'I need to ask you a few questions.'

'Why didn't you come to my office?'

'This was more convenient for me.'

Szegedy looked away. 'Ah, but it's not convenient for *me*, you
see,' he replied pointedly.

András gave a smile. 'Are you telling me to leave?'

Szegedy reiterated, a bit peevishly, 'This *is* Sunday. A day of rest. I'd like to think that even I was entitled to that. I've had a very trying week, I'm very tired, and I know I'm not going to be very good company.'

'I'm not looking for good company. May I come in?'

'Is this about Stefán?'

'Yes, it is.'

There was an uncomfortable pause, and then Szegedy shrugged. He made way for András to step inside.

They were in a small, surprisingly ornate vestibule, its walls painted a deep red. The light was dim, the windows shaded by curtains. To the left of the door, a miniature marble fireplace supported a pair of antique *cloisonné* statues on its mantelpiece. To the right, a smaller door led into a wood-panelled corridor, the cornices lit by muted lampshades.

András followed Szegedy down the corridor and into a large and spacious room, painted ivory. A grand piano stood in one corner, its lid flipped open. Above the piano, a narrow, elongated window opened out to a glade of leafy trees, their trunks and branches streaks of black against a field of dazzling sunlit green. In the spaces between the trees were what appeared to be gravestones, their shades varying from brown to mottled grey. The sun glistened off their planes and reflected into the room.

Szegedy walked over to the piano and tapped it with a proprietorial air. He moved to the window and glanced outside, his hands in his pockets. He appeared to be composing himself. When he turned around again, his face had assumed a calm superiority, all traces of discomfort erased. He straightened his smoking jacket, patting down the creases. His bearing was poised and erect, almost rigid. There was still an affronted air about him, but now it was tempered with his customary smoothness. 'I'm glad you've recovered,' he said in a tone mingled with irony. 'It must have been a terrible experience –'

'It was terrible,' András replied, 'and tragic. And it's been misrepresented.'

'Misrepresented?'

'Wouldn't you agree?'

Szegedy shrugged ambiguously. 'There's always something

337

that can be said that hasn't been said before.'

'Is there? One would like to think you'd have covered all the angles.'

Szegedy flushed. For an instant, he looked almost embarrassed. 'The investigation's come a long way,' he said.

'And what have you learned that you didn't know already?'

'I'm hardly at liberty to discuss that with you.'

'Surely you can do better than that?'

Szegedy lit a cigarette by way of a reply. He eyed András guardedly, his face partly in the shade. Moving away from the window, he leaned over the piano, his hands running delicately over the keys. With his face still turned to the keyboard, he asked him, 'Do you play?'

'No, I don't any more. I used to.'

'A pity. Personally, I have always found music to be a great solace.' He regarded András with a level stare before leaning over and tapping a key. It made a sharp, ringing sound. Clenching his cigarette between his teeth, he pulled out the piano bench and sat down, his fingers peremptorily flicking a fugato. In the middle of the movement, he stopped and glanced over his shoulder at András. 'I went to Immanuele's final concert, did you know that? It must have been twenty-five years ago. I can still remember parts of it vividly. The ankle-length dress that she was wearing, for instance, and the stage – all dark apart from the candle-lit proscenium. There was a kind of fiendish intensity in the way she played, it was quite an experience . . .' He took a deep drag on his cigarette, turning to look at András in a speculative manner. 'But I don't suppose you were there that night, it must have been before you met her . . .'

'I'm here to talk about Stefán.'

'You want to get directly to the point?'

András raised his eyebrows. 'This *is* a Sunday, Inspector, and I'd hate to take up any more of your time than is absolutely necessary.'

Szegedy got up from the piano and crossed the room, settling into a sofa in the corner. 'Ah yes, of course, the consideration lacking earlier now comes to the fore,' he muttered.

Someone coughed behind András. Startled, he looked around.

338

A thin, slope-shouldered man was standing by the door. He was dressed completely in black. He took off his hat, revealing the indentation left on his forehead by the brim.

'My assistant, József Wagner,' Szegedy offered, with a curious lack of enthusiasm. 'You may have met before.' He cleared his throat clumsily. 'My late colleague, Tibor Brander, was Sergeant Wagner's brother-in-law. József's taken it rather badly.' He cleared his throat again. The presence of the Sergeant seemed to be having an inhibiting effect on him.

András didn't say anything. The Sergeant left and returned with a chair which he placed in the middle of the room, evidently with the intention of sitting down on it.

Szegedy looked at him in surprise. He put on a disapproving expression. 'You may leave, József,' he said with asperity. He nodded briskly at the door. The Sergeant hesitated for an instant, and then he walked out, taking the chair with him.

With a dark glance at the door, Szegedy turned to András. 'Do you remember how Stefán's room smelled that night?' he asked. 'I remember that smell more than anything else.' A look of distaste crossed his face before he carried on, 'But then again, you probably don't. You were in no condition to recall anything.'

'My memory's fine,' András replied.

'Ah yes, memory . . . a creature of quicksilver kindling. And now I expect you'd like to move on to Stefán? What do you want to talk about? Whatever it is, my advice to you would be to desist; I am losing patience with the sort of masochistic impulse that dredges up the past.' He stood up abruptly and gestured in the direction of the trees visible through the window. 'Might I suggest that we go outside before we carry on? It's more pleasant there, with the sun and fresh air.'

They walked down a flight of steps into a covered courtyard. The roof was made of glass, the light muted by a thick shag of ivy entwined around the crossbeams. In the centre there was a fountain shaped like a scallop, its shell-like hollows swirling with water.

They approached a heavy wooden door which Szegedy pushed open to reveal the sunlit grotto of the graveyard, the

339

gravestones interspersed with trees and carefully restored marble statues. Tall brick walls overgrown with wisteria enclosed the space.

There was something markedly supercilious in Szegedy's manner as he turned to consider the effect of the place on András. 'Welcome to my garden,' he said, as he seated himself on one of the gravestones. 'What do you think?'

'It's a graveyard.'

'Is that all?'

András considered his surroundings disinterestedly. 'It's old,' he said, 'and rather cold. What else is there to say about it?'

Szegedy's mouth tightened. 'It's not just any graveyard. It's quite unique. Look around you carefully. Those gargoyles in the corner, for instance. Do they remind you of anything?'

'No, they don't,' András replied, with a glance at the figures indicated.

'Are you familiar with Hieronymus Bosch's masterpiece, *The Garden of Earthly Delights*?'

'Of course. I've seen reproductions of it.' András glanced at the figures again, and then he leaned forward with a wordless exclamation.

Szegedy sat back with a pleased look on his face. 'Exactly,' he replied.

'But how? And why?'

'The work of a medieval artisan, Matthias Zschokke by name, whose signature, following the practice of the period, is engraved on one of the bases. Zschokke, or so I am told by a friend of mine who is an expert on these matters, was an obscure artisan of whom very little is known except that he was at one time an apprentice of the master. He subsequently decided to settle in these parts and practise his trade, the only extant examples of which you see before you. Other than that, the life and origins of the man himself remain shrouded in mystery.'

He paused and surveyed the figures. 'That particular group represents the last resting place of a coterie of merchants convicted of grand larceny. It was originally located in a funerary recess in the western wall, but I decided to have it detached and moved to a more prominent location.

'I like to indulge myself a little,' he carried on. 'One of the fruits of a long and profitable career.' Then he added, 'There are those who envy my success, naturally, but why should I feel contrite or apologetic? I've worked hard to earn my creature comforts.'

Aware that András was gazing at him with irony, he flushed and looked away. 'A man has to cultivate his soul,' he said. 'There's nothing especially original about that sentiment. And the gravestones? – I am interested in what they *represent*. They are what I cultivate in my garden instead of flowers.'

'You've done well for yourself, Inspector,' András concurred.

'I probably have, haven't I?' He gave András a look that was a curious combination of satisfaction and unease. 'And all of this from work that pleases me. I don't know too many people who can say as much.' He turned away from the figures and gestured brusquely. 'But enough of this. What was it that you wanted to ask me?'

András chose his words with caution. 'I've been thinking a lot about what took place that night at Stefán's. The process of remembering has been a painful one, but I keep feeling that something's not right.'

'Do you have anything specific in mind?'

'I'd like to know why Stefán killed himself.'

'And you've come to me for the answer?'

'I've come to you because you know the answer.'

There was a pause, and then Szegedy crossed his hands and surveyed András. 'Stefán killed a police officer and then he took his own life. What is there to explain? At best it might be viewed as an unfortunate accident.'

'There was nothing accidental about those deaths, Inspector.'

Szegedy gave the briefest of smiles. 'Permit me to make a confession, then,' he said, 'and I'll be blunt. But for the letter that Stefán so fortuitously thought of posting to us beforehand, you would have been the prime suspect in this particular instance, or hasn't that crossed your mind?'

'That's your conclusion,' András replied, 'not mine.'

'And what, pray, is your conclusion?'

'I believe that someone deliberately planted that waxwork on the island to make a point about Immanuele's disappearance. I

341

think the waxwork was designed to send a clear message, and to set into motion an entire train of events that would revive the whole slew of unanswered questions about Immanuele. That's why I'm convinced that what's been going on is not a series of random accidents, but something that's been very carefully planned.'

'That's all very interesting but what does it have to do with the facts? And, in any case, it still leaves you in a circumstantially ambiguous position, or haven't you realized that?'

András lowered his gaze. 'Of course I realize that,' he said slowly. 'But I am also beginning to question your determination to dismiss alternative explanations.'

Szegedy stared at him without saying anything. He swung his head in exasperation, and then stood up with his feet placed apart. With an air of exaggerated courtesy, he said, 'Might I interest you in accompanying me back to the house? There's something there I'd very much like you to look at.' His eyes rested contemplatively on András. Then, without so much as a backward glance, he turned and marched off.

They entered a smaller room than the one they'd been in earlier. In the middle was a wooden table with a ceiling lamp trained on it. The rest of the room was in relative darkness, although András could make out the Sergeant named Wagner standing silently in one corner.

A large leather trunk rested on the table. Motioning András to step forward, Szegedy unlocked it and brought out a transparent plastic packet.

There was a worn blue notebook inside the packet, and Szegedy held it out to András. 'I'm sure you're already acquainted with this,' he said. 'We found it on the couch in Stefán's room. Hold it by the spine, the paper is very fragile.'

András held the notebook carefully. He turned it over, eyeing the mouldy and water-stained pages, the binding brown with age and scored by grit.

Szegedy watched him intently.

'Does it look familiar?' he asked.

András flipped through it without answering.

Szegedy stepped forward. 'If you will be so kind as to turn to the inscription on the last page.'

András turned to the end and read what was written in the margin. It was a verse in Latin, the writing so faint that he could barely decipher the lines: '*Superat mors vitam, Homo jam recuperat, Quod prius amiserat, Paradisi gaudium . . .*'

'Do you know what that means?' Szegedy asked.

András replied in an impassive tone of voice: 'Death conquers life, and Man wins back that which, earlier, he lost, the bliss of paradise.'

'A peculiar inversion of the *Mundi renovatio*, don't you think? What's more, it has your name below it. Yes indeed, it's a curious world we live in. Some things fall into place, others just careen off . . .'

András didn't say anything. He made to return the notebook but Szegedy intercepted his hand.

'No, not yet, Mr Tfirst. I would like you to read out what's written at the very bottom.'

András did as he said. Unobtrusively printed on the lower right-hand side of the page was a handwritten inscription: '*András fecit me ita ut sum . . .*'

'Will you translate that for me, please?'

'András made me thus as I am.'

'And below that?'

'The name Immanuele.'

The policemen continued to gaze attentively at András. His eyes were dancing. 'Back in the 1970s, Mr Tfirst,' he said quietly, 'there were all kinds of rumours. Rumours that fed into rumours, so to speak. And the rumours spread and the rumours flourished. I can't say I ever gave them too much credence. In my line of work, you see, one learns never to turn to the rumour mills for information.'

He paused significantly. 'It appears that I might have been mistaken.'

He looked blandly at András. 'It's not even as if I'm asking you for any explanations. It simply raises all kinds of questions, that's all. For instance, how on earth did this notebook find its way to Stefán's room? And what were the two of you doing with it?'

He stopped speaking and extended his hand.

'May I have it back please?'

When András had handed him the notebook, he slipped it

into the plastic packet and put it back in the trunk. 'As a writer, you ought to be able to appreciate this,' he said. 'You see, I'm setting a trap.'

'A trap?'

'Yes. A trap for a very cunning animal.'

When András didn't reply, he leaned forward and prompted him: 'What's the matter, André, lost your voice? It's always such a pleasure to watch a writer inventing himself.'

András drew back. 'Inventing myself – is that what you think I'm doing?'

'How else is one to explain it? Your kind of intransigence must be fuelled by a peculiar notion of innocence. But then again, silence is often nothing other than the first fallow confession of guilt.' He stepped back, his foot brushing against a toy xylophone lying on the floor. It made a forlorn tinkling sound. The door behind them opened at that instant, a small boy running into the room, followed by an even smaller girl.

Szegedy started, turning around and addressing the boy, his voice brittle: 'How many times have I told you not to play in this room?'

The boy picked up the xylophone and stared back defiantly.

Szegedy asked again, 'Well?'

András heard the child mutter under his breath: 'Bogus pucusmucus.'

Szegedy bristled. 'What did you say?' he demanded belligerently. 'I heard that!' He turned to the Sergeant. 'Did you hear what he said?'

'Nothing intelligible, as far as I could make out . . .'

The little boy began edging out of the room. He stopped in front of the door and took out a small cloth animal from his pocket, aiming it at his father like a gun. To András's surprise, Szegedy burst out laughing. Bending down to the boy's height, he said, 'And what is that supposed to be, Zoltán?'

'It's a three-legged whroompie,' the boy replied.

'What does it do?'

'It whroomps.'

Szegedy broke into an indulgent smile. 'No, no, Zoltán,' he intervened, 'what *is* a whroompie?'

344

The child gave him a withering look. 'It doesn't like you,' he said slowly. Swivelling around, he ran out of the room, dragging the three-legged whroompie behind him.

The little girl sidled up to András. 'It flies . . .' she whispered, 'the whroompie flies.' She held out the doll she was carrying in her hand. 'Look at my Lady Laideronnette.'

'Hello, Lady Laideronnette,' András said politely. 'How do you do?'

'Silly, she won't speak to you.'

'Why?'

'Because she's the Empress of China dolls, that's why. You must bow down before her.'

András went down on his knee and asked the child, 'What is your name?'

Szegedy spoke up behind him before she could reply. 'Dea. Her name is Dea.'

The girl gazed at András. 'Do you like my dress?'

'Yes, of course I like your dress.'

'It's very special. It's made of refried yellow beans, and the polka dots are blessings from Karlmarx.'

Szegedy walked over and picked the little girl up in his arms.

'Little Dea is very talkative,' he smiled, 'and, in that, not at all like Uncle András. Uncle András is a storyteller,' he continued, 'and, one day, if you ask him politely, he will tell you a story. A good story, because he's very clever at making them up. But it's time for you to run along now. We're busy here. Go and play with your brother.'

He set her down.

The child looked at András, her eyes glinting. With a quaver of suppressed excitement, she burbled, 'Come back one day, Uncle András, come back and tell me a story!'

She left the room and Szegedy burst out laughing again.

'They're a pair of little devils,' he said, 'in case you haven't noticed that already. They keep me occupied.' His face darkened. 'But I do have another child – a daughter from my first marriage – she's much older. There's not much that she and I have left in common. She's part of a lost generation, a misfit. She's completely wild. I had high hopes for her. She's been a great disappointment.' He paused for a moment, and then walked back to the trunk, the chemistry of the room altering instantly as he did. When he turned around again, András was looking at his watch with studied deliberateness. 'I'm running late for an appointment,' András said. 'I'm going to have to leave now, if you don't mind.'

'Who're you meeting?'

'A friend,' András replied shortly.

'Very well, but before you rush off, may I ask you a personal question?'

'It depends.'

'Where does the money come from?'

András stared at him, taken aback. 'Excuse me?'

'The money to survive. As you haven't published for all these years, I've been wondering how you get by.'

András gave a taut smile. 'Interrogation time again, Inspector?'

'Not at all. Fraternal interest, that's all.'

'I see . . . naturally. Well, in that purely fraternal sense, I freelance as a translator, but you must already know that. Why? Do you have something for me?'

'Sarcasm?'

'Not at all. This is fraternal, remember?'

'Clever.'

'I try.'

'Translating . . .' Szegedy drawled out the word, mangling it, 'so that's what the wordsmith's wormwood impulses come to in the end? No longer even the author of your own life?'

'Charming. Thank you for that courtesy.'

Szegedy shrugged nonchalantly and took out a cigar from his pocket. 'Do you mind if I smoke? Because if you do, you'll just have to get used to it.'

He lit the cigar and blew smoke at the ceiling.

'You might be wondering,' he said, 'why I asked you that particular question. In part, I suppose it's the fact that you artistic types have always been such a mystery to me. My daughter, for one. I've tried hard to understand her, but she's as alien to me as my poor brother once was. There's this notion in her head that a

346

pretty word is worth more than a day's hard work, and I simply cannot seem to make her understand that's not the way life works. And it's not even as if I'm not sympathetic to her aspirations. I've always maintained an active interest in the arts. After all, I went to art school myself – a long time ago, I'd be the first to admit – so I'd like to think I'm as educated as anyone else on that front. You people don't have as much of a monopoly on these things as you would like to believe. The enchantment spins through my life in much the same way as it does in yours. The difference between us lies, of course, in the fact that I've chosen to aspire to the modest certainty of an honestly ordered life. People like you or my poor dead brother or Stefán – what is there to say? What is one to make of your values or morals? And I'm not even talking about the younger generation. I make an exception where they're concerned. They're like animals – degenerate. Nothing can be expected of them. The best one can expect of them is that they will simply disappear after a while ... just go away.'

Satisfied that he'd made his point, he glanced with cold arrogance at András. 'So go back to your writing,' he said with condescension. 'Go back to that cloistered living. There's no place for you in the real world. Living, dying, loyalties, rewards, betrayals – these are things beyond your experience, things of flesh and blood, not cardboard cut-outs. Go back to writing about man's cosmic destiny,' he said mockingly. 'Return to your solitary living, your escapism. Go back to that heavily armoured world. Things have changed and yet nothing has changed. For all your efforts, there's still no place for you in the world.'

'411,' András replied.

'Excuse me?'

'I was detainee number 411 in your world. Or have you forgotten?'

Szegedy lost his composure instantly. He turned dismissively to the man in black, nodding towards András with a clipped, 'Show him out.' He cast a final fleeting glance at András.

The Sergeant led András out of the room.

They walked one behind the other, their shadows dredging through the darkness. They entered a small, pitch-black room.

Wagner appeared to hesitate, and then he switched on a light. The brightness dazzled András momentarily. He gazed around him in surprise. The walls were covered with small, framed photographs. Most of them were black and white landscapes, pictures of mountains – steep slopes and desolate valleys – interrupted by the occasional river. Only one was not a landscape. Tucked away in one corner, about a foot above the floor, was a photograph of Immanuele. He walked slowly over to it and went down on his knees, studying it for a moment before turning to the Sergeant.

'What are these photographs?'

'Landscapes –' Wagner replied, his voice a bit too matter-of-fact, 'one of the Inspector's many interests.'

András pointed to the photograph of Immanuele. 'What about this?'

Wagner glanced casually at the photograph. 'A woman, too, is a landscape . . .'

He switched the light off abruptly and they left the room in silence. They reached the front door, Wagner opening it and squinting into the bright light.

András stepped out into the glare and turned to face the Sergeant.

'What was that you said about the photograph?' he asked.

'You have to leave now.'

'I will in a moment, once you've told me what you said.'

Wagner turned away, his face a resolute mask.

'I didn't say anything,' he insisted.

The door closed behind András. Looking around, he hesitated at the top of the steps, taking in the unusual transparence of the day. It had rained the previous night and under the mid-afternoon sun the city was drying out. Wings of light glanced off rooftops, their radiance dissolving the thin blue line between houses and horizon.

He set off down the hill. On the streets and in the alleyways, people darted to and fro, shadows without features, a nervous urban swirl. Cars skidded along, their wheels trailing smoke and dust and grit. Blind men read newspapers in braille. An itinerant puppeteer displayed his wares under the sun: silhouettes of dangling men, birds stuffed into cages, apparitions of dogs. And all around the city, buildings houses streets hills reared up and down, their impulses trapped.

It was a strange feeling.

Near Batthyány Square, András walked into a crowd standing in the middle of the street, their eyes focused on the roof of a building. 'What's going on?' he asked.

'Someone tried to jump off,' a man replied. 'A young girl, with hair like shining gold, and radiant eyes . . .'

András shook his head and moved on. Across the river, he could see the serrated outline of Parliament House, its sun-dappled windows glinting like mirrors. Above it, formations of clouds raced across the sky.

A young couple was kissing at the entrance to the building that housed Júlia Ambrus's studio. The woman had a hyrax slung from her shoulder, the man carried a painted green lizard on a length of plastic string. András held back for them to finish kissing. Finally, the woman drew away and cuffed the man gently on the chin. She ran down the sidewalk, her eyes catching András's. Laughing merrily, she waved to him. András smiled back as he entered the building and walked up a flight of steps. Shouldering past a pair of slatted swing doors, he entered a large and airy studio, its big bay windows overlooking the Danube.

Júlia was standing in the middle of the room, everything about her an exuberant swirl, robes flowing, hair piled high, hands stretched out with the usual extravagance of her gestures.

András walked over and embraced her.

'András! Darling boy! How have you been? I've heard the most dreadful things! It must have been terrible . . .'

The telephone rang before she could carry on. She hurried across to pick it up. She spoke for a couple of moments, and then she turned to András with her hand over the mouthpiece. 'It's Elemér,' she whispered, 'he says it's imperative that he sees you.'

András took the receiver. He listened without speaking, and then he put the phone down.

Júlia looked at him curiously.

'You're awfully pale,' she said. 'What was that all about?'

'It's nothing,' András replied firmly. 'We've arranged to meet tomorrow.'

Júlia glanced darkly out of the window. 'I have something unpleasant to tell you,' she said. Her voice sounded strained. 'Andor Szegedy was here yesterday. It took me completely by surprise. He's an inspector now, or that's what he claimed. He strutted around the studio, full of self-importance as always, stopping now and then to ask me questions about you, and about Ami and Immanuele. They were mostly personal questions, and I'm never comfortable talking about things like that. I told him so, but it didn't seem to discourage him; he kept prying and prodding until I finally had to tell him to leave. I told him that I'd be obliged if he left me alone.'

She paused in recollection of the episode. 'It made me marvel at how little he'd changed. In a particularly acute kind of way it brought home to me what everyone's been saying for a while now, the fact that it's the same thugs who've held on to the reins of power, only in new guises, that they've merely exchanged their Party cards for business suits. It's a tragedy, but we were fools to imagine it could have been otherwise.'

András smiled in response. 'It's a bit too early to pass judgement, isn't it?'

Júlia glanced at him in surprise. 'What do you mean? Don't you agree with me?' Then she said, a bit irritably, 'Do I take it that you are no longer interested in what's happening to this country?'

András looked up from the floor and saw that she had put on her glasses. It made her look older, and more severe.

'What is the point?' he answered mildly. 'Soon we'll all be dead, or old and playing blind man's bluff. In the meantime, our past and our future are interdependent. Give it time.'

'I don't agree. As artists, we have a responsibility to do something.'

András leaned away; his eyebrows rose laconically. With the slightest of grimaces, he said, 'As artists, my dear, our job is to rejoice. In the past the driving force was ideology, nowadays it's money. What used to focus our intent was disease. Now disease has been replaced by chaos. To survive chaos one must float above it. So whichever way you look at it, we've been condemned to a lifetime of enthusiasm. Our vocation is to rejoice, so we must rejoice, and that is all there is to it.'

Júlia looked taken aback. About to retort, she checked herself and suddenly stepped forward, her hand flying up to her mouth. 'André! – I'm so sorry! I got carried away. Under the circumstances you can hardly be expected to think about these things. I let my tongue run away with me! Will you forgive me?'

She gazed at him anxiously. 'André, I don't want to pry, but are you sure you're all right? Is there anything I can do? All you have to do is ask . . .'

András walked over to the windows and looked out at the river. 'Would you like to come for a walk with me?'

'Of course I would,' Júlia replied. 'Where do you want to go?'

They strolled down to the river by Margit Bridge. They walked slowly and without speaking, András leading the way. By the time they reached the bridge, it had become quite overcast, the light fading rapidly. 'Oh! It's cold and windy here . . .' Júlia shivered. 'Not quite the weather one expects at this time of year.' They walked up to the bridge and sat down next to the river. András took out a chess set from his pocket and arranged the chessmen one by one, Júlia watching him fondly. Setting up took a much longer time than usual because András seemed determined to place each piece in the exact centre of its square. When they were all arranged on the board, he gestured to her: 'Your move.'

Júlia shook her head. She pointed to the storm clouds cutting a broad swathe across the horizon. 'I'm afraid not, André. Look – it's begun to rain on the other side of Castle Hill.'

András advanced the first piece as if he hadn't heard. He was playing white. Júlia stood up. Aware that András was watching her, she repeated: 'I'm not playing, André. It would be foolish to stay out here. Besides, you're not fully recovered yet. We'll both get soaked and then you'll catch a chill. Let's go back to my studio.' She hesitated, András continuing to gaze at the board. Realizing that he was intent on remaining, she gave a quick sigh and ruffled a hand through his hair. 'You stay here, then,' she said. 'Maybe you need some time by yourself.' She turned to leave, and then she hesitated and turned around again. 'I know I've told you this before, but your talk the other day went down very well. I've had all kinds of questions from my students, and the department chairman complimented me as well. He said there was some interest from an American university in offering you a position. He went on to say, and I quote, "they have offered to buy his time".' She looked expectantly at András. 'I don't suppose you'd be interested?'

András smiled drily. 'Your supposition is correct.'

He watched her leave, and then turned his attention back to the chessboard. He lit a cigarette. It was drizzling quite steadily now. A fine sheen covered the board, making it glisten. András wiped his face with the back of his sleeve. He picked up the first piece and repositioned it, playing against himself. He tapped his hand absently on the corner of the board as he contemplated his next move, an old habit. He was about to move the next piece when a sudden commotion from the other side of the bridge made him look up. A pack of skinheads was heading in his direction. They seemed to be in uniform: black combat boots, brown combat trousers, white T-shirts. They stopped when they reached the middle of the bridge and clustered around the railings. They were a high-spirited and raucous lot, and from their conversation he gathered that they were planning to go to a late-night cinema show, a rerun of a Leni Riefenstahl documentary. One of them noticed András and yelled out: 'Delete yourself!' They moved on, still arguing excitedly about the film, the rain closing in on them.

András continued to sit where he was, his eyes staring at the board before him. In the distance, he could see a pair of motor-boats signalling to each other, their bright searchlights bouncing off the water. As he watched, they stopped close to the bridge and a siren went off on one of them. A spotlight began to swing wildly from side to side, like a crazed eye. Then the lights on both boats switched off. They reversed and pulled away from the bridge, each turning a circle in the water, their phosphorescent wakes intertwining.

On a sudden impulse, András put away the chessboard, folding it into a neat little square and slipping it into his jacket. A gust of wind blew against him as he stood up and glanced in the direction of Margit Island. The rain had let up and he could see the soft green lines of the island. Making up his mind, he headed in that direction.

He reached the clearing where the waxwork had been discovered and studied it from the shadow of the trees. The meadow was still scarred from the grim evening's work. The centre of the area had been slashed into a swamp, the grass lifeless and black. Someone had driven a wooden stake into the mud where the coffin had been buried, forcing it into the earth so hard that the wood had cracked right down the middle. András pulled the stake out and approached the pier. He slid it over the edge and into the river.

Sitting on the edge of the pier, he contemplated the Danube, its eddies catching around the rocks in the banks. Framed by the city, the river straddled a single straight line, the rain singing along its length in wind-driven bursts. The water smelled of rain; bits of leaves and black, forked branches drifted with the current. Charged with the freedom of air, a bird in flight curved into the river, intent on gorging itself. It sliced through the water and left it lacerated, weeds trailing from its feet. A stave of wind lifted it from the water and hacked wildly at the weeds. Rising sharply into the air, the bird somersaulted and soared high above the river. The weeds plummeted through space, the bird dangling.

András stared at it, captivated. Against the rain-coloured horizon, the bird looked fever-pale and stark. 'Where are the answers?' András wanted to cry out after it, but he couldn't quite manage the sound. He opened his mouth, but remained without voice, speechless. Feeling his throat constrict, he turned and faced the darkness of the meadow. He leaned into the wind, nerves strained to the quick. It was as if he felt nothing, heard nothing. Defeated by incomprehension again, arc of memory arrested in mid-stride, he let his head fall into the silence, the rain running under his skin. Or was it the other way around? Head falling into rain, silence under skin.

When he returned to the bridge, a chill wind was sweeping across it, the evening slipping into the city like ink.

He crossed the bridge and made a sharp right-hand turn. The

353

street was narrow and winding. He hesitated and glanced back at the island. It looked forlorn and empty in the dusk. He looked at the river for a moment, and then he plunged onwards, the city wrapping around him like a shroud.

By the time he returned home, Ami was already in bed. The nurse must have left later than usual that evening. Ami lay in the darkness with her eyes lightly closed. Standing beside her, András watched the faint rise and fall of her chest. Careful not to disturb her, he pulled out his mattress from under the bed and spread it out on the floor.

It was strangely quiet in the room, almost too quiet to sleep. He stirred restlessly for a while, his mind running over the day's events, and then he gave up. Rising to his feet, he walked over to the window, drawing aside the curtains.

It was windy outside. A car was moving slowly down the street, a grey sedan. It parked two houses away, its lights switching off. A gust of wind swept across the street, a trail of leaves scurrying in its wake. The leaves swirled around the car. The wind made tapping sounds against branches.

András stared at the car, waiting for the door to open. He checked several times to make sure there was no one else around. Eventually, a match flared inside the car and he saw the burning tip of a cigarette. With a gesture of resignation, he stepped away from the window, drawing the curtains shut. Then he walked slowly back to his mattress.

♦

Elemér lived on the outskirts of Pest. His apartment was on the ground floor of a house that backed into a railway embankment. Next to it was a blank wall which bore a fading advertisement for a popular brand of cigarettes. Thick clusters of ivy hung from the wall and trailed down to the pavement.

Elemér's apartment consisted of a single room that led out on to a small yard. The door was ajar, and András walked in without bothering to knock. The interior was crowded with furniture and permeated by a thick smell of photographic chemicals mixed with the odour of old books. In one corner, by the windows overlooking the street, a Turkish divan stood completely overwhelmed with ledgers. A clock twittered nervously on a wooden shelf. Pride of place, however, was given to a massive fireplace that had been converted into a bookcase, framed portraits of Goethe and Galileo hanging impassively above the mantel.

Small and frail, Elemér was sitting on an armchair, his jacket liberally dusted with cigarette ash. He threw his head back when he saw András, his quick, jittery movements and his high, domed forehead reminding András of a bird.

He addressed András anxiously: 'Are you alone?' Without waiting for a reply, he sprang out of his chair and walked to the open door. He scanned the street and nodded his head once or twice, as if satisfied. Then he shut the door, leaning his back against it and gazing at András with a look that was both resigned and defiant. 'Someone threw a brick through the windows earlier this morning,' he said. 'It had a swastika stamped on it. A gift from those who don't like my kind. It makes me wish I could bring such people face to face with my acquaintances who insist we are a European country now. Look – I'd like to tell them – there's your Europe standing outside! There's your Europe – with broken bottles in their hands, and hate in their hearts! Yes, indeed, we're a European country now, with a vision as dark as that of Europe itself!'

He paused and extended his right hand towards András, palm up. 'Evidence of my words,' he said grimly. András saw a vivid scar.

'How did that happen?' he asked.

Elemér walked away. 'It doesn't matter,' he replied. 'It's not why I asked you here.' He walked restlessly around the room, his back to András, his hands behind his back. Sitting down, he studied his visitor with a preoccupied air. 'I've been thinking a lot about Stefán,' he said. 'I can't seem to get his death off my mind. I don't know what his reasons were for killing himself, and I can't really say that I knew him too well towards the end, but I keep thinking about the way things used to be, and his suicide simply doesn't make sense.'

'Is that what you wanted to talk to me about?'

'No, I don't really want to talk about him. What's the point? Some men carry their secrets with them to the grave. But it makes you wonder, doesn't it? First there was János. Then Immanuele vanished without a trace. Now Stefán ends his life. Who's next?'

'Is that why you wanted to see me, then?'

'I don't know,' Elemér replied, 'but you'll agree that we have a problem. Oh, we can pretend these things have happened for very different reasons. After all, tragedy comes and tragedy goes and no one knows why. We're both here now but what's the guarantee there isn't going to be more trouble?'

'There is no guarantee,' András said. 'If that's what you're looking for.'

Elemér turned away, his face troubled. 'Andor Szegedy called me a couple of days ago,' he replied. 'He said he'd have me in for questioning if necessary.'

'Did he say what he might want to question you about?'

'He wanted to talk to me about Stefán, and about Immanuele and the Club.' He paused and looked around. 'I told him those things were part of a distant past. I told him I doubted I could help.'

'And what did he say?'

His face strangely red, Elemér replied, 'It didn't appear to bother him. He said that everyone has a different explanation of reality and that the nature of the present investigation demanded that he speak to all of Immanuele's acquaintances.'

'Did you agree with him?'

Elemér stood up abruptly. 'Look, André –' he blurted out, 'this morning's incident with the brick has shaken me up a bit. Would you mind if we went downstairs? I think I'd feel more comfortable there.'

He walked over to the Turkish divan, pushing it aside and revealing a trapdoor. Going down on his knees, he twisted the latch open, raising a cloud of dust. He heaved up the trapdoor and turned on a light, revealing a series of steep, hollowed-out steps. He beckoned to András to follow him as he hurried downstairs.

They entered a large and dimly lit space, its floor unevenly paved with stones. The walls were plastered over and painted a dark green. More curiously, there were carved wooden fish suspended from the ceiling, giving the room an uncanny resemblance to a subterranean riverscape.

'A sculptor friend of mine designed this,' Elemér explained. 'He wanted to capture the way a river looks underwater.' He gestured around him. 'It used to be my dark-room, but the ceiling began to sag dangerously, so I moved all my equipment to the photography lab at school. My friend took a look at the place and suggested transforming it. We found exact replacements for the beams from an abandoned house nearby and cannibalized them to prop up the ceiling. It took us four months to finish it, but it was well worth the effort. It's become my refuge from the outside world, my sanctuary. I come down here to meditate as a counter to the hoodlums who throw stones at my windows. I've given up trying to explain their error to them. I'm a college professor, I've tried telling them. I have status, leave me alone! But it's no use. The few times I've convinced them to stop, they've been put up to it again by their parents. So I've learned to ignore them. I collect their stones instead and bring them downstairs to add substance to the place. I make piles with them, I arrange them into different contours and shapes. There is no alternative, I think. There's no alternative but to forgive and to forget.'

He pointed to the stones scattered around him. 'It's all a question of sensibility. Immanuele was a bit like that, although she was much more solitary and introverted. The real challenge for her was to heal herself and still be part of the world. But she was also extraordinarily gifted, like my friend, the sculptor. I find comfort in people like that, in artists and painters and poets.' He gave a little shrug, a gesture that seemed to combine approbation with regret. 'I remember the very first time she played the cello for me. She played one of the Bach Suites, and I kept my head down throughout. I didn't look up once. I was in a complete daze. It was extraordinary, as if she'd melded her body to the instrument. And at the very end, when she'd finally stopped, I barely had the strength left to raise my head.'

His eyes travelled the room. 'What's left of all that now? We're all muffled in rags, our consciences cloaked over! What can I say? – one has to earn one's death, but even dying isn't simple any more. It leaves me feeling like a refugee sometimes, a piece of flotsam – wretched.

'I'm so tired, André,' he carried on, 'so very tired. Sleep is becoming impossible. This whole wretched business with the waxwork has taken its toll on me. The newspapers are having a field day, as I'm sure you've noticed. What is it they're reporting now? That I was one of her lovers? That we were drug-crazed fiends who had nothing to do with dissidence? That the Gabriel Club was a front for all kinds of sexual deviance? Where do they get their information? Who's been feeding them this rubbish? We're being dragged through the mud, André, and I can't see an end to it.'

He hesitated and looked around. He nodded to himself, as if coming to a decision. 'But all of this is beside the point,' he remarked, in a harsher voice. 'And the point is that I have a confession to make.'

'A confession?'

'Yes, about a mistake I once made.' He gave András a sombre look. 'If you can forgive my many digressions, that's the reason why I asked you here today.' With a slight intake of breath, he carried on, his eyes downcast, 'Have you ever made mistakes, André?'

Thoroughly mystified, András replied, 'Of course, many times . . .'

Elemér twisted his head sharply. 'No, no, not that kind of mistake. The kind that one lives to regret for the rest of one's days.'

'What's on your mind?'

'I wish it were easier for me to tell you this . . .' He paused with obvious discomfort, his eyes scanning the room and returning to András. 'When I saw Immanuele for the last time, she gave me some of her things for safe-keeping – some poetry, fragments of a novel, a few letters. She asked me to hold on to them without saying what she wanted me to do with them. We were both quite distraught, and I left her house in a state of exhaustion that

358

night. It had been a very emotional meeting. I carried her work back with me in a box-file. I took a tram home, with the box-file on the seat next to me. On the steps outside my house I suddenly realized that I had left the file behind. I had no idea how it could have happened. I'm usually very careful about things like that. Cursing myself, I rushed back to the terminus in a panic. I tracked down the tram and spoke to the attendant, but it was no use. I had lost the file.

'I wandered about in the snow after that, smoking incessantly, and finally, at about midnight, I sat down on a bench beside the river and broke down.'

'You didn't return to tell her?'

'No, I didn't. I couldn't, I was mortified. I kept steeling myself to go back and confess, but every time I set off I instantly lost my resolve.' He looked at András gloomily. 'When I finally went back a couple of weeks later, it was only to learn that she had disappeared, just like the material she'd entrusted to my care.

'Believe me –' he hurried on, 'I was mad with remorse for my carelessness. When she disappeared, I held myself accountable. I convinced myself that she must have left some indication about where she'd gone in the letters she'd given me that night. So I blamed myself for grievously hurting the person I most cared about. Do you know what that's like, André? To blame yourself more than anyone else for what could have happened to her?'

András hesitated. 'It's why I eventually left Budapest, Elem,' he replied.

'I thought as much,' Elemér said guardedly.

András leaned his head against the wall. 'I wanted to forget the city,' he said, 'I wanted to forget myself.'

'You built a house on a hill, I heard. They said you'd become a recluse, a hermit.'

'I built a house with my own hands, out of stone and wood. It was my shelter. I wanted to get away from everyone. I lived there with Ami for ten years. Ten years of solitude, ten years of trying to forget.'

'I wrote to you. You didn't reply.'

'I didn't want any contact with the past.'

With his head lowered, Elemér began to pace restlessly, his

slippers making a rustling sound, like a small bird in flight. 'If everything was as perfect as you make it out to be,' he carried on, a bit stiffly, 'why did you leave this marvellous retreat? What made you decide to return to Budapest? To revive the ghosts from the past?'

'It was because of Ami. Her condition deteriorated. I had to come back to the city to be closer to the doctors.'

'I'm sorry, I didn't know.'

'It doesn't matter. That too is a part of the past now.'

Elemér moved his head so that András could no longer see his face. 'And what about Immanuele?' he said. 'Do you ever think about her?'

'Of course,' András replied, a bit helplessly. 'All the time.'

Oblivious to his distress, Elemér continued, 'The two of you belonged to each other, that much was clear. I tried telling her so the last time I saw her. He's on a platter as a gift for you, I said. Of course, she didn't reply. She acted as if she hadn't heard me.' He shook his head. 'It was her pride that got in the way, I think. She was absolutely alone by the end, André. There was no one to turn to. She was completely alone, and starving.'

András froze. 'What do you mean, starving?'

'She hadn't eaten for days,' Elemér replied, a bit brusquely.

András got to his feet with a groping motion. He hesitated uncertainly, as if waiting for the other to go on.

Conscious of being scrutinized, Elemér began to falter. 'André, what's the matter? Why are you looking at me like that? What have I said?'

András crossed the room suddenly. He reached over and grasped Elemér by the shoulders. He didn't say anything, his silence willing his companion to stay quiet. They remained motionless, as if huddled against the cold. At first, Elemér tried to free himself, but then he calmed down. There was a faintly bewildered expression on his face, and he stole a nervous glance at András, who seemed completely immersed in thought.

Finally, András came out of his trance. He let go of Elemér and turned away.

'André? Wait! Where are you going?'

András was walking towards the steps. He didn't slow down.

'Is it my questions, André? Are they bothering you?'

About to ascend the steps, András checked himself. Elemér shot a glance at him and caught sight of his face, distorted by misery, and his eyes, perplexed and anguished. András hesitated for a moment, and then he shook his head and walked back upstairs.

On the street outside, he turned and looked back at the house. Elemér was standing in front of the open door, the light from the room behind him casting long shadows on the pavement. He raised a hand imploringly. 'André –' he cried out, his lips beginning to tremble, but András was already hurrying away.

♦

The day after his meeting with Elemér, András returned to the house on E-Daj Street. It was late in the afternoon and a clear, prismatic light permeated the garden. He went and sat down by the pond at the back of the house. The water was still and dark, its surface stippled with leaves. A lone swallow dipped in and out, its head cocked watchfully at András.

He must have been sitting there for at least an hour when a sharp male voice interrupted him. 'What are you doing here?' the voice demanded. 'You're trespassing!'

András turned around. A uniformed policeman was standing about five feet away, glaring accusingly at him. András recognized him instantly as József Wagner, the Sergeant he'd met at Szegedy's house.

'Did you hear what I said?' the policeman repeated, a bit taken aback. 'You'd better be moving on.'

'Look –' András began without any preliminaries, 'Why did you show me that photograph in Szegedy's house?'

'The name is Wagner,' the policeman replied, clearly surprised.

'Yes, I know that. Answer my question.'

'What photograph?'

'The one of the woman by the river.'

'There are many photographs in the house. The Inspector is an amateur photographer, I thought I told you that. It's what he likes to do in his spare time.'

'I was referring to the photograph of Immanuele.'

Wagner lowered his head. 'Ah, yes, that one . . .' He paused. Glancing at the house, he said suddenly, 'This case has turned out to be wretched, absolutely wretched for the lot of us!'

'What do you mean?'

Wagner didn't answer him directly. Instead, he turned away, his eyes darting nervously around. He motioned towards the house. 'It's impossible to be in there with a clear conscience,' he muttered. He paused to look at András, his eyes dark and unusually brilliant. 'You used to know her well, didn't you?' About to say more, he tensed suddenly and took a couple of steps back. He waited for a moment, looking around warily. Then he turned and strode resolutely back to the house.

András watched his retreating form with surprise. He stood up, about to follow, when he heard someone behind him. He turned to find Andor Szegedy standing by his side.

'Hello, András.' Szegedy gave him a pleasant smile. 'Funny I should find you here. It's very peaceful, isn't it? The neighbourhood's changed so much since I lived around the corner. It's so much quieter now.' He glanced at the house. 'Forgive me, but I'm a bit curious – what was that little conversation about?'

'What conversation?'

'My man Wagner was just here, wasn't he?'

'He asked me to leave the grounds.'

'He did, did he?'

'Is it your turn now?'

Szegedy raised his eyebrows. 'No, András, I'm not going to ask you to leave. I'm not quite that categorical.' He hesitated for a moment, and then he said, 'Goes by the book, that Wagner, a singularly importunate man. But why don't you sit down? There's a lot we need to talk about.'

'What can you and I have left to talk about?'

'I'm leaving the police force in a couple of months. I thought you might be interested to know.'

'You're leaving the police force?'

'This is my last case before I retire. It's time for me to move on. The environment has changed beyond recognition, and there are many more opportunities to be found. I'm going to New York to explore business ventures. There's a firm there that's interested in joint enterprises. They have the capital, I have the know-how.'

'You're going to be a businessman?'

'I'm setting up an industrial security firm. I've been doing some consulting on the side for the past few months, but I think I'd like to do it on a full-time basis now. '

'Industrial security . . . a euphemism, surely?'

'Call it what you like. It doesn't bother me any more.' He gave a sly smile. 'My collaborators in the States happen to be the same firm that supplied us with handcuffs in the past. Very state of the art. So there's already a certain synergy in place.'

'And what is going to happen to this investigation?'

Szegedy looked away. 'I don't think you follow me,' he said slowly. 'I intend to wind everything up within the next couple of months.'

'And how do you plan to do that?'

Szegedy replied in a carefully neutral tone of voice, 'I think Stefán's death offers a natural resolution to the case, don't you?'

András stood up. He felt sick to the pit of his stomach.

'That's going to be your resolution?'

'An eminently reasonable resolution, don't you think?'

András shook his head. 'This can't be right.'

'I wanted to be the one to tell you. We've already made up our minds.'

'It can't be right,' András repeated in a quiet voice. He made a fist and exploded it, his fingers spreading wide.

Mistaking his silence for compliance, Szegedy carried on, his voice gaining in confidence, 'We've explored every other possibility and concluded that it's time to put the past to rest. What's done is done, and seventeen years hasn't added any clarity to Immanuele's fate. Stefán's dead; he's the one least affected by all of this now. He led an eccentric existence, he brutally murdered a policeman, and who knows what else he might have done in the past. In sum, a terrible end to a wasted life.' He gave András a pencilled smile. 'Though if you really wanted to think about it, if one were to take into account the promise of his early years, something must have gone badly wrong to derail him like that. But that is a matter for a writer or a psychologist or, at the very least, someone given to imaginative conjectures, and I think we've both agreed that I can hardly boast strong credentials in that department.'

'You son of a bitch!'

'*What?*'

András walked over suddenly and seized Szegedy by the collar. 'That's what you think, you bastard!'

'Take your hands off me!'

András let go of him abruptly and pushed him so hard that he stumbled backwards and sat down. They glared at each other, Szegedy's eyes wide with shock. Then András straightened up and glanced across the garden to where a couple of men had emerged from the house with crowbars in their hands. One of them turned to say something to the other, and then they cautiously began to approach the pond.

Behind him, András heard Szegedy scramble to his feet. He raised his hand and waved the men off. He turned to look at András. There was a moment of silence between them, and then András stepped back and walked rapidly down the path.

On the street, he ran down to the corner where there was a telephone booth. He slammed in a coin and dialed Júlia's number. The phone rang stridently before Júlia picked it up. Relieved, András asked if he could come over. 'Júlia –' he said, trying to control himself and speaking much louder than usual, 'I need to see you.'

Júlia was in a loose white dress when she opened the door. She motioned him towards a chair, but he got up almost immediately and began to pace the room in silence. He seemed beside himself. Eventually, he stopped and leaned his head against the wall. More composed now, he turned and said in a tired voice, 'When is this nightmare going to end?'

Júlia gave him a curious glance. 'András? What's going on in your mind? Won't you even sit down?'

364

András looked around exhaustedly. His eyes fell on her piano. 'Do you still play?'

'Sometimes,' she replied, 'when I'm in the mood.'

'Will you play something for me?'

She assented with a quick incline of her head. 'I've been working on a Debussy piece,' she said, 'the *Berceuse Héroïque*. Is that all right?'

'Of course.' He returned to his chair. 'Thank you.'

She pulled out her stool and sat down at the piano. She leaned very close to the keys as she played, her eyes closed. The sombre notes filled the room. When she had finished, she sat still with her head bowed. Then she turned around and gave him a quizzical look.

He shook his head, rousing himself. 'That was wonderful . . .' He looked at her. 'I find myself leaning more and more on music these days,' he said.

'Does it remind you of Immanuele?'

'To a certain extent. It's become my daily sustenance.'

She stood up and walked over, standing behind him and placing her hands over his eyes. She held them there for a moment. 'Fortress and wall, André,' she said. 'You chart the limits of your universe and learn to live within that. It's the loneliness of wisdom, darling.'

'Perhaps it is. I don't know. It's the old fall-back with me, I suspect: withdraw, cut off, shut down. There's comfort in melancholy. It's a familiar element. Besides –' he said, with a sudden, sardonic venom, 'it takes a certain kind of stamina to resort to grief. A certain kind of discipline to opt for constant suffering over catharsis.'

He rose to his feet and headed slowly for the door. At the threshold, he waited for Júlia to catch up with him. Kissing her goodbye, he ran down the steps. At the bottom, he paused, as if reaching some internal conclusion. Júlia glanced at him uncertainly. 'What is it?' she asked.

András gave her a preoccupied look. 'I was thinking about where I have to go next. I'm meeting someone at the Totalitarian Zone.'

'That's a nightclub, isn't it?' She looked surprised.

'It's a coffee-house during the week, and a nightclub at week-ends.'

She gave a mystified shrug. 'And that's where you're going?' She tried to sound disinterested but her curiosity was obvious.

'That's right,' András replied.

'I worry about you. Are you well enough? Have you been eating?'

'I feel fine.'

'Well, enjoy yourself, I suppose.'

András gave her an enigmatic look. 'Oh, I fully intend to.'

She ran back inside to fetch him a scarf. 'It's very windy out-side,' she explained, waving away his protests. 'Take it with you as a favour to me . . . as a favour to an old friend.'

◆

The Totalitarian Zone was packed to the rafters with a bedlam crowd. András found himself pressed against a wall almost as soon as he entered, and was forced to remain in that position until a break in the crowd propelled him inside. By the cloakroom he spotted the person he had come to see. It was the girl he'd met on the bridge by Clio's car. She was staring directly at him, her bullet head shorn and startlingly white. She looked even more emaciated than before, the bones of her face sharply outlined beneath translucent skin. She raised a hand to her mouth and wet it with her tongue, gently bringing it across her scalp. For a moment, András felt dizzy, as if he could see right through her eyes. Then she waved to him and began working her way across the room. She moved swiftly, trying to avoid the mayhem around her. When she reached him, she took him by the hand and led him up a narrow flight of stairs into a tiny glass-fronted room that overlooked the dance floor. She shut the door behind them, instantly muting the sound of music. She fumbled with a ciga-rette, lighting it. She coughed as she drank the smoke in. 'Did you bring the money?' she said when she'd stopped coughing.

'I have it here.'

She took it from him, putting it aside immediately, as if she found the transaction distasteful. Without looking at him, she said, 'I should probably warn you that Clio lives in a rather nasty part of town. It's not far from here, and I –'

'– don't suppose you'll ever be going there again, my dear Vega,' a droll male voice interrupted her.

A giant of a man shouldered into the room. He plucked the girl from András's side as if she were a doll. 'Who's your friend? What's going on here?'

Spotting the money, he set her down. Then he turned his massive head and gazed languidly at András. 'You must value something highly, Mister, to give that kind of money to a half-wit who's going to blow it all on dope.'

The girl winced and pretended to look at the floor.

Ignoring her, András addressed the man, 'We haven't been introduced . . .'

The stranger shook his head and laughed, his mouth opening to reveal irregular teeth. 'It doesn't quite work that way here.'

Vega stepped forward to explain: 'Fabien works at the door.'

András addressed the man. 'You know Clio, I take it?'

'Sort of,' the other replied, very short. 'What do you want from her?'

'I need to find out where she is.'

'And what would you do with that information?'

'Use it with discretion.'

The giant regarded him calmly. 'I don't believe you. She's safe where she is.'

'Oh? And what exactly is it that she's safe from?'

'That's confidential.'

'Perhaps I can help?'

'I don't think so.'

András motioned casually. 'It has something to do with the police, doesn't it?'

The giant started, his eyes suddenly flat and cold. His whole body seemed to tighten and it looked as if he were about to strike out at András. Then he relaxed, letting his breath out. 'I'm not going to tell you anything,' he said, all traces of his former languor gone.

András contemplated his hands.

'They've been here already, haven't they?' he remarked.

'What are you talking about?'

'Frightened? Can it be that you're frightened? A man like you?'

The other gripped the edge of his chair. He indicated the door. 'I think you'd better leave.'

András merely stared at him.

Thwarted, the giant studied him for a moment. Then he stood up abruptly and addressed the girl. 'I don't want to see this man here again,' he said. 'I don't care what kind of arrangement you have with him, but don't ever bring him here again, do you understand? If you do, I'll make more trouble for you than you could ever have imagined.'

He turned to look at András one last time, and then, without another word, he stalked out, the door banging shut behind him.

Vega stirred uneasily. 'I'm sorry . . . it probably wasn't a very good idea to meet here.'

András replied, unnaturally terse, 'It doesn't matter.'

She hesitated before speaking again. 'Wait for me outside,' she said. 'I'll see you there in a moment. I'll take you to Clio's place.'

It was András's turn to look surprised.

'Why are you doing this? Is it the money?'

'No,' she replied. Her expression was troubled. 'It isn't the money. I really think she could do with your help.'

András walked out of the club and sat down on a kerbside bench. In the perfectly quiet darkness, a solitary streetlight burned with a dim glow. A stray dog ran past the bench and barked at him. Overwhelmed by fatigue, he closed his eyes.

A man came out of a neighbouring house. He was a featureless grey man in a shapeless grey suit. He lit a cigarette and pretended to watch the traffic go by. When his cigarette had burned down to a stub, he stamped it out. With a sidelong glance at András, he crossed the street and headed in the direction of the club.

It was only after he had disappeared inside that András opened his eyes and noticed Vega standing across the street from him. Assured that she'd caught his eye, she began to walk away, her head turning every now and again to make sure that he was following. They walked in tandem after that, neither making any attempt to close the distance between them. Above their heads, neon signs scrolled round and round. Reflecting their intermittent glare, the night sky assumed a shade of red.

About to enter a narrow alleyway, the girl paused and waited for András to catch up. She pointed to a dilapidated brick tenement. András couldn't see a single light inside. They walked into the darkness together, making their way through makeshift rooms, past plywood walls, the entire place built of temporary partitions. There were other people around, András could hear their whispers, but the darkness had made everything invisible, and it was all he could do to follow the girl.

They went up a flight of steps and into a small room. The girl lit a candle and froze, sharply drawing in her breath. A man sat up on a bed. Realizing that something was wrong, András turned to Vega. Her eyes were bright with fear, but before she could react any further, the man on the bed had leapt forward, snatching away the candle and hitting her with the back of his hand. As she stumbled back, he slipped behind her, his hands holding her up and yanking down her dress in one violent motion. With a hypodermic needle held to her throat, he dragged her to the sofa and threw her down.

'So Fabien was right –' he whispered. 'And what have you brought today, my pussykins? A knight in shining armour? A new face? Another lost soul seeking consolation?' Going down on his knees, he cupped one of the girl's breasts. With his eyes on András, he cuffed her under the chin. 'She carries herself high in the chest, does my beauty!' he muttered. 'And with reason, perhaps?' He hit Vega again, watching her as she crumpled to one side of the sofa. 'Where will you go to, my lovely? Will the big man here rescue you? Will he beat me up? Not in your dreams, my Juliet. He knows you're for me, he knows you're a trophy. And he knows I can laugh louder than your loudest screams.' Bending over, needle still at her throat, he parted the girl's legs and exposed her to András. 'Look at this –' he slurred, 'once you've stripped off the clothes and spread the legs, the familiarity is hideous.' He smiled viciously, his teeth drawing back into a

369

sneer. Then he straightened up abruptly and let go of Vega, who lurched to the floor. The spirit seemed to have gone out of her. The man kicked a bottle towards András. 'You're looking for Clio, aren't you?' he said, his voice thickening. 'Go to the pier on Margit Island. She's waiting for you there.' He ducked his head. 'I'm going to count to ten. Get out before then.'

With his eyes fixed on the syringe, András began backing through the door. As he edged down the passage, he could hear the man begin to croon: '*Dreams, dreams, mirror my heartbeats . . .*' Taking the last few steps at a run, András blundered out of the darkened house, the sound of breaking glass pursuing him. His footsteps echoing behind him, he swerved through the sleeping streets, running in the direction of the river. Inside his head, he could hear the man's voice rising to a shout, and he could see Vega's unnaturally bright eyes, glazing over and slanting down, her face precariously without emotion.

Chapter Seven

Raintoccata, Fugue and Fever

'András!'

A He started at hearing his name called out. He looked around but he couldn't see anyone. He wondered if he'd been mistaken.

It had taken him an hour to reach the pier. Now he crouched under the trees at the edge of the clearing. He felt exhausted, disjointed, blood was pulsing through his head. On the other side of the river he could see lights winking along the horizon. Behind him the city of wooden ribs probed into the sky, relentless in its silence. The night tangled through the island, starless and filled with shadows, its thick, dark roof shaping over everything.

He stepped out of the shelter of the trees and cautiously circled around the clearing, his eyes scanning every hollow. There was no sign of Clio, and the grassy knoll appeared deserted. When he walked down to the waterline he could see the shadowed river flowing swiftly past.

Stepping on to the pier, he looked up at the night sky. He brought his hand close to his face. He spread his fingers and fixed his eyes on his wrist. Under the surface of his skin, his hand seemed very thin. He lowered his arm, his hand descending as if from a great height. He felt strangely detached. He longed for rest.

He took a step forward and felt the pier tremble below him. Drops of rain began descending.

In the distance, a streak of lightning flashed across the horizon. On the river, elongated waves gently stirred; pleated mirrors. Waves in motion.

And rain.

Water from the sky meeting water in the river.

He was still staring at the water when a cough interrupted the silence in the clearing. He raised his head and stiffened to listen. Someone was approaching the trees, he could sense the stumbling tracks even before he heard a drawn-out sigh. And then, silence.

Without a second thought, he turned around, the pier rocking under him. He moved swiftly towards the trees on the other side of the clearing, his eyes fixed in the direction of the cough. He was about to duck into the shadows when, from somewhere in the distance, a disembodied voice began to traverse the darkness anxiously. It called out his name, but in such a garbled manner that it didn't sound like his name at all. It was a high-pitched voice, gawky with panic, and uncertain. It could have belonged to a woman, it had that tremulous stridence. But when it rose to a shout, it sounded like a man in its harsh discordance.

As he waited in the shadows, careful not to make any sound, András heard footsteps crackling through the undergrowth. They approached him and walked right past, and then they turned around again. A face leaned in through the leaves.

It was Vega, her eyes bloodshot and stricken.

'Mr Tfirst! –' she exclaimed in a choked whisper. 'What took you so long? They've set a trap! You've got to get out of here!'

András stepped out into the open. He scanned the clearing, and then the pier. He was about to speak when she reached over and gave him a shove. She seemed beside herself with fear. 'For God's sake!' she cried. 'Get a move on! Just run! Head for the bridge, and stay away from the path! *Go!*'

András stood staring as she turned and vanished into the trees. Infected by her urgency, he moved away from the clearing. Behind him, he could hear the river lapping against the pier. He hurried on, the trees indistinct shapes in the darkness. He caught a glimpse of movement in the gloom and thought he heard shouts. But the sounds died away.

The rain grew steadier, the wind advancing and retreating in tattered ranks. That rain – a brooding, silver-dark thing – nature mortified, penitent. András wished he could slip under it, gather it around him like a quilt. Instead, he blundered through the trees, his mind straying to thoughts of warmth and shelter and Immanuele. The first time he had met her, it had been raining just like this. The first time he had met her, she had told him he would have to learn to fly if he wanted to live.

He emerged on the edge of an asphalted clearing. On the other side was Margit Bridge and the neon-lit arch of the causeway leading up to it. He was on the verge of crossing the open space when he came to a standstill, a chill shooting through him.

There was someone in front of him.

At first he could only make out a silhouette. Then the rain thinned and he glimpsed a woman standing with her back to him. She was wearing a raincoat and carrying an umbrella. She appeared to be waiting for somebody: she kept glancing at the bridge.

A sudden gust of wind distracted András. He heard the trees behind him bend and creak and when he turned back to the woman she had begun walking towards the bridge. He saw her enter the diffused circle of streetlights at the foot of the causeway. She hesitated and then she knelt down, her head turning in his direction. It looked like Clio, but in that light he couldn't be certain. A moment later, she straightened up and headed towards the bridge. As she approached it, András heard a sharp crack echo through the air. He saw her stagger, one hand flying back in an inordinately languid gesture. She turned in surprise, and then she pitched forward violently, as if she'd been hefted up and projected with an enormous force. Her umbrella flew out of her hand and turned upside-down, the curved wooden handle hooking into the air like a question-mark.

Horrified, András began to run towards her. He lost sight of her momentarily as he skirted past a row of trees. He covered the remaining distance in bounds, sprinting up to the causeway and looking around wildly. There was no one there, or on the stairway that descended to the river.

373

András rushed down the stairway. He took the steps two at a time, his feet skidding over them until he reached the bottom. He was only a few feet away from the river when he heard a shout from above him. Instinctively, he went down in a crouch and looked upwards. A car had swung on to the bridge, its bright headlights shooting through the rain. The lights illuminated a figure running with desperate urgency along the bridge. It was Vega, but no sooner had András realized that than the car pulled up beside her. A door swung open, a man sprang out, and the next instant Vega had plunged over the side of the bridge, her head jerking back as she plummeted.

The car on the bridge switched off its lights and moved on.

A touch of white whispering, and then it was gone.

András ran towards where he thought Vega had fallen. He turned a corner and stopped hesitantly: as far as he could make out there was no one in the water. He ran to the river's edge and looked on either side of him. He couldn't see anyone. Taking one last look around, he began to run back to the steps leading to the turnstile. He raced up the steps, not stopping until he'd reached the bridge. There was no trace of Vega or Clio or of anyone else. Only a solitary tram trundled towards him, its pin-point of light growing steadily larger. He waved at it to stop but it rattled past, its lights illuminating the bridge. It clattered on for about a hundred yards and then slowed to a halt. A slight figure in a raincoat detached itself from the shadows and stepped into the tram's brightly lit interior. András recognized Clio and, even before she had taken her seat, he began to run towards her. He was still a good twenty paces away when the tram began moving, its red tail-lights retreating steadily. He watched it recede into the distance. Then he started running again, his footsteps echoing across the bridge. He knew exactly where Clio was going.

◆

It had stopped raining by the time András reached the house on E-Daj Street. In the wake of the storm the sky was mottled and dark. The clouds had tapered into fox-shaped shadows in head-long retreat. Everywhere the houses were drenched with the anodyne gloss of rain, each exposed roof gleaming and distinct. The trees hung low and heavy, their leaves like chipped crystal. The narrow and cobbled streets appeared jet-black in contrast, their shadows dissolving.

The gate to the house was open and András hurried up the path. In the distance he could discern the dim outline of Castle Hill, but the rest of the city was dark, as if land and sky had merged into a single sheet of black, only the lights of that distant hill hinting at a separation.

The passageway inside the house was waterlogged. Rain had seeped through the ceiling and trickled down the walls, and when András entered the antechamber, he could see that the marble floor was almost entirely underwater. Leaving its narrow confines, he moved into the great hall. There was a candle in the foyer, but it fluttered and went out as he entered, leaving him in darkness. Stepping around its smoky plume, he headed for the staircase and the floor above.

Immanuele's room was deserted; the windows were unshuttered, and the wooden floorboards were slick with rain. András cast a quick glance around before moving out on to the terrace. It was windy outside, and the temperature had fallen. The air seemed permeated with dust, yet everything was clear and sharply defined.

Beyond the terrace, beyond the house and the line of trees that walled off the garden, the overcast sky hung low over the Danube, impressing the night's skeleton on its black waters. The twin cities, strangely subdued in the darkness, crouched on either side of that deep divide. Nothing stirred under the frozen sentence of silence. It was as if the surface skin of the city had hardened to a sullen armour, dressed in the granite shades of sleep. Only the river seemed to contain intermittent signs of life. And that, too, was fleeting.

Turning his back to the night, András crossed the terrace and entered the dark cube of the study adjoining it. A pale umbra of light hung down from the gap in the ceiling. A light rain fell through it, every drop gleaming and distinct. It was like a

375

window to the sky. A pool of rainwater had gathered on the floor below it. András took a step towards it, and then he turned instinctively to the far corner of the room where the darkness was impenetrable.

He heard a voice ask: 'Are we all that is left?' It was a woman's voice, and before he could respond, he heard it again: 'We are all that is left, then.'

She was sitting on an armchair, very still.

He walked slowly up to her.

'Clio?' he asked. He went down on his knees. 'Are you all right?' he said, trying to keep the urgency out of his voice. 'I saw you go down . . .'

She glanced at his hands in response, her own hands sliding off the arm-rests she had so compulsively gripped for an instant. He noticed then that her eyes were red, that she had been crying. She guided his hand to her shoulder where there was a rip through the fabric of her raincoat, and then she leaned away from him and gazed at the terrace. 'Wet . . .' she said, her voice sounding strangely constricted. 'Everything in the city is wet tonight. There's water seeping through everywhere.'

'Are you hurt?' he asked again. 'There were gunshots on the island . . .'

She gave him a fleeting look. 'No,' she said firmly, 'I'm not hurt.' A lock of hair had fallen across her forehead and she brushed it back. 'What are you doing here? Weren't we supposed to meet at the island?'

András hesitated, not knowing what to say. Sensing his confusion, she broke the silence. 'It doesn't matter. You're here now.'

'All these days I've been searching for you –'

'And I was searching for something else altogether.'

'Why didn't you call me? Why didn't you try to get in touch with me?'

'All these questions . . .'

'And you were so convinced you'd find the answers.'

She drew a quick, deep breath and stared at him challengingly. They held each other's gaze, and then she replied, sounding exhausted rather than triumphant, 'I *have* found the answers.'

376

She paused and watched him draw away from her. He clasped his hands around his knees, waiting for her to resume.

'You should never have given up looking for Immanuele,' she said.

He stood up. He knew that a reply was expected of him and that he had none to offer. Instead, he said, 'What are these answers you've found?'

'They're here. They're around us.'

'What do you mean?'

She hesitated for a moment. 'Will you walk with me through the house?'

'What will that do?'

'I want to see the rooms again. This is home to me – this place – the fusion of my past and present. It's always been inside me, never lost, never forgotten. It comforts me as nothing else can.'

'You said the answers were here.'

'They are,' she replied simply. 'They're here in this house.' She turned her head and glanced around her. 'That's why nothing could've been simpler than this meeting,' she said. 'Or more dangerous.'

She made to get up, but began coughing, her face suddenly mottled. She caught his look of concern and attempted a smile. 'I'm fine,' she said, moving stiffly. 'I'm just exhausted, that's all. I haven't slept for days.' She was turning away when she paused, realizing that he hadn't budged. She extended a hand to him. 'Won't you come with me?'

He followed her reluctantly as she left the study. They began walking slowly through the maze of rooms, each resembling the next in all but detail. In the fifth room, or perhaps it was the sixth, András wasn't certain, she paused before a marble fireplace and pointed to its maw. 'This used to be one of my secret hiding places. I still have things in there. It's surprising, isn't it, that no one ever thought to look inside?'

She followed him with her eyes as he knelt before the fireplace and felt around with his hands. 'Is this where you hid the diaries?' he asked.

'No . . .' she replied. 'Not in there.' She didn't elaborate.

When he stood up again, she was staring at the fireplace. 'I'm

377

sorry,' she said, 'being here makes it all come back.' When he remained silent, she continued, 'Do you know what it's like to have your childhood snatched away in an instant?'

'Is that why you came back?' he asked. 'To retrieve your childhood?'

'No, I came back to retrieve my memories. Somewhere in this darkness lies an incident from my past. I came back to confront it and try to understand why it happened.'

They crossed the room and András opened the door leading into the next one. He hesitated as he eyed the sagging floor. She stood behind him, misinterpreting his hesitation. 'You can feel her here, can't you?' she said. 'There's such a sense of presence.' She walked past him.

'Careful,' he cautioned, 'the floor's not too firm.'

She stopped and gazed down at the floor.

'It's funny how things come back sometimes,' she said. 'Childhood episodes. Family traumas. Illusions.'

'Family . . .' he rolled the word out contemplatively. He watched her from a distance. 'Why didn't you tell me at the beginning whose daughter you are?'

She recoiled as if he had struck her. He seemed to have penetrated her command of herself. She turned to look at him with startled eyes, and without answering. When he remained pointedly silent, she asked, 'When did you find out?'

'When I last saw Stefán. He told me he'd witnessed a meeting between you and your father at the police station.'

She looked nonplussed. 'I wouldn't have expected Stefán to have known who I was,' she began, and then she stopped. At length she said, 'I don't know what meeting he could have meant.'

'He said you'd seemed rather distraught.'

'I've had my share of confrontations with my father,' she replied, very terse.

He eyed her distantly. 'You neglected to tell me about them.'

'I didn't think it was necessary.'

'Why should I believe that?'

'Because I am nothing like my father!' she exclaimed, surprising him with her vehemence. 'My father has a graveyard for a soul.' She turned and walked back to him, her face pale and taut. 'I know you've been meeting him. I don't care what he thinks about me. I've spent the greater part of my life living our relationship down.'

'But you decided to come back to Budapest, nevertheless?'

'Not because of him.'

'That's immaterial at this point, isn't it?'

She flinched at his tone of voice. 'I was doing the best I could,' she replied, her voice sounding strangely thick. 'That's why I sought you out.'

'And what did you expect to find out from me?'

'I've already told you that. I wanted to find the source of my pain. I'd been escaping from the pain the world had caused me, and the pain I'd caused through my own ignorance and actions. I wanted to find out before anyone else got hurt.'

'Like Stefán, for instance?'

She gazed at him in silence.

'Speechless?' he said. 'I'm sure Stefán would have appreciated that little confession of intent.'

She kneeled on the floor before him. 'What do you want me to say?'

Suddenly weary, he turned away from her. Behind him, as he walked away, he heard her give a wordless exclamation. He glanced back at her. 'Get up,' he said.

She continued kneeling on the floor.

He gestured with sudden impatience. 'Why are we here, Clio? What are we doing walking through the house?'

She shuddered and seemed to stir awake, as if from a trance. She rested her hands on the floor. He repeated the question.

She stood up suddenly. 'I've been so wracked,' she said. 'I've been so torn all my life.' She made a constrained gesture with her hand. 'Perhaps I shouldn't have come here after all. You, at least, seemed to have found your peace. You seem to have been able to live with the fact of her disappearance. But I couldn't leave it alone. I needed to rest, and the only way was to resolve her fate. Earth to earth, where she was concerned, that much at least. Do you know what I mean?'

'Not entirely.'

'She was my friend, András. She deserves redemption.'

'She was my friend as well.'

'But I was here,' she answered him directly. 'I was here in the house the night that she disappeared. That's why it's been so difficult for me.'

András sat down by the doorway. He looked at her as if at a stranger. She watched him and shook her head. 'It makes you want to laugh, doesn't it?' When he remained silent, she said, 'It's so strange, almost as if I've experienced all of this before, gone over these lines in my head. And it's the first time I've ever spoken of it to anyone.' She leaned her head to one side, conscious of his eyes fixed on her. There was an indelible sadness to her face. 'Don't just sit there,' she called to him in a low voice. 'Come in out of the darkness.'

He didn't move.

She stood up restlessly. Skirting the sagging floor, she walked out of the room and on to a narrow landing with a bannister. When András reached the landing, he saw that she was standing halfway down a staircase that plunged sharply to the floor below.

She began to walk back up the steps to where he stood watching her.

'I was running madly down these steps that evening,' she said quietly, 'trying to get away from the house, trying not to scream. I remember falling, I might have cried out, I don't know . . .' She stood next to him, leaning against the bannister. 'The next thing I knew,' she said, 'I was lying flat on my back on my bed at home the next morning. My nails were full of grit. I lay there remembering snatches of what had happened. There was a mirror to the right of my bed and I saw myself. I looked at myself and screamed. I'll never forget that, the sense of alienation from myself.'

'Two days later,' she continued, 'on my way back from school, I saw the police cars filling up the street. There were more people on that street than I'd ever seen. They said that she was missing, that no one knew where she could be.'

She left the landing and András followed her. They reached the study in silence and she sat down on the armchair.

With a rush of despondency, she said, 'My life changed from that moment on, just as if there had been a cage imposed around

380

me. I couldn't remember clearly what I'd seen that night, and it haunted me. It ruined my sense of security and left me feeling constantly vulnerable. I became terrified of strangers. Every time I tried to recall, it was as if an arm curled around my neck and pulled me back into an abyss. I fought and kicked and screamed but the arm cut off my memory. It cut off that part of my life from me as ineradicably as an assassin.

'Things changed a bit once we left Budapest,' she carried on, 'but not much. I grew older, and by the time I had my own apartment in Paris, I had convinced myself that that part of my past no longer mattered. There was always a sense of unease, the sense of having borne witness to an appalling act, and the feelings of anxiety and guilt stemming from that. But I lived a full life, I was working and taking classes and there was hardly any time to spare for retrospection. It was a good mask, useful to maintain my distance from myself.' She hesitated. 'And then, one night, a stranger knocked on my door asking for directions, and there was something about him that brought it all back. I shut the door on him and nearly passed out. I thought I was going to die. It was then that I realized I would have to come back to Budapest and confront my fears. It was then that I realized that the past couldn't be safely forgotten.

'I began to have the most terrible nightmares,' she continued, after a pause. 'In my sleep I heard whispered lines. A litany of words. Round and round their careening dance . . .' She stopped and looked wearily at András. 'I used to be so confident.'

'And now?'

'Now I know that confidence was a ploy.' She held her hands out before her in a gesture of surrender, palms up. 'A façade,' she added, 'to conceal a sense of complicity.'

He continued to watch her, very still.

'András? Please –'

He raised a hand instead of speaking.

She glanced at him intently. Finally, she said, 'Believe me, if I'd had a choice, I would've forgotten everything.'

'And the waxwork –' András asked, 'what did that have to do with all of this?'

She glanced away so that András could no longer see her face. 'The waxwork,' she replied quietly, 'was a friend, who helped

381

me remember her past history.' She paused, her mouth pinched. 'But please don't ask me any more. I've had to rely on that wax-work much more than I'd expected.'

Rebuffed, András phrased his next query carefully. 'I take it, then, that you've retrieved your memory of what happened that evening?'

She ignored him and gazed at the terrace. He waited for her to say something but she remained silent.

'What are you waiting for?' he prompted.

She drew a quick, deep breath and leaned forward, her nostrils flaring. Just for a moment, she looked arrogant and disdainful. With a feverish calm quite out of keeping with her earlier restiveness, she said, 'I'm waiting to drive it home, waiting to make him remember.'

'Him? You mean . . .'

'Him –' she pointed past András with a sudden lunge: '*Him!*'

The movement pushed back the armchair and sent it teetering against the wall. The impact dislodged grains of brick and sand from the ceiling.

András wheeled around. Szegedy was standing in the middle of the room. His head was thrust forward and he seemed quite oblivious to András's presence, his entire being focused on his daughter. He advanced towards her with an agonizing slowness, almost as if the darkness in the room was physically impeding him. When he was near her, he turned to András and asked him in a gravelly voice to leave.

András ignored him and turned to Clio. 'What exactly is it that you want to make him remember?'

She shivered suddenly, and sat down on the armchair again. She glanced at Szegedy and shook her head. András felt his pulse quicken. With a sharp intake of breath, she said, 'That he was the last person to see Immanuele alive.'

'That's not true!' Szegedy shouted.

András began to feel sick. He ignored Szegedy and urgently addressed the girl. 'Tell me about it. Tell me about that night. What do you remember?'

'Everything,' she replied. 'I know everything. He was there.'

'There? You mean . . . here? In this house?'

'Yes.' She sounded exhausted.

'What happened?'

She looked at Szegedy and then she lowered her head into her hands.

Szegedy exploded. 'This is a charade –' he began, as András cut him off and addressed Clio again: 'Go on, don't stop, go on –'

Szegedy stepped forward before she could reply. 'Enough!' he cried. 'I don't know what you're going on about!' he said savagely. He turned to Clio and threw her a malevolent glance. 'You're completely out of your mind! I don't know what happened to Immanuele. I had nothing to do with it, do you hear me? What's the matter with you? You're my daughter. Have you gone completely mad?'

'I'm not mad!'

'You must be!' Szegedy retorted. His voice rose in indignation. 'Why else would you try to bring me down? You should be ashamed, turning on me like this! Making up stories!'

'But it isn't a story, and I'm not making anything up.'

'What are you doing, then?'

'I'm telling the truth,' she replied dully. 'The truth that you've been concealing all these years.'

'What's that supposed to mean?' Szegedy shouted, the veins standing out on his neck. 'My God! Has everyone gone mad?'

'No one's mad,' András interjected quietly. 'And you *do* know what she means.' He walked up to Clio and put a hand on her shoulder. Szegedy looked at them suspiciously and with contempt. 'What do you think you're going to get out of this?' he demanded.

Clio raised her head. 'Have you no shame?' she said. Her voice began to quaver. 'Do you think this is easy for me?'

'I'm your father! Where is your sense of loyalty?'

She gave him a look dense with grief.

'The loyalty that you never showed me?'

Szegedy crossed his arms. He attempted a smile but it came out as a grimace. 'This is crazy . . .' he faltered. He looked exasperatedly at András. 'How can you indulge her like this?'

Clio countered him with a fierce laugh. In a voice so low they almost didn't hear it, she said, 'How can you ever understand what it's been like to carry your secret? That kind of anxiety, the intimations of horror, the pain, above all the pain – to have everything in life coloured by the pain. I can't do it any more. I need to heal myself.'

'This is nonsense!' Szegedy said flatly. 'Fiction! All this whining about secrets and pain! What is this ghoulish desire to relive the past? Where's the proof of any of this? You've allowed your memories to run away with you! Nothing can be more dangerous than mistaken memories. Far too many years have elapsed for you to have any sense of precision!'

'There is nothing wrong with my memory.'

'How can you say that? You're imagining things! You've imagined you had a secret, and rested your identity on it. There's not a word of truth in what you've said. You've been living with shadows!'

'I have proof,' Clio cut in. 'Do you think I'd have gone this far without proof?'

'Rubbish! Don't talk to me like that! I won't be spoken to like that. This is a waste of time. There is no evidence!'

'I am the evidence,' she replied quietly.

In the deathly silence that followed, Szegedy's face lost all definition. His hands began fumbling at his sides. His eyes widened to the point where his entire face seemed subsumed by them. He made a pleading gesture and turned to András for support. András had never seen a man look so terrified. Not trusting himself to speak, he glanced at Clio. She held his gaze, looking completely spent. 'Yes, András,' she said lifelessly, 'I was in her room that night. I was in her room when he lunged at her and began shouting. I was hiding under the bed. And when he ran after her on to the terrace, I slipped in here and hid behind a pile of antlers in the corner.'

Behind him, András heard Szegedy groan. His shoulders slumped suddenly, as if his bluster had deserted him. 'There were antlers in one corner,' he agreed dully. 'A veritable forest of antlers. I do remember that.' He gave Clio a stricken look, struggling to overcome his emotions.

Ignoring him, she continued in a curiously impersonal voice. 'I heard him shouting at her but I was too scared to make out the

384

words. I slipped out and ran deep into the house. On the way down the steps I banged my head against the bannisters and almost blacked out. It hurt so much I thought I had split my head open. And then I couldn't remember what I was doing there any more, couldn't remember why I was running away or what I was running from, all I felt was terror, blind terror at being found out.' She turned towards Szegedy, her face suddenly lined.

'He was shouting at Immanuele?' András asked.

'Yes, but I was too scared to hear what he was saying.'

'And what did Immanuele do?'

Szegedy stepped forward before she could reply. 'She asked me to leave,' he said. 'She asked me to leave and I did. I walked out.'

András turned to him. 'You didn't tell me you were here that night.'

'I was passing by.'

'Passing by?'

'I saw a man stumbling around in the snow outside the house . . . he looked as if he were trying to scale the walls, I thought he was an intruder . . .'

Clio interrupted him. 'I saw a man *inside* the house, and it was you. I saw a man with Immanuele, and it was you. There was no one else here that night.'

'You're making a terrible mistake! I wasn't the only one here that night! It could've been Stefán!'

'It wasn't Stefán,' András snapped. 'You know that!'

Szegedy turned suddenly and addressed his daughter. 'Listen to me!' he said, 'You must believe me when I tell you that I might have been here but I had nothing to do with Immanuele's disappearance. I have no idea what happened to her after I left. I was as bewildered by her disappearance as everyone else.'

András stepped forward. 'You saw a man stumbling around outside, you said. What brought you into the house?'

'I was following the intruder, but there were tracks all over the snow, too many to be of any use. So I came inside to make sure that she . . . that everything was all right.'

'But everything *was* all right until you arrived, wasn't it?' Clio countered.

Szegedy gave her a look of confusion and anger, and then he backed into the shadows so that they could only see his eyes. His gaze bore down on András. 'I had nothing to do with what happened to Immanuele,' he insisted. 'And I don't know where she went after I left. We had a conversation, that's all. I made her a proposition, one that I'm not proud of now. And when she turned me down I lost my temper and shouted at her. But she told me to leave, and I did. That's the truth of it. That was the last time I saw her.'

To Clio, he said, 'I don't understand – the damage you have done. What have you achieved? We could have worked through this together. We weren't strangers. This isn't about winning or losing.'

Her whole face convulsed. 'You lost me,' she said.

'I lost you?' he repeated uncomprehendingly.

'Yes. And now it's too late.'

'Nothing's ever too late!'

She shook her head. 'I wish I could believe you.'

'Why can't you believe me?'

'Because I must believe myself.'

There was a silence, and then András broke in and addressed Szegedy, his voice thin with anger. 'Why did you keep this secret for so long? Why didn't you tell me about it?'

'I *know* what I told you!' Szegedy retorted. 'Wouldn't you have done the same?' His voice cracked. 'I couldn't tell you . . . I couldn't tell anyone!' He faced his daughter. 'Why don't you tell him? Why don't you tell him it wasn't like that!'

'I can't,' she said in a small voice. 'I can't dissemble like you do. For years I've carried your secret around in my heart. But I can't deny myself any more.' Composing herself with an effort, she said, 'For the longest time, I couldn't remember what had happened that night, I had a dim recollection of events, but the face – your face – I had completely forgotten. I had no idea who was responsible. Only pieces remained, fragments of recollection that didn't fit together. Only I knew the truth, but it was a truth that escaped me and left me totally wretched.'

She leaned forward suddenly. Her voice shook. 'Oh no, Father, don't close your eyes. You wedded me to silence and

386

that's how I've had to live my life. I couldn't even grieve openly because I couldn't remember what I'd witnessed. I wrote to you from Paris and you didn't reply. I called you only to be told that you couldn't be bothered, that you had a new life, a new wife, new children, responsibilities . . .' She considered him with heavy irony. 'I'd become an inconvenient reminder of everything you were trying to put behind you. But I couldn't leave well enough alone, could I? I kept on debating what was and what should have been. So I came here and met you and you directed me to András and Stefán.' She hesitated. 'What followed was disaster. The guilt that you'd transmitted to me, the guilt that I'd suppressed, was now compounded by my own actions. I'd joined with you in the preservation of your secret.' She gave him a look full of sadness. 'But in a strange turn of fate it was precisely that joining that brought my memory back and made you transparent. I saw through you and there could be no more pretending. The sequence of repressed events had fallen into place, my guilt finally converted to sorrow.'

She clutched the sides of her chair and began to cough. 'So tell me the truth now –' she managed. 'Tell me where you took her –'

Szegedy stared at her in surprise. 'I didn't take her anywhere. She didn't leave with me –'

She interrupted him: 'She didn't have a choice, you didn't give her one!' Still coughing, she bent over in the armchair. Her pale face looked cadaverous. She clutched at her throat as the coughing died down.

'What do you mean?' Szegedy asked her nervously.

'You hit her,' she said in a choked voice. 'I saw you.'

She raised her eyes to meet his.

'I saw you hit her . . .' she repeated, straining over every word, '. . . I heard you shout . . . there were falling sounds . . . and then . . . nothing.'

András turned to the policeman. He wanted to speak but he couldn't find the words. His mind seemed to have shut down; it was as if he'd been suddenly distanced from his surroundings. He reached out and leaned against the wall. He felt his eyes burning into his head. In a voice that sounded strange even to himself, he addressed Szegedy, 'What did you do to her?'

'I don't know what happened to her,' Szegedy began unsteadily. 'Believe me when I tell you I don't know.' He looked at András in anguish. 'You must believe me when I tell you I didn't mean to hurt her.'

'You assaulted her.'

'There is an explanation for everything . . .'

'What is your explanation?'

In a barely audible voice, Szegedy whispered, 'The hunger . . . do you know what it's like? – do you have the faintest comprehension?' He pressed his hands to his cheeks. 'I loved her. As God is in heaven, I loved her . . .'

He faltered and looked imploringly at András. 'I fantasized about her. She was my phantom lover. She moved within the shadows of my life. Her music, her courage, her particular symbols of life. She was the source of my grief, and because she wouldn't give me anything, she stayed in my mind all the time.' He covered his face with his hands. 'Before you judge me please consider how much I loved her. Without her knowing it, I protected her, I protected her friends, I protected her club. I made my conscience a fugitive. I took impossible risks to ensure that she'd be safe. Eyes followed my every move, ears listened to my every sound. What did I get in return? What did she give me in return? Disdain and contempt in equal measure. Not even a single civil answer. What can I say? I cauterized my grief. I lost my way travelling a road seldom taken. One moment dreaming of light, and the next there was only darkness. Blackness everywhere. Even my brother did better.'

'She's dead, isn't she?'

'I don't know! What can I say to convince you that I really don't know? I loved her – I wouldn't kill her! I wanted to look after her. I wanted to care for her. Even after she disappeared, I maintained this house, I paid all the bills, I kept things just the way they used to be . . .'

In the absence of a clear response, it was Clio who breached the silence. 'Why were you here that night? What were you after?' Her voice broke. 'Why won't you give a direct answer? Is there to be no solace?'

He looked at her dully. 'If I've been wasting your time, maybe you never learned to listen. Do faces belong to bodies? Does the glass globe belong to its shadow, the mirror? I was chained to her by spirit. She was in my blood. I had to reach out to her to prove to myself that I was still alive.'

There was a sudden, despairing cry as Clio swayed forward from her chair, her hands clenched, her head thrusting to one side. With a spasmodic effort she hurled herself at Szegedy, but she hit the floor with a compelling force before she could reach him.

They waited tensely for her to get up, but she continued to stare at them glassy-eyed, her hands resting motionlessly on the ground.

Suspicious of her stillness, András crossed the room and bent over her. He touched her face and her head fell to one side. Going down on his knees, he nudged her raincoat aside: there was a dark stain on her chest. Feeling suddenly suffocated, he brought his shoulders forward. Then he lowered his forehead and rested it against hers.

Behind him, a nervous voice broke the silence: 'What's the matter with her? Why isn't she saying anything?'

András didn't reply.

'András?' Szegedy repeated, breathing noisily. 'What's wrong?'

András gathered the girl gently in his arms and picked her up. He turned around and stepped forward.

Szegedy looked at him, pleading.

'András?'

When András refused to answer, he burst out: 'What's the matter with you? Why don't you speak?' Then he saw the stain on Clio's shirt. 'Oh, no . . .' he whispered. He stared at her in horror. '*How?*'

András bared his teeth in a snarl. He said nothing.

Szegedy shook his head, wide-eyed. He seemed petrified.

András carried Clio across the room, her raincoat trailing behind. He crossed the terrace to Immanuele's room and laid her out on the bed. He took off her coat before straightening up and staring at the man standing before him.

Szegedy sat down on the bed. He seemed to have gone into shock.

András watched him for a moment and then he turned away and walked out on to the terrace. He sagged against the balustrade, his head in his hands. He was panting from the tension. With an effort, he looked towards the street, his eyes picking out details at random. A gate to a neighbouring house swung in the breeze; it was painted a bright orange. A sudden gust swept through the trees in the garden.

He had no idea how long he'd been there before he realized with a start that Szegedy was standing right next to him. He coughed dully but András turned away without acknowledging his presence. Oblivious, Szegedy addressed him, sounding dazed. 'It doesn't make sense . . .' he whispered. He paused and seemed to draw into himself. 'She's my daughter . . .' he said, 'my first-born . . .' He made a sudden gesture, ducking his head and clasping his hands. 'I'm so tired. I'm so tired. Who could have known? Everything's spun out of control.'

His face began to pucker. He straightened up and shook his head unsteadily. He seemed to be struggling for words. 'It's going to take some time to work through all this . . . I need a little time, that's all. A little time before you carry on and draw your own conclusions . . .'

András hesitated, and then he held up his hands. 'Look at my hands, Inspector,' he said slowly, 'I'm growing eyes at the tips of my fingers.'

Szegedy looked at him, uncomprehending. 'What do you mean?'

András lowered his hands. 'So much deception . . .' he said. 'And in the end, to what purpose?' He left the terrace and returned to the room. Standing next to the bed, he reached out and touched Clio's face with the back of his hand. She was cold. A grey pallor had already spread over her features. He considered her steadily, his eyes fixed and glinting.

He heard Szegedy shuffling towards the bed and turned to confront him. His face hardened. 'You did this,' he said, in an unnaturally calm voice. 'You had her shot on the island.'

Szegedy took a step back and crossed his arms, and then he uncrossed them again. He began to tremble.

'I saw her go down,' András continued relentlessly, 'I saw her go down on the causeway.'

'She wasn't supposed to be on the island,' Szegedy whispered. 'She wasn't meant to be there.'

'Another lie?' András replied. 'You lured her there by telling her I would be waiting by the pier. You lured me there in the same way. But something went awry in your trap, didn't it? Your men didn't perform as expected. The rain must have thrown them off. They let us both slip away.' He extended his right hand and thrust it against Szegedy's chest with sudden violence. As Szegedy staggered back, András turned away and knelt beside the girl. He felt around in his pockets, and then stood up and covered Clio's face with a handkerchief.

Szegedy made a choking sound. He went down on his knees by Clio and pressed his ear to her chest. When he straightened up again, his face was crumpled and wizened. He picked up her raincoat and held it in the air with frozen introspection. He tried to speak, but his voice subsided into a gasp. He dropped the raincoat and grasped the side of the bed with both hands to steady himself. His shoulders began to tremble. He crossed himself. 'What are we going to do?' he whispered.

András drew back sharply. His face distorted with fury. He raised his fist and stood completely still. Then he lowered his fist and began to walk towards the door.

'Wait!' Szegedy called out in alarm. 'Where do you think you're going?'

András kept walking as Szegedy fell into step beside him. Szegedy's shirt was soaked with sweat and he kept mopping at his neck with a handkerchief. 'Listen to me!' he said urgently, 'you can't just leave, don't you understand? It's your word against mine, don't you see?'

András left the room, Szegedy running down the steps behind him. 'What happened on the island was an accident, André, it wasn't intended! It was an accident! Can you understand that? I made a mistake! A terrible mistake! And now everything's spiralling, God help me! Everything's spinning out of control!'

At the bottom of the stairs, András stopped and held Szegedy off with his hand. The policeman looked at him in desperation. 'We can come to an understanding, André, an arrangement –'

András attempted to walk around him but Szegedy blocked

391

him. 'Give me your hand, André . . . give me your hand, and the rest can be silence.'

András slapped him across the mouth. Szegedy staggered back, reaching out as he fell. He hit the wall with his shoulder and sank down in a heap.

András hauled him to his feet, his eyes blazing.

Szegedy wrenched himself away. 'Listen, you!' he cried. 'Give me an answer – why would I have looked after this house all these years if I had known her to be dead? Why would I? Answer me that!'

András didn't reply. Instead, he moved into the shadows of the hall, his receding form instantly sucked into the darkness.

Behind him, Szegedy's voice rose: 'Don't be a fool, André! Don't be a fool! No one's going to believe you. There's no tidy version of good and evil here. There's much more to this than meets the eye.'

As he headed towards the antechamber, András heard Szegedy again. 'Your turn will come!' he was shouting. 'Your turn will come!' András slowed down, wondering whether he ought to stop. Deciding against it, he picked up his pace and continued walking towards the front door. He was almost there when he heard footsteps running up. A hand descended heavily on his shoulder. He swivelled around to find Szegedy standing behind him, his face distorted with panic. There was a gun in his hand. He pushed András, who stumbled and nearly fell. Before András could get out of the way, Szegedy pushed him again. Then he lurched forward and placed himself between the door and András. 'What are you going to do?' he said hoarsely. 'What are your intentions?'

András gazed past him in silence, his eyes on the door.

Szegedy gestured him away. 'I can't let you go, don't you see? To let you go at this point would be suicide!'

He motioned with the gun. 'I'm only doing this because I'm desperate! I have a wife and children to look after. You have no responsibilities, and I ask nothing of you save the decency to stay quiet. Suspend your rush to judgement. We're in a void where nothing can be proven. There is no evidence here, only hearsay. Tonight I've lost a daughter, but I will not lose everything I've lived for. I'm not going to be a fugitive, I won't be held hostage.' He pointed the gun at András. 'You must believe me,' he said. 'I didn't kill her.'

With his eyes on the gun, András began to advance slowly towards the door. Szegedy looked imploringly at him. 'What am I asking of you? Eventually something quite unimportant! You can't refuse! Give me your word that you won't betray me.'

As András continued to approach the door, he crooked his finger around the trigger. 'There'll only be one story between us, André, and you'll be the one to tell it! We're the only men in the universe now, and there'll only be one story between us or, as God is my witness, you're not leaving this place! If I'm to go down, it won't be on my own!'

András shifted his eyes to the floor, his head held low against the darkness.

'Well?' Szegedy whispered. 'What do you have to say?' When András remained silent, he made as if to press the trigger, and then he suddenly withdrew the gun and pointed it at the opposite wall. The trigger snapped back, the explosion echoing through the house.

Across the room, a chunk of plaster detached from the wall and clattered down to the floor.

András stared at the wall, the shot still ringing in his ears. Szegedy was rubbing his wrist; he turned unsteadily and extended the gun towards András. 'Go on –' he said, 'take it. A bullet to the head. One bullet and I'm dead.'

András said nothing. Szegedy pressed the gun into his hand. 'Go ahead, do it! End it! We're hooked into each other. To let me go and carry on hating; not to let me go and hate yourself. These are your choices.'

With a look of complete contempt, András pushed him away. Szegedy caught his expression and blanched. He fell back with a grimace of indescribable bitterness.

'Silent to the end?' he said thickly. 'To the end you refuse to speak? Silent to the very end, Immanuele?'

He lunged forward and ripped the sheets away from the bed. 'I've reached the end of my patience, then! This is where the story ends! It's the perfect moment, isn't it? You reserve your words and I go around in circles. Which part of the heart hurts most in this cul-de-sac? Hell must be this silent!'

He paused and pricked up his ears. He thought he'd heard a sound. He wondered if he should investigate. Deciding against it, he made a visible effort to compose himself. His eyes scanned the room and came to rest on the terrace. 'What we have here is a touch of snow,' he whispered, 'soon to be replaced by darkness.'

He removed his hat and sat down heavily on the edge of the bed. He felt suddenly out of breath, his anger burning into exhaustion. One of his hands rested slack and motionless beside him; the other kept time to some secret rhythm with an almost forensic precision.

'What I will never understand,' he said, 'is why you ostracized me. You meant the world to me, that must have been obvious. I would have given you everything.' He gave her a look filled with despair and longing. 'What got in the way? I could have been your benefactor. I would have respected your freedom. I wouldn't have taken away your liberty.' He hesitated, the blood rising to his face. 'Why are you shaking?' he said with fierce resentment. 'Are you cold? Is it me?' He reached forward, and then drew back instantly. 'You burn when I touch you,' he said bitterly. 'Where is the justice in this?

'Your turn has come,' he continued, much more calmly. 'I'm not following the rules any more. I've waited for too long. There'll be no more walls between us. Nothing to hold me back, no more empty longing . . .'

He glanced at his watch and attempted an air of sardonic detachment.

'The end has come, Immanuele,' he said. 'You didn't take me seriously, and now it's too late. You no longer have control over your circumstances. Your immaculate life. Your quest for truth and justice. What an enormous and difficult task you set yourself.' He shook his head. 'But it doesn't matter any more, it just doesn't matter. You dragged me into the void and I've finally come to claim my share. I will be your master of solitudes. Your hands of ice, your lips, your face. So many virtues. So many twisted fates. What can I say? I've waited for the night to fall. I've run away with myself. I think of you, and it's pouring rain inside my head again. Carrion hopes cascading down. I feel cheated, defeated.'

He stood up, gathering his bulk about him.

'Close your eyes now, my dear,' he said, with a sudden gentleness.

'Close your eyes . . .

Let us make an end.'

♦

He stumbled out of the house and opened his mouth wide, drinking in the air. It was damp and dense: difficult. He waited for an instant on the steps and steadied himself. It was only when he was half-way down the path that he realized it was raining. All around him raindrops were plummeting out of the sky. He watched them fall, break up, and fall again. He felt the spray on his face. The darkness rippled before his eyes. He felt his knees give way and sat down abruptly on the edge of the path.

A burst of rain ricocheted off a branch and struck his face.

He remembered the house.

Now a collection of memories, brittle bones within.

A wave of nausea passed through him, but he managed to compose himself and look back at the house. The rain had formed a screen around it. He couldn't see anything. Pressing his hands to his mouth to keep from crying out, he staggered to his feet, the night swimming around him. He felt very cold . . .

Very old.

He reached the end of the path and leaned against the gate. It swung open and he saw water rushing down the street like a river. Wading into the flow, he felt the cold travel instantly through his bones. Thick columns of rain cut off his line of sight. Already he felt one with it, sundered from the earth.

The colour of the rain resembled sleep.

The colour of the rain resembled silence.

Notes

p. 10   Immanuele's 'mangled citation' is from Pier Paolo Pasolini's 'Roman Nights' in *Roman Nights and Other Stories*, translated by John Shepley (The Marlboro Press, Marlboro, 1986, p. 23).

p. 138   One of the charges against which Dostoevsky was convicted as part of the Petrashevist conspiracy was 'the attempt, along with others, to write works against the government and circulate them by means of a home lithograph'. Cited in David McDuff's introduction to *The House of the Dead* (Penguin, Harmondsworth, 1985, p. 10).

p. 189   *'La muerte entra y sale de la taberna!'* ('Death moves in and out of the tavern!') is from *Malagueña*, by Federico García Lorca (Penguin, Harmondsworth, 1967, p. 20).

p. 293   The lines cited here are from 'Your Right Arm Beneath My Neck', in *Miklós Radnóti, Under Gemini: A Prose Memoir and Selected Poetry*, translated by Jascha Kessler, with Maria Körösy (Ohio University Press, Athens, 1985, p. 79).

        The second extract (p. 294) is from the very last entry in the Bor Notebook, dated 31 October 1944, and entitled *Razglednicas* (Serbo-Croatian for 'picture postcards'). The notebook was found in the pocket of Radnóti's corpse, exhumed in 1946 from a mass grave. Radnóti died during a forced march from Serbia. The translation is by Jascha Kessler, with Maria Körösy from *Miklós Radnóti, Under Gemini: A Prose Memoir and Selected Poetry* (Ohio University Press, Athens, 1985, p. 105).

p. 350   'Our job is to rejoice,' is a quotation from Dmitri Dmitriyevich Shostakovich, as cited by Daniil Zhitomirsky, in *Shostakovich: A Life Remembered*, by Elizabeth Wilson (Princeton University Press, Princeton, 1995, p. 177).